ON LONESOME ROADS

A *PETER O'KEEFE* NOVEL

DAN FLANIGAN

For information about this title or to order other books and/or electronic media, contact the publisher:

Arjuna Books
5301 Pawnee Lane
Fairway, KS 66205

ISBN: 979-8-9855614-1-8 (print)
ISBN: 979-8-9855614-2-5 (eBook)

Cover Design by milagraphicartist.com
Book Interior Design by Amit Dey

Publisher's Cataloging-In-Publication Data
(Prepared by The Donohue Group, Inc.)

Names: Flanigan, Daniel J., 1947- author.
Title: On lonesome roads : a novel / Dan Flanigan.
Description: Fairway, KS : Arjuna Books, [2022] | Series: A Peter O'Keefe novel ; [3]
Identifiers: ISBN 9798985561418 (print) | ISBN 9798985561425 (ebook)
Subjects: LCSH: Private investigators--United States--Fiction. | Bombings--Investigation--United States--Fiction. | Mafia--United States--Fiction. | LCGFT: Detective and mystery fiction. | Thrillers (Fiction)
Classification: LCC PS3606.L3587 O5 2022 (print) | LCC PS3606.L3587 (ebook) | DDC 813/.6--dc23

Printed in the United States of America

"Out of this nettle, danger, we pluck this flower, safety."

William Shakespeare,
Henry IV, Part 1, Act 2, Scene 3

CHAPTER ▶ 1

EVENING HERALD

JANUARY 2, 1988

WHO BOMBED PETER O'KEEFE?
DOUBTS PERSIST.

Last October, Private Detective Peter O'Keefe turned the key to start up his specially equipped van.

It exploded, severely burning the left side of his body from his ear down to his feet.

O'Keefe was the victim of a simple makeshift car bomb. Recovery from severe burns can be an up-and-down, one-step-forward-two-steps-back process. He still wears special pressure garments wrapping his left arm and hand and leg and foot, undergoes frequent painful bouts of physical therapy, still walks with a slight hitch in his step, and is learning to run again.

Although O'Keefe says he is rapidly recuperating and expects to recover to nearly all of his pre-bombing range of motion, he wonders if the bomber or bombers have all been identified—or if someone who tried to kill him is still at large.

At the time of the bombing, O'Keefe was investigating the death of Beverly Bronson, his high school friend. Her death was originally assumed to be an accidental death from a heroin overdose or even suicide.

But the investigation turned up evidence of murder, not suicide, and uncovered suspicious connections between Bronson and yet another high school friend of O'Keefe's, prominent real estate developer and leading mayoral candidate, Jerry Jensen, as well as David Bowman, a convicted felon who grew up in the same neighborhood as Jensen, Bronson, and O'Keefe.

The resulting scandal was a city-wide sensation.

Soon after the bombing, Bowman himself met his own violent end, and Jerry Jensen died under mysterious circumstances, apparently by his own hand.

"Many people, including me," O'Keefe says, "assumed it was a certain person, David Bowman, but I wonder if it was really him, and even if he was the primary one, surely he had some help."

According to O'Keefe, "After Bowman's death, a fog of complacency descended on everyone involved, starting with me, but unfortunately also including the police, the FBI, and the ATF. I think they all just stopped looking." (The "ATF" he refers to is the Federal Bureau of Alcohol, Tobacco, Firearms, and Explosives.)

Many have assumed the explosion was the work of local mafioso (often referred to, by themselves and law enforcement, as the "Outfit") due to their penchant for bombing each other, and because of O'Keefe's violent confrontation with suspected Outfit gunmen in Arizona two years ago. But O'Keefe doesn't think so: "This was amateur hour, and those guys are professionals. Plus, I really think they have better things to do than bother with me."

Still, many others wonder.

The investigation also disclosed that both Bowman and Jensen were associated in unclear capacities with Cherry Pink, a "Gentlemen's Club" located in the county, outside city limits. "That's a real snake pit out there with some real snakes in it, and no snake charmers," O'Keefe says.

Asked to name who he might be referring to, he demurred, saying, "it wouldn't be right to just throw names around publicly based only on suspicion." But he does believe that law enforcement should be investigating in that direction, which is complicated by the county being a different jurisdiction than the city.

"That's the Wild West out there," O'Keefe says. "City slickers, even the ones with badges—especially the ones with badges—aren't welcome."

"But that's where the FBI and ATF come in," O'Keefe asserts. "The Feds can cross those lines. But they haven't shown any interest at all. I have good private security in place, but it's really expensive and, frankly, a real pain in the you-know-what to be living under guard all the time."

Responding to requests for comment, the police, the ATF, the FBI, and the U.S. Attorney's office replied only, "We do not comment on open investigations."

O'Keefe's comment: "*What* investigations?"

●   ●   ●

O'KEEFE REGRETTED THAT he was not in a better mood only a few minutes before his weekly high-security visit with his daughter Kelly. His recovery from the burns that had flash-fried the left side of his body when the car-bomb exploded was not going well these days. Or maybe this was the good kind of hurt, a sign of healing. But the dull ache was always there, punctuated occasionally by burning sensations as if the flames still danced along the crackling flesh. Or by sudden tiny lightning bolts at the borders between his old skin and the new, grafted-on skin. Or by an itching in a place too tender or too difficult to reach to scratch. Or by mysterious sparks of stabbing pain as if an enraged poltergeist darted madly and randomly around the archipelago of scar tissue that stretched from his left shoulder down his arm, engulfed his left hand

and fingers, skipped his torso, but resumed at his left hip bone and zigzagged down the side of the leg to the tip of his left foot.

Sometimes it was stings, sometimes ripples, sometimes darts—like miniature neon signs flashing on and off, the burnt-out nerves growing back and rehearsing their purpose to inflict stabbing pain as a warning that something much worse might be coming soon. When his skin didn't ache or sting or stab, it itched, especially two troublesome spots on his back, underneath each shoulder blade, where they took the healthy skin to graft onto the wounded areas—"harvesting," they gruesomely called it. Similar spots pocked a knee, an inner thigh and the back of his thumb, and alarming sores had popped up in the crooks of his knee and elbow.

Scar bands in his left hand began at his fingers and extended downward and, like erratically arranged spokes of a wheel, joined into stigmata at the center of his palm. They gently but constantly pulled his fingers downward toward a shrivel, relentlessly determined to close his hand into a claw. He had difficulty turning a page with that hand and currently could not type with it, which meant he could not do much more than "hunt and peck" on the computer. But the doctors assured him that he would regain nearly all of his range of motion if he assiduously followed through with their prescribed daily physical therapy routine, which required him to dip his wounded hand in hot-as-he-could-stand paraffin, allow the paraffin to congeal and soften the scar tissue, then submit to the deceptively petite, pretty, and pleasant physical therapy nurse's torturous, forced straightening of his bent hands and fingers. They also instructed him to wear, whenever possible (and he knew he should be wearing it more often), a specially designed splint covering the area from his forearm to his fingertips that stretched his fingers and kept them straight.

He suffered superficial face burns as well, but he must have turned his face away from the blast just in time, so those burns were only of the second rather than the third or fourth degree like his other burns. He considered it a randomly vouchsafed beneficence that his face was only slightly scarred, a small patch of rough tissue on his cheek next to his ear lobe that paired with an older, smaller scar along the ridge of his left cheekbone from a whizzing chunk of shrapnel that had nicked him as he fired his machine gun into the Vietnam jungle from the helicopter descending into a hot landing zone. He tried to be grateful for this and similar mercies amidst the physical pain and the vague aura of dread hanging over him.

A homecare nurse arrived each morning to strip off yesterday's wrappings and swathe him anew in compression "garments" to keep the grafts secure and control the scarring, all amidst his constant frowns and winces of torment and occasional muffled howls when a strip of skin ripped off with the cloth. The garments, plus the staples they used instead of stitches to attach the grafts, were the only things holding his new skin precariously to his otherwise raw flesh, and he wondered if it would really all bond together as they assured him it would.

After the nurse helped him dress and then departed, he religiously forced himself into the office. But concentration proved difficult. His stinging arm, shriveled hand, and drug-and-pain-addled brain sometimes made the simplest tasks difficult. The prescription Percocet, opioid pain pills, bestowed a partial and superficial relief but shut him down in another way, relegating him to lying on his office couch drifting in a zombie-like state.

He was not holding up his end. His partners, Sara and George, had to handle everything with little useful assistance from him, and the absence of any significant financial contribution from work performed by him was compounded by the added expense of the security guards, both at his office and at home, and the bomb-sniffing dogs accompanying the security guards. He had failed, until weeks after the bombing, to understand the implications for his future of the uncertainties surrounding the case—the assumption by the authorities, without actual proof, that the bombing had been the work of the now deceased David Bowman and the continuing rumors that it was really the work of the Outfit. Conspiracy theories abounded. In this cloud of unknowing, his former wife Annie, who was still afraid that their daughter was insufficiently safe in his company, and, literally, gun-shy, after an incident two Halloweens ago when he and Kelly had been attacked by Outfit goons while trick or treating, understandably wanted to take no chances, insisting that his visits with Kelly now occur only with maximum security, which he did not believe necessary but thought he had to accept

Unfortunately, this attitude spread far beyond Annie. Most of the world that knew anything about him, especially including his neighbors, wanted badly to avoid him, as if he brought with him something worse than a communicable disease. Although he was happy with his new residence, a rent-to-own deal an enterprising broker had negotiated for him, he still much regretted having to leave his prior one; but, given the furtive and often downright hostile looks from his neighbors and the brusque attitude of the upstairs tenant, he could not claim surprise or cast blame or even argue when, shortly after he left the hospital, the landlord called and asked him to vacate despite their long and friendly relationship.

"I'm sorry, Pete," the landlord said. "The upstairs guy and even the next-door neighbor are threatening to leave or even sue. My insurance agent says if you're still there when the policy expires, they won't renew it."

"No problem," O'Keefe said, "I'm already looking."

O'Keefe couldn't blame any of them for wanting him out. Although he doubted there was any danger of a repetition of that explosion in his driveway that had reduced him to his current state, he couldn't offer any proof of that.

He wanted to remain in something that seemed more like a house than an apartment and also hoped for more space. But detached, single-family homes were seldom available for rent, and he doubted that his unstable income, combined with the debt load he had taken on to support his current business initiatives—to say nothing of his checkered past and current notoriety and the precariousness not only of his health but even, apparently, his life itself—would ever allow him to qualify for a home loan. Setting out hopefully on what he worried was a hopeless quest, afraid he was doomed to end up in some high rise or garden apartment complex, he drove by a "for sale" sign in front of a house in a neighborhood near the downtown area of the city old enough and with a lushness of trees that, like a magician's trick, almost camouflaged the fact that it had once been a suburb too.

The house itself Annie would have characterized as "darling." But what appealed most to him—the recluse in him anyway—were such things as the position of the house, deeply set back from the street; its rough and unwelcoming, but still strangely appealing, gravel driveway; the twelve-foot high hedgerows in the front and on the sides of the property; the oak, pine, and fir trees that covered the house in shade; and the smaller trees—redbud, crab apple, and pink and white dogwoods—randomly strewn around the rest of the double lot. Even on this early winter day he could tell that in the warm weather a profusion of green and flowering plants, including ground roses and rose bushes, would spring to life haphazardly around the yard. It did have an unkempt look about it, something like Beethoven's hairdo, but that appealed to him as well.

"That's a lot of work," his realtor said. "You'd do all that?"

"Not a lick. But I'd find somebody good and pay 'em well."

He was not immune to the "darling" part either: yellow-painted with white trim, a large stone birdbath and stone walkway leading to a custom-made front door featuring an artistic design in etched glass, a flower box under a bay window, a screened in porch on one side and a patio off the other, both accessed by French doors.

"See if they'll rent it for a year and give me an option to buy at the end," he told the broker.

"Fat chance, but I'll ask," she said.

The same day she called back. "I'm dumbfounded. They agreed but on the condition that you pay the current price plus ten percent at the end of the year, though they'll credit your rent payments. But here's the rub. You won't get a real option. They're very worried they won't like their new home. If they want to move back in this one at the end of the year, they can terminate the whole arrangement then."

"Fair enough," he said without hesitation, "as long as that can only happen if they move back in themselves."

When he showed the place to Kelly and Annie, he could tell that Kelly was delighted but Annie skeptical and a bit jealous. "This house does not say Peter O'Keefe," she said. "Who'll do all the gardening work?"

"Kelly."

"Not a chance," Kelly said.

"Even for big bucks?"

"Not even for very big bucks."

CHAPTER ▶ 2

LOOKING OUT HIS front window now, he noted that it would be quite a while before any gardening work would be required, as it was early January, very cold, with unmelted patches of snow dotting the yard in various shaded places. The car he'd been waiting for entered the driveway and parked. The guard escorted her up the walk. *She's getting taller.* Her backpack hung over her left shoulder. In her right hand, crooked in her arm and pressed next to her chest, she held a book that she had apparently been reading in the car. Her hair now reached down to her shoulder blades. For a long time her blondness had been slowly turning into a light brunette with blonde streaks. Even though at age eleven she was passing through a gangly, awkward stage, she was unquestionably pretty and might even end up beautiful, less of a blessing than people thought but probably better than the alternative. Her typical facial expression was one of skeptical amusement, on the verge of bursting out in sudden laughter.

When he opened the door for her, she examined him up and down and said, "How are you?"

"Better all the time…but still hurting a bunch."

"Are you taking those pills? You got that big bottle from the doctor."

"Not much."

"Why not?"

"Don't like the way they make me feel."

"But don't they help the pain?"

"Some. Most of the time not enough to make up for what they do to my head."

"What do they feel like? Not good?"

"Yeah…good…but they shut me down. I hate that."

She opened her eyes wide and looked to the ceiling, appealing to heaven for relief and shaking her head at the incongruity of preferring the pain to whatever the pills did to relieve the pain. He wondered if she wondered how he had been so fond of cocaine and alcohol and not the Percocet. He could have told her it was because those things charged you way up, at least at the start, and this had the opposite effect.

She marched to the couch, dropped the backpack on the floor, kept the book in her hand, her thumb acting as a bookmark, and sat down. She seemed unhappy, even sullen. He sensed he needed to take the initiative. Indicating her book, *Secrets Can Kill*, he said, "You like Nancy Drew?"

"She's okay."

Yes, sullen. He hesitated, evaluating whether to tiptoe gingerly around her mood or address it directly.

"Want to do something?"

"What's there to do? We can't do anything anymore, stuck here under guard."

"I'm hoping that'll end soon."

"How?"

"I think the danger's passed…if it was ever there."

"How you know?"

"That's the problem. I know but can't prove it. I have to find a way to satisfy myself, then your mom, then everybody else."

"It'll be too late then."

"Too late for what?" But he was pretty sure and pretty afraid that he knew what she meant.

She squirmed, looked down at the cover of her book as if she might be able to find the answer there, and said, "Just too late."

"I might miss the rest of the basketball season, but I'm hoping it won't be long after that."

"She'll be married by then."

There it was. Bag, cat out of it. "What's that supposed to mean?"

"Why can't you come back home?"

She hadn't directly confronted him on this for a long time. Hoping to blunt this line of attack with humor, he said, "I think it'd get crowded in there with a mom and two dads."

Mistake.

"I don't want another dad."

"Well, he won't really be your dad."

"Why can't you come back?"

She was crying now, gasping a little trying to control it.

"She doesn't want me back. She's moved on."

"Have you asked her? Have you given her a chance?"

"I can't do that."

"Why'd you leave us in the first place?"

He didn't really know how to deal with this. She had raised it directly a few times before but not for a long time.

"You know why. We just couldn't get along. Not uncommon. Last I looked the divorce rate was over fifty percent."

"What about me? What about my vote?"

"And I out of control…the drugs and everything, you know that."

"You're in control now."

He waved his sheathed, fried-crisp left arm at her, forced a short laugh, and said, "Does this look like 'in control'?"

"Not funny, Dad."

He knew he could shut her down with anger if necessary, but he tried a gentler way.

"I'm sorry, but it's too late now. We all have to live with the situation."

"Why do *we* have to? *I* don't want to."

He didn't respond, hoping for a deliverance from somewhere, until she said, "Why don't you ask her?"

He was not sure he would want to ask her or whether he would want it to happen even if it could happen, but he was surely not going to parachute in at this late date and complicate her life that way. It made him sad that Kelly felt so badly about this, seemed so desperate and afraid—also sad that Annie seemed to have relinquished him, might not take him back even if he begged her; sad because he didn't know if he would go back even if she would take him back; sad because he couldn't trust they would be able to make it work even if he screwed up his courage and returned and she accepted him back, his grandstand play, even if temporarily successful, maybe snatching from her a chance at real happiness with someone who could actually make her happy. All this was now further complicated by the death threat hanging over him. He had wandered too long. Now it was too late for reparation.

Finally, he said, "I can't go barging in now."

"You barged *out*, but you can't barge *in*?"

His face flushed with anger, an involuntary reaction at first but then a stare deliberately prolonged and aimed directly at her.

"I hate you," she said, sprang up from the chair, hurried into the bathroom, and slammed the door.

His left side lit up like a row of maniacal pinball machines in a nightmare arcade, bright lights of torment dancing along his burnt-through nerve ends, invisible spiked balls of pain bouncing madly around. He thought about going after her but didn't know what to say and thought he should let her work it out on her own.

After a while, she came out of the bathroom and said, "I want to go home now."

That made him even sadder, but he didn't try to persuade her to stay. On the front porch he waved at the security guard parked in the driveway. The guard rolled down the car window. "She's going home. I'll drive her," O'Keefe said. The guard would follow them, a protocol they had worked out on previous visits. O'Keefe punched a button on a small remote device hooked to his key chain. His new Jeep Grand Wagoneer, big and black except for wood paneling on the side, had been customized in several ways, including rigging it to start from a distance. At least they would not be able to blow him up in that particular way again.

The headlights flickered. No explosion.

As they walked to the car, he could tell she was carefully observing him. There was only a small hitch in his step now, caused more by flinching from a temporary condition of discomfort than true disability. Climbing into the driver's seat, he winced in frustration and physical pain, but the slightness of the pain was an improvement as well.

They remained silent most of the way to Annie's house. As they drew close, he said, "I hope you'll forgive me one of these days."

"I'm sorry, Dad, I don't hate you. But why won't you *do* something? This is the worst thing that could've happened."

"Is he really so bad?"

"He's not my dad."

•   •   •

Now she saw that *his* car was parked out front. She didn't want to tell her dad that she did not like the way *he* looked at her, how *he* would sidle up too close to her, and some of the things *he* said…she couldn't think of a word for them…they just struck her as weird. She thought about asking her dad to keep going, find something else to do for as long as possible so *he* might be gone by the time they returned. But something held her back. Several things. The quarrel with her dad. The whole thing with the security guard following them, a royal pain. And something else she could hardly recognize or understand, something she had inherited from her father, a hesitation to fully disclose, an unwillingness to open a door that she might not be able to shut. Once in the house, she could just say hello with a fake smile, then rush on up to her room, shut herself in, and maybe finish *Secrets Can Kill* that afternoon.

•   •   •

O'Keefe had also seen the car, and he felt her consternation even before he observed it from the corner of his eye in her body language as she abruptly straightened her posture and shifted restlessly in her seat.

"Bye, Dad," she said, her eyes sparking in either anger or pain or some of both.

"Bye, Pal," he said. "I want you to know I'm working on this. Hope to have a solution before too long."

"Solution? To what?" she said energetically, hopefully.

Another mistake.

"The security thing, I mean."

"Oh," she said, opened the car door and, shoulders stooped, walked slowly up her front walkway, climbed the steps of the front porch, and, without waving goodbye or even looking back at him, let herself in.

Although he made a half-hearted effort to rationalize himself off the hook Kelly had hung him on, he could not dodge the truth that he had found a way to make her life more difficult than it ought to have been.

● ● ●

The front door of the house opened to a small vestibule. The living room was on the right; straight ahead, a stairway to the second floor; beyond the stairway, a short hallway leading to the kitchen. They were in the living room drinking wine and chatting away but at least not cuddled up together on the couch. The first time she had seen that she had nearly gagged. She knew she could not get away with just saying "Hi" and skipping over to the stairway and up the stairs to her room, so she took a few steps toward the living room, stopped at the opening, and gave them a quick wave of her open palm.

"You're early," Annie said.

"Yeah…He wasn't feeling very good."

"The burns?"

"Yeah. Same ol'."

"How about the Percocet? They're not working?"

"I don't think he takes them. He says he doesn't like the way they make him feel."

Annie didn't say anything, but Kelly could tell her mom was pleased he wasn't taking the pills. She had been worrying that all the drugs they had been feeding him since the explosion would hook him again.

"Those Percocet are a fabulous thing," *he* said, eyeing her with that look of inspection and appraisal that made her uncomfortable, "they free people from unnecessary suffering."

Who asked you anyway? Darren...what kind of name is that anyway? Her mom thought him handsome. To Kelly, his smug leer of a smile and smarmy air canceled out any handsomeness.

"I'm heading upstairs. Got a bunch of homework and want to finish this book."

She turned around and headed for the stairs, pretty sure Darren would be watching her. In her room, before she settled down with her book, she reached into her coat pocket and took out two Percocet she had taken from the big bottle in her dad's medicine cabinet. She didn't know why she took the pills or what she would do with them, but she needed to find a good hiding place where her mom wouldn't accidentally come across them.

A little over an hour later, her mom, after a quick knock, opened the door, sat down on the Queen Anne chair across from the matching chair that Kelly sat reading in and said, "How are you? Something seemed...out of sorts...when you came home."

"Is *he* gone?"

The same anger flashed in her mom's eyes as she had seen in her dad's earlier that day. "You mean *Darren,*" her mother said. "You mean, is *Darren* gone?"

I won't say his stupid name.

"You're really gonna do this, Mom?"

"What?"

"Marry him?"

"I surely am. Why are you punishing me like this? You don't want me to be happy?"

"What about me? Why don't I get a vote?"

"Don't keep doing this, please. It'll work out, I promise. He's a good man."

He's not. I just know he's not. "How do you know that? He's not even from here."

"So what? What kind of comment is that?"

"What if Dad asked to come back?"

"He left us."

"He's different now."

"What makes you think he'd want to come back?"

Kelly maintained a tactical silence, her mom's comment being better than it could have been, better than "I wouldn't take the bastard back if he crawled on his knees and begged me to."

"I waited for him too long," Annie said. "I'm done with him. I deserve some happiness."

Kelly exploded in sobs. "I wish I wasn't born. You two shouldn't've had a kid anyway."

Kelly could see the tears glisten in her mom's eyes. But Annie seemed to fight them back, wouldn't let them out to roll down her face.

"Kelly, I'm begging you. Don't make this so hard. It will work out fine."

"What if I want to go live with Dad?"

"Yeah. And maybe get shot or blown up along with him."

"Better than what you're about to do to me."

Annie stood up. "It…is…going…to…happen. Accept it."

As Annie left the room, Kelly said again, "Where's my vote?"

As the door slammed shut, Kelly threw her book on the floor and flopped on the bed, face down, still crying. No, she was not going to accept this. She couldn't stand the way he looked at her or anything else about him. She had to find a way to stop it. What would Nancy do?

CHAPTER 3

AFTER TAKING KELLY home, as O'Keefe tried to figure out what to do with the rest of a cold, dark Saturday to counteract the miasma of physical pain and brooding self-pity that had engulfed him, the phone rang.

"Hey, Boss, got a few minutes for me?"

George.

"When?"

"Now. Or soon?"

"I guess so." O'Keefe could not tolerate suspense, part of a chronic condition of hypervigilance developed initially in his childhood home fraught with domestic disputation and frequent violence, then decisively tipped over into Post-Traumatic Stress Disorder during his tour in Vietnam. But it was not something he was wise enough to seek help for, just another thing to live with.

"What's the subject?" he said, but George Novak had quickly hung up. The two halves of O'Keefe's chest seemed to clench together, and he felt his face flash hot. *What does this mean? Is he gonna tell me he's quitting?*

It had happened before, back in October 1986, fifteen months ago, when O'Keefe seemed to be sliding into a pit of self-destruction and maybe pulling others down with him. Recently, he had loaded a lot of responsibility on George, his employee who O'Keefe had recently made his partner as well, though George still called him

"Boss," ignoring his new status as near-equal just as he had previously ignored the fact that they had been pals since kindergarten. But then there had always been a hint of sardonic mockery in George's tone when he said the word "Boss" that undermined the implication of respect that the word was supposed to carry with it.

The upside for George in their new partnership was the chance to build his own branch of the multifaceted investigative firm that O'Keefe intended to build from his previously solo, off-the-cuff operation, and O'Keefe hoped that, lurking deep within George, was a profound desire to create something of his own. *But he's such a fuck-off. Or at least affects that ethos.* Yet O'Keefe had been a fuck-off too—well, worse than that—until his lawyer buddy Mike Harrigan, his blood brother since the third grade, had offered O'Keefe the very thing O'Keefe now wanted to offer George. But even Harrigan had serious doubts about their friend. When O'Keefe told him what he had in mind, Harrigan said, "Don't know about that one, Pete. Doubt he can hack it."

"Can't believe you're saying that. How about me? How could there've been a more burnt-out case than mine?"

"Totally different. You had a fire burning your whole life, and it was still burning… roaring even…just out of control…George…I think he was born fireproof. All asbestos. Great guy, but neither kindling nor a spark to light it."

Or maybe George still didn't quite trust O'Keefe, didn't want to put so much of the rest of his life at risk with O'Keefe in the way the new venture would demand. Maybe he didn't trust O'Keefe to maintain either his sobriety or his sanity. And even if he did, O'Keefe didn't seem quite made for spending a long time in this world. It might be a lot smarter to purchase a life insurance policy on him than make a life commitment to him. He was certainly a magnet for attracting deadly metals and other lethal substances.

By the time he heard George's tires crunching on the gravel of the circle drive in front of the house, O'Keefe had worried himself into a sorry state. Rising from his chair, correctly anticipating a slight jolt of pain surging through his left arm and leg, he took the few steps to the picture window at the front of the house and saw George talking to the security guard who maintained watch from his car parked in the driveway. O'Keefe moved to the front door, and as he opened it, saw the security guard drive away.

"I told him he could take a break," George said.

O'Keefe lingered in the doorway. George, being one of those people who never got cold or at least never showed it, stood there in a thin leather jacket and an open-collared shirt. Tall, with mostly blond hair rapidly receding, powerfully built, he'd been one of the top pulling guards in the city in high school and had been offered a couple of college scholarships that he had not been wise enough to accept. Instead, he wanted to be a cop. At least he wanted that until he became one and the street duty quickly extinguished that ambition. "It taught me the meaning of that phrase 'hours of boredom punctuated by moments of sheer terror,'" he'd said. He had gone only slightly to seed now in his mid-thirties, overweight but not too much, and still tough, as he had always been, the kind of friend you wanted with you any time a brawl might be brewing. O'Keefe thought he was pretty tough himself, but George had easily whipped him more than once in their younger days.

"Come on out here and enjoy the fresh air."

O'Keefe yelled back, "It's colder than fuck out there. You know I can't stand suspense. What's up?"

"Okay, killjoy," George said, and walked to his car.

"Where you going?"

"Grab a coat and come out here. Got something to show you."

O'Keefe, mightily relieved that George did not seem to be about to announce his resignation, decided he had better humor George in this. When he had retrieved his coat, tucked his chin into his neck, ventured outside and stood on the porch, his breath forming tiny clouds in the frozen air, George opened the back of his white four-door Jeep Cherokee, and what looked like a German Shepherd, but all black instead of black and tan, stepped out, fronted George, sat back on his haunches, focused his gaze on O'Keefe for a few moments, then craned his neck up to look at George as if requesting instructions.

Maybe he's asking, should I eat this guy on the porch?

"Let's go around back," George said.

"Come on, George, what's the damn deal?"

"Just come on, gimp, I guarantee it'll be worth it."

"That dog looks like the devil's dog, soot-black from hellfire."

"Not so. He's a gentle man going placidly through the noise and haste…unless, of course, he's instructed by his master to do otherwise."

"You've been reading *Desiderata*, have you?"

"What's that?"

"The book that quote came from. It's *amidst* the noise and haste, I think."

"I was born this century. *Through* is better"

At the rear of one corner of the backyard, the previous occupants had built a festively decorated gazebo with built-in cushioned bench seating and a small writing desk, also built-in, with a cut-out underneath for the writer's legs.

George gave the dog a signal. It started sniffing, headed for the gazebo, climbed the two short stairs of the structure, and disappeared inside. They followed the dog, and O'Keefe could see that the dog appeared to be sitting still and rigid, facing one of the bench seats.

"That means he found something," George said. "Let's go look."

O'Keefe, mumbling to himself, grudgingly followed. George climbed the gazebo stairs. The dog held its ground and George had to maneuver around him as the dog kept his steadfast gaze on the seating area, built so the seat could be lifted and items stored in the empty seat chamber.

George lifted the seat, looked down, and said, "Well, well. Come have a look, my amigo."

"Jesus," O'Keefe whispered and climbed into the gazebo, now tightly packed with two men and a large dog. George had opened the seat that lidded the chamber and beckoned O'Keefe to look inside. There O'Keefe beheld two items: a pile of dried dung lying next to what appeared to be a stick of dynamite.

"What?" O'Keefe said, "How did that get there?"

George turned to the dog and gave him a doggie treat, took a ball out of his pocket and threw it into the yard. The dog rocketed out of the gazebo, chased down and leaped on the ball, and came trotting back with the ball in his mouth.

"Good boy!" George said twice with great enthusiasm, then addressed O'Keefe's question. "I put them there late last night. That pile was a special gift from my friend here."

"So much for your security man out front."

"They can only do so much. This just shows how easy it is for someone to put you in harm's way."

O'Keefe said nothing, trying to absorb what this might mean.

"And," George continued, "I can tell by the increasingly shrill pitch of your constant bitching that you're gonna make me pull the security pretty soon. So, if you'll just accept the company of my friend here, you'll have your own personal bomb detector. And he'll be a damn good watchdog too, and he probably even remembers a lot from his patrol-dog training. It won't solve everything, but it's cheaper, less a pain in the ass for you, and probably even more effective than what we're doing now."

"What's the cost?"

"Just food and the occasional vet visit and other incidentals."

"What a deal. Where'd he come from?"

"I've still got some good connections with the force. He's a police dog they're retiring. He's not quite the age for retirement, but his handler was Ron Brentano?"

"Name's familiar."

"Killed last Christmas Eve of all days."

"I hope not by a bomb."

"No, this gentleman here," indicating the dog, "wouldn't have let that happen. Ron was off-duty and driving his civilian vehicle when another driver started screaming at him and giving him the finger. They stopped, got out of their cars to duke it out, and the guy pulled a gun. What a world."

"Guns."

"Second Amendment."

"Myself, I'm trying to give them up."

"Be careful there. They do come in handy sometimes," and, pointing to the dog, he said, "but this guy could help with the transition. They'd usually put him with another handler, but he's so close to retirement, they don't think it's worth it. Know what they usually do with retired police dogs when their handlers can't take them home anymore?"

O'Keefe shook his head.

"They destroy them."

O'Keefe looked at the dog whose return gaze, O'Keefe would swear, was brave but plaintive.

"Some stupid thing about they might bite someone without their handler around. So you'll be helping yourself while also doin' a good deed for man's best friend here."

"How old is he?"

"Seven or eight."

"Shit, man, he'll die in five or six years. Last dog I had, I wanted to crawl in the grave with him. I couldn't stop crying."

"You were a kid."

"I'm still a kid, maturation-wise anyway."

"Don't worry about it. The rate you're going, you'll go down well before he does. Don't be a silly-ass loner now. Take him."

"That's a lot of responsibility. You've got to plan your whole life around a dog."

"Here's a deal. We'll own him together. If you need me to take care of him some days or weeks or months, I'll do it. If there are times I can't, we can board him at a nice place. Or, who knows, Sara might want to do it. If you don't want him after you get out from under this shit hanging over you, I'll take him back."

George kept closing off escape hatches.

"What's his name?"

"Karma."

O'Keefe pondered that for a moment. "How can I say 'no' to a dog named that?"

"Yeah, maybe his past lives were well spent…make up for yours… Okay? Are we partners on this beast? Just like in the business?"

"I'll try him for a while, but you'd better be serious about taking him back on demand. I'll have no compunction about sending him back."

"Compunction smunction. Deal." And, finally acknowledging the cold with a shiver, he said, "Let's go in. You got any booze left in there?"

Once inside the house, he ushered George to a seat at the long dining room table, large enough for a feast for ten, but it would almost never be used for that; instead, as now, it would most of the time be covered with large and small piles of business documents and newspaper and magazine segments with articles O'Keefe had set aside to read or that he had read and wanted to keep and store in a filing system that he intended to create but never accomplished.

The dog followed behind George, paying no attention to O'Keefe, and stood waiting for instruction until George issued him the command to "*Sitz.*" Then he found the nearest corner and, in a business-like way, with a dignified self-possession and grace, lay down on his stomach, resting his head on his front paws, eyes wide open and watching George with utmost vigilance.

"Sits?" O'Keefe said. "Your grammar's gettin' even worse, if that's possible."

"It's a 'z,' not an 's.' It's German, shithead. Police dog commands are in German."

"I won't ask why."

"Doesn't matter as long as you learn them. I'll get you a list."

"What's some examples?"

"'Stop' is '*Halt,*' just like the English word."

"'Stand' is '*Steh,*'" which George pronounced as *Sh-tay.*

"'Quiet' is '*Ruhig,*'" which he pronounced as *Roo-ig.*

"That's a damned important one. You don't want him barking like crazy when you're tryin' to sneak up."

"And 'Bite' is '*Packen.*'"

"You sound like Colonel Klink," O'Keefe said, as he set a small tumbler in front of George, poured Wild Turkey until George signaled to stop, placed the bottle on the table within George's reach, and sat down.

O'Keefe looked over at the dog. "He seems to be your boy. Will he obey me?"

"If you've got the right attitude and, of course, the right words, Colonel Klink. And you'll need a couple of long sessions with the canine squad gang. They'll show you some magic and wonders."

"Any risk he'll bite me?"

"None."

"How about other people? Annie is scared enough without throwing a killer dog into the mix."

"He's multiple-trained…for detection and tracking and what they call protection but means attack. He's pretty rusty on the tracking and attack stuff, but he's almost certain to go after anyone wantin' to hurt you."

"Otherwise he's friendly?"

"In a distant way. He's no cuddly, tail-wagging, jump-on-you, pet-me-pet-me type. One problem is people are prejudiced against German Shepherds. And this all-black guy here, as you've already said yourself, is even scarier. You'll have people jump right to panic when they see him coming, grab their kids and all that, or they might not let you come around with the dog ever."

"I guess fuck 'em if they can't take a joke, huh?"

George gave a little grunt of a laugh and took a drink.

"So how's business?" O'Keefe asked, being careful not to seem aggressive, importunate, insistent, or even eager. George had been extremely busy lately, even harried, not a state of being consistent with George's usual persona. He hoped George wasn't in too deep too quickly.

"Boss, I can't believe it. Once you and I and Harrigan started putting the word out, I'm gettin' calls. Lots of calls. And from big-shit people. And big jobs. Security for buildings, warehouses, events, every damn thing you can think of. I can't hire people fast enough.

And remember our old buddy Larry Considine? He's head of a big company now, lots of locations, and wants to meet with me to talk about designing a security plan for the whole thing."

"You okay with that?"

"Yeah, so far anyway. But it's work, I'll tell you that…like havin' to get in shape after the off-season."

"You've gotta stick with me. Don't leave me hanging. You need help?"

"Hell, yes. Sara's helpin' as much as she can, but it won't be enough, and she's got her own line of work to handle."

"Don't be waiting 'til the water's up to your nose to call for more help."

"Okay, here's the call. Gurgle, gurgle."

"Monday we'll meet. How 'bout the bodyguard angle? Anything happening on that?"

"Personal security," George said, rolling his eyes in self-mockery at his use of the fancier term. "Not yet."

"Might not make a lot of money at that, but it might be interesting."

"Something for *you* to do, eh?"

"Gotta contribute somewhere somehow."

George turned the glass up and drank its contents, set it down, and said, "Boss, I think you might have something big here."

"*We…we* might have something big here…"

"Okay…*we*."

"There's a guy in New York who's built this large investigative firm, mostly doing big-time background checks and due diligence for companies and banks and all kinds of things growing out of that."

"New York? That might as well be Tim-buk-fuckin'-tu."

"I don't mean *going* to New York…just the idea…" O'Keefe brought himself up short. The hook might be in, but George could still wriggle himself off before he was flopping around in the boat, and O'Keefe didn't want to scare him with grandiose plans. O'Keefe guiltily wondered if he was doing his friend good or harm with this new enterprise.

"Back to Karma," George said. "I already showed him around the offices so he's familiar with that. Problem is these dogs are working dogs. They can't just laze around. They've got to be active. They need a lot of strenuous play if they're not working, and he won't really be working at all anymore, not like he's used to anyway."

"Bad news there. I can't be playin' around with a dog all day."

"It won't be all on you. Sara's in on it, and we'll take some turns, and I've got a whole list of people that love these dogs who'll come by and pick him up and take him somewhere to chase balls. And by the way, the ball-chasing is a much bigger treat to him than the eats. We'll wean him off the really heavy exercise by degrees, until he's more or less a slug like his new masters."

"I'll give it a try, but I don't see how it can work."

"Worth tryin'. Especially right now. Doesn't have to be forever. You've got yourself way deep in the shit, Boss, and you just have to put up with some inconvenience. This'll be better than what you're puttin' up with now."

George stood up to leave, and the dog stood up too. "I've got a bag of food out in the car to start you out. And some treats and toys. Those are important. And lots of enthusiastic 'atta boy' reward talk."

O'Keefe and Karma followed George to the front door where George commanded, "*Sitz.*"

"Hope you mean the dog," O'Keefe said.

"Which reminds me, I forgot a couple of commands."

George lowered his voice to make sure the dog would not think he was actually issuing commands to him.

"'*Bleib,*'" which he pronounced as *Blibe,* "means 'Stay.'"

"'Come' is '*Hier,*'" which he pronounced as *Hee-r.*

"'Down' is '*Platz,*'" which he pronounced as *Plotz.*

"And 'Heel' is '*Fuss,*'" which he pronounced as *Foos.*

After George deposited the bags of food and treats and big bowls for food and water, O'Keefe watched Karma watch George climb into his car and drive away. His fears about George seemed to have been misplaced. George acted entirely committed to the program. So far anyway. After George drove out of sight, the dog whined a couple of times, worrying O'Keefe, but then looked back at O'Keefe as if to say "Well, what do we do now?"

Reading the gentle but insistent question that so often seemed to be on the dog's face, O'Keefe responded out loud, "Well, Karma, I really don't know."

CHAPTER ▶ 4

BEFORE THE BOMBING and the burn ward, O'Keefe habitually rose at 5 a.m. and performed a short but intense exercise routine, accompanied occasionally by a television morning news program when he could force himself to bear both the distressing news and the distressingly chipper way the local news people broadcast the stream of tragedies, scandals, and ineptitudes. After an intense twenty minutes of exercise, he would flip the switch on the coffee maker he had pre-loaded the night before, shower and shave, pour a cup of coffee "to go," drive to the office and arrive there between 7 and 7:30. But these days he had taken to arriving much later—"banker's hours," he grumbled to himself—because of the combination of sleeping later due to the trifecta of pain, itching, and Percocet that had turned his nights into bouts of bouncing between desperate wakefulness and troubled sleep, followed first thing in the morning by the required daily session of bandage changing and wound dressing with the home healthcare nurse.

George's prophecy about people reacting negatively to German Shepherds came promptly true in the case of the nurse, who asked that Karma be shut up in another room.

"He's really a nice guy," O'Keefe tried to assure her.

"Please," she said. "I don't like them."

The security guards—one stationed in front of the building, the other at the door of O'Keefe's office suite, both there at O'Keefe's expense in an only partially successful effort to mollify the three other tenants in the building who had threatened to move out—felt quite differently about the animal, every day grinning and nodding their heads in affirmation as if he had arrived with a beautiful woman on his arm. And in his waiting room, Sara, looking sharp and crisp in a violet silk blouse and black skirt, welcomed them with an excited hello. The enthusiasm of all these people on beholding a man and his dog brightened O'Keefe's mood.

Sara, still doing receptionist duty until they found a replacement, after which she could work full-time from the new private office they had finished out for her, picked up the receiver, punched a button, and said in her smoky voice, "George, your best friend is here...and Pete too."

Hanging up, she said to O'Keefe, "George wanted to be told as soon as Karma arrived."

O'Keefe sensed Karma could feel George coming and that the dog could hardly restrain himself from lunging to greet him but managed to maintain his dignified presence alongside O'Keefe.

"Release him, okay?" George said.

"What's that mean?"

"Tell him he can come to me."

O'Keefe didn't know what to say. Pointing, he said, "Go, Karma. Go to George."

Karma stayed put.

"The command for 'Go' is '*Lauf*,'" which George pronounced as *Loaf*.

"Karma, *Lauf*, to George," O'Keefe said awkwardly and pointed at George.

With a tail swish or two, Karma moved to George and gave him his head for a pat.

"Now call him back," George said.

"Karma, *Fuss*," O'Keefe said, and the dog immediately, without a hint of the reluctance O'Keefe expected, turned away from George and returned to O'Keefe's side.

"*Sitz*," O'Keefe instructed, and Karma obliged. "Why does he stare up that way?" he asked George. "Looks uncomfortable."

"They're trained to look up for a hand signal. You'll need to learn those too. The K-9 cop gang can show you those. But now what are you gonna do?"

George was testing him.

"Treat?" O'Keefe asked.

"Right on. Not one but two."

As O'Keefe fed the treats to Karma, George turned to Sara. "I've got appointments out of the office today. Can you take him out?"

"You mean Pete?" she said.

They all chuckled.

"Sure," she said.

George looked her up and down, silently questioning how she would do that the way she was dressed.

"I brought some other clothes, Big Fella. Trust me."

George nodded and turned to leave, and O'Keefe thought he detected a ripple of movement somewhere in Karma toward following George.

"Stay, Karma," he said, then remembering the German word, said, "*Bleib*," and Karma complied, though not without watching George intently until he was out of sight.

Sara said, "You look good on that dog, or that dog looks good on you, I don't know which. Can't wait for Harrigan to see him. He'll be here soon."

"What for?"

"He wouldn't say. You think he's got something for us?"

"There's a rumor to that effect."

"Okay. God, I hope so," she said. "We need the work, *I* need the work."

He and Karma took up positions in his office, Karma lying in the corner with his head resting on his front paws and O'Keefe at his desk. His arrival at the office had pumped some adrenalin through him, but now, as it subsided, the dull pain replaced it, and the choice would soon be to clench his teeth and suffer it or surrender to the Percocet and the mental fog that came with the pills. He needed something to do, something to concentrate on, something to distract him. He thought about calling Harrigan and urging him to come right away.

Sara gave her quick knock and came right in with papers in her hand.

"You know," he said, "one of these days you'll do that, and I'll be changing clothes, and you'll catch me with my pants down."

"I'm sure I won't notice anything of significance," she said.

She set the papers on his desk. "Sign these sometime today. And I've got a candidate here for the receptionist job that you ought to meet. You feel okay? You willing now?"

He really didn't feel like meeting someone new, but he couldn't say no. He had to lift the burden from her of doing both her old job and her new one.

"Sure," he said.

"I'm still not believing this," she said. "More than I ever hoped for or even could imagine. Thank you. Truly. Bottom-of-my-heart thank-you. Top too."

He responded with a slight nod of his head and said, "No thank-you necessary. You deserve it." She had come there when he had first opened and didn't really know anything business-wise, not revealing much about her past, her present, or anything else. She signaled reluctance to tell and he decided not to ask, and they joined in an unstated conspiracy of silence about who she really might be. Any employer in his right mind wouldn't have hired her without more of a background check, but something she exuded, some combination of energy, brains, and, he had to admit, sex appeal told him not to let this person elude him.

Hired as a secretary, receptionist, and all-around girl-Friday, she eagerly grabbed at every chance to do detective work, often plunging into depths far above her head and aquatic abilities, but surviving somehow, and educating herself on her own time in every way she could about the profession and the business until he suspected she knew a lot more about it than he did. He wondered if she had ever perceived, though she was surely too smart and intuitive not to know, what he really felt about her, which was simple. One small signal of welcome from her and they would have been together. But she gave no such signal, and he managed to hold himself in check. It had been long enough now that he had accepted that nothing would ever happen, and, as time went on, he had moved from painful longing to calm acceptance, training himself like a ballet dancer determined to maintain his weight, with only occasional tormented moments of thwarted desire.

She left and returned leading a tall, young woman with an athletic body topped with an explosion of unruly red curls who seemed ill at ease in her dress and short-heeled shoes.

"Hello," the young woman said, in a bright, high voice and reached out her hand in a manly way while casting a wary eye at Karma in the corner.

"Is Fido there well behaved?" she said with a sparkle.

"I think so," he said, smiling, "but I can't swear it. I haven't known him long."

Sara said, "I'll leave you three to get acquainted."

"Pete O'Keefe," he said, holding out his hand.

"So I figured. How about Fido?"

"What about him?"

"His name?"

"Karma. His name is Karma. No last name that I'm aware of."

"Cool name," she said.

"And your name?"

"Dagmar…Dagmar Sibelius. That's Si, like Sister, Bay like San Francisco, Lee like Robert E., and Us, like you and me. Si-be-li-us."

This girl had promise. The rest of the interview seemed unnecessary, but he felt obliged to continue.

"Is that Greek?"

"No," she said decisively, with a touch of irritation. "Everybody asks me that. It's Swedish/Finnish. You never heard of the composer?"

"Well, now that you mention it, I've sort of heard of him. *Frederick Sibelius?*"

He should have known from the pale skin and vibrant blue eyes there was nothing Greek about her.

"That's the dude, sir. My dad says he's some kind of remote ancestor."

"Did you inherit any of it?"

"I can bang on a can, but I don't know a chord from a cuckoo bird."

"Education?

"JUCO. I have my associate degree."

"Want to go on to university?"

"Not really. Not right now anyway. I can't afford it. I'm a diver… high dive…and a dancer…but you can't make a living at either. I have to learn to do something to make a living."

"Why this job?"

"Seems different…maybe even exciting. I read about you in the paper last year."

"I'm hoping it won't be that exciting ever again."

"I get it," she said, but he sensed a bit of disappointment in her tone.

"Sara told you about the salary and the benefits, few though they may be?"

"She did."

"You okay with the dog?"

"If the dog's okay with me."

"Sara and I'll talk, and she'll get back to you soon, one way or another."

"That's it?"

"I forgot to tell you at first. Don't assume anything by the length of the interview or the stupidity of my questions."

She leaned toward him, the top of her body over the front of his desk, not in a come-on sort of way but in utmost earnestness. "I'll tell you one thing, sir. If you hire me, I won't disappoint you. I don't disappoint."

"Guaranteed?"

"Guaranteed."

"Who could turn that down?"

She nodded her head slowly, decisively. "One more thing. Do I have to wear this getup every day?"

He hesitated. Sara always dressed upscale. She was scrappy but dressed very feminine. This one was a tomboy all the way. *Surely she wears Birkenstocks.*

"Not the heels," he said. "Flats are okay. Leather though. Not tennis shoes. Maybe the dress…or a skirt. Not always. Pants might be okay too…"

He realized he didn't know what the hell he was talking about.

"…You can work it all out with Sara. But we *do* work with lawyers and bankers—straitlaced, proper, uptight—at least on the surface…so we can't be too loosey-goosey."

"I won't disappoint," she repeated.

As the girl stood up to leave, Sara knocked and brought Harrigan in.

After some shuffling around, Sara said, "Mike Harrigan, this is Dagmar. She's interviewing for my job."

"Old job," O'Keefe said.

"Dagmar," Harrigan said, appreciating the name.

The girl reached out her hand. As they shook hands, O'Keefe said, "That's Dagmar Sibelius—Si like Sister, Bay like San Francisco, Lee like Robert E., and Us like you and me. Sibelius."

"Yes, sir," Dagmar enthused.

"And Mr. Harrigan here is one of those straitlaced, proper, uptight lawyers I was telling you about."

"Only one of those adjectives is correct," Harrigan said.

"Dudes!" Dagmar blurted happily, "and Sara and Fido too! What a deal! Sorry, sir."

"That's okay," O'Keefe said. "You can call me 'Dude, Sir' or 'Sir Dude' from now on."

He could tell she didn't know whether to take him seriously.

"Actually, it's Pete. We're first-name around here, though this is *Mister* Harrigan."

Harrigan made a scoffing noise.

Sara led Dagmar out of the office.

Harrigan turned to Karma, who was now sitting upright and alert, seeming to anticipate the possibility of being called into action. "And this is *the dog!* Can I pet him?"

Harrigan was acting like he was eight years old again.

"Definitely."

Harrigan approached Karma carefully, and the dog allowed him to start with a couple of general pats and follow with a more vigorous rub of the head and some enthusiastic backbone scratching.

Harrigan returned to O'Keefe's desk and sat down in the chair in front of it.

"Let's have him over closer here. It'll be like FDR and Churchill and 'Fala'...That was Roosevelt's dog's name."

"I know that, dickhead. Don't patronize me. I even know who FDR and Churchill were."

O'Keefe summoned Karma and instructed him to sit, then lay down. "I guess I'm FDR because I've got the dog?" he said. "You have any more grandiose delusions this morning?"

"Here's for real. I got that Central Bank portfolio."

The bank, plagued by having made more bad loans than good, had failed in the previous year, part of the ongoing S&L crisis that had already crippled, and was daily continuing to cripple, large sectors of the U.S. banking system as the decade staggered toward its close at the end of Ronald Reagan's second term.

Harrigan continued: "A group from Texas bought the entire loan portfolio and hired me to handle the whole recovery effort."

"No problem with you-know-what?"

"Amazingly, no. I disclosed it, and they just shrugged it off. Maybe a criminal prosecution is a badge of honor down in Texas."

"Well, you *were acquitted.*"

"Yeah, but if it was me in that position, I'm not sure I'd give that kind of responsibility to somebody sloppy or stupid enough to get himself indicted in the first place."

"They must've checked you out, got the whole story." Then he added, casually, not wanting to seem too pathetically eager, even to his old friend, "Anything for me in there?"

"Hell, yes. You were part of my sales pitch. It's perfect for Sara. She's great with numbers. You guys are not only cheaper than lawyers but better for a lot of this work. Most lawyers don't know a financial statement from a wad of toilet paper."

"She'll be incredibly happy. When do we start?"

"ASAP. I've got to scope it out first, but that won't take more than a week or so."

"We're ready."

Harrigan again turned his attention to the dog, contemplated for a few moments, then said, "You're not FDR. You're Rusty. Corporal Rusty. From *Rin Tin Tin.* You've got your own Rinty. You're living one of our boyhood dreams."

O'Keefe couldn't help laughing but quickly turned serious. "No dream. A nightmare. This is like being in prison and having to pay the guards myself. I need to solve this."

"How might you do that?" Harrigan scoffed.

"I'm thinking I'll go talk to the people running the Outfit now that Carmine Jagoda's dead."

Harrigan's eyes widened to express his shock. "You've had many really bad ideas in your misguided life, but this one may be the worst of all. You think they've got a Grievance Committee or something? They're not exactly the United Nations or the World Court."

"Whatever happens, it couldn't be worse than this."

"Horseshit. Death is incurable and forever."

"How else can I get out of this trap? I can't even have a decent life with my daughter unless I prove a negative…that the Outfit *didn't* do it. How do you prove a negative?"

DAN FLANIGAN • 41

Harrigan had nothing readily at hand or tongue to counter that.

"Screw it, I'm goin' for it."

Again, Harrigan did not respond, apparently accepting from a long history with and deep knowledge of his friend that nothing would dissuade him from pursuing this, at least until presented with clear evidence of the folly of it, though by then it might be too late.

"So, I repeat," O'Keefe continued, "who runs the Outfit now?"

"You're suffering from many maladies, apparently including a case of mistaken identity. *You're* the detective, not me. Can't George or Sara find that out for you?"

"No way am I gonna tell them."

Harrigan shook his head like a dog shaking off water. "Secrets. Really bad idea."

"I don't want to scare them. We're building this business. I don't need them to be worrying about what I'm doing."

"Don't kid yourself. I'm sure they're *always* worried about what you're doing...How about that cop, Ross? Surely he knows."

"Not the worst idea."

"Of course you couldn't tell him your purpose. Another secret..."

CHAPTER ▶ 5

DETECTIVE ROSS'S VOICE dripped with suspicion when O'Keefe called him to ask for the meeting.

"What's up?"

"Just want to find out where the bombing investigation stands. If it's allowed, I'll treat you to breakfast, lunch, dinner, or a cocktail."

"Well, not to receive a bribe under false pretenses, I can answer that right now with two words—nothing and nowhere. Sorry about that."

"Indulge me, okay?"

They met for breakfast at Ross's designated place at 6 a.m. Ross was no "doughnut" cop with a big belly and jiggling jowls. He ordered one poached egg, dry wheat toast, and a glass of milk while O'Keefe ordered one blueberry pancake, one egg, and a side of toast.

"Not to be disrespectful," O'Keefe said, "but it seems like the police don't give a flying fuck about my case."

Ross's eyelids slowly closed and opened again. "First," he said, wearily, "it's not my case. I started on it because it was connected to your friend Beverly's case and the Jerry Jensen scandal...but once those resolved, it passed quickly to someone else's jurisdiction. I did check with them once, and there was just nowhere else for them to go with it. It seemed obvious...everybody knows it was surely David Bowman that did it, right?"

O'Keefe said nothing.

"Right?" Ross said, a question that was more like a command.

"I thought so, still think so, but that's just an assumption. No prosecutor would've taken that case to court without more evidence."

"Prosecutors. Pain in the ass."

O'Keefe could tell he was losing Ross. The detective did not have a good excuse for the laziness of his colleagues but could not admit that and was about to close up entirely. But O'Keefe persisted. "Meanwhile, apparently everybody in the world, except maybe you and I, think it was Carmine Jagoda's people, and I'm living in a prison of security guards and bomb sniffing dogs and nobody wanting to be anywhere within explosion distance of me. I can't even go to my daughter's basketball games, can't even shoot around with her anymore, can't even have her visit me except under guard."

Ross looked genuinely sad about that but offered no solution or even solace. He just shrugged and said, "Shitty deal...but better than dead."

"I'm not so sure," O'Keefe said, unsmiling. He took a couple bites of his breakfast and let Ross do the same, then said in a casual way, hoping it would seem like an innocent and harmless bit of curiosity, "Who's running the Outfit these days?"

But Ross remained guarded. "It's not clear right now. Might not be anybody at all. Free-for-all. Why you ask?"

"Just curious." But he decided he might as well go with this, try to draw this buttoned-up man out a little bit, but he needed to word it carefully.

"It's occurred to me to try to get a powwow with somebody...try to bury the hatchet."

Ross's face folded into a look between concern and contempt. "The only hatchet that'll get buried'll be in your skull."

"Better than what I'm living through now."

"Forget it. You're desperate and crazy. Go see a priest or a shrink instead."

"They're saying Russ Lord is organizing a special grand jury to go after them."

Ross chuckled. "Just trying to take advantage of the disarray... finishing off the wounded...coup de gras."

Ross's face formed into another look, more squint-eyed with suspicion, that told O'Keefe that Ross considered O'Keefe to be crazy, maybe like a fox. O'Keefe thought he had better move on.

"You think your guys handling the case, my case, would sit down with me? Maybe there's some way to prove that Bowman did it instead of just assuming. What if it *was* someone else? Not Jagoda's people but someone other than Bowman, or in addition to Bowman."

"Maybe...I'll ask."

"I hope you'll do a little more than ask."

"It's Sergeant Trowbridge. I can't make him talk to you, but since you're the victim, he should be willing anyway."

And O'Keefe understood that this line of conversation was definitively...*closed.*

● ● ●

As Lieutenant Ross drove away from the meeting, he hovered between a discomfort something close to fear and an anger something close to rage. O'Keefe seemed idiotically determined to poke his stick around in the Outfit snake pit. He remembered from the police report what O'Keefe told them that Jerry Jensen had said to O'Keefe when Jensen realized that O'Keefe had brought about his downfall: "You're an inconvenient man." Now O'Keefe might be inconveniencing Ross.

Ross had managed to win O'Keefe a reprieve from a death sentence (O'Keefe being unaware to this day of either the death sentence or the reprieve) that Carmine Jagoda had pronounced on O'Keefe from his prison hospital bed shortly before Jagoda's own death, but that had been more of a selfish than a charitable act on the Lieutenant's part, more a reprieve for himself than O'Keefe, since Ross was the one ordered to do the hit as repayment of a debt he owed the Outfit for a problem they had solved for him long ago when he was very young and very stupid. He had hoped that was all behind him but maybe it never could be. Maybe he would have to keep cleaning this mess up the rest of the life. He was on a promising trajectory that could lead to the Chief job someday, but that aside, no matter what, he surely didn't want to be exposed, ruined, maybe even put to death (his state law still prescribed capital punishment for certain crimes), or, maybe even worse, end up as a cop in prison. But it went beyond that. The shame. His parents were still alive, his sister and brothers, his wife, children. Yes, for sure he intended to do anything necessary to keep his secret buried.

•　•　•

Sergeant Trowbridge agreed to the meeting but played it wary and tight-lipped. He was an ugly fellow: long-faced and slack-jawed, a donkey-face, with a large, purple birthmark on his right cheek and more hairs sprouting from the birthmark and his nose and ears than from his scalp. O'Keefe tried to feel sorry for him but couldn't manage it as Trowbridge seemed to be indifferent to O'Keefe's case and perhaps to everything else in the world, revealing an absence of personality traits of any discernible kind, but an absence that he still managed somehow to decisively convey, expressing itself in mannerisms and voice so laconic as to promptly induce his listener to pine for the deepest possible sleep.

"What can I do for you, Mr. O'Keefe?" he said with insincere politeness.

"I just wanted to get an update on how my case is progressing."

After a ponderous silence terminated by a heroic sigh, Trowbridge said, "Don't we think we know who probably did it?"

O'Keefe knew the answer but waited, wanting to hear Trowbridge say it.

After a further silence, Trowbridge said, "David Bowman of course...and he's dead."

"Is there any actual evidence of that...I mean that Bowman himself did it...as opposed to one of his buddies?"

"There's really not much evidence of anything except the explosion itself. We interviewed all the neighbors. Nobody saw or heard anything...until the explosion anyway."

"Yeah, I do guess they heard that. Certainly *I* did. How about the assholes at that *Cherry Pink* strip club?"

"Problem is that's the county. Not our jurisdiction. We're city only, and they're not too cooperative out there."

"Could Bowman really have pulled it off by himself...nobody at all to help him?"

"Maybe. Probably. It's not that hard. Pretty simple really. Just embed some blasting caps in the explosive material...likely some form of dynamite...could be as simple as maybe some gunpowder and charcoal, sulfur, potassium nitrate...pack it up and attach it to the car starter."

"Any evidence the Outfit boys were behind it?"

"Nah," Trowbridge growled and shook his head, the only thing close to animation that he had exhibited, and even that was a muffled, long-distance thing.

"Is there a way to prove that?"

"I don't see how you prove a negative like that, but I guarantee you, if they did it…well, let's put it this way, we wouldn't be sitting here talking, I don't think."

"What's next? Or is this case really just cold now?"

"Not officially. But practically…probably, yeah…especially when we're almost sure who did it and that person's dead. You can only justify using so many resources on a case like that. Unless we get a break, some kind of tip, a snitch, something…"

"Probably." "Likely." "Maybe." What a fucking joke. O'Keefe's PTSD was shooting Roman candles across the night sky of his mind. He could hardly resist reaching out and smacking this butthead. But he knew he not only could not do that but had to refrain from showing his disgust as well. No good would come of insulting Trowbridge. He tried to still his rapidly beating heart and said, with the faint hint of a plea in his voice, "So if it wasn't Bowman, or if Bowman had a partner or partners, there's maybe a killer or killers out there that might just want to finish the job?"

A rhetorical question as far as Trowbridge was concerned. No answer.

"Not to be insulting or whining, but I guess I'm not the category of victim that sparks enough outrage to galvanize the effort?"

"Look, it may not seem like it, but I really do feel for you, but there's nothing more we can realistically do. I shouldn't say this, but ya know…you're a detective…"

"And that means…" O'Keefe said, even though he well knew what it meant.

"I think I'll leave it at that."

Walking out of the police station, it struck him—a realization that would make it even harder than usual for him to sleep that night, and many future nights. By raising the issue, starkly, not just to Trowbridge but to himself, whether Bowman had acted alone or had help or even a proxy in setting that car bomb, he had opened an even uglier can of worms. Many assumptions that he and others had not bothered to fully explore and analyze had now to be reconsidered and challenged, not just the bombing but going back to what had led to the bombing—the murder of O'Keefe's old friend (you could almost say, old flame), Beverly Bronson. Who really had killed her? Maybe not Bowman himself, or at least not Bowman alone. The old, corrupt, angry energy flared within him, the same energy that surged through him long ago as he fired machine gun rounds into the smoky dusk enveloping the shrouded jungle canopy as they swooped down into the chaos of human suffering sprawling all over the landing zone to extract the living, the wounded, and the dead. When he left the parking lot, he hit the accelerator hard, the Wagoneer lurched forward, tires screeching, and in seconds he was driving well above the speed limit.

●   ●   ●

For the second time in his life, O'Keefe drove on this lonesome road through the shadows cast by the viaduct bridge overhead that for more than half a century had constantly whined from the sound of wheels spinning on metal, carrying automobile traffic over the river-bottoms area of the city. There the stockyards, slaughterhouses, and packing plants had enabled successive waves of immigrants to engage in decently paid toil and conferred on the city its national reputation for the rendering of cows and pigs into fresh meat oozing blood in the butcher's case. All gone now, the soul of it anyway, nothing left but the decaying buildings, some of them abandoned entirely, others occupied in an offhand, half-hearted, shambling sort of way by the kinds of enterprises that needed a lot of space but couldn't afford to pay much for it—body shops, salvage operations, storage places for items one step away from the junk-heap, warehouses for items not worth anyone's effort to steal.

Off by itself, amidst a parking lot that seemed far too large for it and was never full, stood a dirty-white, part wood but mostly metal one-story building that housed a bar named Angie's. His first visit to the place, two years before, and the adventure that had taken him there, had not turned out well, and he had no good reason to hope this visit would end up any better. But he didn't really care. He was just surrendering to a fatalistic impulse to plant himself in the way of things, even if those things might turn out to be harmful to him, as long as they might provoke a change in the current unsatisfactory condition of his existence.

He didn't know exactly who owned the place now, but he knew from his previous investigation back in 1986 that for many years "Donald Praeger" had been the name on the liquor license and that Donald Praeger had been for decades the lawyer for Carmine Jagoda, the real owner of the place, and the boss of what passed for a Mafia in this city that always seemed more like a town. O'Keefe guessed that, through whatever special mechanisms, or more probably just winks and nods, of informal decedent estate administration were honored by the Outfit, some individual or group of individuals, or just the collective organization, if it could be called by such an exalted name, continued to enjoy whatever meager benefits the Angie's enterprise might yield. Just as he did on his previous visit, he observed that the cars in the parking lot were much fancier than this nondescript joint would seem to be able to attract but for some special magnetism not readily apparent to the viewer's eye.

He did not know who he was looking for or what he would do if he actually found himself in the way of one or more relevant personages, but he did know he was more likely to find them here than in most other places in the city. He parked and gingerly let himself down from the Wagoneer driver's seat, noting with gratitude and hope that each time he engaged in it, this essential maneuver, necessarily repeated several times daily, kept getting easier and less painful to accomplish—progress he could measure almost daily now.

He took from his right coat pocket a key with a round base larger than the usual base of a key, about the size of a silver dollar. The prong of the key extended from its base about three inches to a sharp point at the end. He didn't remember, if he ever knew, what this key actually unlocked, or even how he had come to possess it, but he had immediately sensed, without really understanding it at first, that this rather long key, thick at the base but narrowing and sharpening toward its end, could be quite useful for a purpose that had nothing to do with the unlocking of anything. Now sure he had the key with him, he dropped it back into his coat pocket.

Maybe twenty customers were sprinkled around the place—a couple of separate pairs at the bar, several in booths, a pair playing pool, and another pair perched lightly on stools, gripping cues, watching the play, waiting their turn to challenge the winner or maybe for a doubles game. Streaks of cigarette smoke lingered in the air. Nothing played on the jukebox, and there was little sound other than the periodic click of a pool ball against others and the murmur of mostly low voices punctuated only occasionally by a shout or curse of anger, joy, or surprise. He at once became the object of a more than casual amount of scrutiny. A couple of his observers nodded at him in a slit-eyed ambiguous gesture of possible but conditional, though less than trustful, welcome. He could not recognize any of them from memories of grainy photos in the newspaper or the much clearer mug shots he had at various times been shown of certain of them. He wondered if any of them might recognize him from his own photos in the newspaper when he had killed some of their associates who had been trying to do him the same favor.

He planted himself on a barstool and ordered a diet cola with lime and a package of beer nuts. Aware of the bartender eyeing this odd teetotaling new customer, O'Keefe retrieved from a holder on the bar a small plastic-covered menu with fading print that looked like it had been produced decades earlier. He knew this visit would almost certainly not come to much. He had been hoping to somehow find some evidence to help prove himself correct about there being no lingering danger from them, which would allow him to confidently provide the same assurance to others. Despite his previous deadly confrontation with them and his own rather dubious claim on respectability, he still retained the status of a "civilian," a person who could not be harmed without risk of bringing down on the perpetrators the wrath of the appointed keepers of civil order. But if he was wrong about that, he might as well try to provoke a confrontation and a denouement of some kind. Worth the risk, he thought, because his current situation seemed intolerable.

He decided on a trip to the bathroom, though he did not need to go, thinking maybe he would attract someone to follow him in there and check him out, someone like the young olive-skinned tough guy staring at him with dark eyes from his perch on a stool by the pool table, his slick, shining black hair swept back from a long forehead and tucked behind his ears and flowing down onto the top of his shirt collar. O'Keefe reached into his coat pocket and maneuvered the key to place it between his knuckles and closed his hand into a fist. Now a quick punch with the protruding key could cause its human target the severest pain, or if the situation justified it, a quick jab could drive that key prong into an assailant's eyeball, immediately terminating both the contest and the sight in that eye.

He asked the bartender, "Can I get an Italian steak sandwich to go?"

"Sure."

"And where's the john?" he asked, though he knew its location from his previous visit.

"Back, to the right."

He moved through the back room, dark and empty, as it had been the last time he had walked through it, and he wondered if anyone ever actually played the dusty electronic bowling machine or the forlorn looking shuffleboard. Entering the room, he made a right turn and headed toward the bathroom. Beyond the bathroom was a door to what he believed to be an office. On his previous visit a yellow light had oozed from underneath the door frame. Now it was dark. *As dark as Carmine Jagoda's tomb.*

The bathroom contained two urinals side by side and a toilet stall along with a small sink and one of those hand drying devices consisting of a single cloth towel that rolled out of the device when pulled. He walked up to the urinal, unzipped his pants, but did nothing else. If someone attacked him, it would be difficult to respond with his dick in his hand. And indeed, someone did come in—an old man who hardly bothered to notice O'Keefe as he shuffled into the toilet stall, locked the door, and soon produced a series of sloppy-sounding farts, which O'Keefe could not help but interpret as a commentary on the worth of his current quest. He smiled at the indignity of it, gave the empty urinal a flush to keep up the appearance that he truly needed to be there, and returned to his barstool.

The bartender brought the sandwich to him wrapped in butcher paper. "Need a bag?"

"No thanks."

"Chips? Something to drink?"

"No thanks."

O'Keefe swallowed the remainder of the cola, left the half-full bag of beer nuts on the bar, and departed.

As he drove under the viaduct, climbing back up from those lower depths of the city, it came to him that he had been flopping around like a caught fish on a boat deck and that he had failed to bring to his mind that the only human accessible to him that might possess the answer, or at least know where the answer could be found, was Oswald Malone, who arguably owed O'Keefe a favor or two.

CHAPTER ▶ 6

BUILT IN THE 1930s as a WPA project, the United States Courthouse seemed like a limestone pledge to the citizenry that the U.S. government would not only survive that decade's world-shattering economic crisis but long endure thereafter; and so it had endured for half a century thus far. Occupants of that blandly boring but stolidly reassuring edifice included the lawyers of the Office of the United States Attorney, advocating for the government's interests in both criminal and civil matters in courtrooms throughout the building. The head of that office in this judicial district, Russell Lord, the "United States Attorney" (the lawyers under him being referred to as "Assistant United States Attorneys"), like each of the other individuals who held such positions in judicial districts across the country, received his appointment to that position directly from the President of the United States, such appointments being deemed so politically important that all ninety of them were expected to offer their resignations at the beginning of each new presidential administration.

Russell Lord had been appointed by President Ronald Reagan soon after Reagan took office in 1981. During Lord's tenure, Carmine Jagoda had finally been put in jail, an accomplishment that brought Lord much acclaim, not just locally but nationally. But he had not been so successful, so far anyway, in prosecuting the white-collar miscreants allegedly responsible for inflicting on the nation the "S&L Crisis" of the 1980s that was producing financial and economic collapse across large swaths of the banking system. For example, Lord had recently brought against O'Keefe's lawyer friend Michael Harrigan a highly publicized prosecution for bank fraud that was rumored to have been less an act of civic duty than a personal vendetta arising from rivalry over what the rumor mill called "a hot babe" named Maura Davis. Indeed, the facts behind the case, which had been slowly leaking in dribs and drabs out of the Courthouse, once fully disclosed and understood by the public, might suggest villainous machinations out of a cheesy soap opera, not the dignified rectitude to be expected of a public servant, sinking any chance of Russell Lord achieving what he most wanted in life—the appendage of the words "United States Senator" in front of his given name.

If Lord was even mildly disappointed by his recent experience in the Harrigan trial, he disguised it so well as to be undetectable by any of those several personages (all male, except for a secretary invited only to take notes and, in fact, the only attendee *permitted* to take notes) sitting at the long conference table in the high-ceilinged and otherwise imposingly proportioned "Public Affairs Conference Room" in the Courthouse. Each such personage was a representative of federal or local law enforcement, each carefully chosen based on their disinclination to even conceive the notion of blabbing about today's proceedings, whether under excruciating torture, or perhaps even more difficult to resist, the pressing interrogations of a nosy spouse.

Lord, presiding at the head of the table, thoroughly self-possessed and otherwise exuding "senatorial" in every respect—tall, slim, endowed with a head of thick silver hair that showed no sign of thinning now or ever, his finely sculpted face regarding the world before him, now as he always did, with an air of unmistakable contempt—called the proceedings to order: "You all know Max

Trainer, right?" he said, referring to a diminutive man who sat next to Lord and looked a bit like a ventriloquist's dummy, so small in stature was he compared to his boss. In further contrast to Lord, Trainer had managed to preserve only a few strands of reddish-brown hair slicked back on his head and combed over in a vain attempt to disguise how few strands of it were left to him.

"Max will do the detailed briefing today, but before I turn it over to him, I want to thank you for coming. I can promise you won't regret it, because this is the beginning of what I believe will be a great achievement for all of us, a great service to our city and our country… because we are going to *crush*…" and he paused for extra emphasis, "…the Outfit once and for all…Our first blow, which of course several of you here deserve a lot of the credit for, was to put Carmine Jagoda himself in jail. And very shortly after we put him away, he did us the favor of dying. The King is dead. And I do mean 'the King.' After he took over decades ago, there was never even a distant second in command.

"And now, his handpicked successor, his son-in-law Robert Sciorra, has disappeared. We don't know what happened to him. He may return, but maybe not. He may have been involuntarily dispatched to that land of no return. But no matter what, they must be in real difficulty these days. Very vulnerable. It's the time to follow up and…" his palm slapped hard on the table, "…*crush them!*"—which caused several of the assemblage to visibly flinch and then look a bit ashamed of their lapse in manliness while others looked bored, embarrassed, or even disapproving of the melodramatic gesture. In the ensuing silence a vibration from the hand slapping on the table seemed to linger faintly in the room for a few moments.

Lord leaned back in his chair, apparently a signal that Trainer well understood. Max was what they called a "career prosecutor" (meaning, not a "political appointee" like Lord) who had shown himself early in his career to be less than impressive as a trial lawyer but brilliant in every other way, especially at developing the nuances of prosecutorial theories and creatively fitting the evidence to those theories in a way that jurors could understand. His combination of intellect, dedication, hard work, lack of a certain kind of ambition and attendant disinclination ever to try to hog the limelight had made him nearly indispensable to his boss.

"Good morning, gentlemen. Of course, several of you here know all the things I'm about to tell you as well or better than I. You can resume your daydreaming. The rest of you please listen up. We want everyone on the same page. As Russ said, the local 'Outfit,' as they call themselves, but the 'Mafia,' as most of the rest of the country calls them, has lost not one but two leaders in the last year. Also as Russ said, Jagoda did us the favor of dying and now his son-in-law and designated successor, Robert Sciorra, has mysteriously disappeared. He could be on the lam, or hiding from his own confederates, or maybe he's at the bottom of a body of water, or ground up like sausage and scattered for the birds to peck at. We don't know and may never find out. Not that we won't be trying to find out, especially if he's still alive somewhere. But that's not really the point. The point is they must be in disarray. In fact, it's hard to believe some sort of war isn't brewing."

Trainer was not surprised when always-eager-beaver and often-smartass Bart Rowland, Deputy Special Agent-in-Charge of the local FBI office, interrupted: "We have our own ideas about who's running the show now. What're yours?"

"Well, that's a perfect segue into the next thing I want to talk about. Which is who's who, so to speak. First, there's the senior guy, Vince Sorvino, the guy who has been around the longest, the guy that Jagoda always trusted completely. He's never been interested in doing

more than making his own way—as well as a helluva lot of money, by
the way, almost all ill-gotten of course—without treading on others
but willing to murder those very same others if he thought they were
threatening to the Outfit or if Jagoda ordered him to. In some ways
he would've been the natural successor, but he's got no stomach for it.
He's not your typical goombah either. He's said to have a substantial
library in his house, is a history buff, and occasionally quotes from
Shakespeare.

"Next is Paul Marcone, reputed to now be at least the acting boss.
He's been a solider in the Outfit since he was a teenager, ending up
as Robert Sciorra's driver and bodyguard. But that's about the only
thing that qualified him for his new position...other than the fact
that Vince Sorvino was Marcone's mentor, so to speak, and might
have thrown his weight in Marcone's favor. You do have to wonder
if Marcone had something to do with killing Sciorra if that's what's
happened to him. But we don't know a damn thing about the guy. He's
just been background scenery, a cipher. But we're told that he's careful
and tough and maybe even smart.

"Then there's Ricky Vitale. He's been around a long time and
long ago carved out his own special gambling niche, especially
sports betting...and recently some fairly new initiatives, like
financing drug dealers and some moves into the porno and sex
business including a massage parlor or two, a topless bar over on
South Street, and an escort service. As you know, Bart, from your
own informants, though they haven't been too damn reliable in my
opinion..." which drew laughter, especially from the local police
representatives, "...he might believe that he ought to be the new
leader. And what we do know about him for sure is that he can be a
hothead. Carmine was able to keep him under control and people
who know the situation wonder what will happen now that the great

man is gone. And we know for sure that Vitale is both a degenerate gambler, which forces him to constantly be scratching around for money, and a *roué* as well—"

"What the hell is that?" someone said, which provoked general laughter.

Trainer looked exasperated at having to tolerate such militant ignorance, and, sighing, said, "A rounder, a skirt chaser, a rooster in the barnyard. Which, like the gambling, makes him vulnerable, my friends…" And locking eyes with his comedian manqué interlocutor, he said, "…*Get* it, Mr. Investigator?"

Rowland jumped in, showing off again. "And then there's the lady."

"Yes, the lady. Rose. Daughter of Carmine Jagoda. Wife of Robert Sciorra. It seems impossible, but there is some credible evidence that she's having some involvement in the Outfit's affairs."

This produced some low grumbling, and someone said, "They'd take care of Carmine's daughter no matter what."

Trainer wagged his finger and shook his head. "No, it's more than that. She seems to be meeting with Marcone rather often."

"Well, duh," someone said, "Maybe she's fuckin' him."

A couple of them flinched, and one of them pointed to the secretary.

"Oh shit, I'm sorry, Doris."

"Believe me, I've heard it before," she said, "even done it a couple times."

Which got the best laugh so far.

"But really," the embarrassed kibitzer said, "that could explain everything, including Robert's disappearance."

"And," Trainer resumed, "that's one of the many things you'll be finding out, with the wiretaps and otherwise. And we'll be squeezing her in every way we can, remembering that she *is* a woman and maybe an innocent widow—"

"Or a black widow."

"Maybe," Trainer responded, "but a woman with not one smidgeon of known criminal history and with two grade school kids. If we play that wrong, we'll end up with everyone from the press to Judge Montgomery after our asses for persecuting her."

"What's Judge Montgomery got to do with it?"

"As most of you know, we're putting the finishing touches on the warrants for electronic surveillance to be submitted to none other than Judge Montgomery."

"Does it have to go to him? Is he the right guy for that? He can be a damn stickler."

"No choice. He's the Chief Judge, he's gotten wind that the warrants are coming, and he's put out the word that he intends to handle those and everything else to do with the grand jury and this entire investigation."

A disgruntled restlessness spread around the table, expressed in leaning and scooting back in chairs; elbows placed on the table; a hand brought to a forehead; one of them whispering to the one next to him, his hand raised to block the reading of his lips.

Max raised his voice an octave or two, trying to settle things back down. "We'll also subpoena her to appear before the grand jury. We'll treat her fairly gently at first. If she takes the Fifth right off the bat, that will be a strike, maybe two, against her, but that might just be what her lawyer advises her to do."

"Praeger," someone said.

"Probably. He did well for her father for a long time. That would be a natural place for her to go."

"Spare us from Praeger."

"But we won't let ourselves get distracted too much with her. There's several other ones—Caruso, Marchetti, Vagnino. In any event, we think someone'll break, and that break may be the one that breaks the camel's back."

Someone whooped. A couple of others joined.

Lord gave Trainer a look that said, "Wrap it up."

● ● ●

A couple of hours after the Courthouse meeting ended, Sergeant Morris Latham, one of the attendees from the city police, received a call.

"It's Ross…Steven."

"Yes, sir."

"How'd the meeting go?"

Latham hesitated, wondering how Lieutenant Ross might be involved and how this might be any of Ross's business, but Ross was rising fast in the department, and Latham could see no good reason to risk irritating him by clamming up, though he did make a feeble attempt to deflect him.

"The Feds think they know it all of course. As usual, we were like their children, to be seen and not heard."

Ross was not deflected. During the decidedly pregnant pause, Latham could almost feel the insistence of Ross's silence through the telephone line. He felt he had to say something.

"They're revving it up. Getting ready to go in for the wiretaps and starting to subpoena people, put on the squeeze, try to get someone to flip."

"Did they mention any names?"

"The ones you'd expect. Sorvino, Vitale…"

"Yeah?"

Ross seemed to be waiting for more.

"They even mentioned Carmine's daughter, Rose."

"Why?"

"They think she might've had somethin' to do with Robert's disappearance. Or just might be a weak link, ya know."

"All of them'll be subpoenaed?"

"Sounded like it."

More silence. But Ross relieved him this time. "How about Paul Marcone?"

It struck Latham as odd that Ross would bring up that name.

"Yeah, I forgot. Nobody knows much about him, but they think he might be the new acting boss. Definitely a target."

An even longer silence this time. Latham clenched his teeth. Finally, Ross said, "Will you be our main contact with the investigation?"

Latham wondered who "our" was.

Finally, Ross said, "I hope you'll keep me in the loop. It touches on several things we're involved in."

Latham hesitated, then said, "Okay. Call me anytime."

"I will. But you call me if something important's coming down. It could make a big difference to some things I'm involved in."

Latham wanted to ask Ross what exactly he might be involved in that information from the upcoming grand jury investigation might make a difference to, but he didn't, and hung up, still wondering.

CHAPTER 7

OSWALD MALONE RETURNED O'Keefe's call right away. As the business and financial news editor of the local newspaper, the *Herald*, his beat often took him to and beyond that borderline where financial manipulations crossed over into crime, a geography where O'Keefe spent most of his working life. His editors valued Oswald so highly they allowed him a roving commission to investigate anything he wanted so long as it had at least a remotely tangential connection to his primary beat. He seemed to have evolved his persona to match his first name. He gave off the air of a dandy, including flashy bow ties and plaid suits. Fastidious, even prissy, though not effeminate, one inevitably pictured him, like John Steed in *The Avengers*, in a derby hat and brandishing a full-length, cane-like umbrella though he never wore the one or carried the other. An atypical Irish American in that, as he frequently and proudly proclaimed, his forbears were not the usual Catholic bog farmers but aristocratic-though-enlightened members of the Protestant Ascendancy, he was usually the smartest guy in the room. Nobody called him "Ozzie."

"Yes, sir," Oswald said, and O'Keefe could sense an eager hopefulness in Oswald's voice that O'Keefe might have important news for him since O'Keefe had an odd history of stumbling into misadventures of public interest.

"Sorry, Oswald, but this time I'm looking for something from *you*. Can you spare me some time? Let's meet at Harvey's, and I'll buy you a drink...dinner too if you want."

"The topic?"

"I'm wondering what's up with the Outfit post-Jagoda, and now, post-Sciorra?"

After a pause, probably to recover from his disappointment, Oswald said, "I'm not at all sure I can help with that. It's not my beat."

"I'm desperate. I need to find the right person to talk to in that bunch."

"One might think you've had enough of that bunch already and, rather, would be wise to avoid them?"

"Just give it a try, please. Ask around there. If somebody there doesn't know something, they should close up shop."

"Well...I do have someone in mind...Our expert on that subject around here is Paschal McKenna...Know him?"

"*Of* him I know. I've read some of his articles. He's a jailbird himself, isn't he? Armed robbery?"

"Well, I have to say, Peter, that I am disappointed in you. That is not a very enlightened or empathetic way to refer to one of the rare redeemed in our fallen world."

"You guys sprung him, didn't you?"

"Yes, indeed, we *sprung* him, as you say. We recognized a superb writer and a very promising journalist, helped him obtain an early release for the best of behavior, vouched for him with the parole board, gave him a job, and he has been ruler-straight ever since. He is not even a parolee anymore."

"I'll take what I can get. You well know about beggars and choosers...being one yourself."

"But he's a quirky and particular sort. He may refuse."

"Tell him I'm almost as interesting as he is…and my own first name is my real one."

"Again, such a judgmental fellow you are today. So is his. He was born on Easter Sunday."

●   ●   ●

O'Keefe arrived at Harvey's early, something he always tried to do for meetings like the upcoming one with the two newsmen. It made him feel more prepared, more secure, a step ahead rather than behind, an owner of the space rather than a mere guest. He also always took the table in the far corner of the back room so that he would have the widest and longest view of anyone traveling through the bar toward him.

Oswald seemed to detect O'Keefe's consternation that he had arrived without Paschal. "Don't be concerned, he's coming," Oswald assured him as he sat down. "I am aggrieved that my lone appearance is so disappointing to you."

O'Keefe responded with an exaggerated chuckle to let Oswald know that he appreciated his wit.

Oswald looked at the cup of coffee sitting in front of O'Keefe. "Are we not drinking today?" he said. "Too early? It *is* after five."

"It's always too early for me."

"I see. I am afraid Paschal and I do not share your affliction, or at least so far have refused to acknowledge it."

"Don't let me dampen your spirits. I'm perfectly okay with it. I did suggest we meet in a bar. It's when I'm alone I need to be careful."

Paschal, or at least a short, dark, intense-looking man that O'Keefe guessed was Paschal, arrived a few minutes later. He wore black jeans and motorcycle boots and a black leather bomber jacket with white fleece collar turned up so it covered his throat and lower chin and jaw. O'Keefe watched the man watch the other customers with a mixture of distrust and an edge of un-lamblike, chip-on-shoulder hostility as he took the long walk through the bar on the lookout for someone he might know. When he recognized Oswald's back, he accelerated a bit toward them as O'Keefe tossed back his head in tentative recognition and welcome.

"Is this our man?" O'Keefe asked Oswald, who turned in his chair and said, "Certainly is."

Paschal looked to be somewhere close to O'Keefe's age and, like O'Keefe, what they called "black Irish." His dark hair, so dark brown it looked black, swept back on each side of his head and the two sides joined together at the back, a softer and less greasy version of the "duck tail" popular with young hoodlums in the 1950s and early 1960s. He approached with a squint-eyed look of curiosity and appraisal. When he arrived at the table, he stood waiting for someone else to say something. O'Keefe waited for Oswald, who quickly said, "Mr. Paschal McKenna, meet Mr. Peter O'Keefe."

Paschal said nothing but reached out his hand for O'Keefe to shake.

"Sit right down, Paschal," Oswald said. "This is like a gathering of McNamara's band, eh? McKenna, Malone, and O'Keefe."

O'Keefe smiled but Paschal just sat down with an expectant look, waiting for someone else to move the conversation along.

"What's to drink, Paschal?" Oswald asked. "Usual?"

"Please."

The waitress came and Oswald said, "Do you have Bushmills?"

"We do," she said, with obviously fake enthusiasm.

"Do you also have Jameson?"

"We do," she said, now with an edge of mistrust in her voice, suggesting her likely thought: *Is this guy gonna be a pain in the ass?*

"Excellent. Two shot glasses of Bushmills for me and two shot glasses of Jameson for my friend here. A small pitcher of cool water on the side."

After a skeptical sneer, she walked off.

"Okay," O'Keefe said, "I can't help myself. They're both Irish whiskeys. What's the difference?"

Oswald turned to Paschal with a mocking smile. "Would you like to explain that, Paschal?"

"Not really."

Oswald went on, "Despite the obvious superiority of Bushmills, Paschal will not forgive it because its distillery is located in Northern Ireland whereas Jameson is in County Cork."

"Nothing for you?" Paschal asked O'Keefe.

"Life-time quota already consumed," O'Keefe said.

Oswald laughed. Paschal emitted a small grunt of amusement. O'Keefe felt as if he had passed some sort of test.

"So, what can I do for you guys?" Paschal said.

O'Keefe waited for Oswald, but Oswald said, "Peter, I think this should come from your own mouth in your own words."

"Okay. Two things. Related things. One, as you're aware, and as you can see from this getup…" and he raised, for emphasis, his left arm and hand sheathed in the pressure garments, "…I had a recent little encounter with explosives. Instead of truly investigating it, the cops have just let it go. They prefer to just assume it was a guy named David Bowman, and since he's dead, no reason to do anything else. But who knows what really happened…whether Bowman really did it all by himself or had accomplices that are still running loose out there?"

"What's their excuse…the police, I mean?" Paschal asked.

"Everything you can possibly think of." O'Keefe continued in a mocking singsong. "'Limited resources…Surely it was Bowman… We can only do so much, and why waste time when we're virtually certain who it was. The Cherry Pink is in the county, and we don't have jurisdiction out there, and the county's in Cherry Pink's pocket…' even though I remind them that I was fire-bombed in *their* jurisdiction, not the county's."

"So they're just leaving it hanging?" Paschal asked.

"Yeah. If you can believe it, they implied I should try to investigate it myself. Like I know anything about explosives. Like I have access to a lab and forensic experts. Like I have any power or authority to strong-arm people into talking to me."

"Bombing's also a *federal* crime, I think?" Paschal said.

"Maybe, but that just turns out to be another crack for the case to fall through. It's the Bureau of Alcohol, Tobacco, Firearms…*and Explosives*, but they don't apparently think it's worthy of inquiry, so that just gives the local police another excuse for inaction."

"U.S. Attorney's office? Russ Lord?"

"They're busy chasing down the Outfit, or what's left of it…"

"And," Oswald interrupted, "given what happened at the Harrigan trial, I'm not sure Lord doesn't wish the bomb had solved the problem of Peter O'Keefe forever."

O'Keefe raised his eyebrows in affirmation and resumed, "Oswald's articles really helped expose that Cherry Pink snake pit, but it needs a constant light shined on it. Based on my partner Sara's experience out there, it's no telling what they're doing to those ladies."

Squirming in his chair in mild discomfort, Oswald said, "As you know, it isn't my beat. Once the financial-political angle was not there anymore, I had no excuse to follow up. That's where Paschal comes in."

O'Keefe looked hopefully at Paschal, who said matter-of-factly (enthusiasm did not seem an emotion he indulged in much), "Actually, I think it's worth working on. Lots of meaty stuff in that story. Lots of bureaucratic indifference, insensitivity, incompetence, and, I'd venture to say, downright incontinence. Good stuff."

"Well, there you are. Easy enough. What's your number two issue?" Oswald asked.

"Pretty simple. I'm trying to figure out who's in charge of the Outfit now that both Jagoda and Sciorra are gone."

Paschal smiled. "Looking for a job interview?"

O'Keefe smiled back. "Actually, that's not a bad idea. At this point, if they offered, I might accept."

The waitress brought the whiskeys and the small pitcher of water. Oswald poured a bit of water into one of his shot glasses and took a sip, swallowed, and pursed his lips in satisfaction. Paschal passed up the water and drank the entire contents of the first of his two shot glasses, a prelude to taking off his coat and recalling the departing waitress. "Another round for me…Oswald, how 'bout you?"

"Not quite yet, Paschal," he said, squinting in mild disapproval.

Now, with his coat off, Paschal sat in a black short-sleeve T-shirt, his inner forearms covered in tattoos in a florid script that O'Keefe could not decipher without staring inappropriately. He wrapped his hand firmly around his second shot glass as if it might escape his grasp if he did not hold it tight and fixed his gaze on O'Keefe, which O'Keefe took as an encouragement, even an instruction, to proceed.

"I experienced some difficulty a couple of years ago with the Outfit down in the lakes area and out in Arizona…"

Oswald's laughed suddenly and loud. "Yes…difficulty…for sure."

"…and last year," O'Keefe resumed—

"The car bomb," Paschal interrupted.

"A lot of people, wrongly in my view, think those two incidents were connected. They weren't. You know why, I assume?"

"You're still *on* this earth and not *in* it?"

"Exactly."

"But this…misconception…is ruining my life. I can't even visit my daughter without a security guard chaperone. I can't even go to her basketball games because my presence would clear the gym. I got kicked out of my apartment. I'm trying to build a business and some people don't want to do business with me. I need somehow to show everyone, starting with my ex-wife, that I'm not their target. So, my one and two are connected…like Siamese twins…That is, one: find out, meaning *prove,* who really planted that bomb—for sure…no assumptions, no guessing, and, meanwhile, two: get a pass from the Outfit. Nice to have both but either will suffice."

Paschal's face reflected a mixture of amazement and contempt. "What the shit…you want, like, a note to give the teacher?"

Oswald, also appalled, said, "They're more likely to kill you."

"I don't think so. They've got enough trouble without killing a civilian. But I don't care. It's worth the risk."

"What do you have to bargain with?"

"Surely I've got *something* worth trading, especially if they're not really carrying a grudge, right?"

"Well, what they want might not be…likely wouldn't be…legal. What about that?"

"I hope I get that choice."

"Badass and dumb-ass, all mixed into one," Oswald said.

"Just indulge me, okay?"

Paschal looked at Oswald for direction.

"He's been a good friend," Oswald said, "let's indulge him."

The waitress brought Paschal's second set of drinks. He quickly downed the remainder of the second glass of his first round, slid the new double round directly in front of him, favoring them with a longing glance, and said, "It's hard to know for sure, but everything I hear is that Paul Marcone has the top position…at the moment. But it's fragile and contested, and he's at the risk of a challenge from Ricky Vitale. But here's the fun part: I'm also hearing, and from good sources, that Marcone's sharing power with…guess?"

"I don't know. Vince Sorvino?"

"Nah," Paschal scoffed. "Vince is way too smart to step into a shit-pile like that…Here it is…none other than Carmine Jagoda's daughter, Robert Sciorra's *wife*."

"Hard to believe," O'Keefe said. "They're not exactly a feminist group."

"Which could mean a number of different things," Paschal said. "One: she's terrorized into playing this fake role to keep things together. Or two: Robert's dead, and she had something to do with killing him, or at least didn't object. Or three, and maybe most likely: Robert's gone on the lam for some reason, and she's serving as his agent, mouthpiece, and pipeline."

O'Keefe shook his head. "Those gentlemen surely won't put up with a woman giving orders."

"I don't know. If Sorvino's supporting her and she's got her father's ghost, and that's a big ghost, hovering over her in blessing, who knows? It's a new world, and—Jagoda dead, Sciorra gone—they're in the deepest possible shit now with this grand jury comin' down on them in the middle of all the rest of it…"

"Actually," O'Keefe said, "it seems like a pretty good time for a dumb-ass bad-ass, mostly dumb-ass, to enter the picture."

"That's the dumb-ass talking," Oswald offered.

"You know Angie's?" O'Keefe said.

"Of course," Paschal said. "Jagoda's old place. One of my watering holes, in fact. Why you ask?"

"I was down there the other day."

A snort of disgust from Paschal. "You won't find anyone you want to talk to there."

O'Keefe thought about the flatulent old man in the bathroom stall.

"The real hangout, for the people that count, is Maria's. Ricky Vitale's place. Originally his mother's place, hence the name. And it also happens to be the local headquarters for sports bookmaking and betting."

O'Keefe was amazed at the things he didn't know, despite living in this town his entire life and joining only recently but deeply a profession in which it would seem such information might have naturally come his way. He knew of Maria's, of course, but not as a notorious gambling den. Maria and her husband had established it as a traditional "red tablecloth" place before World War II. For decades it thrived on visits from families from both in and out of the neighborhood who especially enjoyed the "Sunday Supper," as the menu called it, traditional Italian dishes in generous portions served family style.

"Do they do that in some backroom?"

"All over the place, especially at the bar…full all the time with those high and low roller types that like to be seen hanging out on the edges of 'the life.'"

"You go there?"

"Sometimes. Not to drink. I drink in honky-tonks. But they've kept up that Sunday Supper tradition and it's kind of fun. The Italians and lots of others still flock in there on Sunday even though it's not that old-country anymore. That, plus the Super Bowl just around the corner, will fill the place this Sunday, one week before the big day."

"How 'bout I buy you supper on Sunday? You can show me around."

Paschal's face turned hard. "Do they know who you are, what you look like?"

"The ones I encountered are all dead."

Oswald piped in, "Several courtesy of Peter here. That's the badass part."

"Not really," O'Keefe said, "just a dumb-ass who stumbled into something he had to turn badass to escape."

"False modesty, they say, Peter, is just another manifestation of the sin of pride."

"And," O'Keefe said to Paschal, "it's Pete, not Peter, despite Ozzie there…" as Oswald winced at the unwelcome use of the nickname, "who insists on calling me that. But nobody else gets to."

"Okay, it's a date, Peter," Paschal said, and crooking his head around, looking for the waitress, he added, "And I need another drink. Maybe two."

O'Keefe noticed a look of concern rippling across Oswald's face as he stared down at his first drink, which he still had not finished, and muttered, "I hope we all survive this match-up."

Meanwhile, O'Keefe was pondering a discovery he had made during the conversation. As Paschal had moved his arms around, gesturing while speaking, O'Keefe had managed to decipher the tattoos on Paschal's forearms.

The left one said "Destiny," the right one "Oblivion."

CHAPTER ▸ 8

TINY SAL'S DELI, barely clinging to precarious existence in a small wooden building on a corner at Third and Birch Street, in the old neighborhood—the old neighborhood that had once crackled with the sounds of children playing in the streets and half-deaf old men shouting at their wives in the house or their lifelong buddies across the street—all eerily silent now and increasingly bedraggled and unkempt with too many empty storefronts and run-down houses with overgrown yards and peeling paint on the fences. The area had once been all Italian. Now the Italians had dwindled to a few, most having fled, due in part to general upward mobility but also to flee from the influx of Vietnamese on one end of the neighborhood and African Americans on the other. But Sal still hung on, still selling miscellaneous specialty Italian grocery items on the increasingly sparsely stocked shelves, and fresh-made Italian sandwiches that Sal lovingly prepared and wrapped in white butcher paper, and pastries that he had once served on thick white ceramic saucers but now only on saucer-sized paper plates because he couldn't find adults or even kids to wash dishes for him anymore and didn't want to do it himself. A widower for more than a decade and now in his late seventies, he had saved enough to endure these unprofitable days and years. He stuck it out because he had no idea what else to do with himself. His good customers, some journeying there once a week or so all the way from the suburbs just for Sal's and old times' sake, expected to one day find him slumped over dead in his shop, giving his last measure of devotion to the place that had provided him the only way he knew how to navigate the remainder of his life in this world.

There were two tables for four, and two tables for two, where customers could sit with their sandwiches, chips, and a soft drink, or a cornetto, cannoli, and a cup of espresso. At one of these tables, after Sal had locked the front door, pulled down the shade, and closed for the day, sat Paul Marcone and Vince Sorvino, each with an ashtray and one empty and one partly full espresso cup in front of him. Vince smoked a cigar and Paul a cigarette. Although the two talked or met on some sort of business several days of the week, Paul had asked for this special sit-down at this special place where they were unlikely to be interrupted, including by any of their associates whose lips would curl in contempt at the thought of hanging out in such a feeble joint. They talked low even though they doubted the aged Sal could hear what they said and knew that Sal certainly didn't want to hear it, wouldn't try to hear it, and wouldn't tell anyone if he did.

Although Paul had been the one to request the meeting, Paul was, technically, Vince's superior in the Outfit, only recently having assumed leadership after somewhat reluctantly but dutifully strangling to death, with a long, thick rope, Robert Sciorra, who had himself been elevated to the "Boss" role only a few months before his death by way of succession from his deceased father-in-law Carmine Jagoda. But Robert had turned out to be both an embezzler from the Outfit's own coffers and a homosexual, the latter crime not quite, but nearly, as offensive to his criminal colleagues as his intramural thievery, thus guaranteeing himself a death sentence once caught. Vince, the most respected elder, especially by Paul himself, had helped engineer what

Vince and Paul had hoped would be a brilliant pairing of Paul with Rose, Robert's widow, but more importantly, the daughter of the legendary and fearsome Carmine Jagoda. Only a few knew for certain that Rose was a widow, since only a few knew for sure that Robert was dead, one of which few was Rose herself because she had helped introduce Robert to oblivion in a frenzy of vengeful rage once she discovered that he had not only betrayed her with a lover but intended to abscond with that lover and a lot of the money from both his family and *the* "family," never to be seen or heard from again. But what she deemed most unforgivable, what sent her all the way over the edge, was her terrified certainty that he had infected her with the AIDS virus to boot.

● ● ●

Paul—slight, dark, handsome, his standard facial expression serious, almost hostile—no chatty opening pleasantries being required or welcome—said, "Things aren't goin' so well."

Vince showed no surprise, but the perpetual frown on his large, long, swarthy face creased a little further.

Paul went on: "This new grand jury Russell Lord's set up…" He paused, waiting for a reaction from Vince.

Vince briefly closed, then opened, his eyes, an unspoken affirmation.

Paul continued, "Devoted to rooting out 'organized crime,' they say."

Vince's frown creased even further, and he said, "Little does Mr. Lord know we ain't so fuckin' organized these days."

"And that's another thing…Ricky…Vitale."

"Bein' a pain in the ass. No surprise."

"Worse than a pain in the ass."

"Well, I warned you."

"What should I do?"

Vince looked very weary as he pondered, then shrugged, said, "Hard case."

"I thought I'd try to make him happy, give him more."

"Won't work. He's one of those insatiable fuckers. Maniac. Megalo all the way."

"What if I made him Number Two…officially, I mean?"

"He'd just be that much closer to your back to stab you in it."

"So then…?"

"Yeah, I think so," Vince said, silently filling in the blank. "And better sooner than later."

"With the Feds seriously after us now, I think I oughtta try the peaceful way first."

"Fuckin' Feds. Since they discovered electricity or radio waves or whatever, we're fucked. Can't keep our mouths shut and we're all for sale. I could be wired right now. You could be wired right now."

"Not us."

"Don't be stupid. You think at my age and facin' the rest of my short and decrepit life in prison I wouldn't rat? I can't be sure…even of myself. We're not all willin' to die in prison like Carmine. I'd like to be walkin' on the beach in Miami right now, not in the middle of this shit show."

"Bullshit. Not you."

"Maybe not. But somethin' ta think about. Can anyone really be trusted?"

They both finished their espressos in quick gulps.

"Sal!" Vince yelled, extra loud.

Sal grunted back.

"Two more espressos," Vince yelled back.

Paul chuckled.

"He's gettin' deafer by the day," Vince said. "Me too."

They sat quietly and listened to the espresso machine. When Sal brought the espressos, Vince said "*Grazij.*"

"*Di nenti.*"

"You still hanging on here, buddy?"

"Barely," Sal shrugged.

"You need anything, Goddammit, don't be a tough guy, let me know."

Sal responded with a quick dismissive nod of his head and shambled off.

"He's almost over with," Vince said. "The whole neighborhood's over with. For us anyway. We're gone. Play it cool and get what you can, Paulie, because the truth is that our thing is on its way out. This neighborhood…neighborhoods like it all over the country…made us. Now where do you and I live? The suburbs."

"Ain't that progress?"

"Progress to nowhere. *Cosa nostra*…our thing…ain't a suburban thing. Back then they bottled us up here. If we went uptown, the cops'd stop us and send us back. No Italians. 'Get the fuck out. Get your ass back where you belong.' The bastards. And we were poor, and on the make, and lookin' for a way ta live large. We provided them things they were forbidden to have. Liquor during prohibition. Gambling almost to this day. We'd be nothing without gambling. And now the government's in our numbers business…state lotteries, nothin' left for us there. And before long they'll make sports bettin' legal too. They treated us as outcasts, so we learned to traffic in the forbidden…but now everything's allowed."

"That's a real pep talk, Vince. I'll go in the back room now and shoot myself."

They drank their espressos.

"How's Rose?" Vince asked.

"Okay," Paul said weakly.

"I'm afraid we made a mistake there."

"No."

"No favor to her and none to us."

"Why you say that?"

"Woman Boss. People don't like it. Think it makes us weak…or at least *look* weak. Inclines them toward an asshole like Ricky, who's made no secret about how stupid an idea that was."

"Bullshit. She's super tough. She sat there across that table knowin' I was gonna kill Robert and damn near spit in his face."

"Woman scorned. Heat of rage. Would she have done it herself? Would she do it to someone that hadn't screwed her over the way Robert did? She might have to do somethin' now to show she won't tolerate any disrespect. Somethin' really nasty. As a woman, she might have to do it double to prove herself and scare the shit out of them. You think she could do that?"

Paul shrugged. "I can't say for sure, but my guess is…yes."

"Maybe she should be the one to solve the problem of Mr. Vitale?"

Paul shook that off. "You think she's in danger?"

"No. Not yet anyway, at least from our people…for the same reason she's not respected…ya know, a woman. But how 'bout Russell Lord and the Feds? They'll surely be comin' after her along with everybody else. A sonuvabitch like Vitale, or even a person like your true friend right here across the table from you, might think she'd be a weak spot, easier to break than the rest of us…a woman…"

Vince let the implication hover over them.

"They wouldn't do it to a woman…" Paul said, but more of a question than an assertion.

Vince snorted in disgust. "Ask Tamara Strand if they'd do that to a woman."

Paul looked confused.

"Long before your time…She was rich. Stupid rich. Loaned Glick, the front guy for the Vegas casinos, some money and claimed he promised her a piece of the ownership. She even sued him, I think, or threatened to. That earned her five bullets in the head."

"Well, it's done. Rose is where she is. Can't be undone now."

"You're not fuckin' her, are ya?"

Paul hoped Vince could detect the steel in his voice when he said, "No."

"But you can't tell me you don't have a hard-on for her? That's impossible. *Truoppu bedda…Regina Seducente…*to the max."

"Why can't I tell you that?"

"You tellin' me 'no,' you don't?"

"That's exactly what I'm tellin' you."

"I hope that's the first lie you ever told me, Paulie…and the last…"

"No lie."

"Well, if that's so, you must be Goddamn ready for the Pope ta fuckin' canonize you. And even if true, I doubt it can last either. It's eventually gonna 'pop up,' if you get my drift. But if it ever happens, that'd be the worst possible thing. So if it does, you just get the hell out of there and go someplace and jack off. That's another mistake we made…I made…constant temptation whether she intends it or not. *Regina Seducente.*"

CHAPTER ▶ 9

AS PAUL DROVE away from Sal's, he tried to analyze what significance to assign to the fact that he had indeed told Vince the first lie he had ever told him—not the part about fucking Rose but the part about him not wanting to. And he had kept to himself his vehement disagreement with Vince on whether it would be a bad idea for Paul and Rose to get together. As Paul saw it, that would solve the problem, not complicate it further. It would be one of those dynastic-type couplings. She could step back behind the throne, exercising power or not as she might wish, through her new husband. But he had to admit that he was afraid for her, and himself. Robert had to be eliminated, but it had made both of them bullseyes immediately, targets for Ricky Vitale types from within and U.S. Attorney Russell Lord and the FBI from without. He could not have taken over at a worse time. Up to the task? He had to be. No other choice now.

They were to meet that day. When they started this, he assumed they would meet often, but they both soon realized that would be unwise. Law enforcement and others, even including Robert's family, had quietly assumed that his disappearance, whether voluntary or not, was likely a necessary and unavoidable consequence of his occupation, but why and how he had vanished, being unknown and mysterious, fostered suspicion and rumor.

• • •

For her part, Rose quickly came to understand that she had sentenced herself to a special prison, and within that a confinement almost solitary. She avoided the public and even old friends all she could, and she turned to the world the face of a bewildered, beleaguered, and bereft abandoned wife. She told the children she believed their father had needed to go somewhere, she didn't know where or understand his reasons, but surely he would return, and they should be hopeful and patient. When Bobby came home weeping because another boy had said, "So they bumped off your daddy, huh," she told him that could not be true and not to believe such garbage.

In an atmosphere of constant, slowly swirling dread, her meetings with Paul had quickly become furtive affairs, elaborately choreographed in preparation, approach, execution, and exit. Today's meeting, like most of them, was scheduled to occur in the office of her father's longtime lawyer, Donald Praeger, now representing Rose, Paul, and others similarly situated.

•   •   •

Paul arrived an hour early after following a convoluted itinerary to evade any possible tail and waited for her in one of Praeger's conference rooms. When she entered the room, swaddled against the January cold in a black shearling parka, black gloves, a white cashmere turtleneck sweater, and white cashmere slacks, he stood up to greet her, hoping she could not detect his boyish eagerness or hear his thumping heart. Her long, thick black hair draped over her shoulders and fell down the front of her, almost to her breasts. She wore earrings, small ebony hoops smattered with small flecks of gold, and no makeup as far as he could tell. She had her father's olive skin and sharply chiseled nose, cheekbones, and chin, her face a sculpture so precariously engineered and poised in space that it seemed it might snap of its own weight. She had also inherited his dark eyes, but hers were large and round, unlike his, which had narrowed into permanent slits from many years of looking at the world in a certain way. Today, uncharacteristically, she seemed harried and distracted, and the dark circles that had begun to develop under her eyes over the last couple of years had deepened substantially in the last few months, but they seemed to Paul only to enhance her beauty—*Regina Seducente.*

"What a trek," she said, her voice deep, almost husky, as if on the verge of laryngitis. "I drove my car to the West Hills Mall, parked in the underground parking lot, called a taxi from a pay phone in a department store, had the taxi pick me up at one of the side doors, drop me off in the underground parking lot of the building next door, and took the underground walkway over to this building. Hope all that's worth it."

She sat down next to him, her perfume almost intoxicating him, and ventured a quick smile. He slid over to her a small cloth bag containing stacks of ten, twenty, fifty, and one hundred-dollar bills and pushed in front of her a legal pad full of handwritten notes that would be shredded after the meeting. She accepted the bag with her left hand, nails painted in a white polish closely matching the color of her sweater and placed it in her Louis Vuitton purse. With her right hand she extracted a pair of black glasses with large clear lenses, which she shook open with a flick of her wrist and slid on with another quick movement, and began to study the numbers and words on the pad. He rolled his chair closer to her, further inhaling her perfume, and he could not help his arousal. This creature had besotted him from the first time he beheld her regally riding her bicycle down the sidewalk, not a drop of sweat on her anywhere despite the sweltering summer day. He was ten and she a distant eleven, almost twelve, those two years an unbridgeable adolescent gulf between them. But he had never in these many years made a single lustful move in her direction, terrified that one such move, if it turned out to be unwelcome, would kill his dream forever, and she had not once fulfilled his hopes by making such a move herself.

Trying not to think about her body under the exquisite cloth, he moved his index finger down the legal pad as he talked. "Of course, there've been additional deposits into the bank accounts as usual. That's the top number here."

Those deposits would be the legitimate, or at least well-laundered items, that could be reported to the tax people. He paused to let her view and absorb the full significance of that large-dollar item, one that especially pleased him as an early signpost on a long road stretching into the hazy future that might lead to enough legitimate earnings to help disguise more and more of the illegitimate, distancing them further and further from a successful tax fraud prosecution.

"As for the rest here, the sports book has been great this year, and the Super Bowl's coming up and that'll be a gusher. But it's been so cold the bars and restaurants haven't done very well all winter. I'm not sure they're worth the trouble. Most of them don't make shit or lose…"

"Angie's?" she asked, which was her father's place, and she felt either affection for it or annoyance, he couldn't tell which.

"It's a small loser before we run some other money into it," Paul answered and continued down the first page of the notepad. "This number here is other gambling income—the card games and casino nights…and what's left of our numbers business, almost all gone, the lotteries are wiping us out. It was criminal for us but not for the government to do the same damn thing. The lending business, same as usual, always better during football season when the gambling is heaviest, guys losing more than they have and needing to borrow for the next bet. And we're doing more and more special lending to businesses that get themselves in trouble and don't have anywhere else to go. Very lucrative."

"What's this?" she asked, pointing to a number toward the bottom of the page with no description of its source.

"The gentlemen's club," he said.

"Gentlemen," she said acidly.

She flipped over to the second page, which listed:

Sales (which meant proceeds of fencing goods from burglaries, warehouse heists, and other thefts including revenue from chop shops that processed the stolen cars that inevitably came their way);

Labor (which meant monies skimmed from the one small union they still controlled);

Partnerships (which meant rents from real estate they owned under straw party names; other legitimate or semi-legitimate businesses, including produce and meat wholesalers; a few parking lots and garages; and a number of other enterprises that they had muscled into one way or another or had just fallen into their lap).

"That's way lower than before," she said, pointing to the "Partnerships" category.

"Winter," he said. "Both car sales and construction are down. Very bad weather so far this year. New limo service doing good though."

"This is just our cut, right, you and me?"

"Yep."

"Next time I think I'd like to see all of it…what everybody gets paid. The crews, for example. This law firm, for example."

She seemed to recognize that her request had made him uncomfortable.

"It's not that I don't trust you," she was quick to say. "But if I'm supposed to be..." she said hesitantly, seemingly reluctant to call herself that, "I ought to know it *all*, right?"

"Right. No argument...And the word you're lookin' for is 'partners'...what we are now."

He couldn't decipher her reaction, but she did not seem to be particularly happy about that.

When they finished with the pad, she removed her glasses and said, "What about this grand jury?"

He shrugged. "Time to hunker down...Fold up into our shells. Don't do anything stupid."

"I think we should meet by phone for a while," she said. "Pay phone. Both ends."

Another stab into his bleeding heart. But he had begun to understand that he was probably better off not to be in her presence. Too painful.

Thinking about his conversation with Vince, he said, "Maybe we made a mistake with this partnership thing. How you feel about bein' in the crosshairs?"

"I made my choice that day with Robert, didn't I? I'll have to live with it..."

Or die with it, he thought, silently finishing what she had stopped short of. That had to be her unspoken thought. When he had killed Robert, she had been there in another room, and she had seemed so enraged he thought she would have eagerly done it herself. She certainly had known what he intended to do and made no attempt to stop him, no plea for mercy. But as time went on, and especially after she received the test result that showed Robert hadn't given her AIDS, the rage seemed to begin leaking out of her, her talk more and more in the vein of what she had just said: "I'll have to live with it."

"On second thought," she said, "I don't need to know those other things. Let's keep it the way it is now…for a while anyway…and how about we get Donald in here and discuss this grand jury thing?"

Could she stand the pressure of an intensive investigation? Could even be an indictment. The U.S. Attorney's office might come after her whether or not they had sufficient grounds for it just to try to break her, turn her. Circumstances could develop where some of the others, like Vitale, might be willing to kill her. Like that woman Tamara Strand. But surely not Rose, who was not an outsider like the Strand woman. But Paul himself was in more danger from her than any of the others since her testimony could put him on death row. He wondered how far he would be willing to go to shield her—from them, from himself. He also wondered whether she would ever lift, even ever so slightly, one of the long, lovely, weightless lashes of her eyes to protect *him*.

● ● ●

Promptly after they summoned him, Donald Praeger arrived in the conference room. He said hello with a special broad smile for Rose. He had known and been fond of her from her childhood, having served for decades as Carmine Jagoda's human armor against the many projectiles flung and fired at him and his confederates by law enforcement. He looked much older than his age, as decades of the stress of balancing on the murky line between representing criminals and being a criminal himself had left marks. And that stress and its fallout probably had also helped produce the girth of the belly that hung over the belt of his suit pants. He wore a French-cuffed, blue-and-white-striped shirt with cufflinks made of gold coins and a garish floral tie that mocked the elegant tailoring of the shirt itself.

The still-brownish curls on his head had become sparse while his eyebrows remained bushy and mostly still brown, but with occasional random, brittle, unruly white hairs sprouting forth here and there like errant weeds. He sat down with a soft, weary thud and accompanying sigh, looking like an exhausted marathoner who could see the finish line but doubted he could make it all the way. Yet his eyes, bright with intelligence and cunning, belied the worn-out frumpiness of the rest of him. He waited for someone else to say something.

"So, Donald," Rose said, "what about this new grand jury?"

"I can't tell you much. Because I don't know much. It's not like they consult me on their plans."

"What's your best guess?"

"It's hard to say. I don't know what they've got. But I really think they're mainly on a tree-shaking expedition. Shake the tree and see what falls out."

"You think they'll be investigating Robert's…disappearance?" she asked.

This might have been an excellent moment for Donald Praeger to inquire of Rose and Paul concerning the circumstances of Robert's "disappearance," but he knew better than to ask about that and really didn't want to know anyway. One of these days law enforcement would likely drag even him, the lawyer, in front of the grand jury and find some way to pierce through the attorney-client privilege and ask him a question under oath he would be required to answer on pain of contempt. Of course he would lie if he had to but would rather not be forced to commit perjury. Thus, in this instance and many others, ignorance was as much bliss as he could hope for given his choice of clientele.

"I don't think," he said, "that's one of their main objectives, but I think they'll see it as a possible 'target of opportunity,' something they'll probe if it looks promising at any point…but I think they assume why he disappeared."

And this would have been a perfect moment for Rose and Paul to inquire what that assumption might be, but neither did.

"So what is it they'll do then…on the rest of it?" Rose asked.

"They probably have something on one or two people, who they'll go right after and try to get them to give up everyone else. Typical stuff."

"Will they subpoena everybody?"

"Probably. They know everyone will just take the Fifth, but they like to do the parade thing for the press and the public."

"Me too? The subpoena? Me too?"

Donald Praeger hesitated, his face clouding with distaste and regret, then said, "I'm afraid so. I hope not. And I'll be doing everything I can to distract and deflect them, but they might see you as a weak link."

"So what should we be doing?"

Praeger's voice raised a level. "Nothing. Or as little as you can. Hunker down."

Rose said, "Should we—"

"Please don't ask me more about that…what you should be doing. I really can't say more about that…You know why…given my position. All of us have to be super careful right now. Lord managed to finally nail Carmine a few years ago, big victory there, but then he screwed up with that Mike Harrigan prosecution, and now he needs something to repair his reputation."

CHAPTER 10

THE WINTER DARK had already descended at 5 p.m. when O'Keefe arrived at Maria's to meet Paschal for Sunday Supper. "You're the first of your party," the hostess said and guided him to a table for four but with only two place settings. A waiter, in his fifties like almost all the other wait staff, one of those types that acted as if he would just as soon slug you as take your order, shuffled over and asked O'Keefe what he would like to drink. O'Keefe said he would wait for the other guest and noticed the irritation in the waiter's face as he turned to shuffle away.

After Maria died a decade or so ago, son Ricky had moved the place uptown into more luxurious quarters, flashy and slick in every way, with the hard and sharp edges of the stainless steel that covered so many surfaces of the place and tuxedoed waiters that made a great show of mixing Caesar salads and imparting at tableside dramatic finishing touches on pasta dishes and flaming desserts. But, sentimentally, Ricky retained his mother's quaint, Old-Worldish custom of the "Sunday Supper." Beyond a marginal interest in things like menu design and interior decoration, Ricky bothered little with the day-to-day running of the place, having too many far more profitable enterprises to pursue, such as illegal gambling, loan sharking, and infiltrating businesses that made the mistake of looking in the wrong place for capital. But he still appreciated how the restaurant cloaked him in an aura of possible legitimacy and a gentler publicity spotlight than did his status as a reputed mob associate, and he made sure to hire strong operating management so he would not have to pay close attention.

The restaurant was packed, mostly with twosomes, but a few larger families were sprinkled around, even including a couple of babies in highchairs. The bar intrigued him most. It was much longer than one might have expected relative to the size of the rest of the place, the stools full of men with the physiques of NFL linemen gone to seed. Several men of similar lumpiness stood behind the occupied stools, sipping drinks and talking to the men on the stools in front of them. He watched as one of the two bartenders answered a telephone and handed it to one of the customers, saying "for you, Jimmy," who took the phone and cradled it between his left ear and shoulder, with his right hand jotted something down on a pad in front of him, handed the phone back, wrestled his considerable bulk off the stool, and headed toward an area somewhere to the side and back beyond the bar and dining area. As the customer began making his way to the back, the other bartender answered yet another phone, said, "Wait a second, Jimmy, got somethin' here for ya," listened for a few seconds, then wrote something on a napkin and handed it to Jimmy who then resumed his progress to the rear of the place.

O'Keefe stood up and asked one of the waiters where the men's room might be, hoping it would be in the same direction Jimmy had headed. His hope fulfilled, O'Keefe found in the back a large area, a hallway down the middle of it, on one side of it three private dining rooms of various sizes, small to middle to large—*like the Three Bears,* O'Keefe thought, and that he really was not unlike Goldilocks herself wandering into this den. Only one of the dining rooms was currently occupied, the other two empty, their doors standing open. He noticed that the smallest one contained a table large enough to accommodate six but with place settings for only three. On the other side of the hallway were the men's and women's restrooms and farther along a series of three doors with an "Employees Only" sign on each. He wondered what might be behind those doors and how much the monthly phone bill of this place might be and if the cops ever cared to look into that. O'Keefe entered the men's rest room and took himself through the same routine at the urinal that he had performed at Angie's. No Jimmy in the restroom. Presumably he had been admitted into one of those "Employees Only" sanctuaries.

On O'Keefe's return to the dining area, he saw that Paschal had shown up, standing at the hostess desk, waiting his turn. He saw O'Keefe, pointed him out to the hostess, and guided himself to the table. Again in black, but more upscale today, he wore black oxfords instead of motorcycle boots, corduroys instead of jeans, a turtleneck sweater instead of a T-shirt. O'Keefe could not decide whether he was grateful or disappointed that the sweater covered Paschal's forearms. Before sitting down, Paschal moved his place-setting to sit nearer O'Keefe rather than across the table from him and with a better view of the dining area. "Better for me to see and both of us to hear our own low and quiet words," he said.

One of the men on the barstools turned around, noticed Paschal, smiled goofily at him and waved, said something to the bar mate next to him, slid off the stool, and waddled in a slouch, listing a bit to his left, toward the table.

"Shit," Paschal muttered. "Arnie Pressley. Wanna-be bookie and gangster. Sole actual accomplishment: buffoon."

"Paschal, my man," Pressley said as he set his glass and himself down without being invited to do so. "Placin' a bet for next Sunday?"

"Maybe. Thinkin' about it anyway."

"Your friend here too?"

"Maybe."

Pressley rose partly out of his chair, straining to lean over both his belly and the table, extended his right hand toward O'Keefe and said, "Arnie Pressley."

"Nice to meet you," O'Keefe said.

Pressley collapsed back into his chair. "No name, huh?"

"Just a friend of mine," Paschal said in a tone to stifle further inquiry.

"Suit yourself," Pressley said. "Who you bettin' on?"

"Hang on. I need a drink. It's five hours after noon. Gotta make up for lost time."

"You must've been asleep."

"I was."

"Sleepin' last night off."

"True enough."

Paschal summoned a waiter and ordered his two double-shot Jamesons without the small pitcher of water that the fussy Oswald Malone had ordered at Harvey's.

"And whatever my friend here wants," Paschal said, indicating O'Keefe, "and I guess," indicating Pressley, "I have to include our uninvited guest here."

"So what's your bet?" Pressley demanded.

Paschal paused, which seemed to reflect indecision amidst ongoing evaluation of the options. "Tough one…but I think I'm the Redskins…"

"Stupid move," Pressley interrupted. "Denver's due. The pattern is the team loses the first one and wins the second one."

"Well, Denver's lost *two*…and by big scores, one of them just last year. They're not due, they're dogshit."

"The oddsmakers seem to disagree, Paschal my friend. How 'bout a side bet, you and me?"

"What's the line?"

"Denver by three."

"I'll take that, but I don't want any of your pissant little bets. I wanna make some real money. Five thousand dollars."

O'Keefe thought he could see Pressley almost gulp. Initially, he looked like he was about to sputter some excuse, but said, "Okay smart ass, go 'head and insult me. Done."

Paschal held out his hand palm up.

"What's that for?"

"You might as well just go ahead and pay me now."

"Asshole," Pressley said and, with difficulty, pushed himself up from the chair using both hands, one on each chair-arm. "I'll be lookin' you up a week from tomorrow night. And you'd better have the money, Mr. Cub Reporter. And goodbye to you too, Mr. No-Name."

As Pressley lumbered back to the bar, O'Keefe said, "Pretty big bet."

"Yeah, but couldn't help myself. Such a jerk. If I lose, maybe I'll have to borrow from Vitale at five percent a week like the other dopes."

"Do you hang out with these guys?"

"Not 'out,' but 'around.' I drink a lot of places, some of them are theirs. You can't believe how many bars and restaurants these guys own in this town."

"You'd think they wouldn't like that…like maybe you're a spy for the cops."

"You'd think maybe so, but never happened. Maybe they're afraid to offend a reporter. Maybe they think of me as a bro'…armed robber, convict, etc."

O'Keefe wanted to follow up on that comment to learn more about this interesting man when their attention shifted toward a small commotion in the direction of the hostess stand where the hostess, the manager, and a waiter were falling all over themselves welcoming a woman and two pre-teen children, a boy and a girl, the boy slightly older than the girl, all of them black-haired and beautiful.

"Well, well," Paschal said, as he and most of the rest of the diners watched the manager and waiter escort the woman and her two charges through the dining area and toward the rear area that O'Keefe had reconnoitered earlier. The noise level in the restaurant elevated noticeably. As if feeling a tremor in the earth, the men at the bar turned and paid the small parade respectful attention that seemed to O'Keefe like a tribute.

"Guess who that is," Paschal said.

"Seems pretty obvious even to one such as I. Is that the right way to say that? Seems weird."

"It's grammatically correct…and yes, the Princess, herself."

O'Keefe remembered the small private dining room with the three place settings on the table.

"Looked like the Queen to me…the Boss."

"Talk about luck. Here I thought I was just gonna show you the hotbed of illegal gambling in town and you get this as a bonus. But restrain yourself, okay. I don't need you making a scene. Might make me unwelcome around here…and elsewhere."

O'Keefe kept his surface cool but was so enthused he could hardly eat his branzino while Paschal consumed a salad, a plate of bucatini amatriciana, an entire basket of bread, another round of whiskeys, a half bottle of wine, a digestif with his after-dinner coffee of not one but two snifters of Courvoisier, and was slurring his words by the end of the meal. O'Keefe was too excited and Paschal too inebriated for any productive post-dinner conversation.

As they rose from their chairs and headed toward the hostess desk on their way out, O'Keefe thought he detected a slight stagger in Paschal's gait. "You driving?" he said.

"I am."

"Want a ride?"

"No need," Paschal said with a decisiveness just short of belligerence.

"Thanks for today."

"I'm sure you'll return the favor."

"I'll do my best."

"Good luck. And be careful. You may be the only guy I know who's crazier than I am."

"Rat in a corner. No alternative."

O'Keefe hung back, but before disappearing out of sight, Paschal turned around and smiled. "You think I don't know what you're about to do?"

Caught.

"You're not gonna confront her, are you? Don't screw things up for me."

"Just gonna leave a note for her with the hostess. The Princess won't even know you were here."

CHAPTER 11

HOW COULD AN eleven-year-old girl, soon to be twelve but still eleven, even begin to figure out how to dig into the past of a man who, until recently, had not even lived in the same city? Kelly thought she had figured out what Nancy Drew might do and was poised to take the first step in executing her plan. Yes, Nancy was older than Kelly, but Kelly would not let that stop her, and she also had in mind that Harriet the Spy was exactly her own age, and she had pulled off even greater feats than Kelly hoped to accomplish.

It caused her a certain amount of guilt that she would be opposing her mom's wishes, but she believed that if she achieved success in this adventure, her mom would have to admit in the end that Kelly had done the best thing for both of them. Although her mom was making a big mistake with this Darren person, Kelly sensed deep down, without being able to bring it to full consciousness and articulate it, that her mom was, in a different way than Nancy or Harriet, but in her own way, something of a heroine herself. After he left them, she had managed to gather up the shards of her shattered world and glued together a decent life for the two of them. Still, even though her dad had done the leaving, was definitely the villain, she knew and understood the phrase, "It takes two to tango." Her mom could be a real tyrant—not so much from some meanness in her but something else, Kelly was not sure what, but it had something to do with that look of sudden fear, near panic, that Kelly often observed on her mom's face before it wrinkled into gritty determination followed by angry self-assertion demanding that all around her come to order. Only later would Kelly fully understand the fear of losing control, of losing her grip and slipping further down the mudslide of respectability and reasonable accommodation in a world that did not leave much room for error.

Her dad was a whole different thing altogether. He was like some wounded monster. She still loved him, even idolized him, some parts of him anyway, but she was not sure exactly why. He had been a soldier, but he didn't seem particularly proud of that so she could not tell whether she should admire him for that or not. On television they portrayed being a private detective as an exciting job, but the job seemed to be trying to kill him. He seemed to instinctually seek the outer edge of things and find himself in trouble there. Often gentle, he would sometimes go shockingly wild with an anger out of control. She could see a lot of good in him, a generous and caring person basically, but incomprehensibly locked into a cocoon of selfishness or carelessness or something that had led him to abandon them. Her mom often called him a "druggie" or a "drunk" though he seemed not to be doing those things anymore. He often referred to himself as coming from "one rung above trailer trash," but he read all kinds of things, even poetry, and listened to that Bach stuff, which she abhorred but knew was supposed to be a very high-class thing. Something she had heard her mom say stuck with her: "He's the original bonehead *Rebel Without A Cause*." Kelly still had not seen that movie, an old one, and she didn't know how to get access to it without causing a fuss that would irritate her mom.

In the year or so after the two of them separated, it did not seem so bad to her; really it was sort of nice as she and her mom buddied up and created a dollhouse little world of their own, and she would every other weekend stay with him in whatever lair he was not so much living as lurking in at the time, and they would do certain things her mom would never even think of letting her do and would vehemently disapprove of if they came to her attention. Kelly thought it better not to report to her mom about some of their mis-adventurous excursions in the woods or some of the PG-13 movies he had taken her to see.

Best of all, once her parents parted ways, she did not have to lie in her bed and listen, in fear and sometimes full panic, to their lacerating arguments that made it seem like the world was about to shatter and crumble to nothing and seemed to give the lie to those other moments, maybe even the great majority of their moments, of peaceful, good-humored banter and gentle teasing, the scorching eruptions making it seem like the good times had never happened before and could never happen again. And there was all the upset over his "carousing," as her mom called it, his failure to come home until late at night, sometimes not until the next day, and eventually, what Kelly only later understood to be his descent into the mad world of cocaine addiction, which even now at age-eleven-almost-twelve she did not really understand, only that it was big trouble and caused big trouble.

But whatever seeming fun she had in that first year soon turned bitter. Everything in her world—from what she could observe of the lives of her friends' families to television shows like *Family Ties* and *The Cosby* Show—emphasized to her what she was missing in not having a real family of mother, father, child. She knew that divorced people often—well, *always* it seemed—married again, to new people. While, at times, such an outcome seemed promising, a chance to experience that ideal family life portrayed in about every place she looked, memories of the stories about evil stepparents in the fairy tales she had absorbed in early childhood gave her pause. But most of all she sensed that a remarriage would forever crush all hope that the three of them, the original crew, would ever get back together and be what they ought to have been all along.

When the bombing happened to him, she actually hoped that his latest injury might be a good thing, might make them somehow see how much better off they would be with each other, in support of each other, all of them together. But it had turned out just the opposite. Now the fear that those Mafia people would never stop until they killed him, and the danger that caused to everyone around him, threatened to cut him out of her life even more than before, like this stupid "under guard" thing, their inability to do much except sit around, and him not even able to attend her basketball games.

But worst of all, it must have caused her mom to abandon even a faint hope of reconciliation, his latest misadventure rendering the possibility of it truly, finally, irrevocably hopeless, leading her to agree to marry this man Darren Maefield who Kelly knew, fancy doctor though he might be, was wrong—for her mom, for Kelly, for everything. She just knew it. She did not know how she knew it, but she knew it. Her mom wouldn't listen, had just lost her mind. Her dad refused to interfere, though he had caused this whole thing. And she blamed herself some too. All those times she had cried to her mom, with always a suggestion of blame (not just of her dad but of her mom too): "Why can't I have a dad like everyone else?" It turned out to be the very thing she kept hearing everyone say, though it had never made sense to her before now, just another irritating thing adults tried to foist off on you: "Be careful what you wish for." Now she understood that phrase and that she might be the only one willing to try to do something to save things.

Utmost on her mind now was a scary movie she had seen at a slumber party the prior year, *The Stepfather*, about a lonely, divorced mother with a teenaged daughter who married a new man; and that man, it turned out, had slaughtered his previous family and was now about to do the same to his current one. The mother had remained oblivious to the very last minute and only the daughter's suspicions and heroic actions saved them from the most brutal fate. Maybe Darren was not *that* bad, but she knew he was bad somehow, she didn't know how, but somehow.

So this time, when her mom told her the three of them were going out to dinner that evening, she did not do the usual whining and arguing that she didn't want to go; that she had homework to do; that if her mom was foolish enough to insist on hiring a babysitter for a girl who didn't need it, Kelly herself would pay, with her own meager savings; and anything else she could think of that might have a chance of prevailing. Instead, she perked up and said, "Okay, where? Can I get pizza there?"

At the restaurant, she ordered a cheese pizza, and the two adults, healthy eaters both, ordered broiled fish.

"How about a bite of fish?" Darren said, offering his fork with a disgusting piece wiggling on the tines.

"No thank you."

"You know, that pizza will ruin your nice figure before long."

She only blushed. *Is this the kind of fake dad stuff I'll have to put up with 'til I go to college? I'll run away from home. And what figure? And why is he noticing it?*

She moved to change the subject and start the conversation she wanted to provoke. "I was thinking of becoming a doctor."

Her mom gave her a look something between skepticism and scorn as Kelly had never revealed anything close to such an ambition before.

"Great," he said. "I'll be glad to help you."

"What kind of doctor are you?"

"I'm an orthopedist."

"What's that?"

"I deal with problems of the musculoskeletal system."

He smiled what she thought to be a nasty little smirk, deliberately holding her ignorance over her.

"What's that?"

"Neck, spine, back problems. More broadly, I treat people with chronic pain."

"What's 'chronic'?"

"Persistent, continuing, prolonged, hard-to-go-away or won't-go-away…usually with a cause that seems mysterious at first. I'm a bit like a detective."

"My dad's an actual detective."

Now her mom flashed her the look they described as "with daggers."

But she persisted. "How come you moved here?"

This time they both gave her a look. Her mom's said, "What are you up to?" and Darren's seemed to say, "How am I going to answer this?"

After an awkward blank space in the conversation, Darren said, "I had a very tough divorce," at which he shot a sympathetic glance toward her mom, who looked interested in the answer, "and I was sort of spinning my wheels in my medical practice, just an employee at a clinic. It was a 'nothing happening' sort of town, and I thought, '*Why not start over somewhere else, somewhere without bad memories every place I go and where maybe I could make something of my own?*' So I came here and put up my shingle."

"Shingle?"

"It means like a sign, like an advertising sign."

"When was that?" she asked, as innocently lighthearted as she could make it, but she noticed her mom looking at her suspiciously again.

"Two years ago."

Kelly had run out of questions. She didn't know what else to ask, and she could tell her mom was about to blow. She took a bite of pizza. Darren took a forkful of the mushy looking boiled asparagus that came with his fish and said, "Maybe you could come to my office someday and see how it's done. I help people. It's called 'a helping profession.'"

She tried to look enthusiastic about that and took another bite of pizza.

At home, after Darren had dropped them off, her mom said, "What was that all about?"

"What?"

"That interrogation…third degree…of Darren."

"Just trying to be nice. If he's gonna be my dad," and she visibly and purposely gave a shudder, "I need to get to know him, don't I?"

One more distrustful look from her mom, but then she left it alone.

Kelly had already known about his divorce and that he had only recently arrived in their town, so the only new thing she had learned at the dinner was the actual year he had arrived. She needed to figure out how she might find out more about him. The next time she visited her dad, she said, "I have an assignment in school where they want us to find out what happened in the past in some other town. You're a detective. Do you have to do that sometimes?"

"How far in the past?"

"Just a few years."

"It depends. Usually, I'd try to figure out if I know someone in that town and ask them about it. If it was important enough, I'd try to find another private detective like me. I might even hire him. If it was likely to be something that could've made the papers, I'd consider researching the old newspapers."

"They keep old papers?"

"Usually not the papers themselves. They take a picture of them and put them on what they call microfilm."

"Where do you get those microfilms?"

"At the local library in that town."

She shrugged and sighed. *No way for me to get there.*

After a few moments of quiet, he said, "You might be able to get some through what they call interlibrary loan. Our library would borrow them from the other library and let you study them at the library here."

"How do you study them?"

"They have reading machines that magnify it on a television-type computer screen."

That's more like it. Microfilm. It seemed like a very grown-up thing to be doing. Something Nancy might do.

She told her mom the same story about the phony research project and asked her to drop her off at the public library for an hour on Saturday while she found out about the interlibrary loan.

Pulling up in front of the library, her mom said, "Is an hour long enough?"

"Think so."

"If I have to wait a bit, that's okay, but not too long."

Kelly wended her way through the room where the library kept current local and national newspapers and magazines attached to bamboo poles. The room was spotted with homeless men, "bums" as she had learned to call them—which seemed wrong somehow but that's what everyone called them—who used the library as a daytime refuge and took more of an interest in her than she liked. She had just begun to deal with the experience of men, and not just these "bums," staring at her, and she felt distressingly exposed in their gazes.

She hurried past them to the reference librarian's area where a counter almost as tall as Kelly herself separated her from an untidy work area in front of metal stacks with oversize books and manuscripts and other strange and daunting looking items strewn here and there that seemed the essence of *boring*. At a desk in the work area, a pudgy man in a wrinkled white shirt open at the neck, with unpleasant looking black and gray hairs sprouting from the opening focused intently on some sort of reading material lying on his desk. Also on the desk, facing out to her, a holder like the ones used to hold the letters in Scrabble, contained a metal plate on which was embossed the name "Brandon Terbovich."

He didn't notice her until she cleared her throat. He squinted up at her but said nothing, waiting for her, so she launched into a recital of her mission and how her dad (hoping that her reference to an adult authority figure would provide some immediate credibility) had told her about the possibility of borrowing microfilmed newspapers from another town, Darren's former town, on library loan.

He pushed his black-rimmed glasses back against the bridge of his nose, rose up from his chair with a grunt of discomfort, shuffled to the counter, and said, "Do you have a library card?"

She had it right in her hand. "Yes, sir," she said with a lilt of triumph and set it face-up on the counter with a modest but emphatic terminal flourish, like decisively laying down the winning playing card.

He had apparently expected that she would be unable to produce the precious card and seemed quite pleased with her for doing so. "Okay, Miss Kelly O'Keefe," he said, looking down at her name on the card, "what time period are you interested in?"

"From 1985." She had chosen a one-year period beginning three years ago, a year before Darren had arrived in her town.

"I'll check it out. It'll take a few minutes."

He moved back to his desk with noticeably more energy than he had journeyed therefrom, pulled out a book, and looked until he found something that seemed to satisfy him, apparently a phone number, which he dialed. When it appeared that someone answered on the other end, he gave them his name, the name of his library, and his title of "Chief Reference Librarian," and asked for the person in charge of interlibrary lending. Although eager to hear the outcome, Kelly's attention wandered during a long pause that ensued after he explained his purpose and they apparently set about tracking down the proper person at the other library. She had no intention of returning to the room of the ogling bums so she wandered through a few of the stacks near the reference desk, looking at titles, until she heard her name called, "Miss Kelly O'Keefe?"

Holding the phone with one hand covering the talking end, Brandon Terbovich, Chief Reference Librarian, said, "They'll send some of it but not too much at once. Definitely not a whole year. How about a month?"

She had no idea how long it would take to go through a particular time period, but she wanted to obtain as much as she could as fast as she could. Darren and her mom had not set a date, but it could happen at any time, maybe without much warning.

"Will they send two months…three?"

He asked them what they could do, said "that would be fine, we appreciate it," and hung up.

"Three months."

"When will it get here?"

"It'll take a week or so."

She exaggerated for his benefit a face of disappointment, close to desperation.

He said, "I'll let you know as soon as it comes in. How can I reach you?"

"Can I call you?" she asked. "We don't have an answering machine," she lied.

He chuckled. "Looming deadline for the project, huh?"

"You bet," she said. Yes, *dead*. Sort of…well, exactly…what she hoped for, regarding the marriage anyway. She thought about asking her new Chief Reference Librarian friend Brandon Terbovich, who looked at her only as if looking at a little girl, not a budding young woman, if there was another way out than the way she had come in, but, instead, resolved to brave it and walked briskly, eyes straight ahead, through the reading room and out the big glass main doors of the library.

When she got to the car, her mom said, "What happened?"

"It's coming," she said.

"Good for you," her mom said, proud of her daughter's initiative and enterprise.

Kelly felt a twinge of guilt. It was good for Kelly maybe but not so good for her mom. But if she was right about Darren, it would be the very best for her mom in the end. She had told some whoppers to get to this point, but for the best of causes. The guilt disappeared quickly. To the contrary, as they drove away, she congratulated herself. Surely neither Harriet nor even the great, almost-grown-up Nancy could have done better.

CHAPTER 12

UNLIKE SARA, WHO tended to do a quick knock, not seeking permission but signaling that she was coming right in, like it or not, Dagmar Sibelius knocked and waited for O'Keefe's invitation to enter. Karma in his corner had quickly come to recognize Dagmar's knock and did not even raise his head until she entered, then opened his eyes as if to verify she was unaccompanied. Wide-eyed, she said, "There's a lady out there, quite a knocked-out *babe* by the way. She says you left her a note, which she apparently has in her hand."

It had been several days since he had left the note at Maria's. In the interim he had been extra vigilant, not knowing what the consequences of leaving that note might be. It could be a range of things, from indifference to an attack. He had concluded that his admittedly desperately quixotic approach at Maria's, as at Angie's, trying to just get in the way and see what might happen, was a bust. Now, hearing that Rose Jagoda Sciorra was there a few yards away in his waiting room, his adrenalin surged, and not in the usual bad way. This was the good stuff, not the PTSD stuff.

"Good. Show her in."

Dagmar left, and he heard her saying something coaxingly pleasant in the waiting room. Her voice became more distinct as she approached his door, saying, "By the way, there's a dog, but he's a good guy, don't worry 'bout him."

"A dog?" the other voice said with a touch of distress, but then she was in the room, looking at the very dog, who now stood in the corner while O'Keefe stood at his desk, like two soldiers coming to attention at the entrance of a superior officer. Dagmar gave O'Keefe a quick glance that welcomed any instruction he intended to give. Once she recognized that he intended none, she quickly disappeared, shutting the door hard as if to close off any possibility of escape.

The lady stood before him, wearing tight black jeans, black boots, a partially unbuttoned black waterproof parka, and underneath that, a gray ribbed turtleneck sweater. The soft leather handles of her purse were hooked over her right forearm and in her left hand she held what appeared to be his note. Her wary attention focused mostly on Karma.

"That's Karma," he said. "He's friendly."

"He doesn't look friendly. He looks like the hound from hell."

"Just looks. You know, book and its cover. Please have a seat. Can we get you something to drink…coffee?"

"No. I'm wondering why you left this note…for *me,* of all people."

He thought the direct approach would be best, as direct as she had been. Lay it out there. "A couple of years ago I had some unpleasant business with some people who other people have said were your father's people. More recently, someone tried to incinerate me in my car…"

"I read the papers," she said.

"Certain people, wrongly in my view, very wrongly, believe your father's people were behind that. It's causing me a lot of trouble. And if not already, it'll eventually cause your father's people trouble… trouble that in this case they don't deserve."

"And because I just happened to've been born into a certain family, no choice of my own, you think I can do something about that?"

"I'm trying to be straight with you. I mean you no harm. Can't you do the same?"

"Oh, I should trust you, should I?" she said as with her left hand she waved the note slowly above her head like a cowboy's lasso, motioning toward the walls, the corners, the baseboards of the room. O'Keefe understood her concern about recording devices. Those had brought her father down and were achieving similar results for similar gentlemen all over the country.

"I know you have kids," he said.

This tipped her face over into anger, so he hurried to explain himself. "I have a daughter. Eleven years old. I can't go out in public with her. I can't even see her anymore except under guard."

He had gestured with his left arm, and she stared at the pressure garment that sheathed his left arm and hand. He thought he detected a softening in her face. "What can *I* do about that?" she said. "You say yourself that you don't think 'my father's people,' whoever that's supposed to be, did it…and like they would listen to me anyway."

He thought it best not to challenge her pretense of non-involvement, at least for the time being. "I have the hope that you'd consider what it'd be like to be in my position with your own children. Then I'd hope that the respect you're entitled to…on your own but in any event because of your father…would put you in a position to put out the word somehow, some way, that I'm like any other civilian…off limits."

"And even assuming anyone would listen to me, why do you think I'd do that?"

"I don't know, but I'm prepared to trade."

"For what?"

"For anything, you name it."

"Anything?"

"Just about."

She approached the chair in front of his desk, sat down, set the note on the lip of his desk, arranged her purse on her lap, put her hand in the purse, extracted an ebony pen, wrote something on the back of the note, stood up again, and said, "Mr. O'Keefe, as I said before, you're talking to the wrong person. You're misinformed about the nature of my father's business and his 'people,' as you refer to them, and you are especially misinformed if you believe I have ever had anything to do with my father's business or his 'people,' as you call them, other than as my relatives or as friends of my family. My husband has disappeared, I don't know where. I'm devastated but still trying to raise my children as if he might return someday…or not… whichever. It's a hard-enough life without having to deal with the kind of rumors that caused you to leave me this note. So I am asking you and telling you *to leave me alone.* I'm tearing this note to pieces right here, and I never want to see you or even hear your name again."

She held the note up for him to read what she had written on the back of it in large block-print letters. "I MIGHT CONTACT YOU." She then slowly and methodically tore up the note into the smallest pieces she could manage and dropped them into her purse, closed the purse, rose from the chair, and walked out of the room, leaving O'Keefe somewhere between amused and amazed.

•　•　•

Two days later, the phone rang on the desk of Dagmar Sibelius.

Dagmar recognized the voice—the "knocked-out babe" with the note.

"You know who this is?"

"I…think so."

"Is your boss there?"

"I don't…Yes, I think so…," Dagmar stammered.

"Tell him I'm out front in my car. I'll wait for him for seven minutes, no longer. Tell him to leave all recording devices, and the dog, behind."

When Dagmar came in and excitedly blurted out this latest development, O'Keefe moved quickly from his desk to the big windows behind him that looked onto the street. Yes, a car out there, not the big black Lincoln Town Car he would have expected, but a minivan, quite suburban. He said "*Bleib,* Karma," and hustled through his waiting room, out into the building hallway, down the stairs (which he navigated more nimbly than he would have thought his injured body could manage) and out onto the street. He approached the van carefully, trying to see inside through the tinted windows. She hit a button that rolled down the window on the passenger side.

"Get in. Cold out there."

"Maybe I should have a look first," he said, cocking his head toward the rear interior of the van.

"Suit yourself," she said contemptuously, and pressed a button on her side that disengaged all the door locks.

After satisfying himself that the back seat and cargo area were empty, he climbed in.

"You seem to get around pretty good," she said.

"Getting better."

"How do I know you're not wired?"

"I wouldn't've had time."

"Didn't grab a little recorder and stuff it in one of your pockets or stick it in your undies?"

"You can pat me down if you want."

"A little too crowded in here and a little too cold outside. If you've got one on you now, 'fess up. If I ever catch you with one, we're done. And not only are *we* done, I'll try to make sure that *you're* done."

In an ensuing moment of silence, he contemplated that possibility.

"I've got nothing to hide," she said—for the record again, he thought. "But no telling how your cop buddies might figure out how to splice things in a way that would make me look guilty."

"They're not my buddies."

"I've checked you out as best I can. Seems like you're not a bad guy. Kind of a fuck-up but otherwise okay."

"I appreciate the positive review."

"And you and your lawyer friend putting an ass-whipping on Russell Lord, that was music to these ears. I'm afraid I'm gonna need some of that myself PDQ."

"Not sure I can help there. That was a special situation."

"That's not what I'm looking for."

"Good. I wouldn't want to take the risk of disappointing you."

He smiled, and she smiled back.

"Are you willing to meet me at my house?"

O'Keefe hesitated, wondering if this was a test, maybe of the extent of his desperation.

"Seems like that might be a stupid thing to do. Seems like a neutral place would be the smarter thing to do. For me at least. Until we get to…you know what they say…get to know each other better."

"If the thing you want can be done at all, it would seem there has to be some level of trust."

"Trust but verify…like our President says."

"Not my President. I always thought that was about the dumbest thing I ever heard."

He was getting to like her.

She continued, "Assuming you believe I'm a killer, do you really believe I'd do it in my house? I have children."

He still hesitated. *My Mommy Was A Mafia Don.* Would the Italian word for a female version be Don-a? Of course he would go there. He only hoped a tactical silence would tempt her to voluntarily relinquish.

Not so.

"Come on a weekday. Bright sunshine. Curtains open. I won't ask you to go down to the basement."

"When?"

"You say. You're the one with the problem…and the proposition… though it seems only one-sided right now. We'll have to see what might be in it for me."

Yes, he was desperate. "How about tomorrow?"

"Fine. 1:30. The kids get home at 3:30."

Yes, Mommy Mafia Don…a.

"No firearms," she said. "No knives. No weapons at all."

"And how about you?"

"You wanted this meeting. You'll have to take the risk."

He considered whether to switch now, try to insist it not be at her home but in some public place. But that didn't really make sense for either of them.

"And no dog either."

"I told you he's not vicious."

"That's not it. I also checked out German Shepherds. They shed like motherfuckers."

"I'll be there," he said, got out of the car, and shut the door.

She lowered the passenger side window. "One more thing. No commando."

Unsure of her meaning, his brow furrowing in confusion, he was about to tell her he had been a Marine but was not some sort of special forces soldier, when she said, "Wear underwear," and drove off.

He stared after her, amazed again.

As he walked toward the security guard who had been watching with great curiosity from just inside the glass front door, O'Keefe thought, *Yes, she's a "babe" alright, body and mind,* and he hoped that would not end up complicating things.

CHAPTER 13

THE NEXT DAY, driving through listless suburbs to keep his appointment with her, he kept thinking he should turn back. How could this end well? Surely she could not be trusted. Even if she could be trusted to make some effort on his behalf, why would they listen? And even if she could be trusted and they would listen and give him the pass, how could that be accomplished in such a way as to provide reliable assurance that others, starting with Annie, would be willing to rely on? What did Ms. Jagoda/Sciorra plan to demand from him in return and what trouble would that make for him? A bargain with the devil? Maybe not, but for him anyway, a devil's bargain.

But see it through.

Robert and Rose Sciorra had established their household in this bland subdivision, which had attracted a diaspora of Italian families escaping the old downtown neighborhood. Their house was only two blocks from the home that Carmine Jagoda had lived in for three decades and where Rose had grown up and only a few blocks from where Robert Sciorra's and Paul Marcone's families had also lived. Carmine's house was one of the nicer ones on its block but no mansion and not even any kind of "statement." If the house said anything at all, it said "nothing is happening here." It was a bit larger and a bit nicer than Rose and Robert's, but they didn't move into it when Carmine died because they didn't want to send any kind of dynastic succession message, however modest, to the law enforcement world or, especially, to their own crew, some of whom, like Ricky Vitale, would have been prone to carp, even seethe, at Robert's presumption and overreaching. "Little too soon ta be anointin' himself," Ricky might say. Robert and Rose decided on their own to sell the place instead of moving into it, but, before a final decision, sought the opinion of the oldest soldier, Vince Sorvino. "Smartest thing you could do is stay out of there. Hell, it ain't even as nice as yours. The thing is fallin' apart. After Sophia died, he stopped carin' about it."

O'Keefe had decided to rent a nondescript car for the visit. He also thought it might be smart to park not in the street like a stranger would, but in the driveway like a friend or close acquaintance. She came to the door in baggy sweatpants and sweatshirt, droopy white athletic socks, her hair tied back into a ponytail. He wondered if she had decided to deliberately play down her looks, suppressing any suggestion of sexuality. He was grateful for her effort, but it didn't work. It only conclusively demonstrated the superficial adornments to be nice but nonessential enhancements.

"Okay, she said, this time I *am* gonna pat you down." She smiled. "Trust but verify."

She made the first pass over him, a rough and thorough investigation except on the burned areas where she proceeded gently but just as thoroughly, then demanded he take off his shirt, which he did without any resistance, and then his shoes, which she checked carefully.

"Okay, big moment now," she said. "No commando, right?"

"No. Never. Uncomfortable."

"Drop trou."

And, yes indeed, she went about that quite thoroughly too, rubbing both hands roughly over his butt and quickly cupping her hand firmly over his groin and just as quickly letting go.

"Well, we survived that," she said with the hint of a smile. "No Thunderware."

"Is that a joke?"

"You still have some things to learn, Mr. Private Detective. It's underwear the FBI uses with a pouch built into the dick area to disguise a gun or a little recorder or whatever."

Once he had climbed back into his clothes, she said, "Let's go in the kitchen. I've got a fresh pot of coffee brewing."

The interior of the house proved far different than the unprepossessing exterior. No expense spared anywhere, the paintings on the walls were originals, abstracts of striking colors. The furniture expressed a cool, modern sensibility but still looked comfortable.

"Beautiful place," he said.

"Thank you. But Robert gets the credit. He has great taste. I learned from him. My parents' house was decorated 'early Dago.'"

In the kitchen she gestured toward a cobalt blue table in a breakfast nook just large enough to accommodate a family of four. Across from the place she had designated for him to sit she had placed a small pile of documents. She set a mug of coffee down in front of each of them, sat herself down, and looked at him with eyes so dark brown they seemed to be black, the first time he had seen those eyes express anything close to innocence, humility, hope.

"Who goes first?" she asked.

"You know what I want already."

"Okay—"

He interrupted, "It can't be criminal or even close to it."

"Just the opposite," she shot back at him with an angry edge.

She hesitated. She looked like she might be about to dive off a cliff into a pool of uncertain depth.

"I want out."

He sat silent for several seconds trying to absorb her statement and figure out what to say next.

"*Out* of *what,* exactly?"

"Out of all of it…including out of town."

"Why?"

"Lots of reasons. Most of all because I have children, and now that Robert's not here…but that's not even it. I don't want them to grow up in it. It's doomed. Only the ones that grew up in it like my father could pull it off at all and look where he ended up anyway. What's left…just remnants. Different people, different upbringing, different world. And they won't let them get away this time. This grand jury thing…I expect a subpoena any day. What do I tell my kids about that?"

"I doubt you can do anything to avoid that subpoena…except cooperate."

"Maybe not the first subpoena, but if I'm both clearly not involved, and gone, out of town and living a different life, an undeniably legitimate one, maybe there won't be a second subpoena. But no matter. I think it's my only chance."

"What about…cooperation?"

Her eyes changed. He saw something in them to be afraid of.

"Forget it. That will not happen."

"*Omerta*? You've drunk the Kool-Aid?"

"Maybe some of it. But don't be a dumb-ass. I don't want to have to hide, and I don't want my children to have to hide, the rest of our lives in a witness protection program. So no chance of that. I'll never do it. And I don't want you trying to talk me into it. Makes me worry about what you're really up to here."

"Just trying to achieve my purpose. I thought there wasn't any way out of 'the life.'"

"I can't be certain. But given who I am…my father and all that…and my situation…and what I might be able to give them in return…"

She broke off there, and he didn't really want to know what that last thing meant, at least not right now, so he asked, "How would I fit into that approach?"

"I think I need someone, a complete outsider…I can't trust anyone close to me now…to help me put it all in place. I don't want to go to them until I'm one hundred percent ready. So, you see, if you hadn't shown up, I'd've had to find you, or someone like you."

"Where might you go?"

"I'm thinking Tucson. If that doesn't work, then somewhere in southern California, maybe Santa Barbara."

She slid the pile of documents in front of him. "I've done a lot of prep work, there's not much left to do, but I need someone to help me execute it. I can't be gallivanting around the country. I've identified several businesses I like, several houses that look worth buying…schools…all that."

She waited for his reaction. He kept her waiting as he tried to figure out what might be wrong about what seemed on its face to be legitimate.

Finally, he said, "Where's the money coming from? I can see someone coming after me for a money laundering conspiracy."

"Every dollar to buy the businesses, the house, the whole move will be from a traceable legitimate source. Between what Robert and I have…," and she hesitated a moment after that word, "on our own and what I inherited from my father, I have a lot of real estate, and some stocks and bonds too. No way to trace that back to anything crooked, for a generation anyway. I'll mortgage or sell enough of it to pay for all this, and the proceeds will be directly traceable to that."

"How do you do that without Robert around?"

She hesitated, apparently thinking about how to answer that. "Most of it's in my name anyway. That's the way my father and Robert wanted it. The rest of it's in a straw party's name, who'll do what I ask."

"As we move along, you'll show me that's all true?"

Her smile seemed something between ironic and bitter. "'Trust but verify.' I will, best as I can."

He knew it couldn't be perfect. There would be unknowns; it's not like he could bring in an auditor. But it seemed like she had thought it all the way through and their interests would be aligned in achieving this with complete legitimacy.

"And," she said, "of course, I'll pay you for your time and expenses." Surprise. A bonus there. Seemed unfair. To her.

"I'm not being charitable. It just makes sense that you'd be paid. And we need a contract for your services. That'll make it even more legit."

"I'm no lawyer, no accountant. Not sure I'm right for business acquisitions."

"No, but you can hire them. You'll just be a high-level go-fer, presumably a little smarter than most…and tougher if I need that. Well, *hopefully* tougher anyway…Should we proceed?"

He nodded.

"One thing more," she said, shifting into her fearsome mode. "If you're lying to me…if you betray me…it will go very bad for you."

He said nothing, thinking it might go "very bad" for him whether he betrayed her or not.

"Okay," she said, "Next time we talk art and car washes."

Driving away from her home, he thought, *Both of us in the same boat. Desperate gamblers…But I wonder how many lies she told me.*

● ● ●

He had decided to tell only one person, Harrigan, and he recoiled, mentally and almost physically, thinking about it, not expecting a welcome reception. They met at Harrigan's office. He brought Karma with him.

"Rinty and Corporal Rusty," Harrigan said as O'Keefe arranged himself in a guest chair in front of Harrigan's desk and Karma laid down next to him, "Sergeant Biff O'Hara here."

"You remember all that shit?"

"All of it."

O'Keefe ran through the Rose situation quickly.

"Can you guess what I have to say?" Harrigan said.

"I could recite your speech myself. But save it. I'm only telling you because someone else needs to know, and I may need some legal advice along the way."

He could see Harrigan's jaw clench as if to keep the words he wanted to say from escaping his mouth.

"And she'll need some legal advice too…acquiring a business, real estate, all that."

"It'd be way too stupid of me to represent her, especially with Russ Lord hovering over me and pissed off that he didn't put me in jail last year."

O'Keefe didn't know what to say or do except look forlorn and abandoned.

It did no good. Harrigan was unrelenting. "And you'd better worry about the same thing. He might be more pissed off at you than me. You're the one who pried Maura Davis out of her hiding place. And like I've told you before: 'If you don't carry a lunch bucket to work, you've probably committed at least one financial crime in your life, knowing or not, if they wanna pin it on you.' And hangin' out with Rose Jagoda is a long way from carryin' a lunch bucket."

O'Keefe thought he might start crying.

"But I *will* advise *you*," Harrigan said, coming partly to the rescue. "If that indirectly helps her, fine, but nothing direct. No asking me, 'what should *she* do?' only 'what should *I* do?' And I'll steer you toward good lawyers in Arizona or California that you can hire to represent her in the transactions. And since you're gonna be a half-ass unlicensed lawyer for her without a malpractice policy, I'll get you some materials on due diligence and other issues in business acquisitions."

"I'd like that anyway," and he told Harrigan about the New York-based corporate due diligence investigation firm and his intention to re-create a version of that.

"God, what have *I* created here?" Harrigan said. Then, looking proud of himself, he added, "Very smart though. I'll help all I can. Need to get past this shit ASAP."

"Before you bring it up, I've already asked her about the source of the money. All demonstrably legit, she says."

"Good for you. Under no circumstances let any of the money pass through you. Let that be between her and her lawyer. No more conversations with her about the source of the funds. But keep your antenna way up, and if you suspect anything at all, let me know right away."

Harrigan stared at O'Keefe and O'Keefe stared out Harrigan's floor-to-ceiling windows. Finally, Harrigan said, "I can't resist. How do you know that she didn't go right to her evil pals and they're setting a trap?"

"Pretty elaborate ruse. And for what? What would be the point?"

"Who knows? I've given up trying to fathom why people do the shit they do. I just plan for the worst and get ready to clean up the mess."

"I have to take the chance."

"It's bad enough to die before your time, but those guys like to torture people before they kill them."

O'Keefe shrugged, though the prospect of it terrified him whenever he had the misfortune to think about it.

"You want to satisfy everyone that the Outfit wasn't behind the bombing. There's got to be a smarter way to try to do that. You need a Plan B."

O'Keefe told him about his conversation with Sergeant Trowbridge and all the loose ends and unresolved issues from the aborted investigation, concluding with, "The damn guy actually seriously suggested I do any further investigation myself."

Harrigan cocked his head, produced his trademark not-quite-smirk of a smile and said, "Well, duh...take the hint. That means they'll probably give you some help."

"Jesus, man, don't I have enough on my plate already?"

"That's what happens when you have such a large appetite. And you've got Rinty there. Rusty and Rinty cannot fail. And Sergeant Biff O'Hara will be here, standing by and on alert."

CHAPTER 14

GIVEN HIS POSITION, Paul Marcone could have commanded his own driver and bodyguard, but he enjoyed driving his black Lincoln Town Car himself as he had done for years for others in the Outfit including the prior Boss, Robert Sciorra. But given how Paul himself had recently become the Boss and his tenuous hold on that position, he wished not to seem overly and too hastily pretentious at this early stage of his insecure ascendancy. But, most important, he wanted never to be so dependent on any single person. Such a dependency had contributed to Robert Sciorra's downfall, killed by his own driver and bodyguard, Paul Marcone.

Ricky Vitale sat uneasily in the passenger seat, occasionally stealing glances behind him at Vince Sorvino who occupied the back seat directly behind Ricky. Paul obtained great enjoyment from Ricky's discomfiture. He and Vince had planned it this way. Ricky expected it to be only he and Paul, but Vince came along as a surprise guest, invited by Paul without Ricky's permission.

"I really want to hear what Vince thinks about this," Paul said after Ricky had installed himself in the Lincoln and they were already a few blocks away from Ricky's place, "so I invited him. No use having to catch him up later. Hope that's okay."

There was nothing for Ricky to do but growl, "Sure, no problem."

They didn't intend to harm Ricky that day, just make him squirm, and, indeed, Ricky started squirming when Vince climbed into the backseat and placed himself directly behind Ricky. To Paul's inner-amusement, a few beads of sweat popped out on Ricky's forehead on this winter day. "That," Vince later said, as he and Paul laughed about it, "was the sign of a man with a guilty conscience."

Ricky "owned" a place similar to but way downscale from Cherry Pink—"owned," that is, in the peculiar way the Outfit recognized ownership, requiring the passing of some of the profits up the chain of command and with no promise that "ownership" would transfer to heirs pursuant to the usual niceties of estate planning and decedent estate administration. He also ran a few higher-class prostitutes through an escort service in town.

Ricky had arranged this meeting and briefed them on the way. "No tellin' what kind of story he'll try to sell us, but I think Wayne Popper's in way over his head. The twerp was just the bouncer at the place until that Bowman-Jensen situation put him sort of in charge by default, and he's no business genius, that's for sure. Might be a good opportunity for us. High-class joint, good-lookin' broads, upper end customers that like to make big bets on the games, cops looking the other way."

After a tour of the premises, which included a raucous visit to the dancers' dressing room full of half-clothed ladies who had been warned to look and act their best for these visitors, they met with Wayne Popper and Marty Lansing, the club's manager, in Marty's well-appointed office.

Marty's semi-college-boy, semi-hippie good looks came in handy in the recruitment of the ladies, both for dancing in the club and fucking on his couch in the office or the big waterbed in his apartment. He was not indiscriminate about it, choosing only the most appealing ones for the second of these activities. If they demurred, they didn't last long at the club. Rejection just did not make for good employer-employee relations going forward.

Wayne Popper sported a high flattop haircut, held erect by ample butch wax, a style that had been in fashion for about a month thirty years ago. He had been David Bowman's sycophantic sidekick, first as grade-school-age juvenile delinquents, earning two stints in reform school before they were out of their teens and, in their early twenties, short prison sentences for a slew of burglaries. They were suspected of much more villainy but received the protection, in the form of indifference or worse, from law enforcement authorities since Popper's relatives were honeycombed throughout county government including the Sheriff's office, a happy circumstance that also facilitated the establishment and profitable operation of the Cherry Pink. Indeed, its license was in the name of Wayne Popper's eighty-four-year-old uncle who resided in a nursing home.

The investors had never wanted direct involvement in the operation or any publicity whatsoever, all participating under corporate and straw-party names, and they wanted even less possibility of exposure after eruption of the recent scandal involving David Bowman and mayoral candidate Jerry Jensen. Bowman's demise left a confused power vacuum that Wayne Popper presumed to fill though he had never before served in any capacity other than the club's chief bouncer and part-time handyman since he did have some mechanical skills. He had no title but issued orders around the place, including to Marty, though he had to defer to Marty's superior expertise and style on all things other than thuggery.

They sat around a conference table amidst a pall of cigar smoke—Cubans proudly proffered by Marty though Marty himself preferred stogie-sized, hand-rolled joints of the finest cannabis that could be procured locally. He had also ordered the best looking, most competent waitresses to report early this day to make sure the guests enjoyed a constant flow of alcohol and semi-lascivious attention. Ricky imbibed freely. Vince, pacing himself, only sipped at his scotch and water. Paul left his whiskey untouched and rolled his unlit cigar slowly in his fingers, only occasionally bringing it to his lips.

"So, what ya think?" Wayne said with boyish enthusiasm that almost overcame his perpetual sneer and made him seem almost tolerable.

"Top of the line," Ricky said. "And out here in Dogpatch ta boot."

Wayne's acne-scarred face went dark when he heard the word "Dogpatch," his relatives being some of the mangiest dogs in the patch, but it passed as he turned his attention toward Vince and Paul for a reaction.

"Nice," Vince said without enthusiasm. Paul nodded in agreement with Vince.

Ricky rubbed his thumb and forefingers together. "But how's the moolah these days?"

Wayne nodded his head toward Marty.

Taking the cue, Marty said, "Great from a profit and loss and cash flow perspective."

"That Jensen-Bowman-O'Keefe publicity didn't hurt?" Ricky asked

"Actually, it seemed to help. So many of these guys seem to want to walk on the wild side."

"Pissants. Gotta love 'em," Ricky said.

"But that ain't true of our investors," Wayne said. "The chickenshit bastards are in hiding and wantin' out. Which leads to this meeting. It creates an opportunity...for smarter people, braver people, not a bunch of chickenshits."

"That's us, Baby!" Ricky said, "meaning the smarter and braver of course."

Smiles and chuckles around the table.

"And there's a lot more to it than just this place," Wayne said, again cueing up Marty with a nod, who again took over the pitch.

"Well, first, there's the obvious. More places like this…and yours too, Ricky…in just the right spots. These make a lot of money, but even more important, they give us, let's call it the 'infrastructure,' and I mean by that, *the pussy!*"

Wayne and Ricky guffawed and whooped, Vince laughed, Paul smiled. Ricky said, "You got it, Baby!"

"And with that *pussy* infrastructure you build the rest. Start with fuck movies. Places like Cherry Pink here, and your place Ricky, you well know, they suck in a lot of capital, no pun intended, you need to keep spending to keep 'em up."

"Well, mine ain't no Taj Mahal like this place."

Marty pressed on. "The movies don't cost near as much. Amateur talent, cheap talent, recruit the girls from your dancers, find some big-dick guys to work mainly for the free snatch. You get it? You know how much they made on *Deep Throat*…on *Debbie Does Dallas*…on *Behind the Green Door*?"

Ricky started to say something, but Marty held up one finger to politely silence him. "I know what you're about to say…that they don't all make that kind of money. That's true, but if you have some decent production values, good looking people, you can make plenty, and every once in a while, you hit the big one. The ROI is fantastic."

"What's that?" Wayne said. Ricky laughed out loud, and the others smiled patronizingly at this hopeless Dogpatch dunce.

"Jesus, Wayne," Ricky said, "ROI is 'Return On Investment.'"

But Wayne appeared still not to get it. Marty, doing his best to disguise his contempt, explained, "It's how much you make vs. how much you put in. If I make one dollar off a ten-dollar investment, that's okay but not the kind of return, only ten percent, that we're in this business for. But you get ten dollars on ten dollars, one hundred percent, and even more sometimes, now you're talking."

Wayne seemed to know they were looking down on him. "Okay. Obvious. Fancy word for somethin' obvious."

Vince asked, "Can you film that stuff in a straight-ass town like this? Wouldn't they just shut you down?"

"First, it would take them a while to catch you. Second, you'd have a chance to pay somebody off. And we're in the perfect place for that. 'Dogpatch' you might call it, Ricky—"

"I didn't mean nothin' bad by that," Ricky interrupted, glancing at Wayne. "Always liked that Daisy Mae."

Everyone laughed but Wayne.

Marty continued, "But we damn near own this patch out here, dogs too, but our most valuable asset: the pussy. And if they do come down on you, you'd bring in the cavalry, the lawyers. That's the kind of partners we're looking for—people who don't just have the loot but the lawyers and the loins, the cojones, to fight. And if they stop you, or make it too expensive for you, you just move on. It's not like you need the Warner Brothers movie lot or something. You need a room…at most a house."

"Marty, tell 'em about the phone stuff," Wayne said, excitedly bouncing a little up and down like a baby in a high-chair.

"Yeah," Marty continued, "the best of all really."

"I think I've heard about this," Vince offered.

"Yeah. They call the 800 number or whatever it is, 970 now I think, and they start talkin' and start ringin' up the tolls, *ching ching ching*, the phone company gets most of it, but they split it with…us."

"So," Vince said, "you pay some broad ta talk dirty...you pay for the phone and the broad and whatever advertisin' ya have ta do to get the horndogs to make the call, and that's pretty much it?"

Wayne responded, "And it don't even matter what she looks like. Can be the fattest, ugliest pig in the world, but nobody sees her. They can imagine whatever they want."

They drifted into small talk and smoked and drank for a few more minutes until Paul said, "So how much do your investors have in this and how much does it cost to get them out?"

Wayne answered: "I'm guessin' they'll take fifty cents on the dollar, maybe less."

"What if you threatened to expose 'em?" Ricky asked.

"Might help, but ain't that called extortion?"

"Yeah, duh," Ricky said. "That's what you might call a specialty of ours."

"Who'll talk to 'em?" Vince asked.

"I'm thinkin' Marty's the right guy for it."

"Maybe along with one of our people," Vince said.

"Yeah," Marty said, "I'll tell 'em that all this bad publicity has us on the edge of the cliff, and I might be able to put together a group of investors to rescue the place and get some of their money back, but they can't be greedy."

"What if they want some due diligence...or negotiate some... before they sell?" Vince said.

Marty looked stumped by that one.

"Yeah," Vince said, answering his own question, "that's why you need one of our guys with you. We can help on stuff like that."

"How much do the investors know about the operations, the P&L?" Paul asked.

Wayne looked perplexed again, like he didn't know what that meant either, but this time he held his tongue.

"Not much," Marty said. "Bowman was very stern about that. Did you know him?"

"No," Paul said.

"A little," Ricky said, "by reputation."

"Well, he was a real tough bastard, and he just stonewalled them on that kind of stuff. They just got checks regularly. Big ones. That's all they really cared about anyway. And I've been holding back those checks since the big blow-up about Jensen and Bowman and that O'Keefe guy…"

"O'Keefe," Wayne said. "That cocksucker needs to be eatin' dirt… and that cunt that works for him too. They've caused us untold bullshit."

Paul said, "You got a budget for all this other stuff…the films and the phone calls?"

Marty said, "No, but I can do one up for us."

Ricky butted in, "And a detailed business plan too, okay?"

Paul tried to avoid looking irritated. He turned to Wayne. "How much of the place do the investors own?"

Wayne squirmed, revealing the guilty hesitation of a man figuring out how to tell a lie.

Marty jumped in, as if he were afraid of what Wayne might say. "In terms of actual ownership, all of it. In terms of practical reality, none of it. Wayne and I think, as a matter of practical reality, that *we* own *all* of it."

Ricky butted in again. "How much do you want and how much do we get for whatever we put in…and our other services of course?"

Vince looked pained and strained, as if he might be about to pass a particularly large and spikey turd, realizing that Ricky was making it a contest between himself and Paul, a contest about which of them, after they left, Wayne and Marty would say, "That guy was the Boss."

Marty glanced nervously at Wayne, looking fearful that Wayne might blurt something stupid again. "We're not quite able to answer either of those questions. Today we just wanted to see if you might be interested. Let me get the budgets together..."

"And the business plans," Ricky said too loudly.

"And, yes, the business plans."

"And we *are* interested, and you Goddamn well need us, Baby!"

●   ●   ●

When the meeting wrapped up and Ricky, Vince, and Paul left the room, Wayne said, "Well, what ya think?"

"I think those are very scary guys. I wish you'd let me talk to my people out west."

Wayne's face instantly and categorically rejected that idea. He said, "We can go a long way with these guys. We're not the only ones in a crack. With Jagoda and Sciorra gone, *they're* in some trouble themselves."

"Which of those guys do you think is the Boss?"

"No question. Ricky, obviously."

CHAPTER ▶ 15

"THIS FUCKING WAYNE Popper, what a moron," Marty thought. He had taken this job for the money, the drugs, the pussy, and what he called "the edge." But that edge had gotten way too sharp, and too narrow, and too high. Though undone in the end by his uncontrollable thuggery and insane addiction to violence for its own sake, David Bowman was at least competent in the basic daily affairs of life and possessed some ability to accurately assess a person or a situation, whereas this Wayne Popper, Bowman's lifelong idiot acolyte, was bone-dry brain-drained—of everything, especially one microscopic spittle of good sense. How had he fallen into this guy's net? Greed. Too greedy. Marty had thought recent events would give him a chance to take over, slide it away from the remaining chicken-livered investors and build this into something like he had described today to those Mafia assholes. But he had not counted on Popper actually believing he could take over from Bowman, and it quickly became apparent that Popper would not accept one word of challenge or dissent, and that he would, without hesitation and happily, do grievous harm to Marty or anyone else who interfered.

Just when Marty was about to bail out, ske-fucking-daddle back to the coast and as far away from these redneck cowboy creeps as he could get, Popper announced what at first looked like a flash of brilliance by bringing in the Wops. Marty thought that surely they would recognize Marty as the guy who knew how to make their money make more money, and a lot of it, in all kinds of different ways. But that stroke of brilliance turned out to be a pathetic little brain fart. Wayne had picked the wrong horse, Ricky, when the two other guys, Paul and Vince, were obviously the bosses, and they did not seem to have much use for Ricky, immediately recognized Wayne as a cretinous nincompoop, and undoubtedly had no intention of doing anything other than muscling out Wayne and the investors for sure, and probably Marty as well unless he could figure out a way to maneuver through this jungle.

Oh man, he had come such a long way from San Francisco!

●   ●   ●

In the parking lot Ricky said, "Pretty sweet, huh, boys?"

Neither Paul nor Vince answered.

"Well?" Ricky demanded.

"It's got promise," Paul said.

Vince added, "Depends how much they want and what we get."

"What we *take,* you mean. We can squeeze those investors."

"That might not be so smart," Paul said, trying to phrase it diplomatically. "Who knows who they are, who they know, what shit they could bring down on us. The ones to squeeze are those two bozos in that office. Let them squeeze the investors, then we squeeze them."

"Yeah," Vince said, "and we need to see a lot more before we give those bozos any money. That Marty seems smart enough, but that Wayne is a fuckin' numbskull."

Ricky's face was turning red, his eyes bulging, and his hands clenching into fists. "Look, if you assholes can't see a good deal right in front of your faces, get the fuck out. I can do this all by myself."

"Not very brotherly of you, Ricky," Paul said.

Ricky seemed to realize he had made a mistake with that eruption and needed to retreat a bit. "Ah, I'm sure you guys'll come around. You'll see how much money I can make us out of this. Like I always do. Let's not forget who's been the biggest earner for years now. And with nobody's help by the Goddamm way. Nobody's. Not even Carmine's, though he took plenty *from* me."

Paul knew he should give Ricky some affirmation, yet he couldn't bring himself to do it. But Vince sprinkled a meager drop of oil on the troubled waters. "Let's not get out ahead of ourselves. Let's see what they've got. We'll get it right."

Paul and Vince turned to walk toward the car.

Ricky stayed put. "I'm gonna stick around a while. I got my eye on a couple of them girls."

"Auditions?"

He grinned. "In a manner of speakin'…I guess so, yes,"

"For your club?" Vince asked.

"Not quite, Chump…For my dick."

Paul smiled but wondered how Ricky could help but see that his smile expressed only contempt.

"You guys oughtta join me."

"Too much work to do," Paul said.

"Too old," Vince said.

"Chumps!" Ricky said and headed back toward the club.

Driving away, Paul asked, "You think he's really a threat?"

"He's probably already makin' his moves, but he's not used to the really hard stuff."

"I was thinking," Paul said, "when they were describing that phone call sex racket, those callers would be providing credit card information. Can you imagine what we might be able to do with all that credit card info?"

Vince thought about that, then said. "Smart, Paulie. Ya know, you're quiet but way smarter than Ricky or any of the other guys. I hope you're as tough as he is. Tougher. That was Robert's problem. Not tough. He'd never've made it even if he hadn't fucked up the way he did. Ricky would've eaten him alive."

"Well, who dealt with Robert? I think I proved plenty there."

"Yes, you did."

"But when it's time, can I count on *you*?"

Vince thought about that an even longer time. "Here's how it is. I'd never go against you. But whether I'd help is a 'maybe.' I'm old…"

Paul's face expressed his disagreement, and he started to say something, but Vince wouldn't allow it. "No. I'm old. I'm tired. I wanna be in Miami, not in this shithole I've been stuck in all my life. So what I'm sayin' is that I'm not gonna do somethin' stupid. You've gotta make the right moves between now and then on your own."

"Well, I might need a little help with those moves…and at the end…"

"I'll try…do my best."

"I can't believe we're hearing about that O'Keefe guy again."

"Yeah, what's with that?"

Paul said, "Can't figure it out. The guy manages to piss people off, I guess." He thought, *Carmine was obsessed with him, ordered Robert to kill him, and Robert had strong-armed Lieutenant Ross to eliminate the guy. Ross only managed to wiggle out of that by trading the info on Robert for a reprieve on the O'Keefe hit. Now, here O'Keefe comes up again. Somebody else wants him dead. But how funny is it that O'Keefe's the one that's still alive? Maybe messin' around with the guy just brings very bad luck.* He wondered if anyone other than Robert and Paul knew about Carmine's hit command or that Robert had ordered Ross to do the deed as some kind of payback for a favor done long ago. He didn't think so. And surely nobody but Paul knew that Ross had provided him the information about Robert and got himself off the hook that way. Paul hadn't even told Rose about any of that. Could Carmine have told her? That didn't make sense. He thought about telling Vince right now but held back, not sure why.

They rode in silence for several minutes, until Vince said, "We gotta do somethin' about Rose. We made a mistake there. My fault. I should've known better than to let you do that."

Paul turned to look out his side window so that Vince would not see the pain in his face.

●   ●   ●

Ricky and Wayne sat at a table in the late afternoon appraising the dancers as they appeared on the stage one after the other.

Ricky said, "You think you can *persuade* that little one, Pixie Dust, with the silver hair and the giant tits? Are those real?"

"The hair color's fake, the tits are real. But I intend that one for me."

"No sharin' with your new pal?"

"I've got a better one for ya. Fellatia."

"Really. That's her name?"

"Stage name. Fellatia Maxwell. You heard the phrase 'she could suck the chrome off a car bumper?' That's Fellatia. Named herself that all on her own…Hey, wipe that shit-eatin' grin off your face."

They had another drink and ogled more dancers and waitresses, and the conversation turned to the larger business issues, what David Bowman and Jerry Jensen had built here, and how to nudge out the investors.

"Just give 'em the old hip check like those broads do in Roller Derby," Ricky said. "Great sport, eh, Baby!"

Marty emerged from his office in the back, waved at them, and said something to the bartender.

"That Marty's a pretty smart guy," Ricky said.

"Yeah, but he's just a front man type. No balls. Wouldn't swat a fly. Couldn't even if he wanted to. And by the way, he doesn't own shit here."

"You need those guys sometimes though."

Wayne shrugged, and his eyelids slowly closed and opened again as if something heavy had pressed on them. "You and Vince and Paul…hope you don't mind me askin', but since we're about to do some business, I thought I oughtta know…who's the Boss?"

"Depends on the deal. It shifts around some, depending on the deal."

It was Happy Hour now, the place filling up, Marty making the rounds, glad handing with old customers and introducing himself to new ones.

"No new Big Boss yet?"

"Not yet. Not really."

"And on this deal?"

"That's me. You can depend on it. This is *my* line of work. Neither of them knows shit about this business. They just get their cut of it."

"Pretty good deal for them."

"Yeah, too good."

"If this thing here works out, you think I could join up, ya know, be one of you guys?"

"Well, not all the way. You gotta be Italian to get in all the way. But there's a place for others. Associates, we call 'em. There's a couple'a Irish guys, even a couple Jews. The Jews're too smart to keep 'em out altogether. Irish just muscle, they're dumb fucks."

"I thought Jagoda was a Jew."

"Nah. He had a Jew name, some goofy story there, but he was all Sicilian."

"What are you?" Ricky asked.

"What am I?"

"Yeah. Nationality."

Wayne looked confused, thought for a moment, then said, "American."

Ricky chuckled. *Boy genius.*

"Ya know," Wayne said, "we've got somethin' else in common…"

"Other than bein' American," Ricky said with a smirk.

"Well, that, but I mean somethin' in common other than this place and all the other stuff we talked about today."

"What's that?"

"A guy who fucked over both of us…big time."

Ricky's face asked the question. He waited for the answer.

"That asshole, O'Keefe."

"I don't quite see it that way. He never did anything to me."

"But he did to your Outfit. How can you let that go? You can't let that go."

Ricky shrugged.

Wayne said, way too loud, "Well, I want him dead, can you help me with that?"

Ricky cringed, looked around at the crowd. "Not here," and nodded toward the back, toward the office.

Wayne waved Marty over. "Say, we need to use the office for a talk. Any problem with that?"

Marty hesitated, which irritated Wayne. "What's the problem?"

"I have to make a phone call. Give me fifteen minutes and then it's all yours."

"Okay, hurry."

• • •

After relinquishing his office to Wayne and Ricky for their confab, Marty hung out in the club for a while and had the kitchen make him a sandwich, which he ate while standing at the bar. When Wayne and Ricky returned, Marty said he had to pick up a few things to work on at home. He sauntered back to his office, locked the door behind him, crawled under the conference room table, removed a tape recorder he had attached to the table's underside, and exited through the rear door. Once home, he poured himself a glass of red wine, relieved himself, checked on the sleeping dancer in his bed who had gotten sick and checked out early that day, and returned to the living room. He extracted the recorder from his briefcase, sat down on the couch, opened his stash box and rolled a fat monster of a joint, took a long drink of the wine, lit the joint, inhaled deeply, and punched the play button on the recorder.

By the end of the recording, neither the wine nor the joint could keep his face from turning pale, his hands from trembling, or his mind from wondering what in the fuck he was going to do now.

CHAPTER ▶ 16

THE NEWSPAPER MICROFILMS had arrived, and Kelly proceeded deliberately, eyes straight ahead again, through the gauntlet of ogling bums in the periodicals reading room of the public library where Brandon Terbovich stood waiting for her behind his counter with some intriguing-looking small, square boxes stacked in front of him. She could tell that, despite his air of impatience at the beginning of her last visit, he now seemed almost eager to assist her, and she felt that her previous approach of earnestly seeking his help with utmost sincerity and courtesy had been just right, how Nancy would have handled the situation, and, after all, just Kelly's own true self anyway.

He took her to the microfilm reading machine and showed her how to load the film and operate the machine.

"Thank you, Mr. Terbovich. I'm not sure I'll be able to do that all by myself when I get to the next reel…"

"If you get stuck, just call for help. I could do that blindfolded and in a swimming pool."

She had never bothered much with newspapers, never read them at all other than occasionally the comics. The microfilm stayed interesting for a while. She couldn't help getting distracted by the more sensational stories, especially the crime stories, that had nothing to do with her task at hand. When it threatened to get too excruciatingly boring, she revived herself by freshening up her expectation that at any moment a headline would pop up with Darren's name in it, revealing all the crimes he surely had committed and had fled to her city to hide from.

After two hours had passed and she had just started on the third reel, she felt, first, very heavy, then very sleepy, and, before long, ready to abandon the entire project. She took a break, again braving the walk through the reading room, carefully looking behind her as she ducked into the bathroom, nervous that one of the men from the reading room would follow her in there, turned on the sink faucet, and splashed water on her face. Then back to the drudgery.

The following week, when a new batch of microfilm arrived, she put herself through another Saturday afternoon torture session, but this time it was even worse than before because she could not muster up even a slight realistic hope of an eventual exciting discovery. And her mom had also grown impatient, saying, "When do you think you'll get this done? Seems like you've done plenty already."

By the end of that second Saturday afternoon, she was convinced that whatever evil deeds Darren had surely done, he had either cleverly concealed or they had not roused the interest of the local newspaper. She needed to find another way, and the only other way she could think of seemed too scary for her to undertake all by herself.

●   ●   ●

The first thing was the key.

Kelly knew her mom carried a key to Darren's house. When her mom arrived home, she would habitually unlock the door, drop her purse, and, separately, the key ring, on a small table set against a wall near the front door. Although Annie would sometimes later retrieve the purse from the table if she needed something in it, the key ring always stayed on the table until she left again. On the next Saturday, when it seemed that her mom had settled firmly into her tiny nook of a home office for "market research" on the IBM desktop computer that her dad and his friend George had installed for her (in that better time before Darren), Kelly put on her coat but didn't zip it, and with her gloves in her hand approached her mom.

"Can I go over to Jamie's?"

Frustratingly, her mom hesitated, keeping her in suspense. The kids' parents always seemed terrified any time kids ventured out to the street away from their parents' direct gaze. Her dad had told her that it didn't used to be that way, in his childhood, in the time before serial killers. He said that he and his friends would leave their houses in the morning and play and roam unsupervised all day, maybe only checking in for lunch. When very young, they might have to stay in earshot of their mothers' calls, but by the time they were Kelly's age, they could be out until dinner time, not even checking in for lunch, and then sometimes go out again after dinner even when it was dark as long as it wasn't too cold, until nine or even ten o'clock.

Her mom looked her up and down. "I guess you've already arranged that?"

Kelly could see no value in responding.

"What's up over there?"

"She's rented a movie."

"What movie?"

"I don't know. She said it was a romantic comedy." She knew that would go down well with her mom.

"Good. No scary stuff. I couldn't get you to stay in your own bed for two weeks after you watched *The Shining* at that slumber party."

Whoa! What if she knew about The Stepfather?

Again, Kelly could see no value in a response other than a look of exasperation.

"How long?"

"Three or four hours?"

"Be back before dark. That's absolute. In fact, an hour before dark. Call me when you get there and when you leave."

Problem. She needed time between leaving her house and getting to Jamie's. "Okay. But I'm supposed to stop at the store on the way and pick up some popcorn and stuff."

"Okay. But be careful. I'll expect a call within thirty minutes max…and just before you come home too. I might walk out and meet you halfway."

Done. Get out now. "Thanks," she said, sincerely this time.

On her way out she slipped Darren's key off the ring.

In her neighborhood, both a hardware store and a drug store copied keys. The drug store was the most comfortable place for her, but the clerks there were chatty types well acquainted with Kelly and her mom and always started up a conversation. She envisioned one of them saying to her mom at some point, "Saw Kelly the other day when she brought that key in to copy." So she went to the hardware store where she asked a clerk with a long, scruffy beard and a dark sweater with dandruff flakes on the shoulders how much it would cost to make the key her mother had asked her to get copied for her.

"Let me see it."

He examined it and quoted her a price that she could cover with the money she had on her. Suddenly she was afraid he might not be able to do it right away. She had not thought about possibly having to wait a long time. Thinking about her thirty-minute deadline, she couldn't afford to wait at all.

"Can you do it now?"

"You in a hurry?"

"Yes, sir," she said, looking back over her shoulder toward the store entrance as if someone was waiting for her outside. "My mom needs it pretty bad."

"Sure," he said.

She followed him to another area of the store to the key-making machine. He kept looking toward the entrance, watching for another customer to arrive, and she worried that if one did, he would go to assist that customer and leave her hanging as minutes kept ticking away. He put on safety glasses. When he looked at Kelly, she bounced a little on the balls of her feet, showing nervous impatience and increasing desperation.

But once he got going, he progressed rapidly. Having exhausted only twenty of her minutes, she hustled to Jamie's house, jogging the last half block. She knocked but immediately entered and confronted the startled Jamie who had been on her way to answer the door.

"Need your phone," Kelly said, rushing past Jamie.

"What's the deal?" Jamie said, but Kelly brushed past her to where she knew they kept their phone.

"You're so weird," Jamie said.

After reporting to her mom, she hung up and turned to Jamie, "You remember that movie called *The Stepfather?*"

●　●　●

The second thing was the boy.

Matt Gardner. Her friends kept saying Matt liked her and teasing her about it, embarrassing her in public by sing-songing:

"Kelly and Matt sittin' in a tree,

K-I-S-S-I-N-G"

And she might be kidding herself, but the looks he kept beaming her way seemed to confirm his interest. Cute, one of the best athletes in the school, and a whole grade ahead of her, a very prized boyfriend. She wondered what attracted him to her. There were prettier girls in the school. She appraised herself in the mirror. Not bad though, and if her parents would just let her wear a little makeup…forget it. They stood united on that. At age thirty-eight her mom still didn't wear any.

Most days, Kelly was what they called a latch-key kid because she arrived from school to an empty house, her mom not arriving home from work until 6:00 and sometimes later. Kelly deputized her friend Jamie to let Matt know that she would take a phone call from him and that the best time to call would be right after school. He called her that day. They engaged in the usual pre-teen, boy-girl awkward talk punctuated by many even more awkward silences. Finally, she mustered the courage to say it: "I'm all alone here every day after school. You should come over sometime after basketball practice. I can cook. I'll bake cookies."

"Really? When?"

"Any time's good. Why not soon? Tomorrow…the next day…or the day after that."

"Wow. Let's say day after tomorrow."

"You like chocolate chip?"

Sure he did. Or any other kind she might have mentioned.

Two days later, when she opened the door for him, he looked disheveled and unshowered from basketball practice with a sheen of sweat on his forehead. She wore a short skirt that showed plenty of her long legs, a baby blue sweater, a thin gold necklace, and a silver bracelet that drew attention to her long thin fingers with nails that she had not bitten down to the quick for a long time. Perfect. She had him at a disadvantage.

She helped him off with his coat and laid it on the couch in the living room.

"Nice place," he said as he followed her into the kitchen.

"My mom. She's good at that stuff."

A scrumptious looking plate of cookies sat on the table.

"Milk? Iced tea?

"Iced tea."

She poured him a glass of iced tea and set the glass in front of him, set herself down, and held out her hand palm up toward the cookies, inviting him to partake.

After the second bite, he said, "Good. Really good. Damn good. I like them chewy like this. How you do that?"

"I don't know. I just do what my mom does, just like she does what her mom does."

He ate one, then two, then started on a third.

"You know, Michael Jackson's comin' soon," she said.

"Yeah."

"I might get tickets."

"Really?"

"If I do, you wanna go?"

"Heck yes," he said.

"He's kind of *over* now, but it still oughtta be fun. Might have to go with my mom. She thinks she's an expert moonwalker."

"Your parents are divorced?"

"'Fraid so."

"How's that?"

"Terrible. And now the worst is comin'. A stepfather."

"Not good."

"Have you seen *The Stepfather*?"

"No. Movie?"

"Yeah. You should rent it."

"I will."

"I need to stop it."

"What?"

"The wedding. I think he's a bad man. Darren's his name. He just showed up here in town last year sometime. All by himself. He's a doctor."

"How you gonna do that?"

"You know what my dad does?"

"I heard he's a private eye."

"Right."

"Very neat. What a great job."

"I'm gonna be one too."

"Very neat."

"And my first case is gonna be to find out what Darren is up to."

Matt reached for another cookie. "Wow. How?"

She brought out the key, pushed it to the middle of the table, and told him her plan. He seemed fascinated.

"Want to help?"

"Sure. But what if we get caught?"

"If I'm right, we'll be heroes. If not, we might get grounded for a while. But we'll be in it together. I'll take the blame, tell them it was my idea."

"When?"

"Soon. They haven't set a date yet, but that could happen any time. And they could even elope. It could be any day."

As Matt left, he turned to say goodbye at the front door. Kelly moved into him. They were almost the same height, he only an inch or two taller. She kissed him, just like she and Jamie had practiced it. He impulsively pulled her into him, which startled her. She didn't push him away but gently backed away from him.

She put her hand on his arm and guided him out the door, saying, "We'll go there real soon, okay?"

CHAPTER ▶ 17

WHEN KELLY FAILED to respond to her mom's morning wake-up knock and call of her name, fifteen minutes later her mom returned and opened the bedroom door.

"Hey, Sleepy. Get going. You'll be late."

Kelly kept her head on the pillow and said, "I'm really sick. I threw up last night."

"Why didn't you wake me?"

Like so many of her mom's questions, this one was too hard to answer. "I don't know," she said.

"I've got so many appointments today."

"I'll be fine. Just leave the stomach medicine out for me. If I feel better, I'll go to school this afternoon."

"I'll call every so often to check on you."

"You don't need to."

"Of course I do."

"If I don't answer, it's because I'm sleeping."

"Well, you call me at work then, every couple of hours. I'll probably be out showing houses, so if I'm not there, leave me a message. And I still might come by."

Several blocks away a similar scene—not entirely unlike the plot of *Ferris Bueller's Day Off*—also played out in Matt Gardner's house except that his parents and siblings were running late and hurrying out the door as usual and did not subject him to the tight inspection and check-in regime that Annie O'Keefe had imposed on her daughter. Soon after Matt happily found himself alone in his house, his phone rang.

"Matt?"

"The very one."

"You clear?" she asked.

"Yep."

"I have to wait a while. It'll be this afternoon. I'll call you."

At 10 a.m. her mom called.

"How are you?"

"Maybe a little better. If I get better, I'll go to school."

"You don't need to. Get your rest."

They're always telling you to get your rest. "No, I really want to go. I don't like to miss."

What a liar I am, she thought as she hung up, but she felt only the smallest twinge of guilt.

At 11:30 she called her mom's office and left a message. "Threw up again. Gonna try to get some sleep."

She hung up and called Matt to meet her at the agreed bus stop. They had explored traveling by taxi, but it turned out to be more than they could afford. Using maps and a bus schedule, they had worked out an itinerary on the city bus line. She left her house dressed in her school uniform and carrying her backpack and speculating whether someone might see her and someday mention it to her mom. She couldn't figure out how to remove all the risks and would just have to take her chances. If she were caught out like that, she planned to tell her mom she went to school and hope her mom wouldn't investigate further.

They traveled first to Darren's medical office where they checked to confirm his car was in the parking lot. Before catching the next bus, they found a pay phone and, assuming her mom would have left a message on the answering machine if she had called, Kelly used the remote feature to check. No messages.

They had to take two buses to get close to Darren's house. They found another pay phone. She called Darren's office and handed the receiver to Matt, bringing her head close to the instrument to listen.

"I need to speak with Doctor Maefield."

"I'm sorry, he's with a patient right now. Can I—"

Matt hung up. They only wanted to confirm he was still there. After that, Kelly called again to check her answering machine. This time her mom had left a message: "I'm still not in the office. I'll call back soon."

"Are you ready?" Matt said. He looked ready himself, courage screwed up and plucky for the adventure. She wasn't so sure about herself. If she got caught, might they send her to juvenile jail or something? And the shame of it. But who cared about that? Not when a future with Darren Maefield living in her house was hanging above her like the blade of a guillotine. Like she had heard her dad say, "Anything worth doing is worth doing fanatically." But she would feel plenty ashamed for getting Matt in trouble. She was afraid they would kick him off the basketball team, or worse. That would be hard for her to live with.

"Sure. Let's go."

Matt had asked her how to act. "Act like we own the place," she had said. "We've got a key after all. He's my mom's boyfriend, and we're making some extra money to do a special cleaning of his house, the stuff the maids never get to, like my mom is always complaining about."

"What if he comes home and catches us?"

She had prepared for this too. She wished he hadn't asked, and she didn't have to tell him, but thought she should: "We'll tell him we thought this was a perfect place to make out."

Big grin from Matt. He looked way too happy. A jackpot smile, like he had won a big one.

Chins tucked in the top of their coats against a chilly wind, they marched down the street, fake-talking animatedly, blabbering meaningless words at each other. A driveway ran up the side of the single-story house ending in a detached garage with closed doors. There would be a back-door entrance to the house. If he came home, would he come in the back or the front? Surely the back.

When she put the key in the lock, it wouldn't turn. Exasperated, she turned to Matt, her hand still on the key. *God, it doesn't work. But maybe that's a good thing. This is such a bad idea.*

"Jiggle it a little," Matt said. Which she did. It turned.

As she opened the door and stepped into the vestibule, she thought, *Burglar alarm!* Why hadn't she thought of this before? She lived with them all the time. They had installed a fancy one in her house after that terrifying Halloween night almost two years before when her dad had first gotten himself in trouble with the gangsters, and, after the bombing, he had installed his own elaborate systems—electronics, even dogs, in his house, car, office, everywhere. But she heard no alarm sound here. Could it be silent, just wired to alert the alarm company or the police? She looked around and did not see the alarm box like the one at her house.

"Alarm system," she said, and dashed off toward the back door and he ran after her.

Nothing there either. She didn't know where else it might be and would have to assume it didn't exist…at least until the sirens started howling and the police showed up at the door.

"He probably has some kind of home office setup somewhere," she said.

They moved through the house together. From the front door, down a hallway, the living room on their right, past a half-bath to the kitchen; into the kitchen, then through a dining room on the right of the kitchen, to a hallway off the dining room, past a small bathroom, and beyond that, three bedrooms, two of them very small, one of them larger with its own bathroom. The furniture throughout looked like it had been purchased in bulk at a discount store. *Surely I won't have to live in this place.* One of the smaller bedrooms, partly furnished as a home office, contained a swivel chair in front of a parsons-table desk with a single shallow drawer in the center of it. A two-drawer filing cabinet next to the desk seemed promising. She opened the drawer and found only items such as the lease for the house, various insurance documents, a couple of boxes of blank checks, and miscellaneous other uninteresting things.

"Closets," she said.

They searched the closets in each of the three bedrooms and found no cabinets, chests, trunks, boxes, or anything else that might hold something revealing.

They returned to the dining room: on the dining room table two neatly stacked piles of papers; nothing but bills, junk mail, and medical newsletters and magazines; a buffet with a flat top and many drawers yielded not only nothing of interest but nothing at all. *He's a nothing man.* Even her dad did not live such a sparse existence. In the living room, no couch, just a comfortable chair positioned to watch the television; next to the chair a side table with a door opening to a small interior space that held a Yellow Pages and a paperback novel with a cover that identified it as a spy thriller. She hadn't noticed another book in the house. *Nothing man*, she thought again, her new nickname for him.

They stood looking at each other, until Matt said, "Basement?"

Kelly felt a jolt of good energy. "Yeah…has to be one. But I didn't see a door."

Matt headed toward the kitchen, and she followed. At the back of the kitchen, on the left side, a door opened to the outside, to a small porch and a three-step stairway. From the bottom of the stairs a short concrete path ended at the driveway.

On the right side of the kitchen, they found another door. Matt turned the knob and shoved the door open, poised on the balls of his feet to jump backward. No need. A large utility room, a washer and dryer, a vacuum cleaner and various other household maintenance items and tools. Another door faced them on the opposite wall. It had two locks: one a small switch built into the doorknob itself; the other, above the doorknob, a sliding bolt lock. She led this time, sliding back the bolt on the upper lock, turning the lever in the doorknob to straight up, and opening the door.

Darkness. Facing a wall. Between the door and the wall, a stairway landing. She reached around the inside of the wall to her right and found a light switch. When she flipped it on, not much changed, some light but little of it. They looked at each other again, even more apprehensively than they had before. If Matt was thinking the same thing as Kelly, he was thinking how scary basements are and how trapped they would be once they ventured down those stairs.

"Let's go," she said. "It's our last chance."

"Think we need a flashlight?" Matt said.

"Come on," she said, and began to step slowly down the narrow and creaky stairway that had no banister. The familiar damp, musty smell that all basements seemed to exude filled her nose. She heard the door shut. *What if it locked behind them?*

Looking back, she whispered, "Try the door," her voice quavering. "Make sure it didn't lock."

Matt tried the door.

It opened back into the utility room.

"Thank God," she said.

"This is too scary," Matt said in a hoarse whisper.

She was regretting it too, hoping there would be nothing downstairs to find, that they could get done down there and dash back upstairs and out of the house fast, which disappointed her in herself. *Don't be a chicken.*

"School's almost out," Matt said, "we've gotta be gettin' back."

She recognized this as an invitation to stop right here, and flee. But she didn't even consider it. She started back down the stairs. "Gotta finish," she said.

The basement had nothing in it other than old, dusty pipes on the ceiling with cobwebs hanging from some of them, a heating unit, some old boards, and, in one corner, behind a flimsy partition, a toilet crusted with ancient dirt. On the other side of the basement, an area had been enclosed with drywall and a small doorway cut into the drywall, creating a separate room. The door opened to the inside of the room. She put her foot on the door and pushed it open, reeled her torso back slightly away from the door in an automatic defensive gesture. Nothing leaped out at her. She stepped into the room.

A light bulb at the end of a wire hanging from the ceiling protruded from a socket with a switch on it. She reached up and turned the switch. Nothing happened. She grabbed the socket and the bulb, turned the bulb more tightly into the socket, and gave the switch a further turn. Her hand lit up, and when she removed her hand, the room did too.

Her eyes widened. On a shelf along one wall sat four plastic storage boxes, each approximately a yard wide and a yard tall. In the middle of the room, as if intended to be featured there, stood a four-drawer file cabinet almost as tall as Kelly. She moved to it, half expecting it to be empty since Darren the nothing man seemed not to have anything that proved he had a past at all. But when she opened the top drawer, she found it full—of papers, arranged in labeled folders.

"Bingo! Matt, come look."

Matt had lingered outside the room. He seemed to have changed, seemed not very brave now. He glanced behind him, crossed to the smaller room, looked at the file cabinet, and said "Bingo," without enthusiasm.

"I'll do this," Kelly said. "See what's in those boxes."

"Shouldn't one of us keep watch out there?"

"We don't have hardly any time left. We've gotta see what's in all this."

She turned back to the file cabinet. In the top drawer, behind a cardboard divider with the word "DIVORCE" written on it in black magic marker ink in large block letters, numerous documents filled the entire drawer, documents on the long legal-size paper like the documents she had occasionally seen her dad studying. The first item was a "Petition" where a Mrs. Delong sought in the strange language of the law and lawyers to end her marriage to Mr. Curtis Delong and, following that, some other legal papers, and most interesting, a bound booklet with a clear cover that said, "Deposition Of Curtis Delong."

The Deposition was like a play. A "Mr. Logan" appeared to be asking Curtis Delong questions that another person would often "object" to and make a speech about, after which Curtis Delong would give his answer. Mr. Logan accused Mr. Delong of punching his wife on at least one occasion, which Mr. Delong denied. She flipped through many more documents, quickly skimming words and concepts she only vaguely understood or not at all, until she reached the last two, the first one titled "Settlement Agreement" between Mrs.

Delong, identified as "the Petitioner," and Mr. Delong, identified as "the Respondent" and the second an "Order Terminating Marriage."

She looked up and saw Matt leaving the room. She wondered if he had heard something and moved to the door to watch after him. On the side of the basement next to the driveway there was a row of small windows set in window wells, half above and half below ground. He stood in the middle of the basement looking toward the windows, his ear cocked like the picture of the RCA dog hearing "his master's voice."

"What are you doing?"

"Shh, Goddamn it!" he said.

They heard what sounded like a car door slamming.

"Shit, he's come home," Matt said, his face in full panic. He ran to the stairs, and she also panicked when she thought he might run up them and try to escape from the house. But he stopped at the bottom of the stairway, listened for a few moments, and whispered, "He came up the back steps. He's in the house. What are we gonna do? We can't stay in here all night. They'll be lookin' for us soon. Maybe they're already lookin'."

"It'll be okay. He won't stay. He works late. I know that. I'm gonna keep looking."

"I'm staying right here."

She turned around and headed back to the room and the file cabinet. She forced herself to do this though she thought she was probably even more afraid than Matt, plus she felt guilty about Matt, and sorry for him. But the worst possible thing would be to get caught without finishing what they came for. That might be the last chance of ever finding out what Darren might be hiding.

Matt had left the lid off one of the boxes. Not good. She replaced it and straightened the boxes and returned to the file cabinet. The second drawer was empty, the third drawer stuffed full of more legal papers but of something different than the divorce case, a case called "People vs. Doctor Robert Ensley and Raymond Gonzalez, Esquire." The document used the word "said" a lot, not to describe people saying something but as an adjective— "said physician" and "said attorney," accusing Doctor Ensley of conspiring with Gonzalez, a lawyer, in the "said" conspiracy, which had resulted in the submission and payment of false claims based on "said false diagnoses." She thought she understood the word "diagnosis" but still did not understand the meaning or function of the document, only that it contained many accusations against the doctor and the lawyer and someone else called an "unindicted co-conspirator," but she could not find where it identified "said co-conspirator" by name.

She didn't know what prompted it, but her mind's eye conjured up the image of that door that led from the utility room to the basement stairs. Looming largest of all in that image, much larger than its actual size in relation to the rest of the door: the bolt of the lock mechanism, not securely in place like it was supposed to be, but retracted, unlocked. If Darren walked into that room for some reason, he would surely notice it. A wave of fear radiated from somewhere in her stomach up to her chest and ignited a rapid pulsing in her heart. She had to keep herself from letting out a shriek. With trembling fingers, she kept turning the pages of the document, but she had a tough time concentrating. Still so much stuff to go through, and even if they didn't get caught, they didn't have enough time left.

Matt appeared at the door. "You were right. He left again. Let's get out."

She hesitated.

"*Now,* Kelly!"

She closed the file drawer, took a last look, making sure she had left nothing amiss, shut the door of the room, and followed him into the main part of the basement. They cautiously climbed the stairs and slowly opened the door to the utility room. Her heart beat faster again when they reached the door from the utility room to the kitchen. If Darren hadn't left, if Matt had been wrong about that, there would be, as she had heard some adult say, "hell to pay."

But the kitchen was empty.

Matt said, "Let's go out the back. It's right here."

"Can't. My key's to the front door."

Matt hesitated. She started walking toward the front door, leaving him no alternative except to follow. Locking the front door behind them and proceeding down the front walk and onto the sidewalk, they tried to present the same innocent façade to the world as they had done on their arrival.

On the bus, they sat next to each other, saying nothing for a while. She passed her tongue across her lips to wet them slightly, leaned over, and kissed him on the cheek. She really did like him and felt grateful that he had taken such a risk for her.

"You're my hero," she said.

"That was really dumb," he said. "I feel like I'm gonna throw up. Can kids have heart attacks?"

● ● ●

Kelly wanted to get back to that file cabinet as soon as possible. A few days later, at the end of the school day, she intercepted Matt in the hallway as he came out of his classroom and headed for the gym for basketball practice. Other students streamed past them as they talked, some of them smirking knowingly at the two "lovebirds."

Hey," she said, "I thought we'd go back tomorrow or the next day and finish with that file cabinet."

His face registered shocked disbelief. "Are you crazy? It's a miracle we didn't get caught last time."

"We've got to finish."

"You're crazy."

"You won't go?"

"No way."

"You're chicken?"

His face flushed red. "No, I'm just not stupid. The whole thing was crazy to begin with. You're not gonna find anything."

"I have to finish."

"Well, I don't. You may be crazy, but I'm not…I can't be late for practice."

He turned and walked away.

She stood, watching him go and her plan go with him. She couldn't help it, the tears came.

One of her friends, who had stopped a few yards behind to watch the encounter, approached Kelly gingerly, came to her side, then peered around to peek at Kelly's face. Kelly didn't acknowledge her, didn't move, kept crying and staring down the hallway even though Matt had disappeared.

Her friend said, "You two break up or what?"

CHAPTER 18

ONE THING ALWAYS led to another—and one thought always led to another—unless you maintained your vigilance and cut the thoughts off before you lost control of them and they meandered into dangerous territory. On the flight to Tucson, O'Keefe, not paying close enough attention, wandered into a reverie. The first thought so harmless: *Never been to Tucson.* Not surprising since he really hadn't been to many places other than his own town and its mostly dull surroundings, and what he had seen of the world was mostly courtesy of the Marine Corps, not exactly the enriching experience that people claimed travel to be. But he had driven *through* Tucson before, heading south to the Huachuca Mountains, almost to Mexico—not that long ago, only sixteen months ago— pursuing the mesmerizing, haunted Tag Parker, convincing himself that he could protect her, rescue her, save her life, but it was a tarnished quest that had ended in a tragedy in which he had played a shameful role.

After that, many called him a hero because he had killed several of Carmine Jagoda's men in a firefight. He knew better. The quest that had led him to that confrontation had its source in the heedless obsession of a besotted Peter Pan, a boy-man who demanded more of the world than he had the right to receive. Though severely wounded, he had survived that firefight though he did not think he deserved to. He quietly resolved to live a useful life, but he carried with him the burden of this curse, either the actual fact or, worse in a way, the world's belief that the Outfit intended to exact their vengeance and would one day do so. He had, wisely or not, decided to deal with it directly by going straight to the evil source and discovered, apparently, something else altogether, a fellow creature who claimed to be trying to escape the curse herself.

At their second meeting, her house again, early afternoon on a weekday, they had gone through the same drill as before—the bland rental car parked in the driveway, the pat-down that embarrassed him and amused her. "Making sure you haven't gone out and bought some Thunderware now that you know what it is," she teased.

Sitting across the table from him, knowing the documents well enough that she could read them upside down, she navigated him through the pile of papers, explaining their relevant contents, her rationales, emphasizing a particularly important number or sentence or phrase by tapping on it with a fingernail. Even though it would have been far easier to deal with and discuss the documents if they had sat next to each other, she stayed across the table. He thought he knew why and was grateful for it.

She had identified not one but two businesses she wanted to buy and take no chance of losing, pressing him to get out to Tucson ASAP and arrange a purchase contract. The business of one of the companies was to identifiy and select, on a large-volume basis, art works for corporate offices, hotels, and institutions such as hospitals and colleges. Her eyes danced, charged with a child's enthusiasm as she spoke about it: "I think I'd be good at that. The owners are an older couple. They came out of the hotel world. They've made a great start, but they've only dented this huge market. They don't have the capital to take it to the next level, and they'd like to retire early. We need full financial information, but we need to try to tie it up while we're doing the due diligence. Offer them their price. No financing contingency. Due diligence only, and we'll finish that fast. Quick closing too. All that good stuff."

After she answered his questions about the art business, he said, "Now from the sublime to the ridiculous. What's this with the car wash?"

"Super Suds, it's called. And don't laugh. You see those numbers? This guy is the unrecognized Henry Ford of the car wash world. He's refined the touchless car wash to a higher level than anyone else in the country as far as I can tell."

"You've studied it that much?"

"Of course," she said, the big eyes narrowing in hostility to the idea that she would do anything less. "I'll show you my piles of car wash magazines."

She marched on: "He's had this one location in Tucson for a long time, and he's just built another one. I think he's in a bit of trouble getting from his construction loan to permanent. He wants to retire anyway, like the art people. Tucson's warm all year and dusty as hell. Perfect place for car washes. Great return on the investment, a solid income all year. But that's not even the point."

"And the point…?"

"Another opportunity for what they call 'scale.' You know what I mean by that?"

"I think so, but save me the embarrassment of being wrong."

"Flood the country with them, no pun intended. Tucson itself can take at least two more locations. Then you move on to the other places. Pick the prime locations, build it up enough to attract a big-time buyer, and sell the whole thing."

He would never again make fun of the car wash idea.

Finally, she also showed him three different houses she wanted him to look at if he had time. High-end places, but not ostentatious. Shrouded by desert vegetation but not hidden. Private but not fortresses.

"I really need you to get there next week. For all I know they're about to sign with someone else. Plus, I just got a grand jury subpoena. Time ta get outta Dodge."

As he drove away from her house, he thought how lucky the authorities were that this woman would not be running the Outfit.

•   •   •

The pilot announced they would be landing soon. O'Keefe gathered up the financial statements and other documents he had been studying, stuck them in his briefcase, and pulled notecards from his shirt-pocket, which contained the abbreviated schedule she had provided him for the two-day trip. She had choreographed things almost down to the minute, each item with full details of times, addresses, and phone numbers (her touch, not his, such precise planning and scheduling being foreign to his nature).

All proceeded more smoothly than O'Keefe had thought would be possible. He had anticipated that the most delicate moment would be the first meeting, the one with their lawyer, Neal Simpson.

"Art and car washes," Simpson said after O'Keefe delivered his summary of the situation. "Not quite what they call 'synergistic.'"

"The client," O'Keefe responded, "has a venture capital 'incubator' type mentality. It's agnostic as to business models. It's looking for what's innovative, roll-up opportunities, candidates for a big launch, even an IPO. And even though they're very different, both of these businesses are poised for take-off…for scale…for national, maybe even international, expansion."

He was about to gag from buzzword overload, but he knew those words—*venture capital, incubator, agnostic, innovative, launch, roll-ups, IPO*—would tend to create a mystique of sophistication around his client. He wanted to do everything possible, without lying outright but with maximum "smoke and mirrors," creating the aura of cutting-edge thinking and the possibility of many future deals to stifle the emergence of any doubts.

Simpson eventually got around to asking him about the pressure garment sheathing his left arm and hand. He had worked this out in advance as well. "Stupid accident. Burned myself up." And stopped there, with a look of shame and signaling that he strongly preferred not to discuss it any further. This approach worked with everyone who asked him about it.

The meeting on the first day, with the owners of the art distribution business, a couple in their early fifties, the wife the real CEO, the husband more the office manager and bookkeeper, lasted several friendly hours. At the end he believed he had successfully navigated the "mystery client" and "unusual agent" issues.

He drove Simpson back to his office. As they pulled up in front, Simpson said, "We'll start on the purchase agreement right now. I've got a junior standing by to get the first draft done tonight."

O'Keefe asked about residential neighborhoods. Simpson gave him the run-down. All the houses she had identified were in neighborhoods that Simpson described as the finest.

"Of course, my preference is my own neighborhood," Simpson said. "The Catalina foothills, east of Campbell and north of River Road. Close to town but with a country feel. Mountain views by day, blazing sunsets and, after dark, the city lights."

O'Keefe had time before dark to visit only one of the houses, which happened to be the one in Simpson's own neighborhood. He found

Campbell Road and headed north out of downtown, turned right at River Road heading east for a couple of blocks, then turned back north climbing up into the foothills of the Catalina Mountains on Camino Real. He tried to translate the Spanish. It probably meant "Royal Road," but he liked an alternative version, "True Way" or "True Path."

This True Path was narrow and twisty, with side roads and driveways, often gravel ones, radiating off into side streets and cul-de-sacs. Unlike Midwestern subdivisions—orderly rows of houses clearly visible from the street with manicured lawns of fescue, ryegrass, or bluegrass—most of these houses were situated on large lots and fully or partially sheltered by palo verde trees, saguaros, ocotillos, and other cacti. A family of quail waddled along to his front, plunging into the surrounding vegetation as he approached. A jackrabbit, long and lean with large feet and ears, looking not at all like the cuddly bunnies nibbling on the grass in the neighborhoods he had lived in all his life, crossed the road in casual hops, as if paying the giant metal monster little mind, moving just fast enough to arrive safely on the other side before the wheels of the car arrived to crush it. A lizard popped up from the roadside vegetation, skittered along, then stopped as if waiting for the car to pass by. Above, hawks soared in search of prey.

Around one of several sharp and blind curves, a sign offered for sale one of the three houses she had identified. He pulled onto the apron of the driveway, left the car running but got out and looked around. He could barely detect the outlines of a house of painted white brick, not the more typical tan or white stucco. According to the brochure, hidden somewhere behind and to the sides of the house amidst the cacti, orange and olive trees, and hedges of white-flowered oleander and pink and purple bougainvillea were a guest house ("casita" was the local term), a swimming pool, a greenhouse, and a tennis court. To the side of the house, on his right, the ground plunged down into a wash and, above that, on a small plateau perhaps thirty yards on, two horses lolled in a corral. Mountain ranges—bare, gray-brown, sharp, rough, and dry—ringed the city all around, and he could see each of them clearly from his vantage point: the Catalinas to the north behind him; the Rincons to the east; to his front, the Santa Ritas past the downtown area on the south; the Tucson Mountains to the west. He admired her choice of this place and felt a friendly envy of her possible escape to this world of sun and dust and distance, not wild but not entirely tame either.

The hotel she had chosen for him, more a boutique resort than a hotel, was exquisitely landscaped and interior decorated, the balconies, patios, and windows placed with careful intentionality to offer vistas of the desert wonderland of spiked flora, rock, dirt, and sun. He checked into his room, poured a glass of cool water from the silver pitcher that welcomed him, sat in the large leather chair at the commodious, antique-looking desk, and called Rose at the appointed time. When she said hello, her voice, unlike the cool calculation and steely steadiness it had transmitted to him up to then, sounded sharply stressed.

He ventured some light relief. "Well, seems to me you've picked a good place…until summertime anyway. Hotter than hell then."

"Amusing," she said, brusque, cold, impatient.

He recounted the story of the day. She didn't interrupt him. At story's end, she said, "That's it? Nothing negative?"

"Not one thing."

"Seems too good to be true."

"The lawyers are working on the art business contract right now. I might even be carrying it back with me."

"Can you have them fax it to your office? I'll pick it up there."

"Be careful. I haven't told them about you."

"Well, that Dagmar girl knows me…my face anyway…Maybe she could bring it down?"

"Yes, she could. Best idea there."

"And the car wash meeting is still on for tomorrow morning?"

"Yes. And I even got to drive by one of the houses and get some info from our lawyer on the neighborhood. Hard to see the places though. Massive lots, much vegetation, very private. Not sure I can do a bunch of broker appointments and still get back tomorrow night."

"Don't do them," her voice flat, not a hint of enthusiasm. "They're not important."

"I went by one of them. Very nice. 360-degree view…see all the mountains and the city lights too."

No response.

He hesitated, wondering if he should mention what he had in mind, in part because she might take it wrong, in larger part because Harrigan had sternly warned him to avoid anything to do with the grand jury probe and her role in it since a possible obstruction of justice charge lurked around that corner. But he decided to anyway.

"Any more word on the subpoena?"

"I have to go in there tomorrow. We tried to delay, and they threatened to hold me in contempt. They're after my ass, Pete. I don't get it. They've gotta know I'm just gonna take the Fifth over and over again."

He had noticed that she called him "Pete" for the first time. He had been "Mr. O'Keefe" at first, then for a while Mr. No-Name, just "You." Now "Pete." *Can you be trusted, Rosalie Jagoda Sciorra? Maybe up to a point, not beyond.* His life-or-death gamble would be guessing exactly where that borderline might be. He only hoped he had not already crossed to the wrong side of it.

●　　●　　●

After the Super Suds meeting, which took most of the next day, risking a speeding ticket as he rushed to make it to the airport in time to catch his flight, O'Keefe noticed that the town did have its ugly aspects, large parts of it festooned with rows and rows of strip centers and merely functional and characterless buildings. Yet he remembered, and doubted he would forget, the feeling he experienced the day before as he stood in that driveway—not the view alone but the feeling that came with it, a promise of both a long distance and a wide angle, brightness, clarity, the long view to the far-off horizon. Hustling to make the plane, he broke into a run in the terminal that quickly slowed to a jog as his left leg showed itself not quite ready to go willingly to a full-out sprint. The plane lifted off as the sun was setting above the Tucson Mountains, a massive cauldron of fire, brewing and bubbling up dazzling colors of another spectrum than he had ever witnessed, made by Something Like God, a bestowal of grace unearned, a blessing from nowhere.

CHAPTER ▶ 19

AS HE ALWAYS tried to do, Lieutenant Ross answered the phone on the first ring. It was Latham, Ross's involuntarily enlisted information pipeline out of Russ Lord's grand jury investigation.

"Got some news," Latham said. "We know the initial target list. Besides a couple of low-level types that they hope, if nudged, might trigger a chain reaction of falling dominoes, the list includes Paul Marcone and Vince Sorvino. No surprise there, but it's hard to see how they get anything out of either of them. The real heat is comin' down on Ricky Vitale. Apparently, he's got a big mouth, and they've got him on tape…maybe enough on him to put him away on a couple gambling charges and an extortion attempt on a local businessman. They think he's the most likely one to sell out…likes his creature comforts too much, especially the ladies. They think there's no way he'll want to spend all the years still remainin' to him in the jailhouse instead of the whorehouse. And they're gonna try to make it real hot for Mrs. Sciorra too. They think she has to know where her husband is, alive or dead. She's gonna be the first witness, scheduled for tomorrow."

Once Latham paused long enough for Ross to be sure that Latham had no more to tell him, Ross said, "Thanks much. Really helpful stuff. Keep it coming, you'll be remembered, I promise," and hung up before Latham could ask him any questions.

Now it was back to the old dilemma. Who in the Outfit knew about him and the debt he owed? He believed Carmine had kept it to himself, to be used only when he really needed the valuable resource that Ross represented. During the many months of Carmine's indictment, trial, conviction, and sentencing, Ross sweated helplessly, waiting for the knock on the door that would come after Carmine fingered Ross in exchange for a lighter sentence or some other *quid pro quo.*

But the knock never came, only a phone call the day before Carmine surrendered himself.

"Say 'thank you.'"

The instantly recognizable voice of Carmine Jagoda.

They both waited.

Finally, Carmine continued. "I can understand why you can't say it. Who knows who's listening? Best wishes to your family. Enjoy your life."

That's the last he had heard from Carmine, but the debt was still outstanding—and accruing interest. Carmine must have told Robert when Robert took over, and Robert, lacking the innate shrewdness of Carmine, quickly and profligately squandered the valuable bequest, promptly approaching Ross with the order to do the O'Keefe hit. Had Carmine told anyone else? Ross doubted it. Certainly not a mutt like Ricky Vitale. Maybe Vince Sorvino, Carmine's oldest living soldier, but Ross doubted that Carmine had done even that. Surely Carmine had never disclosed such a thing to his daughter. But had Robert maybe told her? Doubtful. But if he had, she could be the most vulnerable one, the most likely to surrender and name names.

Paul Marcone knew, but that was because Ross himself had told him—when Ross had approached Marcone to propose the trade of the information he had on Robert in exchange for letting the Lieutenant off the hook on O'Keefe. Some were saying that Marcone and Rose were now running the Outfit together. Had Marcone told Rose? Probably not. Marcone seemed more like Carmine Jagoda than Robert Sciorra. Whatever. Ross had been lucky that Carmine Jagoda turned out to be the kind of man who would hold fast and long to such a treasure, like a miser with his hidden bag of gold, lovingly caressing the precious coins. Lucky up to now. But Ross didn't know how long his luck would hold, and he had become increasingly convinced that he needed to give luck some assistance. Ricky Vitale was not the only one who didn't want to spend the last years of his life in prison dodging shiv-happy butt-fuckers. Ross considered whether he might be able to eliminate them all in one night of massacre and point the finger of blame at someone who would be far beyond the power to deny it.

•   •   •

Donald Praeger tried to negotiate for his client a discreet entrance to the Courthouse for her appearance before the grand jury, but Russ Lord would have none of it. The appearance, widely publicized in advance, attracted a throng of reporters from all media, local and beyond, plus an unruly crowd of importunate rubberneckers jostling for a look at Rose Jagoda Sciorra on the morning she arrived at the courthouse entrance not in the expected black Lincoln Town Car of a Mafia warlord but in the minivan of the suburban mom.

It turned into an embarrassing scene, mostly for the government, as Praeger and his client had to struggle through the howling pack shouting everything from "Get 'em Rose" to "Didja kill him, Rose?" but mostly "Hey, Rosie, how 'bout an autograph?"

After reaching the top of the Courthouse steps where the video cameras waited, Praeger addressed them. "Shame on the U.S.

Attorney's office. Shame on Russell Lord. What a travesty of justice. This is a disgraceful persecution of an innocent housewife just because she's Italian."

Inside, standing at the imposingly tall doors to the grand jury room, Praeger told his client, "You know I can't go in with you, but it doesn't matter. You just say what we rehearsed, over and over again, to every question, nothing else. He might try to goad you into a contempt citation. Don't fall for that. You're better and tougher than they are."

They first made her take the oath…the truth, the whole truth, and nothing but the truth.

She wondered whether Lord had warned the grand jurors that today's proceedings, like the ones that would soon occur involving Paul Marcone, Vince Sorvino, and Ricky Vitale, among others, were a mere show, a performance rather than a true fact-finding inquiry.

"Please state your name for the record."

"Rose Sophia Sciorra."

Lord said sharply, "Isn't your real name Rosalie?"

"On my birth certificate, yes, but I've never been called anything but Rose all my life."

In a denouncing tone, he said, "The whole truth and nothing but the truth, Ms. Sciorra. No exceptions."

She blushed a deep red. The shaming session had begun.

"What is your maiden name?"

"Jagoda."

"What are your parents' names?"

"Father Carmine, mother Sofia."

"Are you married?"

"I am."

"What was…or is…your husband's name?"

"Robert. Robert Sciorra."

"Do you know your husband's current location?"

"I respectfully decline to answer based on my rights under the Fifth Amendment to the United States Constitution on the grounds that my answer may tend to incriminate me."

"Ms....Do you prefer I call you Ms. or Mrs.?"

"I don't care."

"Mrs. Sciorra, are you telling us that your answer may tend to incriminate you because your husband is hiding out somewhere, either from his former business associates or from law enforcement, and you know where he is, and don't want to tell?"

"I respectfully decline..." and she continued with the Fifth Amendment formula word for word.

"Or, Mrs. Sciorra, are you telling us that your answer may tend to incriminate you because your husband has been the victim of foul play and you know what happened to him?"

Again, the Fifth Amendment formula recitation.

"Or, Mrs. Sciorra, are you unwilling to answer because you were personally involved in some foul play that led to your husband's disappearance?"

And, again, the invocation of the Fifth.

"When is the last time you saw your husband?"

Same response.

It continued for more than an hour as Lord asked hostile leading questions on everything from her knowledge of her father's and husband's business dealings to her current activities, including how she was handling her finances since her husband had disappeared, what she had told her children, her friends, and anyone else about her husband's "strange absence." The questions were obviously designed to intimidate and embarrass her, make sure she knew that everything she did was under the most intense scrutiny, and that she was being hunted down and had no means of escape other than her pathetic incantation of the Fifth Amendment mantra, which she repeated over and over until she was sick of it, and herself for saying it, the Constitution for containing it, and the world for her being in it.

Lord ended with a series of questions concerning any meetings she may have had with Paul Marcone, to which each of her answers remained the same, the Fifth Amendment.

"Any meetings at Donald Praeger's office?"

"Bars or restaurants?"

"Hotels or motels?"

"Your house?

"Other places of assignation?"

And the big finale, as he leered at her: "Have you ever had sex with or any romantic relationship with Paul Marcone?"

As she started to recite the mantra, he interrupted: "I'm wondering, Mrs. Sciorra, why an answer to that question might tend to incriminate you?"

As she started to recite the mantra again, he waived her off. "Never mind that baloney, Mrs. Sciorra. Have you heard of Clytemnestra?"

This confused the court reporter. "How do you spell that, Mr. Lord?"

"C- L- Y- T- E- M- N- E- S- T- R- A."

"I can tell," he continued, "by the look on your face that you haven't heard of Clytemnestra, Mrs. Sciorra. I urge you to look it up."

As instructed by and rehearsed with Donald Praeger, she left the courthouse in tears. But it was no act, those tears were real. Donald had been wrong about her being better, tougher. All she wanted now was to find a hole to crawl into and lick her wounds, or perhaps, except for the overriding need and duty to care for her children, just curl up in that hole and stay in there until she had starved herself to death.

• • •

They had agreed he would meet her at her house as soon as he arrived. But he thought it might be too late now, so he thought he should risk a call. At a pay phone in the terminal he dialed her home number.

"Hello," he said when she answered.

"Yes?" she said, her voice expressing in that single word surprise, alarm, suspicion—that he had called her at her house—something they had carefully avoided up to that point.

"No problem here," he rushed to reassure her, "just wanted to make sure the plan was still the same. Just say 'Yes' or 'No.'"

"Yes."

He had not rented another "bland-mobile," as he had come to call them, in anticipation of this meeting. Thinking he may have become careless about checking for someone following him, he made a stop on the side of the highway and acted as if looking for something in his glove compartment. Farther on, he took an exit and traveled on the frontage road until the next entrance where he re-entered the freeway. Satisfied he had not been followed, he did not pay particular attention to a nondescript pickup truck parked on the street leading to Rose's section of the subdivision.

When he pulled into her driveway, he saw her front curtains move, followed by her front door opening.

"Kids are asleep," she said in a near whisper and tilted her head backward toward somewhere in the rear of the house. "We can do this fast."

She led him into the kitchen where they resumed their respective places at the table that had come to seem like assigned seats. She looked different—with none of the air of shrewd calculation and confidence that he had often previously seen in her. The suggestion of dark circles under her eyes had become more pronounced. As he contemplated this new and unexpected manifestation of Rose Jagoda Sciorra, she said, impatiently, "So what happened?"

He brought out his notes and gave her as much detail as his notes and his memory contained about that day's Super Suds meeting.

"Sounds like it went well," she said.

"It did. I'm sure the lawyer will have at least one of the contracts to us tomorrow, maybe both."

"Send it out here by courier, okay?"

"I will."

He guessed that he should leave, but it seemed like she needed some sort of comfort, maybe at least a question or two of a caring kind, so he said, "Your grand jury appearance?"

She closed her eyes and shook her head. "Horrible."

"I don't know how I can help, but…"

"You can't," she said, paused, and added, "except for what you're doing. That's the best anyone could be doing for me right now."

She was obviously done with him for the evening, seeming to want to wrap herself in the rough cloth of her loneliness.

At her front door, she said, "Nobody out there in Tucson asked hard questions about who your client might be?"

"Not one. But, by the way, who'll sign those contracts?"

"I don't have anyone who can do it but me. I'll have to sign them and take my chances."

She looked harried, haggard, stricken as if she had been physically stabbed, and said, "I've never in my life been as alone and afraid as I am right now."

At that moment, any fear of her, even any suspicion of her, disappeared. Her pain had earned his trust. He wanted to do something physically to comfort her, or maybe it was to comfort himself because it was so difficult for him to stand witness to her pain. But he also knew that would probably be the worst thing he could do—that if she accepted the embrace, it might not stop there, might lead to somewhere ecstatic, but even so, to a lower order of experience than what they had lived together up to now.

"Until tomorrow," he said.

She nodded and held his gaze, as if she knew what that previous moment had meant, the danger that moment had posed, and was relieved it was behind them now.

"You're close now," he said. "You can almost touch it."

As he walked to his rental car, it occurred to him that for the first time she had failed to frisk him.

● ● ●

FEDERAL BUREAU OF INVESTIGATION
INVESTIGATIVE MEMORANDUM

This Memorandum has been prepared by Agents Mark Cornwall and Edwin Dodge, both recently transferred from the Chicago Field Office to provide assistance to the ongoing grand jury investigation supervised by U.S. Attorney Russell Lord into the remnants of the criminal enterprise known as the Jagoda Outfit following the death of Carmine Jagoda and the disappearance of his son-in-law and hand-picked successor Robert Sciorra.

Agents Cornwall and Dodge were assigned to conduct physical surveillance on Rose Jagoda Sciorra (the "Subject") and in connection therewith to identify opportunities to extend and expand current electronic surveillance on the Subject. Cornwall and Dodge were chosen for this assignment because, being new to the city, there would be little chance of physical recognition by members of the Jagoda group.

To further minimize the possibility of recognition of the agents when surveilling Mrs. Sciorra, Cornwall and Dodge adopted a "tag team" approach. Cornwall dressed as a workman and drove a pickup truck, neither new nor old, and otherwise chosen because of its unobtrusive appearance. When Dodge surveilled the Subject, he did so in several vehicles borrowed from various parties, such as local utility companies and the cable television company.

While driving by the Subject's house on routine surveillance, Agent Dodge noticed a vehicle parked in her driveway. That any vehicle other than Ms. Sciorra's own vehicle was parked in the Subject's driveway was itself unusual, and the time of day, approximately 1:30 p.m., was an unusual time for the Subject to entertain a visitor. In fact, it was unusual, based on the surveillance by these agents, for the Subject to entertain any visitors at all.

There are only two entrances/exits from the part of the subdivision in which the Subject resides. Agent Dodge positioned himself near one of the entrances/exits and arranged for Agent Cornwall to cover the other entrance/exit. When the referenced unusual vehicle exited the subdivision at the entrance/exit that Agent Dodge was observing, Agent Dodge followed the vehicle to a nearby rental car facility where the driver turned in the vehicle and left in another vehicle, a Jeep Grand Wagoneer.

Agent Dodge called in the license plate on the Wagoneer as he followed the Wagoneer to an office building in Midtown where the driver parked, exited the Wagoneer, and exhibiting a slight limp in his left leg, entered an older, three-story brick building. The vehicle registration was in the name of Peter O'Keefe.

It was later determined that the offices of Peter O'Keefe's private investigative agency are in the previously referenced building. As further surveillance of Peter O'Keefe seemed warranted, Cornwall and Dodge split their duties, one surveilling O'Keefe, the other continuing to surveil the Subject.

At 12:30 p.m., several days after the first observation of O'Keefe's visiting the Subject's residence, Agent Cornwall observed O'Keefe drive from his office to the same rental car agency as before and leave the agency in a rented vehicle, another "basic" car that might be described as "nondescript." Again, he visited the Subject for slightly less than two hours, exited the house at 3:13 p.m., returned the rental car as before, and again drove his own vehicle back to his office.

Two days later, on a Sunday afternoon, Mr. O'Keefe drove to the airport and took a flight to Tucson, Arizona. We were unable to arrange surveillance of Mr. O'Keefe in Tucson.

The next observation of any interaction between the Subject and Mr. O'Keefe was late in the evening two days after Mr. O'Keefe flew to Tucson. Driving his own vehicle this time, Mr. O'Keefe made a visit to the Subject's residence, which lasted no more than twenty minutes. Surveillance of Mr. O'Keefe was suspended at that point.

CHAPTER 20

DAGMAR BUZZED HIM.

"It's a man named Max Trainer."

"Wait sixty seconds or so and put him through."

Waiting, gathering his thoughts, he could only conclude that this could not be good.

"Hello, Mr. O'Keefe. Max Trainer here."

He could tell that Trainer had called from a speakerphone, likely with Russ Lord and maybe others—Assistant U.S. Attorney types, FBI types—in the room, listening, coaching.

"Yes, sir."

"We're asking over here why in the world that Peter O'Keefe, victim of at least two, maybe three, Outfit attempts on his life, is consorting with the person rumored to be the new co-boss of the Outfit, one *Mrs.* Rose Jagoda Sciorra."

O'Keefe noted that Trainer had emphasized the word "Mrs."

After giving O'Keefe a chance to respond, and no response being forthcoming, Trainer continued, "Would you be willing to come over and talk to us?"

"No."

More silence. He thought he could hear whispers in the background.

Trainer resumed, "What if we keep it off the record?"

"I don't know what that means, and I don't believe that anything is off the record over there."

"You don't have to insult me, Mr. O'Keefe."

"I'm not insulting you. I'm insulting your boss. I wouldn't even have answered the phone if he'd called me."

"What if we assure you that you don't have to say anything…no interrogation, just listen?"

Another long silence. O'Keefe thought he detected a slight sound, likely Trainer putting the phone on mute so he could talk to the others in the room.

Trainer resumed. "I can't promise, but it might help you avoid a subpoena and a consequent public spectacle, which might not be good for your business."

"I'll consider it. Don't call me, I'll call you."

"No call, but if we don't hear from you soon, a subpoena."

● ● ●

O'Keefe consulted with both Harrigan and, at Harrigan's insistence, Ben LeClair, the criminal lawyer who had represented Harrigan last year when Russell Lord tried to put Harrigan in jail for bank fraud. After much debate, the two lawyers agreed that O'Keefe should go to the meeting without a lawyer. That way, Lord might be more candid and unguarded and thus reveal more about what the government knew, its strategy, and what that might mean for O'Keefe. But as Harrigan said, echoing LeClair, "Under no circumstances are you to say one fucking word."

"Should I take notes?"

"No. That might put a governor on him too. Play the doofus bozo. Should be right up your alley. But remember every word those guys say and write it all down right after."

● ● ●

Max Trainer met him in the waiting room and led him into Russell Lord's office.

"Thank you for coming, Mr. O'Keefe," Lord said. "I intend to scrupulously honor our agreement. I'll ask you no questions and will not expect you to say anything at all. But I am very sad that you so dislike me, I really am, and even sadder that we find ourselves at odds with each other a second time, and so soon after the first. And how strange it is this time. Your friend Harrigan's situation was one thing, but here I find us seemingly opposed, surely mistakenly opposed, in this very different situation where we're trying to put away these vicious criminals who've tried to kill you more than once. Why you would end up consorting with those very people is a disturbing mystery to me."

Lord paused, apparently waiting to see if O'Keefe would say something. When he did not, Lord continued, "Again, you don't have to answer this, but I assume you have a good reason to be involved with Rose Sciorra that does not involve some criminal conspiracy. Are you interested in telling us that reason?"

"I thought you were going to scrupulously honor our deal."

"I'm just giving you the opportunity to dispel suspicion that your behavior…for example the rental car maneuver…is creating."

Again, Lord waited until he seemed to be satisfied that O'Keefe would not respond, and O'Keefe was regretting even offering the limited response he had made.

"Do understand, Mr. O'Keefe, that we are not likely to continue to tolerate your non-cooperation. We won't hesitate to subpoena you and put you in front of the grand jury."

"I'll just take the Fifth like everyone else."

"Surely taking the Fifth in such a situation won't help your reputation or your business."

Again, the pause. Again, nothing from O'Keefe. Again, Lord resumed.

"We have become privy to some vital information we think you need to know. Disclosing this information to you is a risk to us in various ways. For example, your disclosure of that information to your new friends, such as *Mrs.* Sciorra, might hamper our investigation by putting these people on their guard."

O'Keefe noted that, like Trainer before him, Lord had emphasized "Mrs.," implying the possibility of a sexual liaison. That and the "new friends" comment O'Keefe regarded as Lord's attempt to provoke him into a response. He did not oblige.

"Assuming, Mr. O'Keefe, that you're willing to learn this information, Agent Rowland from the FBI is in the waiting room and will share it with you. Again, I'm sincerely sorry that we find ourselves at loggerheads. Please don't think this is some kind of personal vendetta. In fact, we're trying to do you a very personal *favor.* You may have what you think are good reasons for your course of action, but it's a dangerous game, in any number of ways."

Lord nodded to Trainer who rose from his chair, which O'Keefe took as a signal to do the same. In the waiting room, Agent Rowland formally introduced himself and asked O'Keefe to follow him. Trainer stayed behind. O'Keefe wondered why.

Rowland led him into a small office empty of anything except a desk, some wooden chairs, and two men who introduced themselves as FBI agents and directed O'Keefe to the only remaining empty chair. He sat down, feeling surrounded in the small space, stifled and overwhelmed by the physical presence of the three agents that seemed to fill the entire room with only a sliver left to him.

Rowland sat behind the desk and said, "Here's the bottom line. If you're innocent, you can help us. You can wear a wire when you meet with Rose or any of the rest of them."

O'Keefe considered whether to respond. He decided to, chasing away the image of both Harrigan and LeClair shaking a disapproving finger at him.

"Even if I was willing, it wouldn't work. She frisks me every time."

"Yeah, I bet she does," leered one of the agents.

Well, the lawyer images were right in shaking those fingers at him. *Next time do not be provoked.*

"There are other ways," Rowland said.

When O'Keefe did not answer, Rowland said, "You know we have wiretaps on all of them, don't you?"

Do not be provoked.

"You think you're the only one she talks to on that pay phone?"

Now *that* was upsetting. He hoped he hadn't shown it.

"They're planning to kill you…just as soon as they've made full use of you."

He was provoked. "Show me the transcripts."

"We can't show wiretap transcripts to a third party. It's illegal."

The leering one said, "But if you come to work for us, you won't be a third party."

"Anything else?" O'Keefe said.

"I guess not," Rowland said.

•　•　•

After O'Keefe left, the leering agent said to Rowland. "Nice move with the pay phone. That got to him. Anybody wanna bet whether he'll be back?"

"Hope you're right," Rowland said. "I've got to go report to Lord."

They let him into Lord's office right away. "He didn't fold right there, but he has to be thinking hard about his predicament."

"Keep the pressure on him. And on her."

●   ●   ●

O'Keefe failed to appreciate the unexpected warmth of a false-spring day in March as he absent-mindedly jaywalked across the street in front of the Courthouse to the parking lot. In the Wagoneer, inserting the key and turning it to start the engine, he cringed, a memory flash of another key turned in another ignition switch, and he realized that during the few minutes it had taken him to navigate from that small office in the courthouse to the parking lot, his conscious mind had stopped working. The turning of the key, no longer an automatic, thoughtless act for him, jarred him back to full consciousness, like awakening from a deep sleep and not immediately understanding where he was. He had never walked in his sleep, but this last few minutes must have been something like that. He attributed the closing of his mind in those few minutes to massive denial, near panic-stricken resistance to what they had told him. It called everything into question.

It called into question this latest quixotic emprise of one Peter O'Keefe. The few who knew of it, starting with Harrigan, and including a part of himself, had challenged it as too risky at best and downright crazy at worst.

It called into question his judgment—of calculating the worth of an undertaking, the odds of success or failure, the balance between wise and foolish endeavors. He could write off this particular failure to desperation. Almost anything seemed worth trying in order to escape the intolerable conditions of his current existence. But it went beyond that, also shaking his faith in his ability to judge people, especially the distaff side of humanity. He had come to believe Rose and believe *in* her too, in her own quest to escape a corrupt existence, to save her children if not herself from what had become a family curse. But that seemed now like a delusion and a trap.

Worst of all, it called into question his hope for a reasonable future where his very presence did not create a danger to everyone he wanted or needed to be with.

He wanted to hurt her—if not that, at least confront her with it, press her until he forced her to admit it—or, maybe, a hope he dared not admit to himself, force her to deny it in a way that would allow him to believe her. He drove slowly out of the parking lot, but once on the street, gunned the engine, ran a yellow light that turned to red as he entered the intersection, stomped on the accelerator, and sped toward her.

As he glided down the exit ramp that would ultimately lead to her house, neon colors exploded across the dark sky of his mind like a night rocket attack in Vietnam. He had always been hot-tempered and not just impulsive but propulsively impulsive, and the PTSD had taken that to new and uncontrollably dizzying elevations. He had never recognized it this early before. He also perceived, reluctantly but with some clarity for once, that he had the chance to re-establish a measure of control over himself before he did something to regret. Now it was a matter of willingness to choose the longer and wiser game, but that choice would keep him embroiled in extended mental torture, unable to obtain, by an outburst of angry action, some resolution or release.

I can see peace instead of this, he kept telling himself as he drove, more slowly now, through the streets of the subdivision that would lead to her house. Then he noticed again, more clearly this time, not entirely consciously but more consciously than before, the pickup truck parked on that last street before the turn onto her street. There again. How odd. And this time he could see someone sitting in it. No conscious realization resulted immediately from recognizing that pickup truck. But, without intending to, in fact intending to do just the opposite, he drove past her street for a few blocks, made a turn into a cul-de-sac, checked for the pickup truck in his rearview mirror, turned around and threaded his way in a different direction through the suburban warren back to the freeway, and, only slightly above the speed limit now, drove to his office.

As he pulled into the office parking lot, he remembered it was his turn to exercise Karma today. He knew he could pass that off to George or Sara or Dagmar, but somehow he knew that he should not shirk that responsibility now.

"Are you taking Karma out?" Dagmar asked, clearly hoping for a negative answer.

"I am. Sorry about that. Today I need it more than you, maybe even more than Karma does."

Dagmar frowned with concern. "Sorry to hear that, Sir Dude," an appellation that she used occasionally to bring a smile from him. But no smile came forth this time.

When he opened the door to his office, Karma eagerly rose to his feet, whined, and slowly wagged his tail, about as enthusiastic as the creature ever revealed himself to be. Regarding O'Keefe, the dog had passed from indifference, to acceptance, to a dignified affection—no sloppy thumping of the tail on the floor, or jumping up, or whirling around in delirious, slobbery joy, just a kind of, "I guess now you are mine, and I am yours, and I will obey and protect you."

Man and dog traveled to a nearby high school football field that the school administration allowed non-students and their dogs to use when the students weren't using it, subject to the strict rule of picking up the dung, enforced mainly by the vigilantism of the users who would scold offenders. Despite the day being almost over, O'Keefe for the first time appreciated its gift of sunshine, warmth, and the promise of more of that to come in the springtime drawing nearer every day. As he walked from the car to the gate to the field and onto the field itself, the dog trotting eagerly but patiently beside him, he realized his limp was gone.

He first took Karma through the standard commands. It had surprised him how disciplined he had been about keeping up the training including the search, heel, quiet, and bite commands. He had obtained one of the bite sleeves the police dog trainers wore on their arms to protect them when teaching the dogs controlled biting—biting only for the purpose of subduing the human targets, hurting them only as incidental to subduing them. He obtained a mannequin, dressed it up, attached the bite sleeve, and, in his backyard a couple of times a week, practiced the bite command, *Packen.* The only problem was that Karma quickly destroyed the mannequin. With George's help, he created a scarecrow-like dummy, which required frequent restuffing but was more practical than buying a new mannequin every couple of weeks.

But now, here at the football field, it was fun time. The dog loved the ball, loved it even more than the treats, loved to chase it near and far, especially far, and return it for another go. The dog's powerful strides chasing and returning really did remind O'Keefe of Rinty in the old TV show. He threw the ball. For the first time it didn't hurt at all, only a kind of phantom hurt, a muscle memory of something no longer there. After the first few throws, he did resort to a ball-launching device, a long stick with a cup at the end of it to hold the ball, which allowed a throw of a longer distance and less wear on the shoulder, but that was unrelated to his injury, something he would have done anyway.

He tried to avoid thinking—about his current dilemma or anything else. Nothing. Nothing other than *throw the ball, watch the dog chase the ball, watch the dog return the ball. Notice the bright sunshine, the crisp cooling of the air in the late afternoon, the brown winter grass of the football field, the gray empty stands, the black and grayish cinders of the track surrounding the field. Watch the dog drop the ball and wait with upturned head and slightly lolling tongue for another throw. Throw again, don't favor the left side next time when you throw, it doesn't hurt anymore. Watch the dog chase the ball...*

As he always did to close one of these sessions, he took treats from his pocket and fed them to Karma. Surely the dog suffered a sense of disappointment in these moments, but he never showed it, just gulped down the treats and took a couple of steps toward the exit, leading the way just as he would do if searching for explosives or a culprit in hiding. O'Keefe had taken to jogging carefully with Karma as a way of loosening up the tight skin on the left side of his body. But not today. His reflecting and analyzing machine had turned on again, and it had a problem to solve. He issued Karma the command to heel, and they walked slowly together off the field.

• • •

Back at his office building, Dagmar said, "I filled his water bowl, and you have a couple of voicemails."

The first voicemail was from Rose. "Please come see me today if you can. Usual time and place."

The second was from Paschal McKenna. "Give me a call, I have some news that might interest you."

CHAPTER ▶ 21

THE CALL FROM Paschal struck him as bitterly serendipitous. O'Keefe had not seen or spoken to him since that Sunday at Maria's. He considered which call to respond to first and decided he was not ready to talk to Rose, not ready to decide what to do about her, how to deal with her, or anything else about her. His anger had been out of control at first, stoked and surging on waves of the PTSD and even more by the shame of being exposed to himself as a fool on a fool's errand. But his mind was colder now, transformed by the session with Karma, as if some of the dog's spirit of detached self-possession had quietly passed from the animal into the man.

"Congratulations," O'Keefe said.

"For what?"

"The Super Bowl bet."

"The weasel hasn't paid. He keeps ducking me."

"Returning your call."

"I just came across some very interesting information."

"Yes?"

"As you might imagine, I have sources inside the grand jury and the U.S. Attorney's office."

"As I might imagine."

"All of a sudden a new player has emerged in the saga…One… Mr.…Peter…O'Keefe."

"Is that so?"

"You don't act shocked, and only a little surprised."

"I'll explain, but what details did you get?"

"Pretty simple. You appear to be consorting with, even working for the Outfit in the form of the beautiful Rosalie. Somehow that rang a bell with me concerning a certain Sunday Supper."

"That's it?"

"That's it. They can't figure it out. Why is a guy who's supposed to be in the Outfit's crosshairs suddenly hanging out with the Princess herself? You've got a reputation as a cocksman, I know…"

Cocksman. An odd phrase that had disappeared from the boys' locker room lexicon sometime back in the '60s, probably around the time Paschal had gone to prison.

"Undeserved," O'Keefe said.

"Too bad. You were my hero. So, what's the deal?"

"Let's meet. Better chance of just the two of us being present, if you get my drift."

"Harvey's?"

"When?"

"I'm ready now."

"So am I."

They met at O'Keefe's usual table at Harvey's, farthest back in the back room, on a slow afternoon. Paschal ordered two shots of Jameson as usual and this time an ale behind them. He looked bad and saw that O'Keefe noticed it.

"Helluva hangover today," he said. "Typical. Nothing new."

"I know what you mean." O'Keefe thought he had better leave it at that. He had no doubt whatsoever that Paschal was an alcoholic. The issue was when, if ever, Paschal would be willing to try to do something about it. O'Keefe, fairly new to full sobriety himself, was not inclined to try to butt in, not until Paschal sunk low enough to reach out for help, and he hoped he could then be useful.

"I appreciate the favor," O'Keefe continued, "you calling me, but I need another one. This conversation has to be off the record, now and forever."

"Okay. But I hope you'll give me something in return one of these days."

"I'll do my best."

O'Keefe set a small tape recorder on the table.

Paschal's face turned sourly cynical. "Don't trust a slimeball reporter, huh?"

"'Trust but verify.'"

Paschal laughed. "Reagan. What a noodle…Okay…if you promise not to quote *him* again."

"'Mr. Gorbachev, tear down this wall.'"

Paschal laughed again.

O'Keefe said, "It's just too important to take any risk. I've taken too many already."

He turned on the recorder. "This is Peter O'Keefe. I'm recording a conversation with Paschal McKenna, reporter for the *Herald*. Paschal has agreed that this conversation will be off the record, now and forever, and it will remain so, in its entirety, unless I sign a written waiver of the condition and then only as expressly set forth in the waiver. I would not tell him what I'm going to tell him now unless he so agreed. Mr. McKenna, please clearly state your assent to this condition and this recording and provide some personal information that only you are likely to know."

"Okaaay…This is Paschal McKenna. I agree that this conversation is off the record."

He then recited various facts including his Social Security number, his grandfather's middle name (Ignatius), and even, with a sardonic smile, his prison identification number.

"Thank you," O'Keefe said, and switched off the recorder.

"Of course I could just breach this agreement, and I'm judgment-proof, you can be sure of that."

"Well, I'd at least get the satisfaction of ruining you as a journalist…But I really do trust you. It's just belt and suspenders. I've been working with lawyers too long. They've gotten into my blood."

O'Keefe told most of the story—how he had communicated with Rose that Sunday at Maria's, the quid pro quo arrangement, most important and most interesting to Paschal, her desire for escape and O'Keefe's agreement to help her. He left some things out, such as her focus on Tucson and the specific Tucson businesses she had targeted, and his trip there.

Paschal shook his head. "What a story…I mean the Rose part of it. But you're probably doing all that for nothing. I haven't told you this because I wanted to make as sure as I can that it's true before having you rely on it, but every source I've talked to, every rock I've turned over, and every snake under every one of those rocks confirms that none of those people care a shit about Peter O'Keefe. They think you're just a chump that stumbled into something a couple of years ago and has been doing his best to leave them alone ever since. If anything, if you handle this wrong, you might just provoke what you're trying to prevent."

"Well, here's what I provoked so far. Lord and the FBI summoned me over there this morning and told me they had wiretaps on Rose and her pals and they're planning to kill me."

Paschal took a long drink from his glass of ale, set it down, and said, "That makes no sense at all. Not a lick. Did they play the recordings for you or show you a transcript?"

"They say it's illegal to show that stuff to a third party."

Paschal thought for a moment. Then, again, that cynical frown. "So why isn't it illegal to *tell* you what was said?"

"They'd lie to me about something like that?"

"Why wouldn't they? It's a crime to lie to the FBI but not for them to lie to you. Who are you anyway? Just some idiot playing footsie with the mob. They'd definitely lie to you, especially if they're desperate, which I think they are. Everything I've been able to find out indicates the grand jury probe is stalled, goin' nowhere. Everyone's takin' the Fifth. They haven't even been able to get to Ricky Vitale who they've supposedly got the goods on. You and a wire strapped to your chest's a possible way to rejuvenate things."

"Seems evil."

"It's a 'means and ends' thing. Does breaking the Outfit, maybe once and for all, justify stringing a dipshit like you along? Do I have to answer that question for you?"

Paschal ordered another double. O'Keefe thought about grabbing a couple of drinks himself but managed to resist the urge as he engaged in the silent process of awarding himself a second "dumb-ass" award in a single day. At least he had managed to play it cool enough not to confront Rose immediately, a bridge mercifully not burned, leaving him some maneuvering room though he was unsure where he should maneuver to.

Paschal broke the silence. "So what're you gonna do?"

"I think I'll go talk to my dog. He's smarter than I am."

"One more thing. If I got this information about you and the grand jury, others are likely to have it…including one or more people in the Outfit."

"Thanks. I owe you."

"Glad you think so. Be careful," Paschal said. "I'd miss you. Helping out a fuck-up like you'll surely reduce my time in Purgatory…that is, if I make it *up* that far."

"Purgatory," O'Keefe said, his voice drifting, trance-like.

"You know what I mean, right?"

"Hell, yes. When I was a kid, I believed in the whole Catechism, every word, without question. I intended to be a saint. How about plenary indulgences? Remember those?"

"Sort of."

"If you said the right prayers at the right time and enough times, you personally released a soul from Purgatory to Heaven…sometimes bundles and bunches of souls. I thought it was the greatest thing in the world. I worked hard at it. Probably the best thing I ever tried to do in my whole life."

"Acts of mercy. Probably the best a little kid could do. You still believe in all that?"

"Not a bit."

"No Church?"

"No Church."

"No God even?"

"If God existed, the world would be even more absurd. We wouldn't have only ourselves to blame."

Paschal raised his glass and laughed. "I'm not sure even the Church believes in Purgatory anymore."

"Don't think so," O'Keefe said, "but I do. It's a permanent condition with just enough moments of relief to keep us going."

"One more thing, not to lose the point," Paschal said. "I could be wrong. They may be trying to kill you just like the FBI said. But surely they have better things to do than waste their time on a bozo like you."

The old Irish teasing, constant and merciless. O'Keefe smiled wryly as he got up to leave. "In case I don't see you before, Happy Easter," he said, "your name day and all. Make sure you live up to it."

Paschal raised his glass again. "Here's to the resurrection of souls and life eternal!"

• • •

O'Keefe returned to the office to pick up Karma, considering whether he should ask Karma to teach him a thing or two, like how to put his tail between his legs.

He found another voicemail from Rose, sounding close to panic. "Are you okay? Please call."

Later on that. He wanted to put more "thinking" and even "sleeping on it" distance between now and his next contact with her.

He would have liked to exercise Karma, and himself, a second time that day, but it was already dark. Instead, he drove home, fed Karma a bowl of his food and himself a bowl of cereal, put a Bach CD on the stereo, and sat down with a book, Karma beside him. But he didn't open the book, just sat there, not unlike the dog himself was doing, something between a meditation and a doze.

Karma heard it before he did. He saw the dog's ears prick up and the dog rise to its feet, and only after that did he hear the tires on the gravel of the front driveway. This eventful day might still have more to reveal. He turned off a light or two so he could see better in the darkness outside without himself being seen and walked to the picture window at the front of the house. A nondescript car, he could not even recognize the make and model. The interior lights of the car turned on as the driver opened the car door, got out, and stood with his left arm resting on top of the partly open door, peering toward the house.

Detective Ross.

Karma barked savagely. He quelled the dog with a word, "*Ruhig,*" went to the front door, turned on the porch light, and walked out onto the porch with Karma following.

"Dog, eh?" Ross said. "Looks like one of ours."

"It was one of yours."

"Let's talk. Lose the dog and get in."

Something in O'Keefe wanted to rebel and defy this command from Ross in his swaggering martinet mode, he'd had enough of that in the Marines, but he thought better of it. Ross had treated him decently up to now, and he probably had somehow picked up the same news as Paschal. Hanging out with the Mafia and then stonewalling yet another representative of law enforcement didn't seem like a good combination. Moreover, he might even learn something if he could manage to keep his cool.

"Back in a minute," he said, took Karma back in the house and parked him in his kennel, grabbed a jacket, and joined Ross in the car.

"So why," Ross said, "even in the craziest of all worlds, would you be visiting Rose at her house? Surely you're not fucking her."

Rowland and the other leering FBI agent, and now Ross. These cops seemed to have what people called a "prurient interest" in the subject, or just envy.

O'Keefe thought for several seconds about whether and what to answer, then said, "How'd you come to know that and why do you care?"

"I ask the questions, you answer."

"Not so."

"You want trouble, I can give it to you."

"I'll just say it this way: I'm on a diplomatic mission."

"What's that mean?"

"I'm looking for a truce."

"By putting your head in the lion's mouth? Or is it something else you're putting somewhere else?"

"No use dicking around, no pun intended. I went straight to the source."

"How stupid."

"Everybody tells me that, but nobody gives me another way out. Especially the police, present company unfortunately included."

"What?"

"Instead of a proper investigation and figuring out who actually bombed me, the police, you included, just decided to sit on their asses."

"Don't be tiresome. We all know it was David Bowman."

"You may think that, I may suspect that, but other people suspect other things, and none of us know for sure, do we?"

"Well, it wasn't the Jagoda people. Otherwise—"

"I know, I know, otherwise I wouldn't be here. But that ain't proof. I need proof. Why don't you kick Sergeant Trowbridge in the ass and get me the proof? What if it wasn't Bowman? Or what if it wasn't Bowman all by himself? What if it was someone else from the Cherry Pink?"

"As you well know, those guys are in the county. Not my jurisdiction."

"You know that's bullshit. The crime was committed in yours."

"It's a question of resources."

"Well, there you are."

"You're gonna end up bringing it on yourself. You're gonna end up dead."

"I'm not gonna live this way. It's a good day to die. I'm told Crazy Horse said that. But it was Custer who died that day."

"Big talk. And what exactly is this diplomatic mission?"

"That's none of your business."

"You're wrong. It probably *is* my business. I should probably be investigating *you*. It's almost impossible to deal with those people without being in a criminal conspiracy. How would you like not death but prison? Misery compounded. Or how about tortured to death?"

"I like my odds."

"Well, Russell Lord and the grand jury are onto you."

"Old news."

"Where from?

"I've got my sources too."

"I urge you to listen. Even if Rose and her pals don't do you in, you'll get caught in a crossfire."

"Call someone who cares. I don't."

"Tough talker."

"Rat in a corner."

"Are you dealing just with Rose or someone else too?"

Ross quickly understood that O'Keefe would not be answering that. He said, "I'm telling you, Rose ain't enough."

"She'll have to do for now."

"And I'm also telling you that you'd better not even step on the line, let alone cross it. If Russ Lord doesn't get you, I will."

"Why do you care?"

"I guess, duh, it's my job. And I told you back when you were in the hospital. I've sort've become your keeper."

"Well, you're doing a shitty job…obviously."

"Okay, asshole, I've done what I can. If someone or something restores you to sanity, and you're still alive and haven't committed a crime, you know who to call."

"Yeah, Ghostbusters."

"I hope you're as tough as you are now when they're ripping out your fingernails and hammering a nail through the tender tip of your little peter, Peter."

CHAPTER ▶ 22

BY THE NEXT morning, O'Keefe had cleared up most of his confusion by accepting that he would have to remain confused. He could not trust anyone at all other than his own inner circle, and even they needed to be left out of the loop, undistracted, so they could attend to their normal pursuits and as far out of danger as possible. He had brought this on and needed to play it all the way out, remaining hypervigilant and trusting no one, neither Rose nor the FBI.

He waited until the children would have left for school. She answered on the first ring.

"Me," he said.

"Thank God! I didn't know what might've happened to you."

She sounded neither angry nor distrustful, but honestly afraid.

"Let's meet," he said.

On his way to her house, he employed several maneuvers designed to reveal and evade someone following him. Today there was no pickup truck parked near the street that led to her house. He didn't know what that meant but refused to deflect his focus by trying to figure out why not.

She opened the door, barefoot but otherwise dressed a bit more upscale than he had become accustomed to for these visits, in a snug black sweater and snugger black slacks that seemed to have been dyed to match her hair, which seemed longer and lusher than ever. Looking past him, she noticed the Wagoneer.

"You drove your own car?"

He put his finger to his lips. She looked confused but accepting, said nothing further, and led him into the kitchen, where she had spread Simpson's drafts of the purchase documents across the table with small colored flags attached to the pages on which she had made handwritten notations. As usual, she sat down, folding one leg underneath the other, saying nothing, looking up toward him like an eager student waiting for instructions from the teacher. He sat down in his customary place across from her but left his coat on. Again, she had not frisked him. How could this new level of trust she seemed to have honored him with be anything other than evidence of her innocence? Or part of some scheme to reduce him to a foolish complacency?

He extracted a small reporter-style notebook and pen out of his coat pocket, flipped up the cover, wrote something on the page, and handed it over to her. She read it, rose from the chair, said "shoes and coat," and left the room. When she returned, she pointed to the papers on the table and whispered, "Bring them?"

He shook his head "no."

A sliding door in the kitchen opened onto a patio and beyond that a yard still showing its winter haggardness, the grass and shrubs and trees mostly winter-brown but the trees revealing a few tiny green buds announcing spring coming soon. He opened the door and waited for her to go out first. He then led her out from the patio to the yard itself, turned to her, and said, "I don't think we should meet here anymore."

"Why? What's happened?"

"Nothing in particular. Just a feeling, but I've found it useful to pay attention to those. Maybe it was talking to you the other night about your grand jury appearance."

"You think they've broken in here and bugged my house?"

"I don't know, but I just feel like it's stupid to take the chance."

"You think they know we're meeting?"

"I don't know that either, but maybe we should assume they either do or will soon enough."

"I've got to get this thing finished and get the hell out of this place," she said, more to herself than to him.

"We can do that. Let's get those documents negotiated and finalized ASAP."

"Where can we meet? Would your place work?"

"My office and house are being de-bugged as we speak. But not my office. Too much else going on there." *Plus, I'm keeping you a secret even from them. Lying to them and to you. Who am I not lying to these days?* "We can meet at my house this once. In the future we'll do a different place every time."

She appeared distressed and confused, perhaps contemplating all the machinations that would be required. He said, "But maybe there won't be many more meetings. Let's get those deals closed and get you to Tucson."

After they worked out the details of a meeting to occur a few hours later that day, she led him back through her house to the front yard. He began to walk to his car and turned around after a couple of steps. "And any pay phones you've used, don't use them ever again, and from now on, never use one twice."

She seemed shocked at the realization that those pay phones might be bugged. He left her there, looking stricken. If true, good. He had been warned about her and, while that warning might have been a lie, was likely a lie, he would remain extra wary and vigilant now while her trust level in him had surely increased. He had the power to wreck her escape plan, at least this version of it, and it would not be easy to create another one, and certainly not one as good as this. She could not really do him harm until the deals closed or cratered.

But what about her Outfit colleagues? According to the FBI, she was plotting with them to kill him. Even if the FBI was lying or mistaken, maybe those bad boys didn't know or care about her Tucson plans and might have a more urgent timetable than hers to finish things. Or if they didn't know about her escape plot and it offended them, they might just kill her too. A woman, yes. But there had been other women killed. Few, but some.

He had called on his friend, electro-device wizard Terry Lecumske, who had been one of those kids that carried a briefcase to school starting in the seventh grade, to handle the de-bugging, first on his house, and then on the office after hours that same day. He expected his business and Terry's to grow together, and if his own business plan worked, he would be one of Terry's major customers, so he invested in Terry's business—a small amount, he couldn't afford much, but it made Terry an even more loyal friend.

Not long after Terry finished and left, Rose rang the doorbell. He came to greet her, accompanied by Karma. She eyed the dog with alarm. "Don't let him eat me," she said, and Karma seemed to respond to that with as friendly a posture and presentation as O'Keefe had ever seen him offer anyone and even an accompanying back and forth tail wag. She seemed to accept that as at least a truce.

Looking back at the front yard and surveying the house itself as he and the dog made way for her and she moved further into it, she was wide-eyed, shocked. "This can't be you. It's too precious."

"You're right. It's not mine. It's a rental. But I've got an option to buy."

"Will you buy it? You should."

"I probably will…if I live that long."

He watched carefully for her reaction to that, hoping it might tell him something important. She said, not looking at him, still inspecting the place, "From what I know you can't be killed. You're like Michael Myers."

She caught herself, reddened slightly in embarrassment. "Sorry. Not so funny."

"Not flattering either," he said.

He had moved his phone, which had a speaker function, from the living room to the dining room and its accommodating table on which he had managed to reserve an adequate but shrinking blank space for the phone and for them to work on the documents. They moved quickly through the few issues that she and the Tucson lawyer had flagged in the documents, agreeing on which issues to raise with the sellers and which to leave alone.

He had notified Simpson they would be calling. "The actual client'll be on the line with me," he had said. "By the way, it's a lady."

"How nice," Simpson quickly responded, seemingly sincerely, and O'Keefe was relieved.

"She's president of the company. Her name is Rose Sciorra."

"Good," Simpson said. "Need that for my records and finalizing the docs and all that."

"She's a real estate broker here, doesn't use her license much, but knows her way around."

The introduction went quickly, and well, she charming but business-like and authoritative, Simpson the same, and they moved rapidly into the issues, resolved them, and worked out the logistics to finish the process.

"When can we close?" she asked, her eagerness not revealed in her flat, controlled tone of voice but in the way she edged to the front of her chair and moved her upper body closer to the phone.

"We could close them in as early as a week or so if you want," Simpson said.

"Let's get it done. It can't be soon enough for me."

• • •

Again, Kelly, in her parochial school uniform and cordovan penny loafers, this time in only a jacket rather than a heavy coat, and this time alone, walked down the street where Darren Maefield maintained his residence. She wore a backpack that looked empty. Without looking around, with confident step and bearing, she walked up Darren Maefield's front walk, inserted a key in the front door lock, and let herself in.

It had taken her a while after Matt had backed out on her to build up the courage to go on with it alone, but she decided she had been mistaken in relying on a boy anyway. She should've involved Jamie or another girlfriend. But involving *anyone* else obviously created complications, and she shouldn't have asked Matt to help in the first place and shouldn't ask someone else now. Persuading them to share the risk when there was nothing in it for them was just selfish. This was her thing, not anyone else's.

She did not have much time. It was almost 4 p.m. by the time she arrived. If he came home early from work for some reason, she would be in big trouble. But she had decided it was too risky to repeat the Ferris Bueller sick-day deception even though it would have provided her a lot more time in the house. Too much could go wrong with that approach, especially her mom's flexible schedule and guilt about leaving her daughter sick and home alone. And this time Kelly knew exactly what to search for and believed she could get in there, find the document, and get back out fast.

She moved quickly through the rooms of the house itself to check for anything obvious that hadn't been there or that she had overlooked on her previous visit. Finding nothing, she descended to the basement and the room with the file cabinet. She wanted the divorce petition filed by Mrs. DeLong and the document about the lawyer and the doctor with the reference to the "unindicted co-conspirator." She found each and stuffed them into her backpack. Mission accomplished, she had little time left, but she could not resist opening that previously unexplored fourth drawer. When she did, she almost gasped. A treasure trove—not only stuffed with documents of various types, but many of them newspaper articles, which would be so much easier to understand than the strange language of the legal documents she had seen so far. Now regretting her decision to abandon the Ferris Bueller sick-day strategy for the after-school approach because the latter left insufficient time to seriously examine these things, she decided the best thing she could do now would be to flip quickly through the items, a sort of scouting expedition to get an idea of the contents so she would not waste valuable time when she returned.

Many of the items covered things she did not understand. The items that did excite her were several newspaper articles covering the prosecution and trial of the lawyer and doctor , seemingly starting at the very beginning when the prosecutor announced the indictment. But she kept thinking she heard things like tires squeaking across the driveway, steps on staircases, and doors opening. Increasingly feeling like something bad was about to happen like last time, him showing up, maybe not for just a quick visit to pick up something, but for the whole rest of the day and night, trapping her in that basement with who-knows-what consequences, she decided to get out of that scary place right away. Grabbing the article announcing the indictment, she shoved the door of the file cabinet closed, stuffed the article in her backpack with the other items, and took off.

When she reached the stairway leading up from the basement to the main part of the house, she looked back and saw that she had failed to close the door leading from the basement to the separate room. Was she doomed to get caught this time? She ran back, closed the door, hurried again to the stairs, rushed up them and into the utility room and to the main part of the house. By the time she reached the front door, she was flushed, sweating, out of breath. She stopped to calm herself, and when she recovered a sufficient amount of her composure, opened the door and left the house, thinking straight enough to make sure to put the key in the door and lock it behind her.

Walking down the front walk toward the sidewalk, she saw in the driveway immediately across from Darren's house a woman standing behind the car she had just parked there, holding a small sack of groceries and staring at the girl coming out of the house of her neighbor across the street. Kelly tendered the lady an insouciant, enthusiastic wave, as if they were old acquaintances not to be forgot, and strode on down the street. She was proud of that performance, very satisfied with herself for a while—until she imagined a conversation between the lady and Darren where the lady inquired who might be the young girl she had seen going and coming from his house a couple of times recently.

●   ●   ●

On the following Saturday, she returned to the library because she could not think of anywhere else to find help with the items she had taken from the file cabinet. She considered asking her dad, under cover of some story she would make up. Too risky. She had considered Sara—also too dangerous because she could not swear Sara to secrecy, could not tell her what she was really up to and certainly couldn't ask her not to mention it to her dad. Thus, Chief Reference Librarian Brandon Terbovich proved to be her only realistic option.

First, she showed him the copy of the indictment she had taken from Darren's file.

"Wow," he said, thumbing through the multi-page legal document, "where'd you get this?"

"Teacher gave it to me. I don't know where she got it."

"Neat."

She took him through the things she didn't understand in it. "Why do they keep saying 'said' when nobody is saying anything?"

He laughed loud, so loud he shushed himself, glancing sheepishly around, and, bringing a finger to his lips, said, "Out of the mouths of babes!"

Since he had found something funny, she smiled back at him.

"I don't know how it developed, but lawyers came to use that word to mean 'previously mentioned' or 'previously stated' or 'previously said'…you know, like 'it's the same thing I said before,' like a paragraph or a page ago."

She also asked and he patiently explained the meaning of certain words that she had looked up in the dictionary but that still didn't make sense to her as used in the document, and finally, she asked, "How about 'unindicted co-conspirator'? What's that?"

He squinched up his face, contemplating the question. "You know, I remember that phrase because they called President Nixon that in the Watergate case."

"Watergate?"

"Hmm…I want to make sure I give you the right answer on that. Give me a few minutes."

When he returned, he said, "An 'unindicted co-conspirator' is somebody who has participated in the conspiracy, but for some reason the government isn't including that person in the criminal prosecution. It can be a confidential informant whose identity they want to protect—

"What's that…a 'confidential informant'?"

"That's a person who works for the police 'undercover' and helps them catch criminals by…infiltrating…you know what that means?"

"I think so."

"Making the criminals believe he's one of them while he's secretly reporting to the police on what the criminals are doing."

"Yeah, seen that on TV."

"Or it could be, not a confidential informant per se, but just someone who joined in committing the crime but is now cooperating with the government by testifying against his former criminal pals… like 'telling on' someone, but in a trial…You know what a 'plea bargain' is?"

"I've heard of it…" She remembered hearing it last year during Mr. Harrigan's trial. "…but I don't know what it means."

"It means one of the people involved in the crime has cut a deal with the government to get a lighter sentence or even get off the hook altogether for his crime in exchange for testifying against the others."

"You mean a rat," she said.

He chuckled. "Well, his former pals would call him that."

"Yeah, a 'rat bastard' they call 'em."

He laughed out loud again and shushed himself again, then said, "Or just for some reason they don't want to or aren't able to prosecute the person. Like President Nixon in Watergate. I think it might be that you can't prosecute a President for a crime while he's in office or something like that."

"Watergate?"

"Never mind. Not important. For this anyway. But do you get it now?"

"I do. Thank you."

"So do you want to order more microfilm?"

"Not now. Maybe later."

I've got a lot easier way than that one.

CHAPTER ▶ 23

HE SUGGESTED THEY travel to Tucson for the closings on separate planes.

"You think they're following us?" she asked.

"I don't know, but let's be cautious and assume they are. And if you can get to the airport without them following you, that would be extra good."

In Tucson, they met up at the small bar of the same resort hotel she had booked for him on his previous trip. "I can't believe I'm here," she said. "I don't think I believed this really could happen."

The rest of their meeting didn't last long and consisted mostly of small talk and logistical details: what time they would leave for Simpson's office in the morning; whether she would be able to sleep that night at all; the sequencing of the closings over the next two days. She had negotiated that the husband-and-wife owners of the art business and also the car wash owner would continue post-closing to operate the businesses for a transition period. Her disclosed purpose in this was to keep them in place until she had learned enough to be able to successfully operate the businesses herself, but O'Keefe guessed she had another, undisclosed purpose—buying time for her to escape her situation, her entire previous life, and her current business "colleagues" who might not be willing to let her go or allow things to happen in the customary commercial way.

The art business closed first. No glitches. O'Keefe thought her smile could be described as quiet, serene, almost beatific after the seller couple left with the certified check in their hands and as she stared down at the papers stacked neatly on the table that had accomplished her purpose.

The next day the car wash closing—more complicated, technical, and difficult, since it involved two operations, equipment, and real estate—took most of the day. Simpson suggested they have a celebratory closing dinner at what he claimed was far and away the best place in Tucson, but she begged off, suggesting they meet for a few cocktails instead. After Simpson left the conference room to gather the lawyers and paralegals and other staff who had helped on various aspects of the deals so they could all head together to the bar, she said to O'Keefe, "I thought you and I should have our own private closing dinner."

After an hour or so at the bar with Simpson and his people, she excused herself and O'Keefe just as the law firm people were getting seriously into the drinks. She asked him to drive because she had a couple of drinks and he none. "Wouldn't be good for me to get stopped for a DUI out here."

They spent a few minutes in their respective rooms, then met in the hotel dining room.

He had called ahead and arranged for a single rose to be left across her plate at their table.

"How lovely," she said. "Thank you for this and everything else."

"Sorry for the cliché. Given your name, you've probably been getting them every time you turn around all your life."

"I never tire of it. Truly."

After they finished dinner, she said, "Well?"

"Well?" he repeated.

"I'm waiting for you to ask when I intend to deliver my end of this bargain."

"Okay. Yes. When are you gonna deliver your end? And how?"

"Do you trust me?"

"I have to. No other choice. But it seems like your end is a lot harder to deliver than mine, given who you have to deal with."

"I have a lot of currency to deal with them…really him, just one."

"So…when?"

"Soon. Your deal will be part of mine. But your part won't be that hard. As you suspect, and I *know,* you're not even on anyone's list, 'hit' or otherwise."

"How will I know?"

"I don't know what proof I can give you. You might just have to take my word for it. Surely you should have known that when we started…But I'll tell you this. Part of my *currency,* a big chunk of it, will be in…let's call it escrow…contingent on your continuing safety."

"I'd like to know how that'll work."

"I don't think it would be good for either of us for you to know that."

"You're not really giving me anything, nothing I can take to the rest of the world."

"Didn't we just essentially agree that you had no reason to expect something like that?"

"Maybe you can't deliver even yourself from it."

"Well, then, we're both, let us say…screwed…aren't we? Our little partnership here didn't come with a guarantee of success for either of us."

"They could let you go on and flush me just to spite you."

"Didn't you hear what I said about the deferred payment?"

He didn't know what further to say. They were just going around in circles now.

"You'll just have to trust me. I'm sorry, but there's nothing else I can give you now. But I want you to have your daughter back. I hope you believe a mother when she says that."

They discussed the next steps. He would be leaving the next day after handling some follow-up details with Simpson's office and each of the businesses. She was staying for two more days. "It won't be long enough," she said, "but I have to get back to the kids. It's touch and go with them now as you might imagine. I feel bad for leaving them this long."

In his room, he stripped off his shirt and removed the small cassette tape recorder strapped to his chest. He turned it on and listened to confirm whether the conversation had come through on the tape. It had. He turned the machine off and flipped it on the bed. *Probably not worth anything.*

He opened the glass sliding door and crossed out to the balcony. He shivered in the cold desert night. The sky was packed tight with stars, 250 billion of them in the Milky Way galaxy alone, many of them even more gigantic than the sun, making his eyeblink sojourn in the infinite universe of no cosmic significance and probably no meaning at all. So put on the bold face, like the bravado tattoos on Paschal's forearms, suspend your disbelief and act as if you mattered.

●　　●　　●

Dagmar knocked on Sara's office door just as she hung up the phone from a status call with Harrigan on the loan portfolio of the failed Central Bank. Still wide-eyed and enthusiastic about the job and the sometimes-peculiar goings-on there, Dagmar said, "Wow. You get some real dames visiting this place."

"And what does that mean?"

"In our waiting room is a lady who says her name is Golden Monroe. She says she's from Cherry Pink."

"Let's have a look," Sara said, shifting immediately to high alert. She rose from her desk chair, brushed past Dagmar, and strode down the hallway and into the waiting room. The lady, very young, somewhere in her early twenties, stood there in big sunglasses, black high heels, skinny legs in skin-tight, black leather pants, a jacket of some kind of fur thrown open to reveal a red sequined tank top advertising her navel at the bottom and more than ample cleavage at the top. Her earrings were large turquoise hoops, her nails and lipstick as red as her tank top, and her hair "big" in the current style, an expansive, profuse tousle of silver-streaked blondish curls that fell to the top of the collar of her jacket.

"I need to talk," she said. "It's private. It's important. Maybe life or death."

"Then I guess we'd better talk," Sara said, trying to keep her cool for Dagmar's sake and her own. "All in a day's work," she said to Dagmar who watched with fascination Golden Monroe wobbling slightly on the high heels, her large, unsheathed breasts jiggling under the red tank top as she navigated along in Sara's wake.

In her office, Sara indicated the chair in front of her desk for the lady to occupy, sat herself down in her office chair, and said, "You mind taking off the glasses?"

"No problem," Golden said, quickly removed them, and set them on the desk in front of her. She wore far more makeup than her pretty face needed. *She looks like a little elf,* Sara thought. *But with giant boobs. Those horny bastards must love that.*

Golden said, "You look a little different today than last time I saw you runnin' through the club naked."

Sara felt herself blush, recalling when she had impersonated a dancer looking for a job and had to show her "stuff" to Marty Lansing in Marty's office, and then to David Bowman. When Bowman had tried to force himself on her, she gave him a hard shove that sent him flying and ran near naked out of the office and through the club to the sidewalk out front.

"You're kind of a hero to some of us," Golden said. "Glad we're rid of that Bowman. Really creepy. I would never ever've taken that job if it wasn't for Marty."

"I guess you're a dancer there?"

"Yes'm. I dance as 'Pixie Dust.'"

Appropriate enough. "You said 'maybe life or death'?"

"I'm not sure what to do. I think I may need to hire you. But it's complicated.

"How?"

"It involves you personally."

Sara managed to stay quiet, waiting for the lady to continue.

"Can you keep a secret?"

"Maybe. Maybe not. And the problem is I can't tell you for sure until I know what the secret is."

Golden tilted her head back and gazed at the ceiling for a moment, then brought her head level again, apparently having decided to tell her tale even without a promise of confidentiality.

"The other night I left work early, after my afternoon dance. I felt sick and down and just didn't feel like goin' on through the night, so I begged off and went home to bed…actually to Marty's. He and I are pretty much livin' together now…though Marty says we have to keep that a secret. I assume you remember Marty?"

"Hard to forget him."

"He's a really good guy, really. He's never hit me."

Not much of a standard to live up to.

"He's seemed really worried lately. Every time I try to ask him about it, he shushes me…"

Golden paused, waiting for a comment from Sara. None came.

"So that night I went to bed early. When he came home, I didn't wake up right away, but half-awake, half-asleep I could feel him movin' around the apartment. The bedroom door was open; it always is, no reason to close it, but he closed it, really carefully, but it still woke me up…the light changing or somethin'. Even groggy, that seemed really strange to me. I didn't remember him ever doin' that, and I wondered if he was gonna do somethin' he didn't want me to see or hear…Well, I couldn't accept that, so I opened the door and went down the hallway so I could see him in the livin' room, sittin' on the couch, his back to me, and he was listenin' to a tape on this tape recorder he uses sometimes. I moved a little closer to try to hear. I couldn't really make out much of what they were sayin', but some of it I could. And I couldn't swear it on a bible, but I think one of the voices was Wayne Popper's."

"The bouncer?"

"Not anymore. I think he's sort of the boss now, if you can believe it. He acts like it anyway. What a creep. He's started hittin' on me, which I haven't told Marty yet. No use causin' trouble at this point. Not unless he goes further with it…"

Her voice quavering with distress, she stopped.

"Go on," Sara said softly.

"So…one voice I think was Wayne's and the other voice I didn't know. One thing they talked about was Marty, and it wasn't good. They've got some plan to take over the place from whoever the current investors are. The other man thought they ought to keep Marty on, at least for a while, but that fuckin' Wayne wouldn't have it. He wants Marty out right away. And there were other things on that tape, things I didn't understand, but somethin' bad's gonna happen…"

"Like?"

"Well…Wayne was braggin'…that he had killed people…how he overdosed a couple girls, one of the dancers even, before my time… then some other woman…killed them that way. That dancer was his girlfriend, too. And here the motherfucker's hittin' on me now—"

Unable to stand the suspense for another moment, Sara interrupted, "You said this involved me personally?"

"Oh…Yeah…Sorry…The voice I think was Wayne's said somethin' like…'I'm gonna get rid of that asshole O'Keefe and that bitch of his too'…I thought that last might've been you?"

Sara tried to keep cool despite the adrenalin rush and the blood surging in her temples. "Maybe," she said, her voice almost catching in her throat. "What else?"

"Then they talked a little bit about how they could help each other. The other man said maybe they could do each other a favor… that he had some people he wanted to get rid of too."

"You remember the names?"

"No. It went quick, and it was a jumble."

"Where's the tape?"

"So…Marty finished listenin', and I backed up a step or two in the hallway toward the bedroom, but Marty just sat there for a long time. Finally, he got up, and I moved back more into the hallway, and he has the tape recorder in his hand, and he starts openin' drawers and things, and finally I see him stash it in one of 'em, and then I scoot back to bed so he doesn't catch me watchin'. So it's in that drawer unless he's done somethin' else with it in the meantime."

"I need that tape."

Golden Monroe gave that some thought, then said, "If you mean that I steal it from Marty and give it to you, I can't do that to Marty."

"Hey, girl. My *life* seems to be at stake here. Screw your romance. What if I go to the police with this?"

"You can't do that."

"Did you hear me? My life, my friend's life…"

"I'll just deny it. And you can bet that tape'll disappear."

"You're a real sweetheart."

"I came here to help us all. To help you…and Mr. O'Keefe…but to help Marty too."

"I can't not tell Pete this."

Clearly this was not turning out the way Golden Monroe had hoped it would. She made no sound, but a large tear escaped from each eye, slowly sliding down her face until she rubbed them off, one after the other, with the tip of her index finger, the left one, then the right.

"First, can't you and I just try to talk to Marty?" Golden said.

"This can't wait."

"What if we do it tonight?"

"Where and what time?"

Golden sat thinking for a few moments. "I think not at the club but at Marty's apartment. I dance the afternoon/early evening session today. The club closes at 2 a.m. He's usually home by 2:30. When he comes in, you'll just be there. Otherwise he'll duck you."

They arranged to meet at the apartment at 2 a.m. As soon as Golden left, Sara hustled to O'Keefe's office. Empty. Dark. Dagmar said he had told her the afternoon before that he would be out of town for a couple of days, he didn't say where. This violated his own long-established policy requiring each of them to notify the other two when leaving town. He had been elusive and isolated lately. Not a good sign.

"When you hear from him, tell him I need to talk to him immediately. It's an emergency."

Where are you? You've gone to ground. Brings back some bad memories.

CHAPTER ▶ 24

TIME MOVED EXCRUCIATINGLY slowly the rest of that day and evening until 2 a.m. came around. It was still "warm coat" weather most nights, as winter had not quite surrendered to spring, but Sara left her coat in the car. Golden let her in the apartment—neat and well appointed, not just decorated in good taste but with a high design flare, just like his office had looked when Sara had met Marty there several months before under the pretext of interviewing for a dancer job.

"No coat?" Golden said when she opened the door.

Sara shook her head.

"And no purse."

Sara shook her head again. She wanted to be as unencumbered as possible, able to move freely, as ready as she could be for what might occur in that apartment. She wore snug-fitting corduroy slacks and, as she had learned from O'Keefe, a rather bulky sweater to both conceal and allow easy access to the Smith & Wesson .38 Special revolver in its holster strapped across her belly. Marty had not seemed like a violent man at their last meeting, but Sara wanted to be ready for the worst. She also had a knife strapped to her calf, just as O'Keefe would have done.

Golden gestured toward a couch for Sara to sit on, but Sara gestured toward the table in a dining nook with straight chairs around it and a clear line of sight to the apartment door.

"I think we'd be better sitting there when he comes in." *Sitting up straight and ready to go.*

Golden shrugged and complied. "Want a drink? We've got all kinds of liquor, and I made some coffee. Doubt you want a joint."

"No thanks."

"I had to smoke one. I'm scared shitless. It didn't help much."

They sat at the table, each sitting straight up in formal posture across from each other and trying to make small talk here and there among painfully silent interludes.

"So scary," Golden said, "you do this kind of thing a lot?"

"Hardly ever. It's pretty tame most of the time."

After more silence, Sara asked the inevitable question. "How long have you been doing this job?"

"Almost four years now."

The next question would naturally be "How did you get into it?" But Sara didn't want to know. The story would likely be a sad one, or, if not sad, a lie. Plus, it might be painful for Golden, and Sara guessed she had suffered plenty of pain so far in her life, (especially when her positive review of her current boyfriend was, "He's never hit me") and might about to be facing much more. But she decided to venture a bit in that direction.

"It's none of my business, but you're very pretty...not stupid either. You don't have to sell yourself this way."

Golden pondered that a bit, then said, "Don't we all sell ourselves, one way or the other?"

When Sara didn't respond, Golden went on: "It's good money too. I don't know where else I could make that kind of money."

Sara had to acknowledge to herself that Golden had made two good points but still thought she shouldn't be allowed to rationalize quite so easily. "Make sure," she said, "that you consider the price *you* pay."

Sara wondered if Marty would really arrive as soon as Golden thought he would, how often he hung out for a while after closing for a drink with the staff or special customers or even for a little couch action in his office with one of the dancers or waitresses. She remembered what he had told her the last time they met, something like "I do this for the money, the dope, the pussy, and the edge." That did not seem to promise a faithfully monogamous approach to a relationship. But he didn't seem like a total sleazeball either. It wasn't just his good taste in furniture design. He didn't wear a black silk shirt buttoned halfway down the front. His shirt had been black, but a preppy button down, only one open button at the neck, and appeared to be simply cotton with maybe a bit of rayon mixed in to give it a slight sheen. No golden neck chains. No Rolex, real or fake. No bracelet of gold or silver. No contemptuous, snarky expression. He looked more like something out of the softer side of the '60s. Wire-rimmed glasses. Dishwater blond hair pulled back into a short ponytail. He looked and acted as if he could easily have ended up a hippie guru in a hot tub at Esalen but had read too many *Playboy* magazines and immersed himself too deeply in the "Playboy Philosophy" and "Rat Pack" values hanging over from the '50s.

A sharp intake of breath from Golden signaled that the man himself was unlocking the front door. He entered the apartment, saw who was sitting at his dining table, and, like a guilty thing surprised, his face changed color from tanning-booth light brown to a creamy shade of pale. He looked behind him at the door as if he might flee back into the night but recovered himself and said, "What the fuck is this?"

Golden, her lips quivering and her voice near breaking, her hands pressing down on the table as if otherwise she might fly away, blurted, "Marty, I listened to your tape. I hired Sara to help us."

Marty's face reddened, and he passed rapidly from stupefaction to disbelief to outrage to rage. "Is it still there?"

Golden nodded her trembling head up and down rapidly, trying to keep the sobs from breaking through and the tears from pouring forth. He turned, walked fast across the room to a cabinet, opened it, pulled out the tape, and turned back to the two women.

"You stupid, worthless bitch."

"I just wanted to help. You need help."

"Fuck you."

And to Sara, "And you. Get out."

"I want that tape."

"Fuck you."

"What can I trade you for it?"

"I don't think you've got what I need."

"What's that?"

"How 'bout a second life? Because if this tape gets out, I'll be dead. This dumb cunt isn't smart enough to get that."

"What if we could arrange that…or something close to that?"

"Who the fuck is 'we'? You and O'Keefe? He isn't long for the world and maybe you're not either."

Then his voice broke in anger and fear. "Out!"

Sara rose slowly. She had been thinking from the moment of his first reaction to her presence about threatening him with the revolver. She was afraid to do that, afraid it might be a mistake, that he would call her bluff, that he would know she would not actually shoot him and that keeping the tape would be worth the risk that she would. But she couldn't just leave, not without that tape.

She pulled out the revolver and pointed it at Marty.

Golden yelled, "No!" and lunged over the table and slapped the gun out of Sara's hand.

It flew toward Marty and bounced on the floor in front of him.

Marty pounced on it, grabbed it, pointed it at Sara, and said, "One more time. Get the fuck out."

Golden kept sobbing and shaking her head back and forth, saying, "No, no, no, Marty no, I'm so sorry, no…"

Sara hesitated, trying to figure out what to do. If she went to the police, would they even care enough to follow it up? As if reading her thoughts, he said, "And I'd better never see you or O'Keefe again. Or the cops either. This tape never existed. It's a figment of her imagination and yours. I'll be puttin' it somewhere that stupid cunts like this one can't find it and where it'll go POOF, right up in smoke, if anyone ever tries to get it from me again."

It seemed like there was nothing to do but leave, figure out a different approach, try again later. But she might never be that close to the tape again, right there a few feet in front of her in a weak man's hand. She could try to rush him. Her jiu-jitsu moves might actually work on him. He was no killer. It would be hard for him to pull that trigger. But in panic he might. Tragedy for everyone then. Better talk to O'Keefe. "Two heads" and all that, which was mostly nonsense but…

On her way out, Sara said, "You'd better not hurt her."

"The only ones who might cause her hurt now are you and herself."

•　•　•

Marty followed Sara and watched closely enough to make sure she drove out of the parking lot, then returned to the apartment.

Golden brought her hands together as if in prayer. "I'm so sorry. I love you. I was only tryin' ta help."

"Well, I don't love you. Pack up your shit and get out of here. I never wanna see you again."

"You're *firin'* me too?"

He tried to gather his thoughts together and make sense of them. He was starting to settle down, re-establishing control of himself.

"Maybe. Maybe not. I have to think about it. That might just tip over the whole barrel of rotten-ass apples around here. Meanwhile, you'd better be on your best fuckin' behavior."

"Wayne's been tryin' to hit on me."

He didn't respond immediately. Her comment puzzled him, then made him even angrier.

"Is that a threat?"

"No, no, no. I just thought you should know. I wouldn't let him touch me."

"He's not the type that asks permission."

"I won't let him."

What's happened? Marty thought. *Madness.* Things had gone completely bonkers, totally off the rails. Beholding her, looking so fine, so weeping and needy, praying to him like that. She was a dumb bitch but loved him, trying to do the right thing, dumb as it was. And she had slapped that gun out of the Sara bitch's hand. Right there, despite everything, he was getting horny for her. He needed to think about the situation, spend some time with it.

He walked over to her, stood in front of her. She looked up at him, ran two fingers lightly down the front of his pants, gently tracing his hardness, unbuckled his belt, pulled his pants down just far enough, took him gently into her mouth and bestowed on him two long, slow, soulful strokes.

He took her head lightly in his hands and gently turned her tears-soaked face up so she could see his face and he could see hers.

"Let's go to bed," he said. "We'll figure all this out tomorrow."

● ● ●

Sara, sure that Marty was watching her, pulled out of the parking lot, drove a few yards where she would be out of sight of anyone watching from the apartment complex, and parked by the side of the road. Now, after the danger had passed, the fear rose high and wild. She felt her heart rate jump and thought she might hyperventilate. Once she settled down, she called O'Keefe's house from the car phone he had bought for her (or *they* had bought for her, reminding herself that she really was a partner now). It rang five times and clicked over to his message machine. She called again in case he had not been able to wake up and get to the phone by that fifth ring. Five more rings, then the message machine again.

"Call me," she said. "Immediately."

She hung up, called his office and left the same message there, hung up, and said out loud to herself, "Where *are* you?"

Was he off on some secret escapade with a good reason for both the escapade and the secret? Or was he in trouble again? There was plenty of trouble right here at home.

● ● ●

Adrenalin-spent, sluggish, suffering the post-closing doldrums, afraid Rose would never be able to deliver her end of the bargain even if she tried her best, O'Keefe was almost desperate to escape Tucson. Worried he might miss his plane, he hurried through his post-closing tasks at the two businesses. What would happen now that he had done his part? The same force that drove him to undertake this half-mad emprise in the first place was now doubling down on him. He wanted more than ever to "get on with it," somehow force a resolution, though he didn't know how to do that or how and where it might end.

He caught the last plane out of Tucson, which did not bring him home until close on 11 p.m. He was supposed to pick up Karma at George's, but it was late, and George wasn't expecting him until the following day, and he was exhausted, depressed, and wanted desperately to immediately get some sleep, which almost always lifted him out of a depression. Pulling into his circle drive and leaving the Wagoneer in the driveway in front of the house, he grabbed the remote for the house's alarm system and a flashlight he kept in the Wagoneer and illuminated his path to the porch. At his front door he punched the remote to turn off the alarm system. As he opened the front door, he jumped back. When nothing happened, he felt sheepish, as if it really might do him any good to be reeling back a few feet if the door had been rigged to explode. *Like the generals always fighting the last war. Next time it won't be a bomb, it'll be something else.*

In the vestibule, he turned the alarm back on and headed for the bedroom. Dropping his bag just across the threshold of the bedroom door, he walked to the side of his bed, turned on the lamp, sat down on a chair to remove his shoes and socks, stood up to take off his shirt and pants and dropped them on the chair. Undressing and dressing had become almost normal for him now. It would not be long before he would not have to wear the pressure garments at all.

He took off his watch and at the same time moved toward his dresser, where he kept his watches and other jewelry items, and opened the top drawer of the waist-high dresser only enough to reach in to place the watch with the others.

A slight sting. Left hand. A bug? Winter. No mosquitoes now. Movement in the drawer. Strong movement. Stronger than a bug. Another sting. Something locked onto his hand. He pulled back his hand, heavy now, weighted with something, something locked onto it and flopping around. Snake. Black and white. Its jaws locked onto the ridge of his palm below his little finger. He shook it. Won't let go. He shook it again. And again. It still held on. Skinny, about a yard long, he could see the tail. Grabbing at it, his hand slipped off. He floundered to grab it with his right hand while its body floundered trying to evade the grab, the jaws still locked on. He managed to grab it in the middle of its body and yanked. A rip of his flesh, only a slight pain as his right hand tore it off his left, its head and upper body now lunging wildly side to side, trying to turn and bite the hand squeezing it. He slammed it down like a whip against the top of the dresser. Once, twice, three times. No movement now. Surely dead. Make sure. He smashed it down again. Spatter of blood and pus streaked on the dresser top. He lifted it at arm's length up to eye level. Striped. Black and white. Prison stripes. Nothing hurt. Where did it come from? What if not dead? Poisonous? In the old movies the hero's sidekick cut into the bite and sucked the poison out. No sidekick here. Those stripes. Seen before. On a screen. Training video. Vietnam. Dreaded "two-step." On your second step you were dead. Or the "WTF." Dead before you could say, "What The Fuck?"

Tourniquet? What to tie it with? Too hard and take too long. He sat down on the bed. Think. Poisonous? Emergency room. No more than ten minutes to the hospital. Faster to drive himself than wait for the ambulance…if he could make it that far. Two steps. Poison speeding through him right now? But not feeling anything. Except waves of fear close to panic. He wanted to scream, "What the fuck!" Not exactly the right thing to say. But still alive. Need to put on clothes. Snake in hand. Not trusting it was dead, he threw it into the dresser drawer and shut it, put on his shirt and pants. Forget the socks, just shoes. They'll need the snake at the hospital. Open drawer. No movement. Dead snake. It jumped!

He jumped back. Peer back over open drawer. Lying still again. Involuntary reflex? Corpses sat up on the embalming table. He reached in slowly and grabbed the snake toward its tail and slammed it again, up against the wall this time. Tiny splash. Snake pus on the wall. Poison spreading, pumping through him? Emergency room. Grab the snake, the special remote, out the front door, down the front steps, almost tripping. In the car. Stomp the accelerator. Tires slipping, churning up the gravel. Don't go too fast. A cop stopping you now might cause a lot worse than a traffic ticket.

•   •   •

Doctor Gary Harmon, the physician in charge of the emergency room on this shift, knew Nurse Bennett to be as unflappable as they come. So when he saw her rush past the window of his tiny office attached to the emergency room and the look on her face when she appeared at his door, he knew something must be very wrong.

"There's a man out there holding a snake and saying it bit him and it's poisonous."

He jumped up and followed her long strides, stopping only to grab a small wastebasket. The emergency room intake area consisted of a counter at the end of a hallway, with an adjacent waiting room; behind the counter a couple of metal desks for the nurses doing the initial intake; behind that a wall and beyond that an open space with treatment tables, more metal desks, scattered medical paraphernalia; off of the central area, in addition to Dr. Harmon's office, several treatment rooms, a couple of which had doors but most had only curtains that could slide closed. On one of the tables a nurse tended to a patient with a bloody but superficial knife slash across his belly. A couple of the treatment rooms were occupied with non-life-threatening injuries or drunken accidents, but several others were empty, a relatively quiet night—until now anyway.

When Doctor Harmon emerged from the treatment area, he saw a nurse behind the counter who seemed to be frozen in place and several people gathered in the opening to the waiting area, gawking at a man standing between them and the counter. Coming around the counter, the doctor faced a man of trembling face and chalky pallor from whose right hand drooped a mutilated, apparently dead snake with unusual black and white bands that looked like the stripes of a prison uniform.

"What happened?"

The man held the snake out slightly, offering it for Doctor Harmon's closer observation. "It bit me. I think it's poisonous."

"Is it dead?"

"Very."

"Put it in here," Doctor Harmon said, holding out the wastebasket and moving closer to the man and the snake.

The man dropped it in.

"Was it a pet?"

"No."

"Why do you think it's venomous?"

"They were in Vietnam. They called them 'two-steps.' You're dead within two steps after a bite."

"When were you bitten?"

"Half an hour or so."

"Hey!" the Doctor said to the two stupefied nurses, sternly but not loud, avoiding the impulse to raise his voice too high and elevate everyone's blood pressure to panic level. "Take him back to a treatment room."

He knew the two-step thing was a myth, but super-rapid envenomization was still possible. And that approached the limit of his knowledge. They trained you for all kinds of things but still missed a lot of the crazy stuff that ended up wandering into an emergency room. This man could be minutes away from death, certainly hours away if not properly treated, and Doctor Harmon had only a vague idea what proper treatment might be for a bite from this particular and still unidentified snake.

Following the nurse and the patient into the treatment area, he drew aside the chief resident. "Snakebite. Don't know what kind but might be venomous. Exotic. Assume for now it's from Vietnam, Thailand, or somewhere like that. Get hold of our toxicologist. Round up all the other help you can get. We need to identify the snake, figure out the course of treatment, whether antivenom's available anywhere. Heart attack's possible. Might have to defibrillate. Or could be complete respiratory failure. Get the crash cart, all the breathing support equipment, everything from nasal cannula to a ventilator. Get the resuscitation room ready in case we have to intubate him right away."

He grabbed another resident and headed into the treatment room where the two nurses were gathering basic information from the patient—name, date of birth, address, phone number, etc. When it came to next of kin, the man said he was divorced with a daughter who lived with his ex-wife, his mother deceased, his father's status and location unknown. He gave three contact names and phone numbers—his business partners George Novak and Sara Slade and a local attorney named Michael Harrigan.

"Call those people," the doctor told one of the residents. He needed someone there who could make decisions. At any moment the patient could suffer complete respiratory failure or neurogenic shock. He gave orders for a mild sedative to be administered immediately with a more powerful one on standby, ascertained that the bite had occurred on the left hand, in the palm area, which was covered with a thin pressure garment to treat burn wounds. Neither he nor any of the residents nor nurses could detect any fang marks as such, but did note a tear in the flesh where the man said he had ripped the snake's jaws from his hand. That the bite had to penetrate through the pressure garment may have impeded the venom flow, but the locking of the jaws potentially indicated the opposite—a substantial amount of envenoming.

"How do you feel now, Mr. O'Keefe?"

"My stomach hurts. It seems to be getting worse. I'm having a little trouble seeing."

The doctor noticed the patient's eyelids drooping, only half of his eyeball now visible. Ptosis.

"How's your breathing?"

"Seems alright."

"If you have any trouble, *any* trouble at all with that, you need to let us know immediately."

"My left arm hurts like hell…my neck too. And not from the burns. Starting to feel sore all over. How you treat this?"

"We're figuring it out. No exotic venomous snakebite experience around here."

"Copperheads? Rattlesnakes?"

"Different. Their venom is relatively slow-acting, and there's anti-venom readily available."

"Not for this?"

"We're hoping to find out soon. We have to figure out what kind of snake it is."

"Can't you just use the rattlesnake stuff?"

The doctor noticed the patient had begun to slur. "No. Almost all anti-venom is bespoke. It has to match the specific snake."

"Those guys, Harrigan and Novak and Slade, whose names I gave you. One's a lawyer, the others are detectives. They can help. Can you call someone in Vietnam…or somewhere else over there…Cambodia or Thailand maybe?"

The patient was growing more agitated and panicky. "My whole body's starting to hurt. What's the course of this?"

"I'm going right now to see where we are on getting the answers."

Outside of the treatment room, the doctor ordered pain medication and sedation. "And get the whole respiration support array ready. Nasal cannula to start, non-rebreather mask, CPAP, and a ventilator in case it gets that bad."

A resident poked his head out of the treatment room and in a low voice said, "His blood pressure's dropping."

Doctor Harmon turned to the nurse. "Fibrillation. Get the defibrillator ready too. Make sure they're calling his partners and that lawyer. *Now*."

CHAPTER 25

ALTHOUGH DOCTOR HARMON had said "*Now*," it took several hours for the hospital to contact Harrigan, who arrived shortly after 9 a.m. George came an hour later, bringing Sara with him. A nurse escorted them to a conference room. Soon after, Doctor Harmon appeared with another physician several years his senior and the usual retinue of residents trailing like ducks after their mother.

"I'm Doctor Harmon. I've been his treating physician since he arrived in the emergency room late last night. This is Doctor Petersen. We'll be transferring him from Emergency to the ICU soon. Doctor Petersen's the ICU Chief."

Before the doctors could start addressing the medical issues, the group began peppering them with questions about the occurrence.

"You'll have to sort all that out later," Doctor Harmon said. "All we know is that the snake was in a drawer, he reached in, and it bit him. He has no idea where it came from."

Harrigan turned to George. "Can you get Lieutenant Ross or some other police here?"

Doctor Petersen said, "I'm not sure we can allow them to interview him until he's past the crisis. Some say the chief cause of death by snakebite is fear and panic. And that's not a joke either. We need to keep him as relaxed and calm as possible, do everything possible to slow or arrest the venom spreading through his system."

"Still," Harrigan said to George, "let's call them. They can get started, go to his house, take a look."

"Let me hear the medical first," George said.

Harmon continued: "Start with imagining how much experience we have with snakebites from exotic snakes neither native nor even existing in the U.S. except maybe in some zoo somewhere. We've been scrambling all night to figure this out. We started with our toxicologist, and it turns out that the Natural History Museum at a local university has one of the leading herpetologists, which is the name for an expert on reptiles. We got him out of bed, and he has been invaluable. We're contacting all the U.S. hospitals with leading toxicology units and all the zoos with extensive captive snake populations. And, by the way, the zoos are more likely to be helpful than the hospitals. This hospital doesn't have—and no other hospital in the country that we know of has—any experience with a bite from this type of snake, which we believe is either a Malayan Krait or a Many-Banded Krait. Their basic range is Southeast Asia including Vietnam. You may've heard of what the GIs over there called the 'two-step' snake. Supposedly, if it bites you, you take two steps and you're dead. That's not true, but these Kraits are among the top five most dangerous venomous snakes in the world. Untreated, the fatality rate is extremely high."

"And when treated?" Sara asked.

"Still a high fatality risk. Still a risk of respiratory collapse or complications from the ventilation support—"

George interrupted. "What's the treatment? Anti-venom?"

"Yes, but anti-venom is snake-specific. You can't mix and match. As far as we can tell, there's none for this snake in the entire U.S. But we're still contacting all the zoos that might have it."

"Not hospitals?"

"The major poison centers maybe, but a zoo is much more likely."

Harrigan said, "How about in Vietnam? Will those people even talk to us now? Or maybe Thailand? I'll get on a plane myself if I have to."

"You wouldn't have to do that. We could probably arrange to get it shipped here PDQ. But it won't do any good. First, it's often not effective in the first place, and, apparently, it's even less effective for Kraits than other snakes. And there are often allergic reactions that are as dangerous as the venom itself. But here's the most important thing: It doesn't do any good unless it's administered in the first twenty-four hours, maximum forty-eight. There's no way to get it from over there to here and into him in time."

"Are you sure? Maybe we should try anyway. What else can you do?"

"Basically, the venom gets to make the first move."

Harrigan was passing from frustration to anger and headed toward rage. "What's that mean?"

"There are many so-called 'dry bites,' meaning that the snake takes a bite, but it doesn't inject venom. The snake itself controls that. It can actually choose whether to inject it and how much."

"Diabolical."

"Based on the symptoms the patient has already shown, the snake did inject venom. The question now is how much. This type of snake and a few other snakes in the world have what are called 'neurotoxins' that attack the central nervous system. It paralyzes the victim's muscles. Everything shuts down including, ultimately, your diaphragm, the muscle that pulls air into your lungs. You stop breathing. Then your heart stops."

"How's that part going?"

"He's having some difficulty but not too much…yet anyway."

"Can you do a blood test or something that tells the extent of the venom in his body?"

"No. There's nothing to do but react to the symptoms."

"And that involves what?"

"I'll let Doctor Petersen take over now. It's now more his game than mine."

Petersen took over. "Since he's already having mild trouble with his respiration, we fit him with a cannula. That's the device with the two tubes hooked to an oxygen machine and the tubes at the other end into the nostrils. After that, a non-rebreather mask, after that a CPAP, and next, the ventilator."

"How's the ventilator work?"

"It can be a life saver, but it has its problems. It requires intubation—"

"And that is…?"

"It means inserting tubes down the patient's throat and literally into his lungs. The patient doesn't breathe anymore. It breathes for the patient, pumps air into the lungs and takes it out again. Odds would still not be all that good for survival, but much better. Lots of complications are possible. Possible longer-term damage from the intubation and the ventilator itself and the extremely powerful sedatives we have to administer for the patient to tolerate the process, sometimes for many days or even weeks."

"Let's avoid that if we can, right?" Harrigan said.

"We will, as long as we can without risking his life…or hypoxic brain damage."

"Brain damage? Holy shit, he's surrounded. Can we do it ourselves…give him artificial respiration? I'd volunteer to do it all day, all night. I'm sure all three of us would…take turns…and there's more people out there."

"That wouldn't do much more than the cannula, the non-rebreather, or the CPAP, maybe not even as much."

"At what point do we know?"

"We should know today or tomorrow whether he'll need to go on the ventilator. Usually, it takes twenty-four to forty-eight hours for the venom to travel all the way through as far as it's going to."

Harrigan looked like a man whose own blood had been poisoned. "Let's try to keep him off that Goddamm thing."

"So," George said, "if I go right out of here and make arrangements to fly to Vietnam or Thailand or wherever and bring that stuff back..."

"It won't get here in time. No possible way."

"Can we see him?"

"When he wakes up. He's sleeping now. Fitfully. But sleeping. Be ready for what you'll see. He's sedated, so he may be groggy. He'll likely be suffering abdominal pain. He's experiencing ptosis, meaning his eyelids are drooping, covering most of his eyes. He may slur his words. His breathing might be labored. He might even gasp."

Upon leaving, Doctor Harmon said, "I'll be turning him over to the ICU, but I'll be staying in touch. You can stay in here instead of the regular waiting room if you want. Feel free to use the phone."

After the doctors left, Sara said, "I have something to tell you," and proceeded to tell the story of Marty Lansing, Golden Monroe, and the tape.

"I'll double up the security here," George said.

Harrigan, shocked, asked, "Should we tell the police?"

George and Sara looked at each other. George said, "What ya think? You were there, I wasn't."

"It's too weird and sketchy...and, I think, too delicate for the police right now. Lansing said he'd destroy the tape. Let's get through this first, one way or the other. O'Keefe probably ought to have a say."

"Let's hope he's around to say it," Harrigan said.

● ● ●

In less than an hour, Doctor Petersen returned. "He's awake now. You can see him, but don't take long and keep him calm. Reassure him."

"Does he know what you told us earlier?"

"Basically. He knows about the venom moving through and the forty-eight-hour window, the progressive paralysis, the possible progression to a ventilator."

The group decided not to ask O'Keefe about the event itself or speculate with him on how a Krait snake came to stake a possessory claim to his dresser drawer. But that was the first thing he asked about.

"No clue," George said. "Just one of your many admirers, I'm sure. We've called the police."

Harrigan said, "Let's get this venom out of you and then we'll worry about all that. But trust…we'll be looking into it in the meantime."

"How you doin', lady?" O'Keefe asked.

Sara could deliver only rapid nods of her head, a forced smile, fighting back tears. She grabbed his right, unburned arm with both of her hands, lightly squeezed it, and turned away so he could not see her face.

O'Keefe said to George and Sara, "Try to make some money while I'm on vacation here."

After they left the room, Harrigan said, "Now the really fun part. I need to call Annie."

He tracked her down at her office and tersely recounted the abbreviated and optimistic version of the story he had carefully prepared and mentally rehearsed, but it still produced the predictable explosion.

"A snake! What the fuck? How does he get himself into these things?"

Harrigan had nothing to say to that. His own reaction when he heard the news was similar to Annie's. These were some of the dues to be paid for having O'Keefe in your life.

But she quickly turned from anger to fear and grief. "I'm coming," she said, trying to suppress her sobs.

"Don't. There's no point. Nothing we can do but wait. At the moment, he's okay. It could get worse, but right now there's no reason to be pessimistic. If things get worse, we'll call you."

"And when do we know for sure?"

"The next twenty hours are supposed to tell the tale."

"But he could die?"

The long pause before he answered, "Highly unlikely," told her all she needed to know.

"I'm coming. School's almost out. I'll pick Kelly up and be there right away."

"You sure that's wise?"

"I couldn't bear it if he died alone."

"He's not alone."

"I mean without seeing his daughter. Or his daughter seeing him."

"I don't know if they'll let her in."

"I'll trust you to take care of that, Big Shot."

• • •

At approximately 4 p.m., O'Keefe's breathing deteriorated further.

Doctor Petersen imparted the news. "We'll be moving to the non-rebreather mask before too long."

"You think it'll get bad enough for the ventilator?" Harrigan asked.

"I truly can't say. It depends on that huge unknown…the amount of venomization."

●   ●   ●

Shortly after Dr. Petersen's visit, Annie and Kelly arrived. Harrigan had prevailed upon Doctor Petersen to allow Kelly a brief visit with her father. When they entered the room, Kelly hurried to one side of the bed, Annie to the other, looked at him and then at each other, failing to disguise their alarm at his pallid complexion, the skin on his neck gone flaccid, drooping eyelids, labored breathing.

When he said, "Hi, kid," he slurred his words.

"Dad," she said, appalled and afraid.

Annie brought her hand to her mouth as if trying to stifle something, but she could not control them, the tears came again and that triggered Kelly's as well.

"It'll be okay," he said, having to catch his breath. "Really. Just trying to stay off the ventilator."

"Screw that. Just stay alive."

"You can't die," Kelly said. "You can't."

"And I won't. Talk to the doctors, they'll tell you."

He tried to indicate with his eyes to Annie that Kelly should be taken out, but his pupils were hardly visible, covered by the sagging eyelids. But she apparently came to the same conclusion on her own. "Kelly," she said, "would you mind leaving us alone for a minute?"

Kelly looked relieved to be going. She kissed him on the cheek and left.

"I'm going to believe you'll be alright," Annie said, "but you've got to stop these insane escapades. Kelly deserves better."

"I swear this is old stuff. Trying to fix past damage. Old sins. If I make it through this, it might be done with."

"I don't know what to do. I'm afraid I'll never see you again."

It was awkward with him lying in the hospital bed, but she tried to hug him. She put her face into his neck and held it there for several seconds. He could feel her breath on her neck. He weakly lifted his injured left arm and flopped it onto her back. She lifted her head and kissed him on the cheek.

"I'll see you tomorrow," she said.

He inhaled shallowly, quickly, three times, his chest heaving, trying to catch his breath.

"And quit resisting," she said. "Let them put you on the ventilator."

Her perfume lingered. A frequently recurring image of her came to him—involuntarily—in a sundress, slightly swishing back and forth as she walked, bare legs and shoulders. He always tried to avoid the troublesome appearance of that image. Once they parted, it was better for him to picture her frowning at him in disapproval.

She had said she was afraid she would never see him again. Surely he would not die here. Yet they said the Krait bite had a high fatality rate even when treated. If they put him on that ventilator…bad sign. Intubation: stuffing a breathing tube down his throat and into his lungs; the ventilator pumping air into him and sucking it back out, itself often causing lung damage; prolonged mechanical breathing causing further problems; the necessary, constant sedation to lighten the pain of the intubation, the tube, the pumping; the intubation process itself, its radical assault on the body, weakening him, sapping his life force. "Eating" through a feeding tube. Unable to speak, locked in, like being buried alive.

His breathing kept slowly getting worse. A nurse came in, wheeling in the crash cart with the non-rebreather, the CPAP, and the ventilator.

The array intimidated him. "What are those?" he asked, though he thought he probably knew.

"We need to put the non-rebreather mask on you now."

"And the other?"

"CPAP next. And getting the ventilator in here and ready just in case we need it."

"But only for just in case?"

"Yes. Just in case."

She came to his bed and began working with the bags and tubes plugged into him.

She noticed the question on his face.

"Giving you a little more sedation."

"Just in case?"

"Just in case. And it can't hurt to reduce the anxiety anyway, right?"

Right. Yes, right. He didn't want to admit it even to himself, and certainly wouldn't tell the medical people until he had reached a state beyond desperation, but breathing was steadily becoming more difficult, the periods of breathlessness increasing in duration in small increments, and toward the end of each period of suspended breathing, he would find himself on the verge of gasping, coming closer and closer to full panic, waiting, in suspense, literally with "bated breath" until that next one could be "caught."

"Before you do the sedation, can you ask my friends to come in again?"

As they came in, each of them gave the breathing devices a long, hostile, fearful look.

246 • ON LONESOME ROADS

"It's getting harder to breathe," he said. "Not sure how long I can stay off the ventilator. If it happens, I won't be able to do anything else, including talk."

He could tell they didn't know what to say, but he was certain each of them knew that phony assurances and insincere optimism would only produce the opposite effect on him.

"The odds are in you favor," Harrigan said. "No shit."

He fixed his gaze on Harrigan. "If I'm going to die anyway, make them pull that bastard out of me and let me say goodbye."

"Fuck you," George said. "You ain't gonna die." He was truly angry but also on the verge of tears, which O'Keefe would have sworn George was incapable of.

"Well fucking stated," Sara said, "I agree with George. We need to get out of here and let you rest. Don't fight it. Let it happen."

She came to him and squeezed his hand.

Harrigan did the same.

"I ain't squeezin' your hand, dipshit," George said. "When you get outta here, I'll slap you upside the head instead. You're such a drama queen."

●　●　●

After they left his room, George took Harrigan aside and said, "I need to get out of here and arrange security for him. Sara too. I don't want to tell her right now though. She might resist. I want it to be a fate accomplished."

"Been brushing up on your French, I see."

George only looked puzzled at that.

●　●　●

He could feel the stronger sedating drug taking effect. He really wouldn't mind drifting off into a sleep-filled haze now and float there until whatever was coming to pass had come and, one way or another, passed. And if it came to it—what Harrigan had once called "The Big Tilt,"—there were many worse ways to die than in this friendly, stuporous haze.

Lay my burden down.

All my trials soon be over.

If he died, what would they all say about him...to themselves... their honest thoughts? Fond of him or not, if honest, they would have to conclude he had been more of a problem than a solution.

Do not go gentle into that good night.

• • •

At 12:15 a.m. they moved from the non-rebreather to the CPAP. Mercifully for everyone, the patient was so groggy from the sedation he didn't protest or even speak, so they didn't have to answer the question the patient would surely have asked though he already knew the answer: "The ventilator is next?"

• • •

Sara had agreed to take the late-night shift that all of them avoided calling by its usual name—the "graveyard shift." When they told her about the CPAP and left the room, she rested her forehead on her arms and sobbed until neither tears nor breath were left to her.

CHAPTER ▶ **26**

SPECIAL REPORT
BULLETS, THEN A BOMB, THEN . . .

By Paschal McKenna

Hovering at death's door had become a dangerous habit for local private detective Peter O'Keefe.

The first time, less than two years ago, that O'Keefe found himself hospitalized on the verge of death was from bullet wounds suffered in a gunfight in the Arizona desert with men identified as members or associates of the local criminal enterprise known as the Outfit. (There was even a corral involved, though not that storied "O.K. Corral" made famous by Wyatt Earp and Doc Holliday in Arizona a century ago.)

Then, only a few months ago, a stream of flame from a car bomb flash-fried the left side of O'Keefe's body.

But the most recent trip to the hospital and to the dark edge of doom arose from the oddest and most unpredictable circumstance of them all: a bite, inflicted by a snake hidden in a dresser drawer in O'Keefe's house.

O'Keefe is not an amateur snake charmer and has never kept a pet snake. It appears that the snake was planted there by an enemy. Moreover, the snake was a quite special one—a Malaysian Krait, one of the deadliest snakes in the world—with venom that by some accounts kills more than half the people it bites.

O'Keefe managed to kill the snake and drive himself to the hospital, snake in hand.

While the hospital declined to comment, citing patient privacy concerns among others, knowledgeable parties attest that the hospital could only stand by and do their best to counteract the havoc caused by the spreading venom. The side effects include creeping paralysis, increasing shortness of breath, and, ultimately, respiratory collapse because the venom-induced paralysis interferes with, and can eventually shut down entirely, the patient's ability to breathe.

In the end, it was the snake itself that dictated the outcome. It turns out that the Krait controls the amount of venom it injects. It could have injected enough to kill O'Keefe, but for some reason couldn't or chose not to.

"They're very shy creatures actually," said Gavin Kokoruda, one of the nation's leading herpetologists (reptile experts). "They usually just want to be left alone. Apparently, it was just a 'leave me alone' bite, not an 'I'm going to kill you' bite."

Another perspective is that, ironically, the pressure garment O'Keefe was still wearing from the bomb-related burns acted as a partial shield, preventing the snake from injecting O'Keefe with a "full load" of venom.

But who put that snake in O'Keefe's dresser drawer? The same people that planted the bomb? As the Herald has reported previously, the bombing attack on O'Keefe has stirred controversy due to the speculation by some that it was a vengeful act of Outfit "payback" for the Arizona incident, a notion that O'Keefe and some others, including in local law enforcement, have mocked as "absurd."

Interviewed at the hospital the day before his scheduled release, O'Keefe refrained from commenting, except to say, "So now we're supposed to believe the Outfit guys are snake charmers? Complete bull-you-know-what. They need to look elsewhere, soon, and thoroughly this time. I don't think I have any more lives to spare."

● ● ●

On the day before his release from the hospital, O'Keefe had several visitors. Annie dropped by, bringing Kelly. "Here we are again," Annie said, "Our annual visit. Three years in a row. It's getting monotonous." She smiled when she said it, but he guessed this had only reaffirmed her decision to leave him behind and get on with her new life with a new man. He did not know what to say. Even a smile didn't seem appropriate.

Annie filled the uncomfortable silence. "I'll leave you two alone. Kelly, I'll meet you out front in thirty minutes."

Kelly wanted to hear all about the snake, the bite, and the poison. Basketball season was over now, so that furnished no conversation. He tried to draw her out on her softball team and its upcoming season, but she seemed indifferent. When she left, at the door she turned to him and said, "You know it'll be coming soon."

Responding to his questioning look, she added, "the announcement," and left without kissing him goodbye.

● ● ●

AGENT ROWLAND AND another FBI agent made their appearance.

"Do you get it yet?" Rowland said.

"Get what?" O'Keefe said.

"Don't play dumb. Your new girlfriend almost got you this time. Unlikely she'll miss a second time."

"Since when does the Mafia try to kill people with snakes?"

"Why wouldn't they evolve just like the rest of nature?"

"You've made a deep study of Darwin, have you? Whoever bombed me also did this, and the bomb wasn't the Outfit either. That was a *federal* crime. Goose your buddies over at ATF or do it yourselves. Tell Mr. Lord to get his grand jury to look at that instead of just parading mobsters in and out of there taking the Fifth."

Rowland looked at his companion and said, "Sounds like the words of a dying man, don't it?"

"If so," O'Keefe said, "I'll make sure the reporters know to knock on your door and ask why you let it happen."

● ● ●

When Detectives Ross and Trowbridge came to see him, he said, "The FBI was here this morning. Surely you won't give me the same line of crap they did…that the Outfit have become snake charmers all of a sudden."

Ross said, "We're looking at it…hard," and stared sternly at Trowbridge, who was looking sheepish and contrite. "And," Ross continued, "the Feds are too, whether they'll admit it to you or not. We're working together. So spare us more newspaper stuff."

"Nothing I can do now, the cat's already out of the bag."

"Well, at least don't set the fucking cat on fire."

Ross looked sharply again at Trowbridge, expecting him to say something. Trowbridge managed to overcome his reluctance to say anything at all to offer ponderously, "Yeah, we're getting some outside help on the bombing materials and re-interviewing your neighbors—"

"And this time," Ross interrupted with a sour glance of disapproval at Trowbridge, "not showing them just David Bowman's mug shot, but photos of Wayne Popper and Marty Lansing and some others."

Trowbridge, looking chastised and penitent, even slightly animated (which, O'Keefe thought made him a lot less ugly), said, "And we're talking to pet shops and exotic animal suppliers and even hired a herpetologist. I thought that was a guy with herpes, but that's the name for a snake specialist."

Ross seemed unamused, but O'Keefe laughed, and said, "Vietnam. Once upon a time, I went to Vietnam. Now *it* came to *me*. Talk about payback. Vietnam just keeps on giving…Look for that, okay? Find out if Marty Lansing or Wayne Popper or any of those Cherry Pink trolls served over there. That's where they could've picked up booby trapping and snake handling too."

"We're trying," Trowbridge said, "to get enough for a search warrant for everything in those two guys' lives, but we don't have *anything*, not one physical item, connecting either of them to the bombing or the snake. If you have something or get something like that, it's what we need."

Trowbridge trying to get me to do his job again.

"What I want to know is how did they get in and out of my house? My alarm was *on* when I got there, I'm sure of it. I turned it off when I got there and back on when I got in the house."

Ross said, "We checked that out. It's really pretty simple. Turns out, if you know what you're up to, you can disconnect that alarm without triggering it and then re-connect when you're done."

"And how does that snake end up in the exact drawer I opened that night?"

"Good guess or just dumb luck. Bad luck for you, good look for whoever put it there. Not surprising if you think about it. Top drawer of a dresser. The most likely one to be opened most often? And anyway, he doesn't much care *when* you open it. You'll open it eventually. If the snake hasn't starved to death by then, it's Ouch! for you, and if the snake has starved to death, so what—one snake dead, no big deal."

As they prepared to leave, Ross said, "How's Rose?"

"I refuse to answer on the grounds that law enforcement personnel may use it as an excuse to continue to lodge their heads up their asses."

"I know you're in denial, but the Outfit could have done that. Would have been a pretty smart thing. Do it in a way that it doesn't look like their work."

As if on cue, after Ross and Trowbridge left, the hospital presented him with a single rose that had arrived without any identification of the sender other than a card in block printing, though with odd, feminine flourishes here and there that he recognized from the small sign she had printed for him in his office that first day to avoid speaking out loud to the much-feared FBI wire: "DON'T BELIEVE IT. DON'T EVEN THINK IT."

Was this sincere or sinister? He felt he had come to know her, not necessarily in the depths of her soul, but deeply enough not to assume the worst of her. If he turned out to be wrong, and survived his error, she would deserve a special place in hell…and he would do his best to place her there.

Sara and George arrived for what amounted to a council of war. Sara told O'Keefe the story she had already told George of Golden Monroe, Marty Lansing, and the tape.

"Is she covered?" O'Keefe asked George, nodding toward Sara.

"I have her stashed best I can, and I put one of our new bodyguards on her twenty-four hours. Hard to make money when I'm using all our people to protect *you two*. Your lousy karma, no pun intended, has rubbed off on Sara now."

"What else?"

"I'm having Marty Lansing watched. Hard to be sure, but it looks like he's slowly and carefully packing up to get out of town."

"And the dancer?"

"Looks like she's still with him."

"We have to get that tape."

"No shit, Sherlock," George said. "But we can't just burglarize his apartment. He's probably got it well hidden by now. Or worse, destroyed the damn thing."

"That would be too stupid. That's his only 'Ticket To Ride.'"

"Or to hell."

"You're awful quiet, lady," O'Keefe said.

She raised her shoulders in a shudder. "That snake was about the last straw for me. I'm afraid to open every door and drawer. I really don't want to go out that way."

"I don't deserve you guys," O'Keefe said.

"We know," George said.

•   •   •

When Ricky Vitale called and said they needed to talk and he was driving out to Cherry Pink right away, Wayne could easily guess what Ricky wanted to discuss. As instructed, he watched from a window in the front of the club, and when Ricky pulled up, he sauntered out to join Ricky in the car.

"It had to be you, right?" Ricky said, eyes wide, bright, and angry.

"Isn't that a song? Is this like that show, 'Name That Tune'?"

"Jesus, Wayne, *we* were supposed to do O'Keefe, not you, remember?"

"I told ya I had somethin' special for the prick. I thought I could save you the trouble and maybe get a rain check…good for a later ballgame. I spent a lotta money smugglin' those snakes in here from Thailand."

"It didn't work, you doofus."

"But it fucked him up pretty good…and it was fun…Bet he shit his pants. And bet there's complications for a long time or forever."

"Fun? And you said 'snakes.' You have more of those fuckin' things?"

"Maybe."

Ricky shuddered. "Get rid of them. That'd be evidence against you."

Wayne grinned. "I'll give it thought. They're damned valuable."

"And you'd better never get any of those fuckin' things anywhere near me. You can't pull this kinda shit. I can't work with somebody who does shit like this."

"Tell you what. I'll do 'em all. Your three and my two. Earn my way into your boys' club."

"You are one fuckin' goofy goon. The deal's off. I'll take care of my own. You take care of O'Keefe yourself. Got that? The deal's off."

Wayne was shocked. "For the Pink too?"

"We'll see about that. That's probably still worth doin' together. But you've gotta straighten up and fly right. I can't take this kinda shit."

"Ain't that a song too?"

"What?"

"'Straighten Up And Fly Right.' The song."

"Yeah, well here's another one, 'Hit The Road, Jack.'"

"'And don't come back no mo'?"

"Get out. Don't call me, I'll call you. Maybe."

Wayne stood on the sidewalk, smiling as big of a cocky and sassy smile as he could call forth, watching Ricky drive away and hoping Ricky was watching in his rearview mirror as Wayne showed him not the slightest hint of regret, just swelled-up-chest pride in his accomplishments. Ricky would be back. The Pink was too big of a prize to pass up. And Wayne knew that he himself also constituted such a prize. Ricky would eventually know him as just the opposite of a "doofus" and a "goofy goon." The snake was just a bit of fun. He would get serious now.

CHAPTER ▶ 27

AT 2:30 A.M. Marty Lansing checked the front part of the club to make sure everyone was gone and the front door locked. He returned to his office, turned out the lights, put on his jacket, grabbed his cigarettes and car keys, and headed for the back door, which led onto an alley with a few parking spots including Marty's. When he opened the door, human shapes lurking in the darkness of the alley moved quickly to him. Brutally strong hands crashed into his chest, pushing him backward into the small hallway. At least two people grabbed him, one on each arm, dragging him, futilely resisting and stumbling, back into the office and flung him down into his chair. One of them smelled of perfume.

A light went on.

"You motherfuckers."

The biggest one, a truncheon in his right hand, planted himself imposingly above him, while the other two, the fucker O'Keefe and the Sara bitch, sat down in the chairs in front of his desk.

He reached for the phone to dial 911.

None of them reacted physically, but O'Keefe said, "You should think hard about what the consequences of that call might be for you."

Marty kept the phone in his hand but looked inquiringly at O'Keefe, waiting for more.

"We're not here to hurt you," O'Keefe said.

"Tell that to Igor here. I think he broke a rib." He nodded his head toward Sara. "And last time I saw this bitch she pulled a gun on me. Thanks for that, by the way, honey. I now carry it everywhere I go."

The receiver in Marty's hand started beeping in protest about being off the hook and nothing else happening to it. He hung it up.

"The tape," O'Keefe said. "All the cops in the world are either sitting on their asses or floundering around in the wrong places. We need that tape to reform their thinking."

"The cops? Really? That's your solution? Fuck you."

"Marty, *your* best thinking is gonna get you dead. We might have a better idea."

"That tape is where nobody but me is ever gonna get it, and if I don't say the right word, it's gonna be erased...automatically. The finger is poised above the button now and all the time. Erased, gone..." He snapped his fingers. "Just like that."

"Bet we could get that 'right word' out of you."

"Goofy assholes that you are, I think you're scared ta go that far. I call that bluff."

"Like I said, 'your best thinking.' Our lives are at stake, Numb Nuts. And you weren't gonna lift one little finger to warn us, you rotten prick."

Marty had nothing to say to that.

"Worse for you, someone else a lot more skilled at it than we are might be having a go at you soon..."

"You gonna tell them about it?"

"Maybe. And for sure we'll tell the cops about it. You don't seem to understand, that one thing leads to another. It's a universal truth."

"That happens, the tape'll be gone, and so will I."

"You think you can really hide from those guys? You think you'd want to live the life you'd have to live to keep those guys from finding you? You don't look like the outdoor, survive-in-the-wilderness type."

Marty looked about to gag.

"What if we could help you negotiate a plea bargain and a witness protection deal?"

"Eat shit and die," Marty said, picked the receiver back up, and dialed 911. O'Keefe casually rose from his chair, grabbed the phone cord and ripped it out of the wall.

"That was just for emphasis," O'Keefe said, "I'm kind of a drama queen, right Igor?"

"Indeed you are," George said.

"And I think you've got a new nickname, *Igor.*"

O'Keefe turned back to Marty who was still holding the useless receiver in his hand. "We're leaving now. We keep our promises. You can rely on us. And we promise you this. If we haven't heard from you by 4 p.m. today, we're goin' to the police and let the chips fall and the shit hit. But if you straighten out your thinking by then and work somethin' out with us, maybe we can all get out of this nasty crack we find ourselves in at the moment."

 On their way out, Marty said to Sara, "You're awful quiet today, Lois Lane. Cat got your gun?"

She fixed him in her gaze, the pupils of her eyes dilated, her irises turning in rapid succession several darker shades of brown, and she said, "You'd better not hurt that girl. She's better than you'll ever deserve. Her only flaw I can see is what she sees in you...Numb Nuts..."

• • •

At O'Keefe's office the rest of the day, each of them, in their separate ways, tried to remain productive while wondering how their fates had come to be lodged in the unclean hands of Marty Lansing. At exactly 3:59 p.m., George and Sara arrived at O'Keefe's office door.

"Nothing, no call, nothing," he said. "But let's not go to the police until tomorrow. Won't hurt to sleep on it."

"Sweet dreams," George said as he and Sara departed.

Karma looked at O'Keefe with the usual question mark on his face.

But five minutes later, George called. "Our guy watching Marty says Marty's on the move. Actually, he's been on the move since around 3:30."

"And your guy's just telling us this now?"

"He had a tough time getting to a phone. I shouldn't have to tell *you* how hard it is to stay on someone's tail."

"Let's hope he's heading here."

Soon, Dagmar came to his door and said, "Sir Dude, there's one of the handsomest guys in the world out in the lobby asking for you. Babes and studs. This place is like a casting agency."

Yeah, Dagmar, but watch out. They're often villains.

"Name?"

"Sorry. Forgot to ask."

"Be careful. If it's who I think it is, he's a rotten sonuvabitch. If he answers to 'Marty Lansing,' bring him back."

And it was Marty Lansing who moments later appeared at the office door, not with his usual cocky air but looking anxious and breathless, and said, "Sorry. Traffic was a bitch. I waited until the last minute. Big decision here."

Two steps into the office Marty noticed Karma and froze. His abrupt stop-motion triggered Karma who jumped to his feet and locked his gaze onto this intruder who was sending all the wrong signals.

"Relax, he won't hurt you…*if* you relax."

O'Keefe gestured toward one of the chairs in front of his desk. "Have a seat."

Marty, the opposite of relaxed, moved slowly to the chair. Once he sat down, Karma returned to his corner.

"You've got a real menagerie. Where's Igor?"

"Down the hall. He's looking forward to meeting you again."

"Keep him in *his* cage. One vicious dog in here is enough."

Marty was recovering some of his smugness. He said, "Hope you haven't called the cops yet."

O'Keefe was tempted to keep the prick in suspense, but it was no time for games. "My hand was on the receiver."

"That receptionist of yours is interesting. A dancer's body."

"Actually, she is one. Not your kind though."

"Too bad."

"Can I bring Sara in?"

"No way. Lois Lane's bad luck."

O'Keefe waited.

"Bet she's a good fuck though, yeah?"

"I wouldn't know."

"Don't bullshit the bullshitter."

O'Keefe wondered if Marty could detect what he was on the verge of doing to him.

Apparently not. "Bet she's the kind who wants ya ta be a little rough."

"You seem to've come here wantin' to get beat up…or…" he gestured toward Karma, "maybe your numb nuts gnawed on some."

Marty seemed to understand that he needed to move on. "Okay, here's where I see things. If I don't give you what you want, you go to the cops, which, at best, causes a lot of trouble for me. At worst…who knows? Which means you've pretty well got me cockblocked. And if you do go to the cops or anything like that, the tape disappears. Which means I've pretty well got you cockblocked."

O'Keefe thought of the word "contretemps," but was afraid to say it—afraid that his French pronunciation would fail and in any event spoil his tough-guy image. And it wasn't quite the right word. After a moment, it occurred to him. "Dogfall…no pun intended."

"I call it mutually assured destruction," Marty said.

"But which one of us is Gorbachev? 'Mr. Gorbachev, tear down this wall.'"

"Nice. Here's my proposal. Actually, it's a demand, a requirement, an ultimatum."

"You're a human thesaurus."

"You go to the cops, the grand jury, the FBI, everybody you need to, and you don't tell them my name or give them anything that amounts to even an obscure hint who I am. And you tell them you know a guy with a tape that they damn well want to listen to because it contains important information about not one but two of their pending investigations. And that guy needs a get-out-of-jail-free card in case anyone thinks *he's* committed some kind of crime along the way and a *guaranteed* witness protection deal to his satisfaction. And, you need to know, and you need to damn sure believe me, I'm not bluffing. If I get a subpoena, or some cop knocks on my door or even calls me on the phone, or I hear they're on their way or even nosing around, or any fucking thing like that, that tape is up in flames, bottom of the river, erased, obliterated."

"I see you're prone to metaphor…and rhetorical, even poetic, repetition."

"Never thought about that."

"You know that would be obstruction of justice, don't you?"

"Tell somebody who gives a shit. I'd rather be in jail than dead… You don't blame me, do you?"

"Not for the repetition compulsion. For the other, I do blame you, because lives are at stake, including Sara's, and that doesn't go with her pay grade."

"Mine's at stake too, and not in my pay grade either."

"But she's not a pornographer, a Svengali, a pimp…"

"I see you can do the repetition thing yourself."

"It's apparently contagious."

"My Goddamm life shouldn't be at stake because you and your lady decided to stick their noses in other people's business. That was your choice, not mine, and you're the one who's exposed her, not me. All I want is a fair trade—my life, for Christ's fucking sake, for the value I created for the risk I took in making that tape."

"A tape you were sitting on even though you knew those people were planning to kill a bunch of other people. And you're still sitting on it. You're a foul piece of shit. You deserve nothing. But like you say, it's a dogfall, mutually assured destruction. So it's a deal. But I'll tell you this. If I keep up my end, and you don't, I might not kill you, I actually don't know, but I'll definitely at least hurt you in a permanent sort of way that you will deeply regret. And even if you keep up your end, if something happens to Sara while you're holding out on this, I will definitely kill you."

"Well, you'd better get your ass in gear then, Partner, Amigo, Pal, Buddy, Compadre, etcetera."

CHAPTER 28

"NEED TO TALK," O'Keefe told Harrigan, "In person. I'm finding out that you just never know who might be listening."

"When?"

"Now. Urgent."

Within thirty minutes, he was sitting in front of Harrigan's desk telling Harrigan the story.

"You seem to've been put on this earth to make my life interesting," Harrigan said.

"You've given me some peak moments yourself."

"This isn't my usual stuff. I need to do some research. I need a day."

"How could it be hard?"

"I don't know. Except I know when you think something's easy, that's when it turns out to be hard."

"Okay, but ASAP, my brother. Not a moment to spare. Who knows where the next snake's hiding?"

Leaving the office, he couldn't help but think about that last look on Harrigan's face, and it troubled him. It had seemed to O'Keefe it would be so simple. *Who said, "the law is an ass"?*

Late the next afternoon, Harrigan called. "Let's meet at that field where you and Karma play ball. I'm getting as paranoid as you."

"Just because I'm paranoid doesn't mean they're not out to get me."

●   ●   ●

He thought he could detect the slightest lilt in the stolid Karma's step and manner when the dog realized he would be playing with the ball for a second time that day. O'Keefe arrived at the empty field before Harrigan. As he threw the ball and watched Karma's long, powerful strides as he galloped after it (*Yeah, just like Rinty*), it occurred to him how exposed he was in this large, open field, how a sniper could from any number of locations easily put a bullet in his brain. So much easier than a snake in a drawer. No way the Outfit did that.

He saw Harrigan's car pull into the lot and park next to the Wagoneer. Harrigan disembarked and made his way across the field, incongruously clad in his Brioni suit and Ferragamo loafers. And when he got close enough, O'Keefe could tell, *Yes, damn it, there's a problem.*

"*Sitz,*" he told Karma, who was waiting impatiently for the next throw. The dog obeyed without hesitation and O'Keefe wondered again if dogs experienced emotions like resentment. Close by was the bench the visiting team would normally occupy. Harrigan led him there, and O'Keefe told Karma to follow. They sat down, Harrigan leaned forward and rested his elbows on his thighs, looked sideways and upward at his taller friend, and said "Not good news. I thought it might be a problem, but I also thought I might find some way around it. Pay close attention, it's complicated."

The first problem, the original sin, so to speak, which tainted everything else, as Harrigan explained in excruciating detail, with references to statutes and citations to case law, Marty Lansing's recording of the conversation was illegal…in fact, a crime…a violation of the U.S. Electronic Surveillance Act.

"You remember Ed Neighbors?" Harrigan said.

"Name's familiar, but not really."

"Local private detective they put away a couple years ago. He represented a husband in a divorce case and bribed a phone company employee to help him tap into the adulterous wife's phone calls."

"So what? This is a little different. Gangsters planning to murder people."

"Doesn't matter. And it gets worse. It's also a crime for anyone who comes to know about the contents of such a tape to disclose any of its contents. That would be this Golden Monroe person, Sara, George, you, and, now, even yours truly here."

"No problem," O'Keefe responded, "I'll only be disclosing to the cops now."

"Yes, problem. The law was mostly directed *at the cops*…protecting the citizens against Big Brother."

"Marty Lansing ain't Big Brother."

"Well, it covers Little Brothers like Marty Lansing too. Basically, unless one of the parties to the conversation consents, nobody can record it except the FBI and then only with a court order."

"Well, the cops'll be able to figure out a way to use that info to take the next steps. And who's gonna prosecute me for that anyway?"

"Russell Lord?"

"Surely not even him."

"It's worse than that. There's two conflicting court cases out there. One says the cops can't even use the information to investigate. Another says they can. But who knows what *this* federal court, that is, our old friend Judge Harlan Montgomery, will decide? The cops could be guilty of the same crime that you've been committing all over town."

"Don't tell me that I have access to a tape where people say they're gonna kill not just me, but Sara too, and I can't go to the authorities to keep them from doing that."

"Even that is technically a crime, but you're trying to do way more than that. You're trying to negotiate a witness protection deal for an anonymous person based on an illegal tape that you don't even know what's on it except some vague shit that a stripper thinks she heard. And the final stake in your heart…Since the tape is illegal, most likely the prosecutor can't use it in court. It's inadmissible as evidence. So what good would it do him to take the risk of doing a blind plea agreement and witness protection deal with an unknown person—a person who's guilty of at least one crime for sure, the taping, and who knows how many others—so they can get their hands on a tape they don't even know the contents of…and even if the contents are definitively incriminating, they can't use it in court anyway?"

They sat in silence for less than a minute, but it seemed longer, until O'Keefe said, "Man, this is real life, not law school shit. Maybe they'll see the law differently than you do, or know of some loophole you don't know about, or can't help themselves wantin' to know what was said, or, God forbid, actually want to keep me, and maybe even the Outfit people they were talking about on that tape, from being killed? Even if they can't use it in court, it's like a smoking gun. It's got to be worth a whole lot. What if they could use it to flip Outfit people involved in it?"

"It's possible. Ya know, they have an obligation, if they hear on a wiretap that some mobster intends to kill another mobster, they have to notify the potential target. But it's a helluva big gamble that they'll see things that way."

"And how about Sara? Surely they'd want to protect her."

"Just give the fucker up."

"I promised I wouldn't."

"You promised? Not to tattle-tale? What the fuck, are we still in grade school?"

"It's not just that. If they come for him, he'll destroy the tape."

O'Keefe looked up and out from the field and the stadium at two tall bluffs and a high-rise apartment building in the distance and thought again of all the places a sniper could fire from. The sniper might miss and hit Harrigan instead. Sara, Harrigan…and how many others…in danger just being near him, a situation that now seemed worse than when he had started all this.

Still staring at the bluffs, he said to no one in particular, "If I don't find another way, I'm gonna have to kill the fuckers myself. Hope I guess right…get the right guys."

● ● ●

"You have to give me more to work with," O'Keefe said, after laying out for Marty some of the legal complexities, dangers, and snares. "I need enough details to have any chance of getting them to take the risk of promising you a deal."

"Fuck all that," Marty said, "I'll be gone out of this town tomorrow and never look back. And the tape'll be gone too. Erased."

"Erasing that tape won't be enough. You know why?"

He left Marty a few seconds to respond. When Marty didn't, he said, "Have you listened to the tape yourself?"

"Of course."

"So you know what's on it."

"Of course."

"Which means you can testify to what's on it. And the only way to erase that is to erase you."

"I thought it was prohibited to disclose to anyone under any circumstances what was on the tape."

"You really think the Outfit will engage in such a complex legal analysis? If you're dead, they have no risk at all."

"They'll have to find me."

"They will. And I'll help them. You won't get out of town without me following you, Numb Nuts. We're both fucked here. Mutually assured destruction. Mr. Gorbachev, tear down this wall."

"I have to think about it. Might have to smoke on it too. Like the Indians used to. Except some better stuff in my pipe."

"When might that interesting decision-making process be complete?"

"Soon."

"Hurry. And by the way, they'll probably kill Golden too."

"Her fault. She should've minded her own business and kept her mouth shut."

"And who said chivalry is dead? You're lower than snake shit. One of these days you'll figure out she probably saved your miserable little wormy life. Hope it won't be too late…for her anyway."

"I'll smoke on that too."

"Hurry."

• • •

Marty called back in a little over two hours, his voice cannabis cool and marijuana mellow. "Is this a clear line?"

"I think so. I'm having it checked daily."

"Well, I won't be sayin' any more than I'm gonna let you tell 'em anyway. Here's what you can say. The tape contains admissions about unsolved crimes already committed and a plan to kill people in the future, and the Outfit is definitely involved."

"And 'the people' to be killed include me?"

"Yeah. It's sort of a trade. The Outfit kills you and the other guy returns the favor."

"What's the 'favor'?"

"That's all you get for now."

"And Sara?"

"The Outfit said they'd think about it."

O'Keefe frowned, squinted in concentration, and said, "Who is 'they'?"

"They?"

"The 'they' in the Outfit. Don't play the dunce. Marcone, Sorvino, Vitale…Sciorra… Jagoda. Who is 'they'?"

"For now that's for me to know and the rest of you to find out."

The thing most on his mind when he hung up was the word "they." Maybe the FBI hadn't been lying. Maybe Rose intended to kill him after all.

CHAPTER 29

AS O'KEEFE EXPECTED, Max Trainer and FBI Agent Rowland had gathered in Lord's office for the meeting.

"Well, Mr. O'Keefe," Lord said, "have you seen the light, so to speak?"

"Got religion?" Trainer added.

"Come to your senses?" said Rowland.

"You guys are a regular barber shop trio. I've got something better than that."

Trainer said, "But, first, I want to know if you've brought your pungi to play for us."

Once the long silence made clear that nobody understood him, Max said, "I am so disappointed you don't know. A pungi is the flute-like instrument that snake charmers use to soothe the cobras."

O'Keefe laughed a little bit, Lord and Rowland not at all. *Maybe they don't appreciate the implication that they're snakes.*

"Before we go on," Lord said, "we don't suspect you of any crime, at least up to now, at least that we know of, so we're not going to read you your Miranda rights, but I do feel the obligation to ask whether you've consulted with a lawyer about your situation?"

"I have."

Lord's eyebrows raised. "And…?"

"That's all I intend to say about that."

The trio looked at each other, each seeming to be waiting for one of the others to speak, which turned out to be Lord. "Alright. We'll honor that. Proceed."

O'Keefe proceeded. He had carefully prepared his speech, even written it out and rehearsed it out loud to himself several times. He wanted to avoid any detail that would make it too easy for them to go on their own fishing expedition and start issuing subpoenas to everyone they could think of. They listened, not interrupting once. When he stopped, Lord said, "Would you mind stepping out of the room while we confer on this?"

Pacing in the long, wide, high-ceiling corridor outside of Lord's office suite, he thought that it seemed to have gone as well as he could have expected. He detected nothing scoffing in their manner or even skeptical. But they were leaving him out there pacing for a longer time than he had expected they would, and almost half an hour passed before they summoned him.

Max Trainer did the talking now, as if they had chosen for their spokesman the one of them O'Keefe would be most likely to trust.

"You have not listened to the tape yourself, correct?"

"Correct."

"And you have not even set your eyes on the tape?"

"I haven't."

O'Keefe was quickly coming to understand that this was not going well.

"You say you consulted a lawyer about this. So are you aware that the alleged tape was illegally recorded and that the person who taped it violated federal law in doing so?"

"So what?"

"And are you aware that even telling the little you have told to us about what's on that tape is a crime?"

"They're trying to kill me, Max."

"And are you aware that we ourselves may be civilly and even criminally liable if we pass on this information to anyone outside of this room?"

"Cut the shit, Max. The Outfit's gonna sue you? And who exactly is it that's gonna prosecute U.S. Attorneys and FBI agents for that?"

Lord intervened at that point. "Mr. O'Keefe, the Justice Department and the FBI can't just pick and choose the laws we do and don't want to obey."

"Tell that to the Black Panthers and Jean Seberg and the antiwar people."

Lord reeled backward and straightened his posture, ready to continue the argument, but Max quickly resumed.

"*And, finally,* are you aware that it is highly likely that what was said on that tape will be inadmissible in any trial of the participants in that conversation or anyone else?"

"Please just get to whatever your point is."

"And you won't identify who it is that recorded the conversation and has control of the tape. Yet you want the government to agree to a very generous plea bargain and witness protection deal for whoever this person is."

"I can represent that the person is not associated with the Outfit, has no prior criminal record of any kind, has no knowledge that he has committed any crime other than recording that conversation, which he didn't know was a crime when he committed it."

Lord had been fidgeting, growing impatient with the banter, and now interrupted. "But this is simple. You just need to tell us who your informant is. We'll subpoena him, and he'll have to turn over the tape."

"Didn't you hear me? He's promised, if you come for him, he'll erase or destroy it."

"Well, there you go. We've already made some progress. We now know your informant's gender."

O'Keefe cursed himself for that slip.

"As we said, the tape doesn't do us that much good. Destroy it or not, he'll have to tell us what was said on it and by whom."

"I thought Max said it would be a crime for him to do that, just like me here."

"You need to just leave that to us."

"One final problem."

"Which is…?"

"I'm not gonna tell you."

"Then, unfortunately, for you anyway, we'll be forced to put you under subpoena and require you to tell us. *Poena*. In case you don't know, that's Latin for 'pain'…in this case, the pain is jail for contempt."

"I'll just take the Fifth like everybody else does in front of your grand jury."

"And we'll agree nothing you say will be used to prosecute you for any crime, which will put you back in the trick bag, and you'll still have to answer the question."

"So, you don't care that a tape exists that might identify people who are trying to kill me, and if you don't care much for me, some other people as well, some of whom may admittedly be even worse that I am, but at least one of which is my colleague Sara?"

"We care a great deal, but we have other responsibilities—for example, not entering blindly into plea bargains and witness protection deals without having full knowledge of the situation, including, for example, the small matter of the identity of the alleged witness."

"That's worth a life? Or maybe several lives?"

"Those lives are in *your* hands. Tell us who your source is and let us do the rest."

"Did you not hear me? He'll destroy the tape."

"So be it. It's not that valuable anyway, as we've told you, since it's inadmissible. But this person might be persuaded to tell us who the people on that tape are and what they said. You're the one keeping us from getting that information."

O'Keefe stood up to leave.

"Before you go, we do now need to read you your rights since you've already committed a crime and confessed to it right here in this room."

And they proceeded to advise him to remain silent, that anything he said could be used against him in a court of law, that he had the right to an attorney, and that if any could not afford an attorney, one would be provided to him.

"There are no words," he said, and left the room.

●　　●　　●

The next day the U.S. Marshal's office called him to arrange peaceful service of the subpoena summoning him to appear before the grand jury two days later. He had thought about skipping town to avoid it but knew that would only postpone the inevitable while a reckoning might be fast approaching for him, and Sara, and the Outfit targets including, possibly, Rose.

Yes, the law could be an ass, certainly so in this instance. Screw all the cops, lawyers, grand juries, subpoenas, and judges. It was time to bring another, near-equal power into play.

●　　●　　●

O'Keefe thought he detected a flicker of mischievous amusement in Max Trainer's eyes as if Max anticipated with pleasure whatever might be about to happen no matter the outcome. Russell Lord's demeanor was decidedly different, more like a man locked into the third day of simultaneous acute episodes of acid reflux and constipation. No pleasantries were exchanged. Lord and Trainer knew this could not be good news. O'Keefe and his two companions, Oswald Malone and Paschal McKenna, had agreed that the companions, not O'Keefe, would do most, if not all, of the talking today. All sat down and waited for Lord to speak.

With the look of a condemned man appointed to preside over his own hanging, Lord said, "It's your meeting. Proceed."

Oswald cleared his throat. "Pete has come to us with a tale that I can only describe, with considerable *understatement*, as…harrowing. We have, after careful consideration, concluded that our duty to the public requires us to publish the story…"

Lord interrupted: "Would you intend to disclose the contents of that tape? I should say the *alleged* contents of the *alleged* tape?"

"We don't see how we could avoid that."

"Then your newspaper, and the journalists, and everyone down and up the chain, including Bruce Nelson if he knows about it and allows it to happen, would be committing a crime. There's no exception in the statute for journalists."

"There's a good possibility there's a murder plot in the works. It may be unfolding, even consummating, as we sit here. We don't see how we can stand by and take the chance of that happening without sending… actually, shouting…a warning. The public is entitled to know."

"Does Bruce know about this? Maybe I should call him."

"We have also consulted our lawyers. At length. And have gone even further. We've talked to the nation's experts on our free speech rights under the First Amendment. We are advised that the

Constitution almost certainly trumps anything in the statute that would prevent our publication of this item."

"*'Almost'*…That's the key word. Pretty big risk to take based on a weasel word like that. Those 'experts' have been wrong before. Wonder how Bruce would like to spend some time behind bars? He might not appreciate the journalists who put him there, might not ever even want to lay eyes on them again."

"Frankly, we don't think you would prosecute anyway. Jailing a bunch of journalists for *'committing'* a public service? You would, to coin a phrase, 'live in infamy.' We think you should do the opposite. If you don't believe *you* can do the right thing here, you should *encourage* us to publish."

Looking at Paschal, Lord said, "I guess this is what happens when a newspaper starts hiring jailbirds."

O'Keefe saw the anger flare in Paschal's eyes and Oswald's pupils almost imperceptibly shift to the corners of his eye sockets, toward Paschal, and Oswald flinched slightly, expecting an explosion. But Paschal let it go.

Oswald seized the floor again. "Of course we understand the U.S. Attorney's concerns and will try our best not to portray the office in a bad light, but the facts might themselves unavoidably paint that very picture."

"When do you plan to publish?"

"Tonight."

"Give us one day."

It seemed Oswald expected that. "We can do that, but I have been advised, again by our legal experts, to insist, in exchange, that, during that delay, you agree not to seek an injunction against the publication of the story."

"I could go get an injunction right now. You know Judge Montgomery doesn't like that kind of publicity."

"Of course you're free to do that, but you'd better hurry. As they say, the 'presses are rolling.'"

Lord clearly understood he was cornered now. "Alright. We won't go today."

"I have to insist that you not 'go,' as you say, for an injunction until this time tomorrow, so the paper will not be prejudiced, timing-wise, in any way by agreeing to the postponement."

"Is that all?"

"Only to say that we are really sorry this situation has developed. We only want the best relations with your office. But our duty to the public sometimes outweighs that."

"What you *are* is, to coin a phrase as *you* say, a bunch of sanctimonious, phony fucking assholes."

● ● ●

"Checkmate," Trainer said to Lord after the door closed behind the departing trio.

"Well," Lord replied, "we played it as far as we could. I didn't like our position. Actually, I'm looking forward to finding out what's on that tape."

"What about our own exposure? What can we do with the damn thing?"

"I read the cases. Like Harrigan told O'Keefe, they conflict. But I think Judge Montgomery will agree with us."

"And if he doesn't?"

"I think we should just go see him and make sure."

"*Ex parte* communication?"

"There's no adversary. Not yet anyway. I don't think he'll stand on that particular ceremony, especially given the stakes here."

After a silence, as the two men mentally studied the possible maneuvers on the chessboard in front of them, Lord said, "That peckerwood O'Keefe pisses me off. He's the living embodiment of the phrase, 'better lucky than good.' I just hope somebody doesn't kill him before I get my hands on him."

● ● ●

Outside, on the Courthouse steps, O'Keefe said, "Oswald, you're one studly dude."

"Before you spread my legend too far, I'll disclose that"—raising his eyebrows in a gesture of sly self-mockery—"to coin another phrase and as they say in the movies, I came close to shitting myself in there."

"And who's Bruce Nelson?"

"Merely the publisher and owner of the newspaper."

"Good that you talked to him beforehand. Lord's probably calling him right now."

"Actually, I didn't. You've heard the saying, 'Better to ask forgiveness than permission'? I'd better get going and catch him before Lord does."

Paschal said nothing, but he nodded at O'Keefe and smiled, then hurried to follow Oswald down the majestic stone steps of the Hall of Justice.

CHAPTER ▶ 30

APPARENTLY REALIZING THAT a fistful of murders could be imminent and they might look very bad if they failed to make at least some effort to thwart them, once Lord committed to the deal, the U.S. Attorney's Office and other government functionaries caught fire.

The *Herald* agreed to hold off on any publication, subject to Lord's oral agreement that the paper would be fully informed of all future developments in real time on an exclusive basis.

The only threat to a deal turned out to be Marty Lansing. First, Marty wanted more assurances than O'Keefe and LeClair could give him that the government would not back out of the deal. Then he insisted on approving his relocation city. "I want it warm," he said, "no Minnesota or North Dakota shit. And no place where the Puritans are in charge. I might want to get back in the pussy business."

O'Keefe could not blame him for negotiating those points, but after Marty tried to extract subsistence payments in an amount and over a guaranteed time period in excess of any that the Marshal's Service had ever agreed to, O'Keefe lost patience. "Marty, if you don't stop this shit, I'm just gonna tell them who you are. Fuck the tape and fuck you."

•   •   •

After the final signatures had been obtained from the government, and the time to deliver the tape had arrived, O'Keefe told Marty, "I get to listen to this bastard first. I earned it."

Marty brought the tape to O'Keefe's office and a copy for O'Keefe to keep. "Volume's got to be way up," he said, "and you need to prick up your ears. You know the conference table in my office? That's where they were sitting, and the tape was attached just under the tabletop."

"Who'll be talking?"

"Vitale and Popper. Vitale starts the conversation. You'll be able to tell the rest of the way. Wayne's the idiot."

Marty hit the play button.

Voice 1: Yeah, this is a lot better than out there. Quite an office he's got here. In a titty bar, for Christ's sake.

Voice 2: Yeah, he thinks he's hot shit.

Voice 1: He seems good though. We should keep him on, at least for a while, at least until we get rid of the investors. He'd be good help with that.

Voice 2: Nah. He's a fuckin' weenie. I can do what he does easy and better.

Voice 1: So here's the deal. You got somebody you want rid of, this O'Keefe turkey, right?

Voice 2: Yeah. And that bitch of his too.

Voice 1: And I've got a similar situation. But no way I can do it myself. Nobody can think I was anywhere near it.

Voice 2: I'm your man.

Voice 1: You're pretty cocky, but what's your experience with this kind of thing? This isn't beatin' up little kids on the corner for their lunch money.

Voice 2: You remember a guy named Slater…Vern Slater?…No?… He was the head of a local motorcycle gang. He tried to muscle in on us here at the Pink. He went off a bluff on his motorcycle. With a little assistance.

Voice 1: I think I do remember that.

Voice 2: There's others. O'Keefe's trailer trash slut, Beverly, that was tryin' ta blackmail Jerry Jensen. Overdose. Everybody thought that was David Bowman. I've done more than one of those. And I did the O'Keefe thing too, the first one.

Voice 1: The bomb?

Voice 2: Yep.

Voice 1: That wasn't such a good job.

Voice 2: Not my fault. Bowman wanted to do it cheap and in a hurry. Mistake.

Voice 1: Jesus, you got quite the history there.

Voice 2: There's more. Another cunt. Cheated on me. Overdose. And one more guy besides those. Knife. Seventeen stab wounds. Dumped him in an alley. Cold, cold case.

Voice 1: The women…that didn't bother you?

Voice 2: Why would it bother me?

Voice 1: Might be a woman involved in my situation…

Voice 2: No sweat. Let me guess. Those guys today?

Voice 1: Just one. The young one. Marcone. The other one, Sorvino, only if he's stupid enough to get in the way. I thought maybe you could invite the young one out here…maybe tell him you don't want to do business with me, just him…he'd like that. Somewhere on his way here or on his way back…he disappears.

Voice 2: And why wouldn't I have every guy in the Outfit out for me then?

Voice 1: Let's see…I can think of at least three reasons. One, we'll figure out how to make it look like somebody other than you did it. Not hard. Second, he's not that popular. A lot of people think he doesn't deserve his good fortune. They won't be anxious to avenge. Third, because then I'll be in a position to keep that from happenin', Baby!

Voice 2: And I can guess the woman is the Jagoda woman…

There was a long silence except for the clink of ice cubes in glasses, after which—

Voice 2 (resuming): Maybe she'd come out here with the other guy. Two-in-one there.

Another lengthy silence.

Voice 2 (resuming): If not, that one could be at her house. A burglary and rape that got out of hand.

Another silence.

Voice 2 (resuming): I've got a woman on my list too. That Sara Slade slut that works for O'Keefe.

Voice 1: Lots of people think O'Keefe's days are numbered anyway. They won't be surprised. They'll never think it was you. They'll think it was…maybe the very people we were just talkin' about. That would be nice. I'll think about it, but I don't think we can risk doin' the Slade woman. Too much heat.

Voice 2: I'd just as soon do her myself anyway…same as the Jagoda woman.

Voice 1: Better if we just do O'Keefe. You do the other.

Voice 2: All I want is *in*. I'd kill 'em all for that.

Voice 1: You know that thing we've got about bein' Italian.

A long pause. More ice clinking.

Voice 1 (resuming): But you could be right near the top anyway.

Voice 2: I understand.

Voice 1: But let's not forget what we talked about here today. We'll dump your investors and move this along just the way Marty said.

Voice 2: And on this, Italian or not, I'm equal. I brought you in on this. I've gotta be equal.

Voice 1: Absolutely. And that's the future. But are you sure we don't need Marty to make this work, right?

Voice 2: I'm sure. In fact, I insist on it. He's as good as gone already.

Voice 1: Alright, let's get this done.

Voice 2: Consider it done.

Marty turned off the tape.

O'Keefe, in angry exasperation, said, "You told me '*they*' from the Outfit were gonna kill me. What 'they'? Who was 'they'? There's no 'they' here. That was one Outfit guy. Just Vitale, nobody else. The '*they*' are the ones Vitale wants killed, Paul Marcone… and maybe Rose."

"Just a figure of speech. 'They.' No big deal."

O'Keefe's mind unfolded through three stages of rage-red, each deeper and darker than the last. Marty must have read it in O'Keefe's face. He flinched. Lucky for him. It satisfied O'Keefe that Marty apparently sensed the extent of the violence that O'Keefe wished to inflict on him, enabling O'Keefe to restrain himself this time. *Maybe later. This guy is in desperate need of reformation.*

● ● ●

Donald Praeger called shortly after Rose returned home from dropping the children at school.

"We need to talk."

"When?"

"Right away. My office. When can you get here?"

"An hour or so. What's up?"

"Please come. Hurry. I can't talk about it on the phone."

Driving downtown to meet the lawyer, her mind ran wild with fear. Maybe they were arresting her, maybe negotiating her surrender with

Donald. Maybe the next time she would see her children would be after they had perp-walked her before the cameras...or even from a jail cell.

•   •   •

Rose would have been even more anxious if she had known that she was the lead car in a small procession—two FBI agents, one in a telephone company panel truck and the other in a slightly rusty and dented-up pickup truck...and Wayne Popper in his new, super-souped 1987 red Mustang GT. Since he was not on any FBI radar at that point, neither agent took any special notice of Wayne Popper and his red Mustang.

What nobody other than Ricky Vitale and Wayne Popper knew now was that Vitale had dropped out of the conspiracy and what nobody other than Wayne Popper knew now was that he had vowed to himself that he would do his best to earn his way into the Sicilian bad boys' club by killing every one of the lucky five. He had already done the snake trick on O'Keefe. It hadn't worked but was fun anyway. Now he intended to go after the ones he conceived to be the most vulnerable, the bitches. He looked for Sara first, not knowing that George had her well hid. He gave up on that pretty quick. He needed not to be wasting time, needed to move along. From what he had seen, he had a slight preference for Rose anyway.

Wayne figured there was no downside in following her close, a target of opportunity, ready to be pounced upon whenever an occasion provided itself. Actually, this was a pretty opportune pounce occasion right here since at this moment they were the only two people on the parking level she had chosen. But before he could gather wits enough to take some action, she screeched into an empty parking spot, jumped out of her car, and scooted into the elevator.

He parked as close as he could get to her car, five spaces away, and sat there, waiting for an opportunity to occupy a space even closer to hers, occasionally turning on his car to listen to music but mostly ruminating about how exactly he would approach her and what he would do to her and how he would do it once he had her disabled and helpless.

• • •

When she arrived, Donald came to the lobby to meet her, something she could not recall him ever doing before. He looked flushed, nervous, and his eyes failed to meet hers.

"Donald," she whispered, "what the hell is it?"

"Conference room," he said, and led her down a short hallway. As he opened the door to the darkened conference room for her, he said, "I'm sorry about this, Rose. I had no choice."

Rose started to ask him what he meant, but he had quickly shut the door behind her, leaving her alone with the answer to her question, who stood in the shadows at the other end of the long conference table.

"Lock the door, Rose."

"Paul," she said uncertainly.

"Lock the door."

She obeyed.

"What you been up to, Rose?"

He moved around the table, advancing slowly on her. She wondered if she should try to unlock the door and run, but she held steady.

"Keeping secrets, are you, Rose?"

She still did not respond.

He moved into her, grabbed her by the throat.

"Peter O'Keefe? Are you fucking Peter O'Keefe?"

She would have laughed if she still had enough breath to laugh. She gripped his wrist and lightly pressed him to remove his hand from her throat so she could speak. He loosened his grip but kept his hand there.

"No, I have not been fucking him. Or anyone else. Jesus, is that all you men care about?"

"I do care about that," he said, then raising his voice above his usual deadpan delivery, and infusing it with unmistakable cold rage, "but what I also care about is the FBI and the U.S. Attorney's Office and the grand jury knowing what you're doing before I do. We're supposed to be partners."

She knew she needed to do something to de-escalate this, keep him from maybe doing to her what he had done to her husband.

"Can we sit down?"

He released her. She sat down and waited for him to sit down next to her. At first she was afraid he would remain standing, but he did finally sit down, right next to her, uncomfortably close, a hostile hovering. She forced herself to look directly into his eyes—dark, deep, inscrutable. She explained to him why their "partnership" was not working, why she needed to escape for her children's sake, how O'Keefe's approach—

"What an idiot," he interrupted. "Like we could give a shit about him. Until now anyway."

"What's that mean?"

"Go on."

"However idiotic," she said, "it opened up a way for me to explore some things, arrange some things, before I came to you—"

"You should've come to me first."

"I don't think so. And you're proving that now."

"You should've come to me first." That voice raised in that cold rage again, almost a weapon in itself.

She needed to retreat.

"If I made a mistake about that, I apologize. But this is good for you. Isolated as I am, I've heard enough to know this 'partnership' isn't going well. It's hurting you, making you weaker than you ought to be now."

His posture straightened defensively.

"And," she hurried on, "you'll be a lot richer. You won't have to split with me."

"Maybe I don't care about that."

"A lot more rewards for you to give out. That's important."

"But maybe I don't care about any of that. Maybe I care about something else."

It took a moment, but she came to understand what he meant. *Aegisthus.* "No way. We can't. Not on top of his grave. We can't."

"He was a traitor…a thief. How could he have done worse to you than he did?"

"But I got my vengeance. You got it for me."

"I had no choice…given what he was doing…not the faggot thing…but the stealing…what he was planning—"

"But I didn't have to help you. I didn't have to revel in it. And it turns out there's a price to pay for that."

He looked away from her. She could no longer read his face, if she could ever read his face.

"I'm a mother. The only thing left to me now is my children. My children whose father I helped murder. My children whose mother is being hunted down by the police and may end up in prison. We can't be fucking on his grave, no matter what he did. If that's a capital crime, you'll have to go on and kill me."

He still did not look back at her. She knew that she had finally said the right thing to him…put it in the bluntest, starkest terms. "And speaking of killing, you know that I'm a weak link…or everyone on both sides of this thinks I'm a weak link. The Feds will press and press and squeeze and squeeze…What happens then? What do you do about me then?"

He said nothing, kept looking away.

"What's it to be then?"

It seemed he was not going to answer.

Finally, she said, "Talk to Vince. Please talk to Vince."

Still he said nothing.

"Can I go now?"

Still, he said nothing.

She stood, unlocked the door, and left him alone in the room.

As she hurried down the hallway and through the reception room, the receptionist, startled by Rose's sudden presence, blurted, "Ms. Sciorra, Mr. Praeger would like to see you before you leave."

Hurrying on, not even looking back at the receptionist, she said, "Tell him I said to go fuck himself."

• • •

Although there had been almost no activity on this level of the garage, the more he thought about it, the more he thought that grabbing her here in the garage didn't seem like any fun at all. She looked like the type that would put up a fight, might even scream. He wouldn't be able to achieve all he wanted there in the parking lot, especially given the possibility of some fool spoiler eyewitness stumbling into the midst of the festivities. One possibility was grabbing her and throwing her into the trunk of her own car and driving off with it. But, obviously, even though any chance might be the only chance and one should take his pleasures as they came and not look a gift horse in the mouth, catching her at night in her house would be so much better.

As he was contemplating whether or not to pass on this opportunity, the opportunity passed on him. She hustled out of the elevator and right to her car. He had expected her to be gone for a lot longer. By the time he understood what was happening, it was too late. But as her van backed out at speed, tires squealing when she hit the brakes and again when she accelerated forward, as if the vehicle itself were angry, he thought, *Good. Better. Best. Much for the best.* At night in her house, hopefully that very night, as he flipped on the light switch in her bedroom and she sat up, her grogginess and confusion rapidly turning to terror, he might put his finger to his lips and say, "Shh! Don't wake the kids…or I'll have to kill them too."

CHAPTER 31

O'KEEFE PLAYED THE tape for Sara.

After it finished, he said, "I'm sorry I got you into all this."

"Forget it. Not your fault. Does the FBI have this now?"

"Yes. The police too. I gave a copy to Ross."

"Apparently every one of those was a crime you committed. And Golden was a criminal for telling me, and I'm a criminal for telling George and you. Screw Marty. We're the ones who need witness protection."

• • •

When he called Rose, she seized the agenda immediately.

"We need to talk. Right away. I have news. It didn't go so well with Paul."

"I have news too. I'll be there as soon as I can."

When in the fading twilight he pulled into her driveway, he didn't have to honk. Her front door opened and she hurried out to join him in the Jeep.

"Kids don't need to hear this," she said in explanation.

He played the tape for her.

"Jesus," she said, "Vitale. What a piece of shit."

"Looks like you're gonna have to hit the mattresses...and not for the fun stuff."

292 • ON LONESOME ROADS

"I have to tell Paul and Vince. Can we play the tape for them?"

"Yeah, but maybe you shouldn't be involved in that." He explained to her that she would be committing a crime. "I've now committed the same crime so many times another one can't matter. But no reason for you to expose yourself. Russ Lord would love that. And I'd like to meet with those two guys face to face anyway."

"I don't know if that's such a good idea. Here's my news."

She told him about her meeting with Marcone.

"What's Sorvino know?"

"I told him everything. "

"Where's he stand?"

"He knows putting me where they did was a mistake. He apologized. Said he would try to bring Paul around."

"Arrange the meeting. My office. Tomorrow. No time to spare."

As they talked, they noticed headlights moving down the street toward them. Both tensed up and said nothing further, O'Keefe looking in the rearview mirror, Rose turning slightly sideways, each attending to the black car that moved slowly past them and moseyed on until out of sight.

●   ●   ●

He had borrowed the black car from one of the dancers (not that she had any real choice in the matter) for scouting Rose's place, his burglary tools in the seat beside him. Wagoneer in the driveway! What the fuck! O'Keefe! He must be banging her. The rotten sonuvabitch. That dirty whore. Although he had never heard the word "cuckold," and wouldn't have known what it meant if he had, Wayne was experiencing all the outraged feelings of a betrayed husband.

He would make both of them pay for this.

● ● ●

More excitement for Dagmar as two swarthy men in dark suits and trench coats showed up trailing clouds of dread as they came, and said they were "here to see O'Keefe." She could barely croak a request that they give her their names. She made her way back to O'Keefe's office and told him a Mr. Marcone and a Mr. Sorvino had come to see him.

"Send them back," he said, his jaw tight and face more serious than she recalled ever seeing him before.

As he waited for them, he opened the top drawer on the right of his desk where he kept a pistol and left it open, then stood up to greet them.

When they saw Karma, they stopped, frozen in place.

"He's peaceful as long as you are," O'Keefe said.

"He'd better be," Sorvino said, "or I'll blow his fuckin' head off."

Keeping his eye on the dog, Sorvino, said, "We understand you have some information for us."

"I do."

Looking up at the ceiling and around the walls, Sorvino said, "Are we alone?"

"As far as I know, and I have it checked every day."

But he could tell they didn't trust him. There would not be many words said in this meeting other than on the tape he would be playing for them, which was already loaded in a small cassette player on his desk. He motioned for them to sit in the chairs in front of his desk, which they did, keeping their coats on.

"Ready?"

He discerned a twitch or two of facial muscles he interpreted to be as close to gestures of affirmation as he was likely to receive.

Listening to the tape, they neither talked nor moved except for occasional knowing glances and stern frowns directed at each other.

When it finished, Sorvino said, "Is there an extra? Can we have a copy?"

"Sorry, no. The tape was recorded illegally. It was a crime for me even to tell you about it, let alone play it for you. And if Russell Lord found out I told you two in particular what's in it, or God forbid, *played* it for you, he really might indict me."

Sorvino accepted that, even seemed impressed.

"And," O'Keefe continued, "I don't want to make it worse by handing copies out. And you have the same problem by the way. You can't disclose the contents to anyone else."

"Well, we sure wouldn't want to engage in any unlawful activities," Sorvino said. His face didn't change, remaining deadpan, but O'Keefe thought he detected the shadow of a smile lurking there somewhere, and Marcone even chuckled, the first clear indication that he was other than a statue.

"Then please play it one more time," Sorvino said.

O'Keefe played the tape again.

At the end, Sorvino said "*Regalu*" to Marcone, who blinked slightly faster than he had previously.

Noticing O'Keefe's incomprehension, Sorvino said, "*Regalu*. A gift. Thank you."

The two men stood up to leave.

"Can I walk you down?" O'Keefe asked.

"We need to make sure you're not wired," Sorvino said, gesturing that O'Keefe should stand up and come around the desk. When he did, Karma stood up and growled.

"*Ruhig*," O'Keefe commanded.

Karma stopped growling.

"*Platz.*"

Karma laid down.

"*Steh.*"

"It's okay," O'Keefe said. "You can do it now."

"Rather go out in the hallway," Sorvino said.

In the hallway Sorvino said, "And close that door, okay?"

Sorvino took the front and Marcone the back, and they gave him a thorough going over. Unlike Rose before them, they showed no tenderness to his wounded areas. O'Keefe thought Marcone especially handled him rougher than necessary.

On the sidewalk O'Keefe said, "They talked about killing Rose on that tape. I assume you'll protect her?"

Marcone scowled. Vince said, "Of course. As soon as we leave here."

"Did she tell you what *I'm* looking for?"

Sorvino said, "Any debt you owe is repaid...any sin remitted... Right, Paulie?"

Marcone nodded and said, a bit grudgingly O'Keefe thought, "What we know about anyway."

They turned and walked toward the parking lot and into the gathering dark.

That would have to do.

● ● ●

No Wagoneer in the driveway this time. This was it. Tonight. He would drive to a diner out by the highway and have dinner...slowly, taking his time...dessert and coffee too...until the kids would've been in bed for a while and sound asleep...then return, park in a good place he had found close by her house...

● ● ●

O'Keefe called Paschal. "Anything new?"

"Yeah," Paschal said. "They're splitting the investigation and any ultimate prosecution between the Feds and the local guys. The Feds will handle whatever conspiracy to murder and related RICO charges they might be able to tag Vitale with from the stuff revealed on that tape. They can't use the tape itself in any prosecution but hope they can find an angle to leverage it, ya know, to put even more pressure on Vitale than they're already doing."

"And all the rest of it: Beverly, the dancer, the bombing, the snake?"

"All local. So Popper will be all local except for the conspiracy with Vitale."

"That might be better, actually."

O'Keefe hung up and called Lieutenant Ross.

"I thought you were my keeper, my guardian, my buddy."

"So what is it now?" Ross said, his exasperation unmistakable.

"I heard about your arrangement with the Feds."

"First thing, it's not my deal. I'm not in charge of the investigation."

"But you surely know what's goin' on."

"Probably."

Ross confirmed what Paschal had said about the division of responsibilities between the two enforcement authorities.

"So the police aren't investigating or even keeping their eye on Vitale, that's all Feds?"

"Yeah."

"You know what they're doing?"

"No. The Feds' idea of communication is one-way. With them, it's a 'hooray and fuck you deal.' 'Hooray for them and fuck you.'"

"So you don't know whether the Feds have someone on Vitale twenty-four-seven?"

"Don't know. But you can bet Vitale won't do somethin' like that himself. He'll have someone else do it."

"Based on the tape, Vitale's the one supposed to be comin' after me."

"You think Vitale did the snake?"

"Not a chance."

"The snake happened *after* that meeting."

"And Vitale acted on the tape like he wouldn't agree to Sara. That would leave her to Popper."

"He's definitely a rambunctious little bastard. Looks like he's wantin' ta do everybody."

"Do you guys have someone on Popper twenty-four-seven?"

"No."

"So what's next?"

O'Keefe chose not to interrupt the ensuing silence. He knew that Ross was deciding whether and how much to tell him.

Finally, Ross said, "They're getting a warrant ready to search Popper's apartment and the club. Keep this to yourself. If you pass this or anything else I tell you to McKenna or Malone or any other reporter, or anybody else for that matter, not only will you never get anything else from me, but I'll find a way to do you harm."

"Ya know, you're like havin' a real nasty prick of a big brother."

"Exactly what you need, Junior."

"Does Popper know you're on his trail?"

"I don't think so. We haven't talked to anyone close to him that would give him a clue. I say, 'close to him.' It doesn't seem like there *is* anyone close to him, at least not anyone that wants to be."

"How long will it take to get the warrant?"

"Can't say. They want to make sure it'll stand up in court when they try to introduce any evidence they find."

"Will you tell me when you serve the warrant? That might provoke him to come after us if he hasn't already by then."

More moments of silence, after which Ross said, "I will. But this has got to stop. Go make a living and let law enforcement do its job."

●　●　●

Hanging up from O'Keefe, Lieutenant Ross thought, *This jackoff O'Keefe is getting a lot more than "inconvenient" now.* Scrounging up that tape from Marty Lansing only complicated Ross's life. The Vitale part of that was very bad news, would put further pressure on Vitale, make him more likely for a prison sentence, more likely to turn on the likes of Sorvino, and worst of all, Marcone, the only person that Ross was certain knew about his past with the Outfit. Vitale might be the first domino in the chain, leading to the fall of others, ultimately maybe Marcone himself, who, despite his relative youth, might be more "old school," unwilling to rat on his associates. But why not rat on a cop? That was some valuable currency to trade for a better sentence. Maybe Popper, fuck-up that he had shown himself to be with O'Keefe, would succeed in eliminating Marcone. Ross would cheer him on from the sidelines but couldn't expect much from a loose cannon like Popper. And even if Popper succeeded, would that be enough? Did Sorvino know? Did Rose? That last one caused him a shudder. He had rolled it around and around. Too much killing required. And who knew what inconvenient item O'Keefe might scrounge up next? It was only ancient history now and hearsay. Inadmissible hearsay, except that he himself had admitted it to Marcone, which made it admissible as what they called "an admission against interest" by Ross. He had made that stupid mistake, why? To duck Sciorra's assignment last year to kill O'Keefe. An act of mercy, sort of. It seemed now it would have been better if he'd just finished O'Keefe off. But he had hoped to keep his own hands and conscience *clean*—clean at least of murdering someone directly, with those very hands. So much for good intentions. Like they say, no good deed goes unpunished.

● ● ●

Nobody tailing Popper. Better make sure Sorvino and Marcone sent someone to Rose.

When Rose answered the phone, he said, "You okay so far?"

"Yes. Now I owe you double."

"I assume you have company of some kind?"

"Two of them. People are gonna talk, all these strange men visiting me."

● ● ●

After dinner and dessert...apple pie *a la mode*, his favorite...and before parking the car, Wayne made a final pass by her house to make sure nothing had changed. Now some other car was in her driveway! And so late! *What a slut. She must be fucking every guy in town.*

CHAPTER 32

PICK YOUR POISON, *Vitale or Popper.*

It didn't take a genius to figure out that Popper would likely soon attempt something homicidal on one or more of the targeted five. Sorvino and Marcone could take care of themselves, and they were presumably taking good care of Rose, though O'Keefe intended to stay in touch with that situation, unable to forget the sinister longing in Popper's voice on the tape when describing his plans for Rose and Sara. This left O'Keefe and Sara as the most vulnerable. O'Keefe was supposed to be Vitale's responsibility, but Vitale had demurred on Sara, and it seemed like Popper had decided to take out everyone on the list anyway. Although nobody would be proposing Popper for admission to the Mensa High IQ Society, he was certainly creative, evidenced by the bomb and the snake attack, both failures, but, as the saying went, "even a blind pig," etc. Who knew what the "rambunctious" psycho might try next?

Since, according to Ross, the police hadn't put a tail on Popper pending the service of warrants, O'Keefe decided to tail Popper himself. He wasn't even sure if he cared if Popper discovered the tail. That might prompt Popper to undertake a preemptive strike against O'Keefe, a struggle O'Keefe knew he could win if not caught unawares as he had let happen with the bomb and the snake. Of course he could not physically devote twenty-four hours a day to this, he would need help, which George pledged to provide him from his growing corps of security people.

"You're making yourself a target, aren't you?" George said. "Human bait."

"Not necessarily. I mainly just want to keep the guy under constant watch, so he doesn't kill somebody else."

"I wonder if the worm ever survives the hook and the bite?"

Since the Wagoneer was the opposite of unprepossessing, he employed the same strategy as on his visits to Rose, renting a car so bland it was not likely to stand out against any background. He took Karma with him for some creature company. Creature company but not creature comforts, for either of them. While Karma didn't whine or otherwise protest aloud, he fidgeted constantly, laying down here, then rising and turning and laying down there, trying to adapt himself to these strange, new, spartan vehicular accommodations, and O'Keefe thought Karma's eyes asked, "Why are you doing this to me?" O'Keefe experienced similar discomfort and found it especially irritating to operate without his car phone, relegating him to the inconvenience and hit-and-miss availability of pay phones.

Except for the Cherry Pink building and a couple of other newer buildings, the industrial "park" was a hodgepodge of mostly one-story, crumbling buildings of a 1940s vintage, several of them entirely unused. On the third day of the surveillance, instead of immediately exiting the area, Popper drove into the potholed parking lot of one of the empty buildings, approached the door into the building, took a set of keys from his pocket, unlocked the door, and disappeared inside. He remained in the building for a long time. When he came out, he looked all around, and O'Keefe thought for sure Popper had seen the bland-mobile parked a block away, and very conspicuously so, no other cars being anywhere around. Popper stared for several moments, then turned to climb into his car. O'Keefe felt he couldn't remain there and take the chance Popper would stop to examine O'Keefe's car inside and out. O'Keefe nonchalantly eased the car toward the park exit and, once out of Popper's possible line of sight, sped away.

A short time later, he checked Popper's apartment parking lot, found Popper's car there, and hurried back to the industrial park, taking the gamble that Popper wouldn't return to the club until the evening. He only needed time enough to inspect the lock on the building and verify that it could be picked with one of his several bump keys. But he decided not to go in now, in daylight, his car prominently solitary in the empty parking lot, inviting investigation. He would need to return at night and on foot.

The county authorities, reluctantly genuflecting to the local Puritans, required the Cherry Pink to close on Sundays. O'Keefe thought that would be the best night, with the entire park empty, to commando in, pick the lock, and find out what business Popper had in that abandoned building. But as it got closer and closer to Sunday night, he increasingly second guessed himself. Ross's comment, "Just let law enforcement do its job," kept bothering him. There were limits to the value of this vigilante stuff. He had already committed plenty of crimes in this case and would only be committing more now, and more serious ones—breaking and entering and trespass and maybe more—and the Popper-influenced county authorities would likely not pass up the chance to put him in jail if the opportunity arose. Worst of all, if there were something incriminating in that building, his initiative, or "interference" it would surely be called, could end up tainting the evidence and compromising Popper's prosecution.

● ● ●

"Okay, Lieutenant," he said to Ross, "I'm following your advice to let law enforcement do its job. Let's see if it can manage that."

"Did you have a visitation from an archangel?"

O'Keefe told Ross about his tail of Popper.

"Taking things into your own hands again, no surprise there," Ross said.

He told Ross about the building. "Can you add that to your warrant?"

"I think so. It's the county, but the Feds ought to be able to help there. Good work. We'll need an affidavit from you though to support the warrant."

"I have to tell you I was gonna do the search myself—"

"The only surprise is that you didn't."

"But I decided, against all the evidence and history here, to put my fate in the hands of law enforcement."

"We'll try to live up to your lofty standards."

"Keep me informed, okay?"

"As already promised."

●　●　●

O'Keefe continued his tail on Popper for the next two days. On the afternoon of the second day, he turned over the tail duty to George's man early enough to take Karma to the football field before dark and put the dog through his paces, responding to the usual litany of instructions and commands and indulging the dog's immeasurable delight in chasing after a ball and returning it.

Just before darkness fell, Lieutenant Ross called O'Keefe's office. There being no answer since it was after hours, Ross left a message on O'Keefe's voicemail: "We hit him with the warrants this afternoon. I served them personally. When he saw the one on that building you

304 • ON LONESOME ROADS

told us about, he almost shit his pants. I supervised the search on his apartment while a couple other squads were hitting the other places. We didn't find anything in his apartment. After we were done, he left right on our heels. I assigned an officer to follow him, but he was gone before the officer could get in position. So he's on the loose and expecting an arrest any time. He might have a mind to try to settle up with you while he's got the chance."

Not long after Ross left his message, which O'Keefe had no way of picking up, George also was also trying to find him. He knew O'Keefe was not at the office and that he had no car phone. He left a message on O'Keefe's home machine: "Pete, we lost the damn guy. The cops served him with a warrant and searched his apartment. Our guy got enthralled with that, left his car to try to talk to the cops when they were finished, and Popper slipped away. I've got people checking for him at Cherry Pink. Call me as soon as you can."

As O'Keefe pulled into his driveway and up to the front of the house, Karma lurched up, as agitated as O'Keefe had ever seen him, his paws scratching furiously on the passenger-side window.

"*Ruhig*," O'Keefe said, the command to "Quiet." Karma immediately obeyed, though it seemed like Karma's every muscle and hair was standing on end, his gaze fixed unalterably on the house, and O'Keefe congratulated himself for working so hard to make sure Karma would maintain silence in a situation demanding it.

"*Sitz*," O'Keefe commanded. Karma again obeyed but clearly did not want to.

He chambered a round in his semi-automatic pistol.

As he climbed his front porch steps, he kept issuing commands *sotto voce* to keep Karma under control, "*Ruhig*" for "Quiet" and "*Fuss*" for "Heel." He opened the front door. The red light button was not on, which told him the alarm had been turned off. He brought the pistol up in front of his chin, barrel pointed to the ceiling, turned on the interior overhead light, which fully illuminated the vestibule and, partially, the large, long living room beyond.

From the moment he turned on the light, everything became automatic, purely reflexive action.

He thought he made out a figure standing at the far end of the family room. The highly agitated Karma had no doubt about someone being there, and the only thing in the world he seemed to want was to be set free to attack it, struggling between his duty of obedience and his duty to protect his master no matter what.

"*Packen,*" O'Keefe yelled.

Karma rocketed across the front room and halfway across the family room before he launched himself, propelling himself through the air at a velocity and height and for a distance that O'Keefe could not believe, and crashed into Popper as Popper fired his weapon.

O'Keefe thought Popper had surely brought Karma down, which overwhelmed him with dread in the seconds it took to mentally absorb the result of the clash. If Popper had brought a shotgun, he might have blasted Karma out of the air, but he had brought only a pistol, which forced him to be more precise, to take aim, while this mighty eighty-pound dog-missile rocketed through the air toward him, a sight to panic the mind, blur the vision, and loosen the bowels, but, most important, to cause the tiniest moment of hesitation, not more than two rapid blinks of distracted, faltering eyes.

Popper did manage to pull the trigger but only at the same time as Karma, a canine cannonball trained to attack the weapon-holding arm, smashed into Popper and locked down on that arm with the massive pressure of his jaws, shaking the arm violently back and forth, as if it were no more than a tattered rag. Altogether, the arm, the gun,

306 • ON LONESOME ROADS

and the bullet veered to the right, blowing out a window but doing no further harm. The gun clattered to the floor as Popper screamed in pain and terror, lurched back several steps until he crashed into the wall and fell, Karma on top, his jaws still locked on Popper's right arm and still brutally yanking it back and forth. As Popper screamed and pounded on the dog with his left fist, Karma let go of the right forearm and seized on the left. Popper, who was now flat on the floor and had no leverage, could only feebly strike the dog with his injured right arm, which Karma did not even seem to notice as he continued to bite and shake the left arm, at one point pausing just long enough to take a quick snap at Popper's face, then returning to the arm.

Popper shrieked, "Get it off. Get if off me!"

O'Keefe shouted, "Halt." Karma did not relent until O'Keefe shouted "Halt" a second time. Karma let go and took a step back but continued to hover over and growl and bark at Popper who was bleeding from the bites in both arms and the bite to his face that had ripped away a chunk of his nose.

"*Ruhig*," O'Keefe commanded.

Silence. A tableau—man, dog, man, still life except for the movement and sound of the heaving chests and desperate breathing of each of the three creatures.

After he caught his breath enough to be able to speak, O'Keefe said, "You did it all, didn't you?"

"*All?*"

"The snake."

Popper said nothing but smiled and nodded his head.

"The car bomb."

Popper nodded his head again.

"Beverly."

Popper nodded his head again.

Popper looked at the dog, at O'Keefe, at the pistol on the floor, considering his options. But he did not move toward the pistol. Was he afraid of another attack from Karma? Or did he see the savagery in O'Keefe's face and his killer eyes? Not quite fully conscious of it, O'Keefe hoped Popper would make the move, allowing him to solve the problem of Wayne Popper forever. But Popper didn't move. O'Keefe still considered shooting him. He could claim self-defense against an assailant who had already tried to kill him twice and was now advancing on him brandishing a pistol. He thought about Beverly, about Popper injecting that killer heroin dose into her, the dancer that Popper had killed in the same way, his intended rape and murder of Rose and Sara. He had no doubt that Wayne Popper did not deserve to live and that his continued presence in the world almost guaranteed that one or many innocent people would pay a price for it, not just premature death, but far worse, the terror and pain they would suffer before they died, when death, after what had gone before, would be a welcome deliverance. His hesitation, to the extent he could understand it in that pulsating, hysteria-charged instant, stemmed both from the fear of punishment together with some doubt deep within him that he had the moral right to kill even this piece of shit, though that would surely be by far the best outcome for all the world. Thus did centuries of moral, philosophical, and sociological discourse, debate, and disputation come to bear down on one troubled man with only a few moments to weigh and parse and turn round and round what he knew of it and apply it here and now.

He chose to spare Popper. Later, he would wonder—often, too often, and would not ever be able to definitively conclude—whether he should have pulled the trigger, and why he had not done exactly that, whether from the fear he would be prosecuted or the fear he would not be able to live with himself for murdering even this despicable scumbag. But he was certain of one thing. It was no act of mercy. The suspicion would thereafter haunt him that his choice was, at bottom, a selfish and cowardly one.

Popper seemed to recognize what had taken place and that he would be allowed to live.

He smirked.

"You think we're done here?" O'Keefe said.

Popper smirked again.

"*Packen,*" O'Keefe snarled.

Karma obeyed.

Popper screamed.

A voice behind O'Keefe: "The worm turns…"

O'Keefe looked behind him.

George.

"…and," George continued, "it *can* survive the hook and the bite…as long as it has a dog."

As they took Popper away to the hospital and then to jail, he sneered at O'Keefe. "Chickenshit. I know you were thinkin' about it. You should've done it. I'll make you pay for those bites someday."

CHAPTER 33

SHE HAD BEEN dreading this. She had heard the two of them planning things, her mom on the phone arranging things. Now her mom had summoned her to the kitchen table and indicated she should sit down across from her, and she looked wary, defensive, near anger already, even before she spoke.

"We're announcing next week."

"What's that mean?"

"We've set the date."

Kelly didn't know what to say so she just shrugged her disapproval.

"I don't suppose you'd be willing to be in the wedding…maybe a bridesmaid?"

"You're kidding."

"Please don't be so selfish. He's a good man."

Good man. She wouldn't argue. She would prove otherwise if she could. There were still papers in that file cabinet she hadn't read. She had kept putting off a return visit. It was too scary. He had almost caught her that time with Matt. A third visit would really be pushing her luck, a phrase both her mom and dad used in accusation and warning. She had been hoping something would happen to make it unnecessary; perhaps some quarrel between her mom and Darren; or her mom surrendering, realizing that she had lost her good judgment and good sense, bringing this stranger into their lives, into their house, their kitchen, living room, bathroom, sleeping with her mom in the bedroom a few steps down the hall from Kelly's. But no luck there. She had also hoped her dad would come to the rescue after all, but in vain. On her next weekend visit with her dad—still frustratingly under guard for her mom's peace of mind, mostly stuck hanging around his house and yard, a nice place, especially with Karma around now to play with, but not nice enough to be stuck in—she tried one more time. Same result. He would not "interfere." But, still, he never said anything like, "It's over, forget it," or, "That's not what she wants and not what I want either," or, "It'll never work." So that kept her waning hope alive.

She thought hard about whether to fake illness again and stay home from school as she had done with Matt that first time. That would give her more time at his house. She could arrive there earlier when there would be less activity on the street than in the late afternoon with schools getting out and people who went to work early coming home. But she saw too many risks in another sickness ploy—her mom maybe suspecting that Kelly was faking it, and, even if not suspicious, she would be checking on Kelly throughout the day on the phone and maybe even coming by the house. There weren't many papers left for her to look at anyway. She should be able to get in and out quickly.

She required no coat now, only her blue uniform sweater, as full-on spring had arrived. She took a long look at the house across the street from Darren's where the woman had observed her leaving his house on the previous visit, but she couldn't detect activity or presence of any kind. She unlocked the front door in the same breezy, entitled way that she had done the other times. She made extra sure to close the door to the utility room behind her, and the door from the utility room to the basement stairway as well, and hurried straight to the basement room and the file cabinet and the drawer and the place in the drawer where she had left off last time. She crossed her legs underneath her, sat down on the basement floor, and pulled out the newspaper articles one by one and read them.

The first articles recounted an FBI investigation of a Doctor Ensley and several clinics he secretly owned, using various business names. She recognized the doctor's name from the indictment document that she had found in the files on her earlier visit and had asked Mr. Terbovich at the library about. Apparently, some lawyers and other people also had a secret ownership in the clinics. Some of those people worked in healthcare companies such as nursing homes and specialty private hospitals, and they referred patients to each other for "referral fees" that the articles called "illegal kickbacks." The clinics provided various laboratory procedures and tests. The FBI claimed that most of the tests were either unnecessary or did not occur at all.

She did not understand all the "schemes" except that they were apparently bad things given the disapproving nature of the language used to describe them, involving such things as "billing for unnecessary medical procedures" or ones never performed at all. The lawyers would send their clients to Doctor Ensley and his clinics where the clients would "claim" they had injuries that didn't exist and the clinics knew were fake. In some cases the "conspirators" staged fake car accidents and "slip and fall" cases, paying people, poor people and drug addicts mostly, to claim nonexistent injuries from the accidents, and the medical conspirators then "certified" their injuries and required expensive treatments, leading to "settlements" with insurance companies. The lawyers then split the money with Doctor Ensley and others. Terms like "mail fraud," "insurance fraud," and "falsification of medical records" appeared frequently.

The investigation, which had included undercover agents posing as patients at Doctor Ensley's medical office and the various clinics, first resulted in the arrest of what the article called "small fry" in the various schemes. The FBI agent in charge of the investigation said, "We'll soon be sweeping up the kingpins, the lawyers and doctors and healthcare executives who orchestrated this whole thing and were the biggest financial beneficiaries of it." All this eventually culminated in the indictment and prosecution. A bunch of lawyers, a few doctors, and others in the healthcare world either pleaded guilty or were convicted in a trial.

The final article, headlined "The Unindicted Co-Conspirator," focused on the young physician in Doctor Ensley's office who the FBI had identified early in the investigation and agreed not to prosecute if he became an "undercover informant" and "whistleblower." He had done things he knew were wrong and then didn't know how to "extricate" himself, and the people involved, who were spread throughout the local healthcare industry, acted as if "everyone" did what they were doing. When the FBI "approached" him and offered him a "deal for his cooperation," he agreed.

At the bottom of the article appeared a photo of the young doctor with his name, Curtis Delong, but, unless he had a twin brother with a different name, the photo was of Darren Maefield.

A shadow fell over her.

"What you got there, little honeybee?"

Her hand reflexively closed on the newspaper article in a tight grip. She looked back over her shoulder. He had managed to come into the house, down the basement stairs, and sneak up behind her without her noticing anything, so entranced was she in those articles. She had been caught doing bad things before, but nothing like this. Something pressed on her chest from the inside. She could feel her temples madly pulsing. No leering smile now. Darren, or Curtis, whatever his name, was angry. Her guilt passed into fear. Nobody knew she was in that basement but him.

"Maybe I should lock you in here so you can finish your reading?"

Hearing that, her heart pounded even harder. She couldn't speak and was too afraid even to cry. She shook her head vigorously "No."

"Come here," he commanded.

She stood up. Her hand with the article in it dropped to her side. He stood inside the room, his back to the open door, his hand on the knob. He swept his hand in front of him, a mock gentlemanly gesture, indicating she should walk in front of him and out of the room.

She obeyed. As she passed in front of him, he grabbed her upper arm.

"Drop that paper."

He squeezed her so hard it hurt. She cried out, but he didn't let up, only grabbed her tighter, hurting her more. She yanked hard, wrenching her arm out of his grasp, and ran. Apparently surprised, and for a moment uncertain, he failed to act, and not until she had reached the steps did he start chasing her. Luckily, he had left the door open. She scrambled up the stairs, emerged into the utility room, slammed the door behind her, dashed into the kitchen, and slammed that door behind her too.

Front or back? She hustled out the back door and raced across the back yard into the yard of the house behind his and kept running. A dog barked close by. She glanced back once and thought she saw him standing at the top of his back steps. Why was he following her anyway? Would he take her back to that basement and kill her and bury her there?

She kept running—through the neighbor's side yard and the front and out onto the sidewalk of the block behind his and on for two more blocks. Winded, she stopped to catch her breath, thinking she might throw up. She looked down the long street. Likely he would get in his car and come looking for her. She needed to get off the street. She began to weave through yards, moving farther and farther away from his street, often blocked by fences or thick hedgerows, sometimes needing to retrace her steps and find some other way, occasionally emerging onto the sidewalk, peering down the street to see if his car might be coming, resuming again her dodging, vagrant progress through the yards and alleys, the barking dogs, and the occasional curious onlookers, all continuously fueling her panic.

But she had the proof now. A good man, not so. Not even his real name. An unindicted co-conspirator. She came to a main thoroughfare. Bus stops. There would be bus stops. She found one within a couple of blocks. The bus driver, and those passengers who were paying attention, looked curiously at this disheveled girl, out of breath, face sweat-streaked and mottled red and white, clutching a ragged looking piece of paper, asking how best to take buses that would get her close to the address she gave the bus driver.

She had thought about fleeing to her dad's house but doubted he would be home, and he would surely immediately call her mom. And anyway, she wanted her mom to see this article right now, to see that Kelly had been right. *A good man, my foot. Not even his real name. What other lies has he been telling?* She had to transfer to another bus line, and the bus that picked her up on that line dropped her off three blocks from her house. As she reached her block and approached her house, she saw her mom's car in the driveway. To her relief, *his* car was not there.

When she entered the house, her mom, on the phone, pacing back and forth, looking frantic and a combination of relieved and angry when she saw Kelly, said into the receiver, "Here she is now."

"Who is that?" Kelly said, her voice shrill and breaking.

"Darren."

"That's not his name," Kelly said, waving the paper at her mother.

"What's going on?" Annie said, seemingly to both Darren/Curtis and to Kelly.

"Hang up!"

Her mom said frantically into the phone, "I have to go."

She hung up the phone.

"You broke into Darren's house? What's wrong with you? Are you crazy?"

"That's not his name. And he's an unindicted co-conspirator. Look at this."

She thrust the paper at her mom who commanded, "Sit down," and started to read. When she finished, she looked up, stupefied.

Kelly said, "There was a big fraud thing he was involved in. He changed his name and moved here. He's a faker and a crook."

"He's on his way here now."

"Don't let him in."

"He said he could explain."

"No, he can't."

"You go to your room. I'll deal with you later."

Kelly wanted to scream. She sobbed in anger and frustration and rushed to the front of the house, ran up the stairs to her room, and watched out the front window. Soon Darren arrived and let himself in the house. She moved out of her room to the top of the stairway.

She heard her mom say, "I feel like I'm in a madhouse. What the hell is going on? Who are you? What does this article mean? Is it you?"

With utmost calm, Darren/Curtis said, "Please sit down."

Apparently, her mom did so.

"Yes, it's me. But I can make everything clear. I don't want you to take my word for it. My attorney is standing by back in my old town. Let's go back to your office and call him on your speakerphone. He'll explain everything."

"What do I call you, Darren or Curtis?"

"It's Darren. That's my official name now. A new man in a new life."

The home office nook was toward the rear of the house next to the kitchen. Kelly moved slowly down the stairs to the entryway and peeked around the corner of the living room. She could not see them, and they could not see her. She moved closer so she could hear.

The lawyer identified himself, saying he had represented Darren in the "nightmare situation" that Darren had the misfortune to become involved in. "At first he was confused and afraid and didn't know what to do," the lawyer said. "He did some things he knew were wrong, but as soon as he got the chance to extricate himself from it, he took it. Not only that, he became the true hero of the case. He became an undercover informant. They could not have made the case they did against all those crooked people without him. They said it would have taken years for them to secure the evidence he obtained for them. They brought no charges against him. With help from the FBI and the prosecutor, we even convinced the medical board not to revoke his license. They agreed to put him on two years' probation, let him continue to practice under the supervision of the Castorp Clinic. He should come off the probation very soon."

"He changed his name?" Annie said.

Darren answered that. "Maybe that was a mistake, but I felt I had to. It was notorious, one of the biggest scandals ever there. I was afraid it would blight the rest of my life. Look what's happening right now."

The attorney added, "The name change was entirely legal. The law allows it. In fact, it's a quite simple procedure. And even the medical board didn't object to it."

They were all silent for a few moments. Finally, the attorney said, "Any questions?"

"Not that I can think of now."

"If you have any, don't hesitate to call. Darren has given me full authorization to answer any question you have, holding nothing back under any circumstances."

When the attorney hung up, Darren said, "I was not going to marry you under false pretenses. I was going to tell you before we announced. But I should have done it earlier. I'm very sorry for that."

"I can," she began hesitantly, "understand…most of this…but not to tell me…"

"I was afraid to take the chance of killing it…you know, in its cradle, before it had a chance to grow and live. I waited too long."

"If you explained it the way you explained it today, I think I would have understood. Maybe I still could. I need some time to think."

Her voice was becoming so soft. Was she about to forgive him? Surely not.

"No," he said. "It's hopeless. Your daughter obviously hates me, and she's willing to go to any lengths. She'll never give me a chance. She's been that way from the very beginning. I couldn't live in that situation. You couldn't either. It would be doomed."

Good.

"This is horrible," her mom said.

"You're the innocent one here. I'm so sorry. I really do love you."

"This can't be." Her mom was crying now. "Maybe we should try to…mend things somehow…give it some time. We can work with Kelly, maybe all go to counseling or something."

Not a chance.

"Let's not kid ourselves," he said.

"My God. This is it? This is goodbye? The end?"

A long silence. She heard her mom sobbing. Then movement seemed to be coming her way, and she quickly retreated up the stairs and listened from the top of the staircase again. But nothing else was said. She heard the front door open and close, moved to her room, and watched out her window at his figure moving in the darkness. The overhead light in his car came on when he opened the door, then shut off when he closed it. He started the car and drove slowly away, Kelly hoped, for the last time.

She remained in her room for as long as she could stand it. She could not read or do anything else other than sit and think about what had happened and what might happen next. Finally, she made her way down the stairs where her mom sat at the kitchen table with a glass and a bottle of wine in front of her, her face red and swollen and wet with tears.

"Well, you've done it," she said. "You've got your way. I hope you're happy."

"I saved us. From him."

"You've ruined everything. How could you do this?"

"How could *you*? Why don't I get a vote…in anything?"

"Do you realize what you did? That was burglary, and theft. If he makes a complaint to the police, you could be sent to reform school for what you did."

"Better than living with him."

"Did you overhear that phone call with his lawyer? You butted in, interfered, and you were wrong about him."

"He's a liar. He changed his name. He was an unindicted co-conspirator."

"He explained all that."

"He's a creep. Should I go live with Dad now?"

"Another stab in my heart. Go to your room. You're grounded. Forever."

"I hate you."

In her room she thought about packing a suitcase and leaving right then. But she couldn't call him and ask him to pick her up. He would probably still refuse to "interfere" in the situation—even after he had been the one who screwed everything up in the first place. She could truly run away from home, away from both of them. Where would she go? How would she get there? Hitchhike? Scary. They were hurting girls out there.

She could not believe this. She deserved gratitude, praise, not this anger and blame. She turned on the radio. They played the new song by Tracy Chapman. "Fast Car." Yes, it would be so nice to fly away in a fast car. The longing, hopeless lyrics only made her cry the more. She thought she might not be able to stop crying. After a while, she fished out the two Percocet from their hiding place, thinking, *might as well try,* and swallowed them.

Gradually, peace settled down on her, soothing her. It was much better than her dad had described. The pills made her even more certain she had done the right thing and that all would somehow be well.

●　　●　　●

When Darren returned home, he poured himself a whiskey and dialed a phone number.

"Darren here."

"It's late. What's up? Anything wrong?"

"Not wrong. But something's happened that might put a spotlight on me for a while. I need to be careful. We'll have to put our project on hold."

"Ouch! That'll take a bite out of our bank accounts. How long? A week? A month? More?"

"I can't tell. Probably not long. I'm just nervous right now. We've got a good thing going. No reason to get greedy and stupid and foul everything up. I saw that before, with my own eyes and at close range."

"What about the patients and claims in the pipeline now?"

"I guess we have to keep those moving through. Just no new ones for a while."

"Can't be long, or we'll have to find someone else."

"Don't do that. I just need a little space right now."

"Can't be long. What happened anyway?"

"Long story. About a shitty little brat. I'd like to wring her neck."

CHAPTER 34

GENTLEMEN'S CLUB FIGURE DENIED BAIL

Paschal McKenna

District Judge Richard Dombrowski yesterday denied the request of Wayne Popper to be released from jail on bail following his arrest on a variety of charges stemming from a home invasion and related assault on local private detective Peter O'Keefe.

"If you were just a flight risk, we could handle that with a money bail," the Judge announced, "but you have been unable to rebut the prosecution's evidence that you're a clear and present danger not just to Mr. O'Keefe, but possibly to others as well. It's in the public interest to keep you incarcerated until and unless a jury acquits you."

Popper allegedly broke into O'Keefe's residence, threatened O'Keefe with a firearm but was subdued by O'Keefe's dog, Karma, a retired member of the canine unit of the local police force. Popper was taken first to the hospital where he received treatment for the dog bites, which required several stitches in various parts of his body including his arms, leg, and face.

Popper is suspected in earlier attacks on O'Keefe, most recently by means of a highly venomous snake hidden in a dresser drawer in O'Keefe's home and another attack last year by means of a car bomb that severely injured the detective, requiring treatment for extensive burns.

If Popper is indeed guilty of the car bombing, this would put to rest a persistent rumor that the bombing was the work of the local Mafia organization known as the "Outfit."

Popper is also suspected of other serious offenses, which the police declined to specify "at this time." The police are conducting searches of Cherry Pink Gentlemen's Club, Popper's place of employment, as well as his residence and other places, and are analyzing the evidence obtained.

Sources indicate that the police have discovered what they describe as "a veritable snake farm" in a makeshift storage space in an empty, decaying industrial building near the Cherry Pink Gentlemen's Club. Police spokesmen declined to comment.

Popper said nothing during the hearing, but, as he was led away, made an obscene gesture to O'Keefe and others in the courtroom.

● ● ●

DAGMAR APPEARED IN his office door and said, "Another surprise visitor."

"Who now?"

"Lieutenant Ross. He says you know him well."

Ross's face showed a mix of reluctance, guilt, and a fierce resolve, which portended no good. O'Keefe tried to steel himself to absorb bad news.

"They've delegated me to bring you the news. A plea bargain. With Popper."

"Am I gonna be happy?"

"Are you ever happy?"

"I guess no death sentence?"

"No, obviously."

"Life without parole?"

"'Fraid not."

"Unbelievable. What is it?"

"Fifteen years."

"How about parole?"

"No condition on that."

"What a ratfuck. Why would your prosecutor do a plea bargain with Popper that not only isn't life without parole but isn't even life? The bastard gets out no matter what in only fifteen years and could get paroled even sooner?"

"I didn't make the deal. Don't shoot the messenger."

"Let's see. He committed the following crimes. Vern Slater. Maybe the authorities are inclined to think it's not a big deal to push a motorcycle gang leader over a cliff, but he also confessed on that tape to overdosing his dancer girlfriend—"

"That tape is his only admission on that, and it's almost certainly inadmissible because it was illegally recorded. And he says he was just lying…bragging, trying to sell himself to the Outfit. Remember, he regarded that session with Vitale as kind of a job interview."

"And Beverly Bronson?"

"I know that's special to you, your old friend. But same thing. Illegally taped confession, and just bragging. We have no physical evidence putting Popper at the scene. Everyone knows or thinks they know that Bowman did it. That will be a very effective defense, the 'somebody else did it' defense."

"The bombing, which, by the way, could've killed innocent bystanders, not just a hapless dipshit like me."

"Same. We do have some physical evidence…some bombing materials, like the ones in the device that blew up your vehicle, in one of his storage places. That evidence is one reason he's getting the fifteen years."

"And the fact that he confessed it to me?"

"Confessed? You mean your interpretation that he nodded his head 'yes' when you asked him that? Forget it."

"And the snake?"

"No evidence there other than circumstantial…that he was in Vietnam, loved snakes—"

"And that little snake farm of his?"

"Powerful but still circumstantial. The snakes we found in that storage space didn't even include a Krait like the one that bit you. We couldn't figure out how he got that snake into the country."

"But he confessed Beverly, the bombing, and the snake to me."

"Yeah, with those supposed nods of his head with a big black German Shepherd chewing on him and your gun pointed at him… and you with every incentive to interpret those supposed head movements a certain way…"

"So I'm a liar?"

"Let's just say you had an understandably strong inclination to misunderstand what that head movement of a terrified man looking into the jaws of a killer dog meant. His lawyer said they'll bring in video of a similarly trained and vicious looking dog attacking a human. Might be pretty effective. And there are gruesome pictures of his bite wounds already available."

"And the last attack? No doubt about that one."

"And he's being punished for that, but he has a story about that too. Once his lawyers found out from your search warrant affidavit that you were following him, he came up with the story that he *knew* you were following him, that you had no lawful authority to do that, you've got a reputation for vigilante violence, and he broke into your place only to try to force you to stop stalking him."

"Surely you don't think this is right."

"What I think doesn't matter. But put everything else aside. Here's the real reason. Russ Lord put major pressure on our people so he could get Wayne's testimony against Vitale. The illegal tape wasn't an issue there because, with this plea agreement, they'll have direct testimony from Wayne that he and Vitale hatched a conspiracy to kill five people. And if Vitale denies it, they think the court would allow that part of the tape as corroboration of Wayne's direct testimony. Or if Vitale gets on the stand and denies it, it could be used as impeachment evidence against him."

"Assuming the Slater killing was deemed to be a public service of a sort, Popper has killed two women, tried to kill me three times, and conspired to kill four other people…Yeah, Sorvino and Marcone are Outfit criminals if that should matter, but Rose, not necessarily so, and oh, by the way, also a housewife and mother that he was going to rape before he killed her. And if Rose is deemed to be unworthy, there's Sara—"

"Stop beating on me, Goddammit. I can't defend it. I'm just giving you the facts."

"I'll be at his sentencing hearing."

"Won't do any good. It's Judge Dombrowski. He'll never overrule the prosecutor on something like that, especially when he knows that the Feds want the deal."

"Can't wait 'til he gets out."

"Somebody'll surely kill the sonuvabitch in prison anyway."

"If not, I'll kill him when he gets out. You'll know who did it and where to find me. Bring the handcuffs."

"Cool down. That kind of talk can get you in a lot of trouble."

"And how about Vitale?"

"Still loose, but the Feds are squeezing him hard. They think they can turn him."

"That'll cause some dominoes to fall."

"Yes, it surely will."

O'Keefe was puzzled by the look on Ross's face. He seemed not to be very happy about that.

GUNSHOTS IN THE NIGHT, A BODY ON THE SIDEWALK: MOB ASSOCIATE FOUND MURDERED

Paschal McKenna

The bullet-ridden corpse of the owner of popular Italian restaurant, Maria's, was found yesterday morning sprawled on the sidewalk in front of a three-story brick apartment building in Midtown.

Ricky Vitale had apparently been visiting one of the apartment tenants. Gunshots were heard at approximately 4 a.m. yesterday, and one of the tenants saw a car speed away from the scene shortly after the shots were fired.

Vitale has been one of the primary targets of the pending grand jury probe, supervised by the U.S. Attorney's Office, into the alleged local criminal group commonly known as the Outfit.

Although grand jury proceedings are required by law to remain secret, it appears from surrounding circumstances and events that the investigation had come to focus, in part, on a possible connection between Vitale and Wayne Popper who has been associated in various capacities with the Cherry Pink 'gentlemen's' (strip) club in the county. Vitale was reputed to be one of the owners of a similar local establishment, The Erection.

Popper was recently arrested and charged with attempted murder by the city Prosecutor's office in connection with several recent attacks on local private detective Peter O'Keefe. Popper is also under investigation for several other crimes including murder.

At the same time, Popper is also a key government witness in the pending federal grand jury investigation of Vitale. Reliable sources report

328 • ON LONESOME ROADS

that Popper has recently struck a plea bargain with both federal and local authorities, obtaining a prosecutorial recommendation for more lenient sentencing for his crimes in exchange for testimony against Vitale.

Popper has been denied bail and is rumored to be held in a secret high-security situation under the protection of the U.S. Marshall Service's Witness Protection Program. It is unclear what will happen now that Vitale is deceased.

Maria's, established by Vitale's mother and father in the 1930s, has been a popular fixture in the city for decades, its popularity unaffected (and some say enhanced) by the notoriety of its owner.

Vitale was married and the father of several children ranging in age from nine to sixteen. His wife was unavailable for comment.

● ● ●

"I'm getting psychic," Ross said when O'Keefe called him. "Somehow I knew it would be you."

"So I read the paper today," O'Keefe said. "I assume that means the plea bargain deal is off."

Ross sighed. "You assume wrong. I guess our lawyers aren't the best. All the deal required of Popper is that he be available to testify against Vitale and to testify fully and truthfully when requested."

When O'Keefe said nothing in response, Ross continued, "And I also have to inform you that you are a person of interest in the Vitale killing. We need to arrange an interview..."

Ross started to read O'Keefe his Miranda rights but stopped when he heard the click of O'Keefe hanging up the phone.

● ● ●

"Thanks, Sal," Vince said, as the old man set down four espressos, two each for Vince and Paul.

"How you doin'?'" Vince said to Sal.

"Pretty same. Ain't gettin' any richer or healthier, that's for sure."

"Damn it, I'm gonna be pissed at you if you need anything and don't ask me to help."

"I'm good, really, no kidding."

Sal shuffled away.

"Jesus, he looks terrible," Vince said. He downed one of his espressos. "Wearin' slippers now…When he's gone, it's all gone," he said, with a gesture meant to encompass the whole neighborhood, the whole small world that had made them.

Not quite, Vince, Paul thought, *not until you're gone too.*

"Thanks for comin', Paulie."

"Of course. No thanks needed, you know that."

"So…what about the news yesterday?"

"No clue, I swear," Paul said. "I had nothin' to do with it. Another *regalu.* From above."

"Not exactly from above."

"You know what I mean."

"But you don't know what *I* mean. The *regalu* was from right here."

"What are you sayin'?"

"What you think I'm sayin'?"

"No way."

"Seemed like the only way."

"Jesus! Be careful. Never know who's listenin'."

"Not sure it matters. There's a problem anyway. The paper said a witness saw a car drivin' away from the scene. My guess is they saw more than that."

Paul considered this, then said, "We could solve the witness part."

"No way. I'm pretty sure who it was. One of his baby dolls. He was comin' out of her place. I'm an old man…not that much time left anyway. I don't want an innocent woman on my conscience even if she was stupid enough ta be fuckin' a gangster. Not worth it."

"Weren't you tellin' me at this very table not long ago that you weren't sure you'd help me with him?"

"That was before everything changed…when we found out from O'Keefe's tape they were definitely comin' for you, and for Rose too, the rotten bastards. You heard that tape. He was gonna let that Popper scum do Rose…rape her too. Suddenly I became the best solution."

"All by yourself."

"Best not to involve you. I wanted you to be clear of it."

"What can I do? I wanna help."

"Not much. Pay Praeger to keep me out as long as possible."

"You managed to stay out all this time. You might die in there."

"Hey. Carmine died there. Why do I deserve any better?"

"Is that all? Or can they go for the death penalty?"

"Not the Feds. If the state people prosecuted it, they could. But the Feds wouldn't let that happen. No glory for them in that. But if they do, I'll be my own hangman, I don't need their assistance. I know I said that about rattin', but I was just illustratin' a point in the discussion."

"What can I do?"

"Other than Praeger, only one thing, though I hope I don't even need to ask. Let Rose go. Do her no harm."

"Of course."

"*Promise?*"

"Promise."

"And there's still that Popper motherfucker alive."

"Goin' ta jail though."

"But alive. If we let him do to one of our women, especially her, what he said he'd do to her on that tape, it'd be the bottom of the pit of shame for us."

Paul nodded.

"We'd hold our manhoods cheap," Vince said.

"What's that mean?"

"Shakespeare…his way of sayin' we'd be dickless dogs, not worth shit to nobody."

"Can't have that."

"Be good ta spare the world from that guy…get rid of him…in prison or wherever."

Marcone nodded.

Sorvino downed his second espresso. "Okay, gotta go. Catchin' a plane later."

"Miami?"

"You bet. You'll find me there…until they come for me."

CHAPTER 35

IT ASTOUNDED O'KEEFE when he answered his car phone and heard the voice not of the secretary, not of his human familiar Max Trainer, but of Russell Lord himself. "Mr. O'Keefe, this is Russell Lord. We need to talk about something important to both of us. And, once again, I'm going to advise you to bring counsel. Can you come in this afternoon?"

O'Keefe figured he probably had some luck left and had not gotten himself in too much trouble operating without a lawyer so far. When Lord's secretary guided him into Lord's office, he received his second surprise of the day. Lord was alone. Even Max Trainer had been left out.

Lord gestured toward one of the chairs in front of his desk. O'Keefe sat down, wondering if a tape was rolling somewhere.

"I had to advise you to bring counsel," Lord said, "but I'm glad you didn't."

He wouldn't say that on tape.

Lord had not read him his rights, but he thought he should check anyway: "Surely you guys don't think I killed Vitale. Before we go any further, if that's what you want to talk about, I do need a lawyer."

"No, we don't think so, and here's why."

Lord flipped the switch on a tape recorder on his desk and played a tape of a wiretapped conversation that had occurred between Vince Sorvino and Paul Marcone at Sal's Deli.

When the tape ended, O'Keefe said, "Well, I guess that tells you that I didn't do it."

"But you did something else."

O'Keefe thought he knew what that meant but hoped he was wrong. "What's that?"

"The tape. Marty Lansing's tape."

"I was afraid you'd say that."

"I don't know how many violations of the Electronic Surveillance Act you've committed by broadcasting what was on that tape far and wide…"

"Like, for example, telling you about it."

"All of the other instances might be excusable, but your disclosure of the contents of that tape to Sorvino and Marcone led to the murder of Ricky Vitale."

O'Keefe felt the shades of the prison house beginning to close on him, the cell door clanging shut. He thought, *I've come all this way…for this.* He said, "I'll say a prayer for his miserable soul. But they probably would've killed him anyway, and if I hadn't disclosed it, there'd likely've been at least three murders, not even counting Sara and me, which would've made a five-pack, not all of them of bad guys. *Failing* to disclose it would've been a lot worse than disclosing it. It would've been unforgivable. You should've told them yourselves. That was your *real* duty."

Lord seemed to shrug that off. O'Keefe wondered if there was anything in the world Lord wouldn't shrug off.

"Rationalize if you must," Lord said, "but, on the other hand, as you know, our strategy was to use the conspiracy disclosed on that tape, not through the tape itself but through Wayne Popper's direct testimony on what was said at that meeting, to squeeze Vitale and get him to turn, which could have resulted in seriously wounding, even extirpating, the Outfit, a nest of vicious killers and thieves, once and for all."

"Coulda, woulda, shoulda."

"Exactly. *Shoulda*. We'll never know because your criminal action ruined our strategy—"

"A strategy that betrayed me and the public by giving that serial killer a ridiculously light sentence when he should have been executed…or at least put away permanently."

"Please let me finish—"

"No. You let me finish. If not for that tape I brought you, you wouldn't even have known about it and *had* a strategy until it was too late. You weren't smart enough to include a clause in the agreement that Vitale had to be alive for Popper to get his benefits under the deal. He could've killed Vitale himself and still reaped the benefits of that agreement. I should have killed Popper myself. I could have too, and probably gotten away with it."

"Now *I'll* finish. You told Sorvino and Marcone about it, which lead Sorvino to kill Vitale. All we've got now is, maybe, Sorvino for the Vitale murder based on that conversation you just heard. We might get Marcone as an accessory after the fact, but we have to show not just knowledge but actual assistance, and that's highly doubtful. You have single-handedly destroyed a major initiative against organized crime in this country. What you did amounted to an obstruction of justice with devastating consequences."

"I wonder if a jury would really convict me for that, once they heard the whole story."

"They'd have no choice. The Surveillance Act violation is clear, and there's no defense. The court wouldn't even let your evidence in."

"Well, I guess we get to put on another show, Mr. Lord, you and me."

"Don't kid yourself. It won't be just you and me. Your partner Sara would have to be part of it too."

O'Keefe tried to keep his head up, but it was difficult. Later, he thought that at that point he must have looked downward at the floor, defeated.

Lord smiled, as if had greatly enjoyed what had gone before and was about to especially enjoy what was coming next.

O'Keefe waited for someone to arrive with the handcuffs.

"But," Lord said, "I really don't want another circus. You'd probably get a lot of sympathy from the public, especially when you've got those two knucklehead journalists on your side already. And it would likely expose a lot about our investigation and our investigative techniques that I'd rather not have exposed."

Now O'Keefe was certain Lord was not recording the conversation, and O'Keefe was wishing that he had brought a tape recorder of his own. "Like failing to warn Paul Marcone and Rose Sciorra that they were in the cross-hairs, which was your duty under Justice Department policy."

Lord smiled. "But, Mr. O'Keefe, that would have been a crime. A crime like yours. A violation of the Electronic Surveillance Act."

O'Keefe wondered if he could get away with lunging hard and fast across Lord's desk and whipping his ass.

Lord continued, "But just as I said, I'm going to let it go. I'm going to let it go even though you have…to put it colloquially…fucked me up and over not once but twice now."

"I suppose your condition'll be that I wear a wire and try to entrap Rose somehow? No deal."

"Not even for Sara?"

O'Keefe had nothing to say to that.

Lord smiled. "You're pretty well fucked now, aren't you? Which one will you protect?"

O'Keefe still had nothing to say.

"But no. I won't demand a *quid pro quo*. I'm just asking you to let it go as well. Don't make a big stink at Wayne Popper's sentencing hearing. Keep your jailbird reporter friend on the sidelines. You won't win anyway."

"But maybe I'll create a record that'll be worth something when the parole board wants to let him out early when he finds God and Jesus about three days after he's sent to prison."

"If you think about it, your record won't really influence the parole board at all. On the other hand, you and Harrigan and your reporter friends haven't ruined my entire reputation, yet anyway, and I'm promising you, I repeat, promising you, that I personally will do everything possible, and persuade everyone I can persuade to do everything possible, to keep Popper there for his entire term. And if he is the man I think he is, he'll commit more offenses in the prison yard, and his sentence will be extended, and I'll personally try to make sure that happens as well. Not just for you. Not at all for you. Mostly for me. I don't want this plea bargain on my conscience if he gets out and does what we know he's likely to do. And surely somebody will kill the bastard in prison. You heard Sorvino and Marcone on that tape a minute ago. Let it be. Let things unfold. Maybe your interventions are not as helpful to the world, and even yourself, as you think they are."

"So I just stand down and hope you hold up your end and don't prosecute me?"

"You're not listening, you ornery motherfucker. You don't need to stand down. There's no *deal* here. There's nothing to trust. Assume I'm lying to you and act accordingly. But I'm telling you that I'm not prosecuting you no matter what, or your partner Sara either, at least for the particular crimes we've discussed here today. I'm just suggesting it will be better for everyone, including better for you, to return the favor. I didn't appeal the Harrigan dismissal, did I? Let's clean the slate. What did Jerry Jensen call you—'an inconvenient man'? Surprisingly, you've been quite resourceful in these contests. I get no glory whatsoever if I beat the likes of you but the utmost obloquy and shame if the likes of you beat me."

● ● ●

After some troubled reflection and continuing consteration, consternation that he knew would long continue, O'Keefe decided that even if Lord was lying to him, he ought to close his eyes, hold his breath, and save himself the brain damage of showing up at Popper's sentencing hearing to make a futile protest, guaranteed to fail, however just and eloquent it might be. As for Lord's statement that he would not prosecute him, he decided he would follow Lord's advice neither to trust nor verify, but, for once, simply bend to the reality on the ground. Yes, always looming menacingly over him now would be the prospect of Popper getting out of prison and taking vengeance, and not on O'Keefe alone.

But there were other things he could and ought to be grateful for. There was the removal, at least temporarily, of imminent daily peril for him and Sara and others close to him, which would continue for many more days and years even with that fifteenth year and possible earlier parole date lurking out there. Maybe somebody really would kill the sonuvabitch before he gets out. There was also the "pass," the boon he had been seeking all along, that he had received from the Outfit, what was left of the Outfit anyway, in exchange for his *regalu*. And he and his fledgling firm had survived financially during this difficult period and were now poised to pursue his business plan in earnest and with much promise of success if it could be pursued without distractions.

It helped his mood too when a check arrived in the mail from Rose, representing a generous premium for his services, an amount that made up in several multiples for his downtime for the last several months during which he had worked almost exclusively for her (and himself). Yet the payment was not so large as to signal something like "payoff," "bribe," "money laundering," or "dividing up the loot."

He asked Dagmar to arrange food and drink for a small gathering at "happy hour" on the day of Popper's sentencing for his "happy few": George, Sara, Dagmar, Harrigan, Oswald Malone, Paschal McKenna, Terry Lecumske, Kelly, and Annie too (though Annie politely declined), and special and most honored guest, Karma. He even thought about inviting Lieutenant Ross, but something about that didn't seem quite right. He made a short speech and could feel the excitement, close to downright delight, that these people, and Karma too, seemed to be feeling. About Karma, he said, "George, Sara, Dagmar, Kelly, this isn't my dog, it's our dog, our community property. Why? Because he saved my life? That's no big deal. Most of you have done that, in some cases more than once. I'm sure, Dagmar, it'll soon be your turn…"

They laughed, after which he continued, "But because I don't want the sole responsibility of taking care of him all the time…"

They laughed hard at that too, after which he continued, "And that's not just a joke…"

A small ripple of chuckling.

"We'll figure out over time how this little experiment in socialist ownership will work out as a practical matter. But in the meantime, in the spirit of one of my favorite characters, Tiny Tim…here's to Karma and to all of us every one."

Second only to Karma, Paschal was the center of attention and some delight, even after he succumbed to his chronic disease—that is, became sloppy drunk. Everyone but Paschal knew he was too drunk to drive home. O'Keefe pulled Oswald aside and said, "What can I do? How can I help?"

"I'll get him home safe," Oswald said. "He'll resist, but I'll threaten to pull him off his current beat and assign him to weddings, funerals, and obituaries, a threat that has brought success on prior occasions."

After the others left, Sara came into his office.

"Got a moment?"

His adrenalin jumped and blood pulsed harder. Surely she wasn't going to quit? She seemed to have taken recent events quite hard.

They both sat in the guest chairs in front of his desk. Brown hair cut rather short, brown eyes, small spray of freckles on both sides of her slightly sharp nose, full lips. She had a Gallic look about her, like some French actresses whose images he could vaguely recall but not their names.

"I've been deputized," she said, "by George."

He waited, anticipating the worst.

"We'd like no more secrets."

She paused, as if she expected at least a minor eruption. There being none, she went on. "We know you'd rather not take the risk of someone talking good sense to you. We also know that sometimes good sense is a mistake. We'll try our best to give you a long leash... no pun intended, Karma. But we'd like, let's say, as a general rule, with appropriate exceptions, no more secrets."

He stared at her long and thoughtfully. He guessed she knew what he couldn't help thinking and that she had just taken a big risk, because Sara was herself a secret, her entire life before coming to work for O'Keefe a mystery, one she apparently intended to keep that way. He had honored that; had vowed to himself, and had ordered George as well, not to pry; had refused to learn and to know; had avoided searching and discovering; not so much afraid of what he might find, but honoring her privacy, trusting that she would tell him if something in her past might affect their work together. He could tell from her anxious expression that she understood the hypocrisy, if that was the right word, of her side of this conversation and seemed to be waiting for O'Keefe to demand that she 'fess up on her own secrets. But he didn't think that way at all. Her secrets were personal; his, at least the ones she was referring to, affected the business, and they were partners now.

When he opened his mouth to speak, she recoiled slightly, incorrectly anticipating the demand he did not intend to make. "Why didn't George do this himself?"

She took her time to answer, until she ventured, reluctantly, "Well, he says he thinks you'd respect it more coming from me."

He groaned. "That's not even close to true. I love him. I respect him too… But I probably do sell him short."

"I won't tell you what to do. I know you. You'll do the right thing, once, like Churchill said, you've exhausted all other possibilities."

She got up to leave the room and at the door turned and said, "And thanks for accepting that without further interrogation."

He nodded.

As she left, he could only think, *What a woman. What a person.*

And after that, *Here I am with personnel issues. What the fuck.*

He reached for the phone to call George.

CHAPTER ▶ 36

ON LONESOME ROADS they travel…

Vince enjoyed his morning walk along the beach more than anything else he could think of, even though it was almost always the most humid part of the day. It was a good thing he could spend some time here in April and May, the least humid months of the year in Miami. But the rest of his timing had not been so good. After May, the last few months that he would likely ever spend in this town he loved so much would be in the muggy summertime. His hometown was muggy too, and there was no beach there to relieve it; and no great seafood; and no Cuban; and certainly not so many beautiful, near-naked women either. He had evolved into a bit of a dirty old man, but kept it under control. "I have sinned in thought, word, and deed," the old prayer went. No deed here unfortunately. *The paper said a witness saw the car driving away. Regret. A stupid thing. If a frog had wings…It had been the right thing to do under all the circumstances. Life's been better than I deserved it to be. Try to just enjoy the time left…before they come for me.*

•   •   •

It still surprised Paul how much he liked to just get in the Town Car and drive. He'd've thought by now he'd be long sick of it since he had done so much of it—for others, now himself. But he could concentrate better, think more deeply on a long, solo drive than at any other time. He would find an uncrowded highway at an odd time of day or night, often very early in the morning, 4 or 5 a.m., still dark, and drive to some little town not far outside the city, drinking coffee purchased from a 24-7 convenience store, a tall cup when he started the trip, another on his way back.

He had depended so much on Vince, who had now withdrawn to Miami; retired without saying so, "until they come for me," as Vince put it. If they did come for him, and Praeger couldn't do his magic, then Vince would be even farther away, in prison, almost certainly for life. At least now Paul could fly down and see him, and they could walk on the beach and talk without fear. But he had avoided that so far. Time to get used to going it alone.

Many in Paul's position now would eliminate Vince, in the most merciful way possible of course, but taking no chance Vince would experience a failure of nerve when faced with losing, for the rest of his life, essentially everything that made life worth living. Vince had come all this way, only one short stint in prison a long time ago, and then to end up like this, the last act of his life. But Paul was willing to bet that Vince was not the kind of man to lose his nerve, even in that extremity. No, he was a brave man, admirable in every way, eminently worth Paul's wager that Vince would hold firm. And no matter what, how could he do that to Vince after all Vince had done for him?

Right now, they had no federal death penalty, so they couldn't threaten Vince with that, a threat that Vince had scoffed at anyway, but it might be different if it was right there in front of him instead of a distant and improbable thing. Answering a hypothetical question, Praeger had said there could be a death sentence if they prosecuted the murder by the state authorities under state law, but he doubted if the Feds would let any organized crime figure escape their clutches and lose the glory of the capture and conviction. Another wager on Vince worth making. And shit, you couldn't live forever, and Vince had lived a long time. That's the kind of calculation Vince would make. If you had to go, the lethal injection thing they had just introduced might be a better way than a lot of others. Ask Robert Sciorra. Strangled with a rope, rough and sharp, scraping across his neck.

He was vulnerable to a death sentence himself. The testimony of either Vince or Rose in a state-court prosecution could put him on death row. For what he did to Robert. That would hang over him his whole life. No statute of limitations for murder. Much as it had thwarted his silly romantic intentions, he accepted that it was all-in-all a good thing that Rose would be out of town and out of the life, and even his life. If she managed to evade the worst from this current grand jury investigation and escaped out West, she would be less and less vulnerable as time went on and not constantly exposed to investigation and prosecution as she would have been under Vince and Paul's misguided plan to make her co-Boss with Paul. As with Vince, he doubted he could ever harm Rose. Maybe he wasn't right for this Boss job after all, just like Ricky Vitale had kept saying.

And Boss of *what?* Less and less to be Boss of. But that gave him a mission. A new world, different and a lot harder to operate in than that old, dead world of a younger Vince Sorvino and Carmine Jagoda. BFD. He knew where he wanted to take it if he survived this latest thing. Not all at once but more and more legitimate over time. The Popper-Vitale debacle and the disappearance of Marty Lansing, the only guy involved who knew what he was doing, caused Paul to shy away from that whole titty-bar, fuck-movie stuff, though the phone sex thing still appealed including those credit card numbers and the authorization to charge on those numbers that would come with it. Keep working on that.

He would seize Vitale's gambling infrastructure before someone else could grab it, had already made the opening moves, and he would nurse it along, being very careful because it seemed like the Feds had so often managed to trip them up on gambling violations. Most of the prison sentences stemmed from that—too social, too public, too many people in a position to rat you out. Eventually, it could be folded into the coming *legitimate* "gaming" world. Legal gambling, and not just lotteries: casinos, spreading now beyond Las Vegas and Atlantic City. Iowa, fucking Iowa, of all places, was close to allowing riverboat casinos. He would try to find a way to grab pieces of those as they came along. Find some brainy lawyer—not Praeger, who was plenty brainy, but he was a trial guy, not a planning and structuring guy, and increasingly looking so pasty-faced, like death warmed over, not that much longer for the world—yes, a brainy young lawyer who could help him figure out how to disguise the tainted source of the money and invest it in legitimate stuff, and then other stuff, and then more stuff until it emerged at the other end of the process fully pasteurized and homogenized. He would have a lot of capital to work with, especially with Rose giving him her half. His heart still ached every single time he thought of her, probably would always or at least for a long time, his only solace being to abruptly stifle the thought before it got too far ahead of him. And maybe it was all for the best, probably better than what he had originally hoped for. As the saying went, familiarity might just breed contempt.

Back in town now, he thought he might drive on over to Sal's... silently raise a cup of espresso to Vince...offer, like Vince always did and sort of in Vince's honor, to help Sal if he needed it...Sal in his slippers shuffling around. Make it a routine, a ritual, until it wasn't there anymore, which it wouldn't be much longer...the end of something.

• • •

Kansas is not nearly as flat and boring as people make it out to be, Marty was thinking as he sped west on I-70 toward Colorado, *but good Goddamm riddance all the same.* Once Vitale was dead and Wayne headed for a long stint behind bars, Marty decided to dump the Witness Protection Program bullshit: having to change his name; having to live in a place the government ordered him to; having to struggle in some shit job that the government made him take so he wouldn't embarrass them. He even gave some thought to hanging around town and trying to take over the Pink and make something out of it and himself rich in the process. But the Pink seemed doomed. It had suffered too much horrible publicity, the Popper debacle being surely the last straw. Even the county government crooks had to turn their backs on it no matter how much money it had put in their pockets so far and might have done in the future. He had spent way too much time already in this nightmare land of, on the one side, prurient Puritan yahoos, and on the other, a bunch of degenerate redneck cowboys like David Bowman and Wayne Popper with some killer Dagos mixed in. Not for nothing was this the land of Charles Starkweather, Dick Hickock, Perry Smith, and such.

And running a gentlemen's club was hard, stressful work, having to worry constantly about undercover cops, psycho lecher customers, women haters and beaters, brawling drunks, minors with fake IDs, and managing mentally and emotionally damaged dancers with every problem you could imagine and some you couldn't, from irregular periods to episodes of the clap to pathological lying to homicidally jealous revenge fantasies. He decided the porn film business was the best niche for him and pointed himself straight ahead to its capital, the San Fernando Valley, adjacent to Hollywood and itself the Hollywood of porn.

"Yeah," he said, out loud this time, hoping to wake her up, "Kansas isn't nearly as flat and boring as people say…but so long motherfuckers."

She didn't wake. Since she begged him to take her with him, he let her come along. She had many good qualities, starting with the fact that she loved him beyond all reason. Which was by no means sufficient for him to keep her around. But she also loved to fuck and was great at it, all of it—the before, the during, and the after. If she wanted to become a porn star, he would allow it, but he guessed she wouldn't, and if he was wrong about that, they wouldn't be together long because, while not looking for the Virgin Mary, he refused to be relegated to a steady diet of sloppy seconds. He guessed she might be smart enough to do a number of things other than get near naked and gyrate on a stage. She could be a production assistant for sure, take care of some of the logistics, maybe even some of the finance and business end too.

• • •

Lieutenant Ross thought he should send a thank-you note to Vince Sorvino for killing Vitale and eliminating a strategically placed domino that, if it fell, could have toppled enough others to lead ultimately to him. Distance…the most important thing. Put as much distance between a deed growing older and older and the evidence of and around it growing staler and staler until nothing remained but rumor and hearsay. Paul Marcone was the only one who Ross knew for sure knew about the old sin, his old crime, and Marcone only because Ross himself had told him, and who would believe Marcone over Ross? And even if they were inclined to believe Marcone, no other evidence of any kind existed to corroborate the statement. There might be a cloud over him, but the department would not even be able to fire him based on that. Robert or Paul may have told Rose, but that would be double hearsay—Rose from Paul from Ross or Rose from Robert from Carmine.

These constituted the components and operations of the calculus of his risk analysis to determine whether he should kill any of these people. It just did not seem worth it given the unlikelihood of it ever coming out, and even if it did come out, the unlikelihood of it damaging him. Most people would tend to consider it a vicious slander of an exemplary public servant. Besides, it would just create more risk to kill someone now to cover up something likely already beyond the possibility of harming him, replacing stale evidence with fresh, because there was always evidence, no perfect crime. There would be this new crime with new evidence and a new timeline, everything all spruced and freshened up. And he had never murdered anyone with his own hands and wanted to keep those hands at least that clean. Meanwhile, Marcone was likely to be within arm's reach anytime Ross needed to reach there. It was good that Rose Sciorra had left town and that Russ Lord's grand jury investigation had turned up nothing worth pursuing on either her or Marcone, thus creating more distance and moving the timeline even further along. Despite that one horrible mistake, he was not a bad man, and he was a good cop, and that was a good thing to be.

Now if O'Keefe could just keep away or be kept away from stirring pots and turning over rocks with snakes—real snakes, for Christ's sake—under them. But how ironic, if that was the right word, that it turned out that O'Keefe had done a lot more good than harm, going back to the mink farm thing, the Bowman-Jensen thing and now with the Popper-Vitale thing. They said keep your friends close and your enemies closer, O'Keefe being a troubling mixture of both, and he didn't know why but he was fond of the damn guy. So he would keep O'Keefe extremely close, in a bear hug, a sort of unofficial partner. He'd be what O'Keefe had called him. A real nasty prick of a big brother.

● ● ●

Paschal was too drunk to realize not only that he would not be able to drive himself home but that he would likely not be able even to rise from his chair; so drunk he had forgotten even to order another drink for some time; also so drunk he could not think in a linear way at all, for example how he might be rescued from what he could not quite recognize as a "plight" that he was in at the moment and who his rescuer might be. He remembered her, and vaguely perceived that, as always, she would still be awake, wishing she could sleep, might even be out roaming from drinking spot to spot hunting for him, probably wishing she could just leave him once and for all. What possibly induced her to stay on?

He did remain vaguely aware of his immense disappointment in himself, couldn't escape that ever. He had come so close. He had become an actual journalist, paid even, respected, his criminal past, that one insane impulsive alcohol-fueled moment, now repented, expiated, maybe even forgiven, pricks like Russell Lord notwithstanding. But the Great American Novel, which he had always felt driven, destined, compelled, put on this earth to write, kept eluding him, having begun it countless times but never progressing past page ninety-seven. He had been so lucky to end up with this crime beat, which furnished so many great characters and stories, so much about human life, right out of Shakespeare, begging for a chronicler who did not glorify it or moralize about it but just laid it out there like Shakespeare did with Macbeth and Lear and the rest. But he seemed incapable of working to anything but a daily deadline and for current payment. In that sense the newspaper job ended up being a curse. If he could just get some publisher to pay him a worthy advance and a deadline came along with it, maybe…or if the right woman came along to inspire him…a muse.

Sometimes he managed to realize that his job, plus getting at least slightly and often stumbling drunk almost every day, plus the tortuous daily process of recovery from getting drunk every day, all by themselves required more than twenty-four hours. The drinking he could not quite bring himself to blame, at least to assign it a central role, let alone *the* central role. If he could regulate certain other things in his life, things he yearned for but could not quite identify, the drinking would then regulate itself. His new acquaintance, maybe even friend, O'Keefe, was managing to stay sober. How did he do that? Why did he even want to do that? Paschal could not imagine living without it, without that eager anticipation and then, at about the second hour in, for a little while at least, the magic of getting thoroughly lost in it, everything else forgotten other than the promise of endless possibility and eternal renewal. But that was coming less and less, puking and problems, dry heaves and depression more and more. He had once, while still on parole, been stopped for a DUI. It could have sent him back to prison. Oswald had persuaded the newspaper to use their connections to get the prosecution dropped and the parole officer mollified. Good guy, Oswald, but the way Oswald watched him now when he was drinking three for every one of Oswald's…He had missed a deadline or two. He had said some foolish things to the newspaper brass at happy hour sessions. He had been beaten up in the honky tonks a few times, even once ending up in the hospital. Things seemed to be closing in, like right now, the lights going off, someone turning them off…*Where the fuck am I anyway?*

●　　●　　●

When O'Keefe pulled up to her house, past the "For Sale" sign in the front yard, and into her driveway, he saw her mightily shoving on a last bag, trying to wedge it in the already packed-full rear of her van.

He parked next to her, got out, and walked around the side of the van.

"Need help?"

She looked sideways at him, sweating and out of breath, and said, "No, I've got it," and administered a final all-or-nothing push and frantically slammed the cargo door shut as if the bag might lunge back out at her if she hesitated even for an instant.

They stood there, awkward, staring at each other. As always, they kept a physical distance, as if some line somewhere in between them could not be crossed without unacceptable consequences.

Finally, she said, "Thanks for coming. I wanted to see you, but now I wish you wouldn't have. I'm not even gonna hug you…not even gonna peck you on the cheek."

"Understood."

"I can't even say anything."

"Goodbye, Rose."

"Goodbye."

"Best wishes."

"Same. Avoid snakes. I may need you again someday."

He climbed into the Wagoneer, backed out, and drove away, without another look or even a glance at her in the rearview mirrors, keeping his head rigid and his eyes firmly fixed on the empty road ahead.

• • •

She drove south and hooked into Highway 40, which would take them through northern Arizona where she could show the children the Grand Canyon before turning south toward Tucson. The children bickered over who would ride up front. Bobby claimed to be entitled because he was older and Sophia because she was younger and a girl. Their mother settled it the easy and obvious way by requiring them to share the privilege and stopping on the side of the road to flip a coin to determine who would go first. The toss favored Bobby.

A few miles out of the city, Sophia said, "You think Daddy'll be able to find us clear out in Tucson?"

Rose almost had to stop on the shoulder again and put her face in her hands and weep into them, but she managed to stay in control, looking away from them, hiding her face from them, and saying, "Oh, yes. He'll know how to find us. For sure."

Before long they were both asleep.

Clytemnestra. Russell Lord had called her that. Nobody in the room but him seemed to know what it meant. At the library she discovered the series of ancient Greek tragic plays, the *Oresteia.* King Agamemnon, husband of Clytemnestra, fomented and organized the invasion of Troy to avenge the supposed "kidnapping" of his brother Menelaus's wife, Helen, by the Trojan prince, Paris. Agamemnon left his wife and two of his children, Orestes and Electra, at home, but took with him one daughter, Iphigenia. The invasion encountered difficulty at the start, threatening to remain forever stillborn, when powerful winds prevented the Greek ships from sailing. The goddess Artemis, who had brought forth the winds, now refused to calm them, making it impossible for the Greeks ever to embark, unless Agamemnon slaughtered his daughter Iphigenia, sacrificing her to the goddess.

And he did it. The blood-soaked warlord sonuvabitch butchered his daughter. And they sailed.

It took the Greeks ten years of atrocity and bloodshed to prevail and for Agamemnon to return. During all those years, one thing dominated Clytemnestra's mind—avenging the death of her daughter. She took a lover, Aegisthus, who had his own murderous grudge against the King, and they ruled together. When the Greeks won the war, and Agamemnon returned in triumph, she and Aegisthus assassinated Agamemnon, seized the throne, and ruled together. The young son Orestes, the natural heir to Agamemnon's throne, presumed to be in mortal danger from Aegisthus, was mysteriously smuggled out of the kingdom somehow, and returned as a young man, under orders of the god Apollo, and, spurred on by his sister Electra, avenged the murder of his father by killing Aegisthus and his mother Clytemnestra.

None wept for Clytemnestra.

Until Paul and Vince had come to her and told her what Robert had been doing and was planning, she had not realized how easy her life had been, how little suffering or even disappointment she had experienced. She had enjoyed the benefits of her father's life, her husband's life, without paying for them. When she learned of Robert's treachery, her shocked sense of betrayal, grief, and rage ran close to madness. That his lover was a man did not cause her any special anger or grief—betraying her for a woman would probably have enraged her even more—except for the atrocity that overwhelmed everything else—AIDS. He had been penetrating her, after dipping his disgusting stick in who-knows-what plague-ridden holes. She could almost feel her insides seething and rotting with the virus, corroding away her immune system. Even more than most people in the world, Robert, closeted homosexual, must have been acutely aware of the AIDS epidemic and its dangers. Maybe he not only didn't care about infecting her, maybe he did it deliberately, hoping to kill her that way, maybe planning to put the word out that she had engaged in filthy liaisons that had led to this tragic outcome, liaisons she had never engaged in, not once, even though men had been trying to seduce her since she was fourteen years old. Did he not care that his children would grow up without a mother? It had driven her near to madness.

She could not have stayed the inevitable killing hand. His sentence was death anyway, that outcome irrevocably fated even if she had not eagerly supported it. But she had gone even further than that, spitting venom and fire at him in his last moments. After they made him disappear, obliterated, into some grave that his parents and children could never find, never visit, never mourn over, she read everything available on the course of the virus, the horrible wasting away, the sores, the ugliness of the death. What would happen to her orphaned babies? Carefully, secretly she arranged for an AIDS test in another city. And once the test results arrived, informing her that she was free of the virus, the rage and vengefulness drained out of her, replaced by guilt and regret for the part she had played in his murder, which now was just as overwhelming as the grief and rage had been, compounded by the constant deceitfulness of playing the role of the grieving widow, lying to everyone including her fatherless children.

Although she kept trying to remind herself they would have been fatherless anyway if Robert had succeeded in his treacherous escape plan, that furnished no comfort.

But she would play that role of Clytemnestra only in the killing, not after. There would be no Aegisthus. Not Paul Marcone, the killer, wanting to fuck on top of Robert's grave. Not even the innocent Peter O'Keefe, though she thought maybe she had fallen in love with him or could easily do so if he campaigned for her, which, mercifully, he had not. That would almost certainly end badly. What if O'Keefe ever learned the truth about her?

No, there would be no Aegisthus. She would live the rest of her life like a nun, in expiation, however insufficient. The only thing for her now would be motherhood and operating these businesses. But she could not deceive herself. All of it was doom-laden, tainted with guilt, shame. She could only hope the pain of it would dull as time went on. Those businesses, the big home with acreage in Tucson, and all the rest of it, fruits of a poisonous tree. That huge duffle bag she had been shoving into the van when O'Keefe arrived: stuffed full of cash, some of it accumulated by Robert, mostly by her father; cash stashed in and retrieved by her from all kinds of places; safe deposit boxes in banks in her city and other cities; throughout the house in safes, behind walls, under floorboards, in books that weren't books, in old luggage and at the bottom of boxes, in the attic underneath layers of antique china or bedding or old clothes. She wished she had the courage to burn it all, hoped someday she would muster that courage and light that fire, but she did not have the strength for it now despite the fear that the failure to relinquish it would somehow bring her and hers to a final ruin.

She looked at Bobby sleeping there. Like Orestes, son of Clytemnestra, would he grow up someday and learn the truth and, perhaps, like Orestes, egged on by his own sister, little Sophia there, avenge his father in that same way? She was fleeing now, she hoped, not to save herself from all that but *him* from all that, smuggle him and Sophia out of that evil kingdom, desperately seeking to escape the curse of the life they had inherited.

* * *

Since that last day in Darren's basement, though she had managed against all odds to achieve her purpose, her life otherwise was not going so well. Matt had taken to bad-mouthing her at school, making up stories, and she had heard the word "slut" a few times as she came near or walked away from a group of classmates. And the counseling that her mom made her endure really sucked. The counselor kept not so subtly trying to convince her, by means of a bunch of annoying questions, that she had been "inappropriate" to interfere with her mom's life in the way she had done. What a crock. They should be touting her, carrying her around on their shoulders for exposing Darren/Curtis for who he really was.

It was pretty chilly around the house for a while. Her mom was not as chatty as before and quicker to anger, until, late one night, she came into Kelly's bed, held her for a while, and said, "I'm sorry for some of those things I said. I love you. It'll all be alright."

She and her dad could do things now, out in the world and without the security guards. His yard was springing to life, and he seemed, to her surprise, to be quite excited about it, an affection for plant life he had never before exhibited. "Before long," he said, "we'll have ground roses, dogwoods, redbuds, and crab apples flowering all over the place." And now he had this wonderful dog. She wished she could have a dog like that. They made a little arrangement where she could "babysit" Karma once in a while.

When she looked in his medicine cabinet, the bottle of Percocet was gone. He must have thrown it out.

• • •

Kelly did have one unconditional admirer, but a necessarily secret one, a wandering Odysseus, guiltily but thoroughly pleased with his daughter, who had so bravely—and so madly, it had to be said—played the role of Telemachus to Darren the suitor. He silently renewed his previous vow to find every way he could to love and support her, if only from afar, and somehow make it up to her for abandoning her in that earlier, evil time.

Given recent events and the raw feelings they had exposed and that remained not entirely healed, and to confirm that he was now "clear" and could resume a normal life again, or at least what passed for a normal life in his peculiar case, O'Keefe thought it might be a good thing for everyone if he took Kelly on a trip at the upcoming end of the school year in late May. His suggestion was met with enthusiasm from both daughter and mother. Early on a Saturday evening, with Kelly out for the night at a slumber party, he invited himself to Annie's house to discuss, he deviously claimed, the upcoming trip, which was merely incidental, however, to his greater purpose.

As they sat at the kitchen table, him drinking a cup of coffee and her a glass of wine, he plunged in.

"So, how've you been?"

"Pretty rocky. Pretty busted up. Two-time loser and all that." Smiling mischievously, she said, "I seem to make unfortunate choices when selecting supposedly lifelong male companions."

"Speaking of that, what would you think about us getting back together? Kind of a probationary experiment sort of thing."

She frowned. "You mean like shacking up? You already tried that a few times a long time ago, remember? I said 'no.'"

Oh, I do remember. And I came to admire you for that.

"The intention would be permanent," he said. "Just trying not to put too much pressure on it at first. Pressure on you, that is. It's your choice. I'm ready, in for it, committed."

Her eyes narrowed. "I've heard of a pity fuck, but not a pity marriage."

"Don't be that way. It's not that. This whole thing's made me think we...I...I, not you...made a mistake back then. I'm the one that needs the pity."

"Did Kelly put you up to this?"

"No. But it would...might...be good for her too. She seems to be sort of teetering on the rails these days."

"So maybe it's not pity for either of us, but for Kelly? A 'stay...' or in this case 'get...together for the children' sort of thing?"

So much for that. Not just a rejection but a pugnacious one. Here they were again, at loggerheads, the thing that had bedeviled them when they were together.

He said, "I've known for a long time it was a mistake. I don't know what I've been wandering around and waiting for. When I heard you were getting married again, I could only think about what I had stupidly lost. But I didn't want to interfere."

"Not lost. Threw away. You walk out on us, stay away, 'wander' as you put it...for years, and you think you can waltz back in here and I'm supposed to melt in gushy gratitude."

"No—"

"I don't know if I even want you back anymore. You broke my heart..."

"Maybe I can help it mend...make amends." He had never thought about the affinity of those two words, *mend* and *amend*. And *repair* and *reparation. Tikkun Olam. Healing the world. Repairing the world. Re-pair. Pair again? The pair we once were?*

"Pity again?" she said. "How about *love?* Maybe it's sort of phony, but better than 'make amends.'"

It is phony. A word that meant so much and so little and was so abstract it meant nothing. It would be too phony just to trot it out now. She would rightly not believe it, scoff at him. There were other words. *Appreciation, yes. Admiration, yes.* He admired her right now, for the bravery and integrity of this rejection of him. And that made him remember their times together and how they expressed what they felt for each other—physically. *Desire. Then. Now too.* He could even muster *devotion.* All of these other words, he *knew* what they meant and that they were true.

So he said, "Love is an action. I'm here."

"Love is a lot of actions," she said, "a lifetime of actions."

Well, that wasn't a test he had passed, so far anyway. "All I can say is I'm here. First step."

"I spent a lot of time waiting for you and finally got tired of it."

"Call it what you want. I don't know what to call it. But *sincere* is one thing it is for sure. And it's not pity."

Well, at least not the patronizing kind of pity you're referring to. The pity he felt for her now, he knew to be a much deeper thing, a compassion, for the wounded, by his own hand. That compassion, and the other things he felt with it, might in fact be love, or as good as love, whatever that was. *I left you alone with a little girl.* But he didn't feel he could say that, sensitive as she was not to fall into the trap of his pity and guilt. Seemed that it would only make things worse.

They fell into a silence. He had apparently screwed this up. He didn't know what to add or how to end this in an acceptable way.

Apparently, she didn't either.

Finally, he said, "Well, besides that, how the fuck are you?"

She laughed. Hard. Merrily even. It made him feel a little merry too, despite her rejection. Maybe that was love.

"Besides," she said, still smiling, "why should I marry a dead man walking."

"The insurance."

"No, you'd have to get a different job. And I bet you couldn't do that. Or wouldn't."

"Or maybe just do the job differently?"

Her look said, "Yeah, tell me something else that'll never happen."

They returned to the conversation that he had falsely claimed to be the purpose of his visit, agreeing on the basic logistics of the trip: destination, clothing and other items Kelly would need to pack, times of departure and return.

"She'll love this," Annie concluded, "and maybe spending a week with you'll make her appreciate me again, and vice versa. I can't believe she's such a little gangster. Her father's genes."

She walked him to the door.

Not knowing what else to say, he said, "Hang in there."

She watched him walk down the porch steps and to his car, noticing the hitch in his step was gone now. He seemed to be able to heal from everything, she nothing. He looked back and waved. As she watched him pull away from the curb and make his slow, distracted zigzag down the street, she was thinking that nothing could have surprised her more than the conversation they just had, and, as it continued to sink in, her adrenalin was spiking a little, her heart was beating a tad faster, her brain was fogging a bit, and, yes, there was even a sort of gushy feeling in her face and eyes and temples—and she was very afraid of what that might mean…

As he pulled away from the curb and made his slow, distracted zigzag down the street, he was thinking that he had broken the thing and then wandered too long and should not be surprised that he couldn't put it back together now. *All the king's horses and all the king's men...*But then one thing did lead to another, sometimes even predictably so...and he did have the dog...

This concludes *On Lonesome Roads*.
If you enjoyed this book please consider
posting a review on your favorite review
or retailer website. Thank you.

ACKNOWLEDGMENTS

Thank you to the now-usual suspects:

Keri-Rae Barnum

Meghan Flanigan

Ericka McIntyre

Travis Tynan

for midwifing this book to a successful birth. We'll see how the child does on its own.

Of course, none of them should be blamed for my misunderstanding or just my unwillingness to follow their advice. In that regard, please note that deviations from punctuation "rules," especially concerning commas, are deliberate based on my own feelings about how the language ought to flow on the page. I sincerely apologize (really) to any readers irritated by those choices.

Thanks to the following for assistance with respect to certain aspects of the story (and who also cannot be blamed for my failures to understand or willful obtuseness):

Ann Darke

Nathan Hass

Gary Jenkins, *Gangland Wire*

Catherine Kozal, Sergeant, K.C.Mo. Police Canine Corps, Ret. (Friend of Karma)

Lee Parfitt

And, with the same caveat re my failure to follow what they were trying to tell me, thanks to the following for their advice with respect to the material in Chapters 24, 25, and 26 (DON'T LOOK!):

David Duethman, MD

Matt Gratton, MD

Vern Lovic

For those of you who find it amusing to search and discover such things, at three widely separated places in the text there are direct or near-direct, very short, unattributed and unmarked quotations from Wordsworth.

ABOUT THE AUTHOR

DAN FLANIGAN is a novelist, playwright, poet, and practicing lawyer. He holds a Ph.D. in History from Rice University and J.D. from the University of Houston. He taught Jurisprudence at the University of Houston and American Legal History at the University of Virginia. His first published book was his Ph.D. dissertation, *The Criminal Law of Slavery and Freedom, 1800-1868*.

He moved on from academia to serve the civil rights cause as a school desegregation lawyer, followed by a long career as a finance attorney in private law practice. He became a name partner in the Polsinelli law firm in Kansas City, created its Financial Services practice, chaired its Real Estate & Financial Services Department for two decades, and established the firm's New York City office and served as its managing partner until October 2022. His legal bio may be viewed at www.polsinelli.com/professionals/dflanigan.

Taking a break from the law practice for two years, he and his wife, Candy, founded *Sierra Tucson*, a prominent alcohol and drug treatment center located in Tucson, Arizona.

Recently, he has been able to turn his attention to creative writing. In 2019, he released a literary trifecta including *Mink Eyes*, the first in the Peter O'Keefe series, *Dewdrops*, a collection of shorter fiction (a novella book-ended by two short stories), and *Tenbrae: A Memoir of Love and Death*, a bracelet of verse and prose poems dedicated to

366 • ON LONESOME ROADS

his wife, Candy, to honor her last illness and death and their 40-plus years together, a work that has been described as "moving," "elegiac," "celebratory," "heartbreaking and exquisite."

The Big Tilt, the second in the Peter O'Keefe series, was published in 2020 and has been described as a "gritty and eloquent crime novel" and "deft, hard-boiled, but literary prose that's reminiscent of Raymond Chandler's best work."

On Lonesome Roads, the third book in the series, was released on April 26, 2022.

In September 2021, Dan won several awards in the 2021 Readers' Favorite Contest. This contest included both independent and bestselling works from publishing houses such as Penguin Random House, Simon & Schuster, and Harper Collins. Among thousands of entries, only five awards are presented in each category: Gold, Silver, Bronze, Honorable Mention and Finalist. *The Big Tilt* received the Bronze Medal in Fiction-Crime; *Dewdrops* also received the Bronze Medal in Fiction-Anthology; *Tenebrae: A Memoir of Life and Death* was a finalist in the Poetry-General genre.

He has also written stage plays including *Secrets* (based on the life of Eleanor Marx) and *Moondog's Progress* (inspired by the life of Alan Freed).

His novella, *Dewdrops*, was originally written for the stage and enjoyed a full-cast staged reading at the Theatre of the Open Eye in New York. Its director described the play as a "powerful" work about "addiction in America—addiction to drugs, alcohol, sex, danger, power, and to finding 'The Answer,'" with characters that are "well drawn, real, and actors love to portray them. "

He has written a feature film screenplay of *Mink Eyes* and a pilot for a TV series called *O'Keefe*.

He serves on the Board of Directors of Childhood USA, the U.S. arm of the World Childhood Foundation, established by Queen Silvia of Sweden, working to end child sexual abuse and exploitation everywhere.

He divides his time among Kansas City, New York City, and Los Angeles.

Learn more at www.danflaniganbooks.com.

THE PETER O'KEEFE SERIES

How did we get here?

Dan Flanigan, after a long career as a finance, banking, and bankruptcy lawyer in which he was both a player in and witness to the dramatic transformations of our modern times, intends to provide at least a few of the answers to that question through a series of novels, recounting, from the 1980s to the present day, the life and adventures of his private detective hero Peter O'Keefe and the assorted characters in the O'Keefe orbit.

Welcome, then, to this chronicle of the scams, schemes, and scandals of the last four decades of American life. Flanigan hopes the series will appeal to every generation—from the Boomers, who lived all of it, down to Gen Z trying to learn its lessons and play the hand dealt to them.

In the first three books of the series—*Mink Eyes, The Big Tilt,* and *On Lonesome Roads,* which are set during the period 1986 to 1988—Flanigan explores such themes as the disruption and decline of the traditional American Mafia; the Savings & Loan scandal that crippled much of the U.S. banking system in the 1980s and early 1990s; the fallout from the AIDS crisis of that era; the emergence of the surveillance society ("Who is watching? Who is listening?"); the corrosive effect of keeping secrets in both public and private life ("We are only as sick as the secrets we keep."); addiction and recovery; date rape and other sexual violence and the blighted lives that so often result.

In these stories, though teeming with plenty of villains, everyday people of mostly good will, confronted with extraordinary challenges, struggle to repair and heal themselves and others, and their world, from their wounds, self-inflicted and otherwise, not merely—paraphrasing William Faulkner—to endure, but, just maybe, to prevail.

MINK EYES
(PETER O'KEEFE BOOK 1)

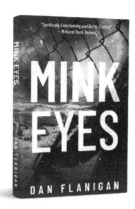

YOU DON'T SEND AN ANGEL TO DO A DIRTY JOB

It is the tarnished heart of the "Greed is Good" decade. Peter O'Keefe is a physically scarred and emotionally battered Vietnam vet. Struggling with life after war, O'Keefe tries to outrun his vices by immersing himself in his work as a private investigator. Hired by his childhood best friend, ace attorney Mike Harrigan, O'Keefe investigates what appears to be merely a rinky-dink mink farm Ponzi scheme in the Ozarks. Instead, O'Keefe finds himself ensnared in a vicious web of money laundering, cocaine smuggling and murder.

Mink Eyes is available in paperback and eBook.
The audiobook will be available May 2022.

"Terrifically entertaining and deftly crafted…"
–Midwest Book Review

THE BIG TILT
(PETER O'KEEFE BOOK 2)

NO GOOD DEED GOES UNPUNISHED

The war in Vietnam didn't kill Peter O'Keefe. Neither did his run-in with ruthless crime boss "Mr. Canada" in the Arizona desert. But chasing after justice in his own hometown just might.

A high school crush of O'Keefe's turns up dead, but the details don't add up. His pal, Mike Harrigan, has put his trust in the wrong people and now stands accused of crimes that could put him in the slammer. And O'Keefe? The mafia has put a price on his head.

The Big Tilt is available in paperback and eBook.
The audiobook will be available Summer 2022.

"...Flanigan manages to conjure deft, hard-boiled, but literary prose that's reminiscent of Raymond Chandler's best work. A gritty and eloquent crime novel."
–Kirkus Reviews

Candace Gambrell Flanigan

April 26, 2011

Death, be not proud